Praise for *Minus Me*

"Medwed's lovely novel of marriage, motherhood, love and loss is so real that at times it feels like non-fiction. It's a timely reminder that in the worst of times, we sometimes rediscover the very best of ourselves."
—Jodi Picoult, *New York Times* bestselling author of *A Spark of Light*

"A profoundly warm and intimate novel about what it means to try to manage the tumult in our life—and the life of a loved one."
—Caroline Leavitt, *New York Times* bestselling author of *Pictures of You*

"A charming and hopeful story about love and destiny. It's a beautiful story about the family you have and the family you choose . . . A perfect read to escape the world."
—Miriam Parker, author of *The Shortest Way Home*

"Such a sharp eye, wry voice, and warm heart at work here! . . . Has there ever been a more entertaining drama queen of a mother? So much to love! *Minus Me* is vintage Medwed: smart, funny-quirky, and so very satisfying."
—Elinor Lipman, author of *Good Riddance* and *On Turpentine Lane*

"A smart, touching comedy . . . Mameve Medwed writes with heart and charm, warmth and wisdom. She knows how to evoke laughter and tears . . . Fans of Medwed's previous novels and newcomers to her work will eat it up as greedily as they would a Paul Bunyan sandwich."
—Stephen McCauley, author of *My Ex-Life*

Minus Me

Also available by Mameve Medwed

Of Men and Their Mothers
How Elizabeth Barrett Browning Saved My Life
The End of an Error
Host Family
Mail

Minus Me

A Novel

MAMEVE MEDWED

alcove
press

Copyright © 2021 by Mameve Medwed

Published in the United States by Alcove Press, an imprint of The Quick Brown Fox & Company LLC.

Alcove Press and its logo are trademarks of The Quick Brown Fox & Company LLC.

Library of Congress Catalog-in-Publication data available upon request.

ISBN (trade paperback): 978-1-64385-643-8
ISBN (ebook): 978-1-64385-644-5

Cover design by Melanie Sun

Printed in the United States.

www.alcovepress.com

Alcove Press
34 West 27th St., 10th Floor
New York, NY 10001

First Edition: January 2021

10 9 8 7 6 5 4 3 2 1

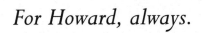

For Howard, always.

Chapter One

Your mother's birthday is June twenty-eighth; she wears a size ten. Your father's is May eighteenth, and a bottle of single malt always works.

Annie pulls up outside Michaud's Quik-Basket. She's too near the hydrant, but for once she doesn't care. She turns off the engine and tries to slow her breathing. She pictures the all-too-cheerful and all-too-serene yoga instructor in the video Sam gave her at Christmas. "Made for type As," he explained. She watched only half. She's lousy at relaxing. The harder she tries to breathe from her diaphragm, the faster and more shallow her breathing becomes. *So what*, she thinks, and opens the car door. *Nothing matters now.* She leaves the key in the ignition; she leaves the door unlocked; she climbs over the ice bank rather than mincing her way along the skimpily shoveled path. To hell with everything. Let her slip, splayed like a snow angel on the filthy sidewalk. Perfect simile.

Raoul, the father, and not the son, Ralphie, who sat behind her in high school social studies, is in front of the cash register— her first stroke of luck. Ralphie would want to yak about their classmates, analyze hockey scores, ask about her mother. Not that it matters either. But today, of all days, she does not want to talk about Ursula.

Mr. Michaud is watching the weather report. It's February first. Will Punxsutawney Phil come out of his hole tomorrow? wonders the grinning, lumber-jacketed, suspiciously orange-skinned weatherman. His teeth are five degrees whiter than fresh snow, shaming the dirty brown-and-yellow mounds polka-dotting her hometown. "Whatja think, Annie?" asks Raoul, his Canadian vowels harsh against the weatherman's broadcasting-school diction.

"Don't know," she says. *Don't care either.* Six more weeks of winter or an early spring means nothing to her now. Annie points to the racks behind the dusty cash register, its fading photos of Ralphie and his sister Marie in their confirmation clothes, twenty years out of date, Scotch-taped to it. "A pack of Marlboros, please." She reconsiders. "Actually, a carton."

If Mr. Michaud disapproves, she can't tell. His face is turned to the TV. She pays. He counts out the change. "You want a bag with that?" he asks.

"Don't bother," she says. Let the whole town see evidence of her vice. Her public relapse.

But the sidewalk holds no witnesses when she exits. No one to ask how she's doing, whether she'll be at the city council meeting tomorrow night, if the new pickle suppliers for the Paul Bunyans are up to snuff, and what about that enchanting mother of hers?

There'd be a pause, then a glance at the carton, followed by "Is everything okay?" Lucky for her, not a single car passes along the street to see her leaning against the steering wheel as she lights up. Oh, happy day. Hunky-dory day!

Of course, the lighter is broken. Of course, she doesn't have a match. With the car still running, she gets out and goes back inside. "Matches?" she asks.

He doesn't look up. "Over there." He points to a Whitman's Sampler filled with matchboxes from Gus's Gas across the road. "Have a good one," he says.

She drives around the block to the high school. She turns into the last row of the parking lot, territory once claimed by the tough guys who used to smoke their unfiltered Camels and rolled their joints over by the pine trees. It's the exact spot, too, where the fast girls unhooked their bras, where she and Sam used to make out—how quaint—in his father's old Chevy when they were teenagers and the movie had ended. By nine, the whole town closed down. At that hour, when glowing living room televisions dimmed one by one along Grove Street, you could almost hear the words "Good night, John Boy. Good night, Jim Bob" from *The Waltons* reruns she used to watch as a kid.

Nobody's around. Hardly surprising, since teenagers have birth control and the comfort of their own beds for overnights. "Better at home than in the back of the car or some cheap motel, since they're going to do it anyway," explained her best friend, Rachel, whose daughter had a boyfriend with weekly sleepover privileges. Not that Annie has that problem.

But the problem she does have is a big one. The biggest. The central theme of literature and music and philosophy—not cigarettes and teenage sex and municipal taxes. Or narcissistic mothers or bland pickles. It's the major enigma-slash-obsession of all time.

She pulls a pack from the carton and begins to tear it open, still wearing the ruffled purple gloves Ursula sent her. The leather is so fine, a second skin, the cashmere lining so fitted to its outer layer that she manages to extract a cigarette even though her hands are trembling. She hasn't smoked since her first pregnancy, except for one or two during Ursula's high-stress visits. But never through the other doing-everything-right pregnancies, four of which ended in miscarriage. And the last, a daughter, stillborn—the never-again. After that, she lost the taste for it.

Is this why? The smoking? Something to keep her hands occupied when she felt shy at a party, a country bumpkin's glaze of sophistication. A no-cal substitute when she looked through the drugstore window and spied one of her friends demolishing a hot-fudge sundae at the soda fountain. This despite so many hard-won tobacco-free years? Despite all those meetings of Smokers Anonymous in dark church basements and shabby cafeterias? Add to that a childhood swathed in secondhand smoke erupting from Mt. Ursula and a teenaged bout of pneumonia, which, according to the doctor, might have compromised her lungs and led to problems in adulthood.

"I'm so sorry," Dr. Buckley said, clasping her hand in both of his, squeezing back tears.

Of course, she thought. Her just desserts. Not only from her original sin and a child's sense of invincibility, but let's face it: too much wine, too little broccoli. Dropping out of exercise class the first week. Her yoga aversion. The extra ten pounds she blames on the Paul Bunyan special—that nutritionally challenged continual source of income and marital harmony and local fame.

"Just bad luck. Just life," Dr. Buckley added.

"Screw life," she says now. She's only thirty-seven, dammit. Not that her mother would appreciate the *only*. "Darling," Ursula demanded when Annie turned thirty, "let's keep your age *entre nous*," in the same voice she'd used to insist that her toddler daughter address her as Ursula, more sororial than the maternity-revealing *Mama*.

Annie strikes the match, lights the cigarette, holds it between the second and third fingers of her still-gloved hand. The cigarette nestles right in, as if she's just restored a missing digit.

Annie inhales, coughs, and feels awful—dizzy, like her twelve-year-old pudgy self when her mother first offered her a Parliament, promising a trim waist. Her mother was right. Annie kept at it. The cough—at least then—disappeared; the pounds fell off. "What a pretty little thing," people cooed. Flaunting the cigarette, she felt worldly, Parisian. Not that that was a quality the boys in her high school seemed to value. Their ideal was less urbane and more juvenile delinquent, a better match for bad boys like Ralphie Michaud, with their nose rings, their moussed-back hair—a single lock bisecting their forehead, a couple of heavy-metal tattoos.

Sam wasn't one of those guys. And she wasn't one of those girls who glued themselves to the side of such boys like an extra rib. She and Sam had gone through Benjamin Franklin Elementary School together, in the same class, their birthdays three days apart. In second grade, he gave her a heart-shaped box of fudge for Valentine's Day. In fourth, he was her Secret Santa. By junior high, he had become so handsome she couldn't stop staring at him. Shy, diffident, a little absent-minded, he never realized how good-looking he was. (And still doesn't seem to, no matter the second glances and flirty compliments.)

But they really found each other freshman year of high school, where they clung together, two outcasts bad at sports, smart no matter how hard they tried to hide it, and only children among big, constantly proliferating families. What's more, they were minorities: he, Jewish; she, Unitarian, in a community centered on St. Peter's Catholic Church. Even worse, they both lived in the fancy part of town, which meant—viewed through the narrow scope of Passamaquoddy, Maine—no tires in the front yard, a half bath tucked under the stairs, an air conditioner sticking out a bedroom window, and a dishwasher in the kitchen. She and Sam were a clique of two.

Now she takes another puff and feels even worse. She opens the passenger side window, stuffs the pack back into the carton, and flings the whole thing into the snowbank. Should she feel guilty for littering? Should she feel guilty for corrupting a minor if some kid comes along and pounces on it? Should she feel guilty for starting some other poor soul on the road to disease? She has a better idea. Forget indulging in a social conscience. She's going to indulge in a hot-fudge sundae with chopped walnuts, melted marshmallows, whipped cream, and a red-dye-maraschino cherry on top. The works.

She drives the half block to Miller's Drug and backs into the parking space someone else is just vacating. Though the never-repaired squeak in the door announces her arrival, nobody looks up. A couple of toddlers with their harassed and exhausted mothers are sitting at one end of the counter. One child has stirred a dozen straws into his milk shake. A little girl keeps trying to grab them. "Some days . . ." her mother sighs, mopping up the spills.

"Believe me, I know," the other mother commiserates.

Annie scowls. *You have no idea how lucky you are*, she wants to shout. She chooses a stool at the opposite end of the counter. "Drowning your sorrows?" asks Mr. Miller when he takes her order. "This seems to be the day for it."

"Really?'

He nods. "Agnes Bouchard was in here just two minutes ago and wolfed down two banana splits. Seems old Mrs. Bouchard died . . ."

"Yes, it was in the paper. I'm sorry to hear that."

"Don't be sorry. Ninety-one years old and as nasty as they come. You can't imagine what Agnes put up with taking care of her. At her beck and call every second. The old lady used to call and scream at me when her blood pressure medication wasn't delivered fast enough. As if she was the only customer in Passamaquoddy. As if we offer white-glove service here. Then she goes and dies intestate." He mops a scattering of sprinkles off the counter. "Without a will."

"I know what intestate means." Annie feels the need to defend herself.

"Now all these far-flung relatives are turning up under rocks and demanding their share. Worse than if she'd left her money to her cat, which Agnes had figured she'd do."

"I hope the banana splits helped," Annie says.

"Not sure. Though I sent her home with a strawberry milk shake. On the house. It's a lesson for us all. I've already made an appointment with my lawyer to do my own will. Never too early . . ."

Or too late, thinks Annie.

"Not that you have to worry," he adds.

"You never know."

"Ain't that the truth. Well, on to more cheerful things," he says. "How is that lovely mother of yours?"

"Great," Annie says, not bothering to muster up the usual fake enthusiasm and present her unembellished report of Ursula's overly embellished life. She's used to this. Over the years, she's become desensitized, like people with allergies who, given increasingly larger doses of what they're allergic to, develop tolerance to the very thing that once caused hives. At the start of every school year, "How is your mother?" was the first question each new teacher asked her. Soon enough, Annie would take preemptory action and, before the words were even formed, announce, "My mother is great. *Great,*" prompting the guidance counselor to send out a memo to staff suggesting they inquire only about Arabella herself. She saw the memo on Miss Cleary's desk once, along with the words *What a sensitive and shy child. Arabella is, alas, so unlike her mother.* Even now, all these years later, that *alas* has—alas—become part of what defines her.

She unfolds the paper napkin in her lap, studies it, pleats it into a fan, then flattens it, her attention clearly and pointedly not on her mother. But Mr. Miller doesn't notice. "I saw her in that series a while back," he continues. "She made the rest of the cast look like pikers!" He squirts an extra turret of whipped cream on her sundae and adds a second cherry as—Annie assumes—an homage to Ursula. "Will she be returning to the old sod anytime soon?"

That's all she needs, Ursula as Angel of Mercy, clad in Dior white, swooping down and seizing center stage, taking over, grabbing all her daughter's sorrows as her own. The role of a lifetime. The role she's been playing all of Annie's life.

When Annie's father died, Ursula, draped in black, a few sequins bordering her décolletage, rhinestone buckles twinkling on her satin shoes, carried on in such a way you would have thought she was still married to the just-deceased instead of on her fourth spouse. Henry Stevens had served a short sentence as number two, just long enough to produce Ursula's sole offspring, whom he had nicknamed Annie, deeming the Ursula-mandated *Arabella* too highfalutin for Passamaquoddy. After the funeral, all the mourners crowded around the sobbing widow, basking in Shalimar and theatrical tragedy while ignoring the daughter, the child who had loved her father and was truly bereaved.

Except for Sam, who never left her side.

Annie shovels the ice cream into her mouth. It tastes like medicine. The chocolate sauce clumps around her tongue. The nuts feel like grit. *Can all the pleasures of the world abandon one so abruptly?* she wonders. She can't even commit the sins of cigarettes and sundaes without such forbidden fruit turning into bitter herbs. She slaps ten dollars on the counter and hops off the stool.

"Something wrong?" asks Mr. Miller.

You better believe it. "Not at all," she lies.

"You aren't going to finish that?"

"As my mother always said, 'A minute on the lips, a lifetime on the hips.' "

"Guess it paid off for her." He looks wistful. "Well, tell her we miss her." He wipes the counter. "And give my best to that husband of yours."

That husband of hers. Sam. Oh, Sam. Dear Sam.

How will she ever tell Sam?

Chapter Two

Feeling lonely? Call Rachel for a movie, dinner, chat. She's number two on my speed dial (after you!).

How *can* she ever tell Sam?

Sam, her cherished cohabitant, her coworker, her co-owner, her co-replicator of the Paul Bunyan. Sam, at her side 24/7—except when she's running errands or sneaking cigarettes or scarfing down sundaes. Or . . . Her breath catches.

Or going to the doctor.

How she hates it when she hears one celebrity or another call a boyfriend, sweetheart, partner, husband, or wife "my best friend." Such a cliché, so trite, so tacky, she always notes. A view that doesn't stop Sam from introducing her as "Annie, my wife and best friend."

"Wife, yes. Best friend, no," she informed him. "Rachel owns that title."

"Just because you and Rachel pricked your thumbs and mixed your blood when you were kids." He held up his hand. "Give me a knife," he laughed. "Seriously," he continued, "you're all I need."

Though she understands how a family of two, biologically limited, might cling together to the exclusion of all others, statements like these make her feel both claustrophobic and contrite. She needs Sam. Of course she needs him. After seventeen years of marriage, he's as much a part of her life as the streets of Passamaquoddy and the scuffed floors of the sandwich shop. Still, Sam seems to lean on her more than she does on him.

"In every marriage, the balance is off," reports Rachel, graduate of a master's-degree program in social work, specialist in adolescent angst, eating disorders, and post-divorce therapy. "One partner always loves the other more."

Annie is sure this isn't true, though she doesn't argue with Rachel. She knows she and Sam love each other equally. But on the playing field of dependency, the seesaw tips.

"I can't imagine not having you by my side," Sam tells her at the shop, in bed, at the grocery store, over a glass of wine, under a shared umbrella, inside the movie theater, outside their front door. "I don't get those couples who lead separate lives. How would I ever cope without you?"

"You don't have to. I'm not going anywhere" is always her answer.

Was her answer. Her smug, satisfied answer. Is she being punished for this certainty? After all, Rachel's husband surprised the hell out of her, running off with that ditzy dental hygienist with the (ironic, oxymoronic) bad breath. Who can predict?

Given their superglue togetherness, Annie was convinced she and Sam would walk into the sunset, hip replacement to hip replacement; they'd occupy matching rocking chairs on their assisted-living porch, then go gently into that good night, if not exactly with Romeo-and-Juliet timing, at least within a few months of each other.

Not that she doesn't know life is unfair. All those people she went to school with popping out kids as easily as blowing their nose. All those people with intact families, healthy-hearted fathers, loving siblings, and a mother who doesn't embarrass them. All those people who didn't have to hold a dead daughter against their breast, a perfect, *perfect* baby with a lace of pale-blue veins fluttering over her eyelids, a sweep of lashes that a Disney princess would covet, a flawless valentine of a mouth, a comic fuzz of hair like a baby chick's.

The nurse had to pry her out of Annie's arms. Finger by finger, wrist, elbow, shoulder. "It's okay. It's okay," the nurse kept saying.

"It is *not* okay," Annie screamed.

"What shall we call her?" she asked Sam, the baby book with their checked-off favorites still tucked into her overnight bag.

"Better not to," he whispered, his words a sob against her ear.

Later, in her narrow hospital bed, as her uterus contracted and bled, he held her all night, his arms the same unrelenting vise with which she had clutched beautiful, anonymous, perfect Baby Girl Stevens-Strauss.

And even later, her husband, who had thrown up before breakfast all during her (his!) first trimester, who'd matched her cramp for cramp at each miscarriage, whose every sore throat signaled pneumonia and for whom the slightest nick meant gangrene, ended up in the hospital. "A depressive episode. Exhaustion," was the official term. "Falling apart. Emotionally fragile," the first-year resident translated. "Talk about feeling your pain."

"It's his pain too," Annie said.

Hasn't she paid her dues? Hasn't Sam?

Now she checks her watch. She knows she should go to the shop. It's almost lunchtime. Customers will be queuing up, a majority of the hungry masses consisting of locals who grab the same place in line every day exactly at noon. "Please open on Sundays," they beg.

"Nothing wrong with peanut butter and jelly," Sam jokes.

"Or a lobster roll," she adds.

She should be next to Sam now, building the sandwiches, *sam*wiches, wrapping the finished ones in the custom-designed waxed paper, chatting with the customers while simultaneously moving them forward—a talent she's honed to an art. She should be ringing up sales, slicing tomatoes, checking in with the suppliers. But Megan's there, Rachel's seventeen-year-old daughter, Annie's godchild, who, younger than her classmates, is taking off the year between high school and college. Megan has volunteered to intern at Annie's Samwich Shop. She hopes to go into the restaurant business, she explained.

"This is hardly a restaurant," Sam pointed out.

It didn't matter. Megan wanted hands-on experience to help her decide between a liberal arts college and a culinary institute.

"Okay, but a *paid* internship," Annie insisted. "And I, like your mother, strongly suggest liberal arts."

"Crack that whip," Rachel implored. "What better way to send her running toward English and art history."

Though Annie agreed to be tough—it was a tough business, after all—she herself had floundered in figuring out a career. What a stroke of fortune when she and Sam decided to buy the shop from the three brothers who had owned it from the time her own father was a child. Three fat, cookie-cutter men of indeterminate age, Julius, John, and Jerome, so pale they seemed dusted with flour, wearing spotless white aprons and white caps. The Pillsbury Doughboys, everyone called them. So much a part of the marble counter and the mullioned windows that everyone assumed they'd die with their immaculate white clogs on, keeled over the last Paul Bunyan of the day with the same lack of fuss with which they spread mayonnaise and sliced rolls. Not a single Passamaquoddian believed the Doughboys would ever desert Maine, let alone sell such a thriving enterprise.

To Annie's amazement, as soon as she and Sam became proprietors, she found herself doing something she loved. The accounts. The buying. The assembling. The spiffing up of walls with flea-market renditions of laden tables and kitchen interiors.

Not that it was easy. The day after the sale, the brothers discarded their aprons, donned Hawaiian shirts, and fled to Florida. Without leaving them the recipe for the Paul Bunyan. Had their lawyer, Bob Bernstein, who'd studied for his Bar Mitzvah with Sam, forgotten to put this crucial requirement in the purchase agreement? Of course not, their affronted attorney exclaimed; they needed to check page seven, paragraph three, subhead *a*. The parties had signed and disappeared without honoring a critical clause of the agreement. Not his fault. Paul Bunyans were his mother's milk. He was addicted. Would he ever have left out the most important line in the whole contract?

Though it took a half hour on the phone, written and verbal apologies, and a bottle of single malt to mitigate the insult to both legal and epicurean know-how, the fact remained that they didn't have the recipe for the most famous sandwich within a hundred-mile radius. Hell, the most famous sandwich in Maine. Natives who moved from the state and found themselves suffering from gastronomic nostalgia would order Paul Bunyans packed in dry ice and FedExed to places as far away as San Francisco. On visits back home, their hosts would wrap up a few dozen for return flights, causing fellow passengers to either relish the tear-watering smell or ask to change their seats. Without the recipe, Annie and Sam knew their business would bomb.

She wrote the brothers at their forwarding address; the letters were returned: *address unknown*. The emails bounced back: *invalid recipient*. The mailroom in Century Village had never heard of them. Had they started their own Florida satellite despite the noncompetition clause? She Googled. She searched Yelp. She clicked on Gourmet.com and typed in *submarine sandwich recipes*. She checked public records and actually paid $49.99 for a search. The Pillsbury Doughboys had disappeared.

"Should we hire a private detective?" she asked Sam.

Sam laughed. He was sure they could use the remaining stock and their collective gustatory memory to analyze the sandwich layer by layer. They would deconstruct and reassemble the prototype, arranging and sifting through its segments like so many archaeological shards. Salami, olive oil, onions, cheese. How hard could it be?

The two of them took notes, made diagrams. Here was the formula: Its base, the soft roll from the local bakery cut down the middle. First came chopped green peppers; second, exactly three slices of tomato, followed by a thick filling of diced onions marinated in oil, salt, garlic, and red pepper flakes and some other mysterious ingredient: Mayonnaise? Worcestershire sauce? Vinegar? (Balsamic? Cider? Wine?) Mustard? (English? American? French?)

Like the Pierre and Marie Curie of home economics, they separated out and sampled each in turn. Using an algorithm Sam devised, they subsequently—and painstakingly—tried all possible combinations until they came up with the closest approximation to the original. Once they nailed the sauce, they placed four squares of unnaturally yellow American cheese, the texture of thin rubber, over the onions. Next, they covered the cheese with three circles of overlapping salami studded with green peppercorns—all garnished with a precise row of five fluted pickles.

Their Eureka moment didn't last, however, because of the unexpected difficulty in finding just the right bricks and mortar for the Paul Bunyan. In the years—*decades*—since the brothers had started their business, even Passamaquoddy, Maine, had begun to embrace the organic. "Nutritious Diets" and "Healthy Eating" sections were colonizing more of the supermarkets' square acreage. Variety stores and fast-food joints were inserting the word *gourmet* on their signs. It wasn't easy sourcing the nitrate-laden ingredients with their artificial coloring and large proportions of fat to lean. The establishments that sold them were in the sketchier parts of town where the shelves were dusty and the shelf life long.

But finally, Annie and Sam managed to paste together a gastronomical *Grecian Urn* that they could reproduce. They held a tasting for loyal customers. "A miracle," declared the local police chief. "Like Helen Keller discovering the word for water," marveled the nursery school principal. "As good as ever," wrote the food columnist in the *Passamaquoddy Daily Telegram*. Though a few curmudgeons voiced doubts, most letters to the editor were positive, striking a you-can't-go-home-again-but-this-comes-close tone of approval.

They also needed a new name. For obvious reasons, *The Three J's* wouldn't work. They brainstormed. Maine Chance? Maine Squeeze? The Big Bite? BUNyan House? With the addition of a Pinot Grigio, they became sillier and sillier. "PtoMaine," Sam suggested, writing it out. By the time they agreed on *Annie's Samwich*, the second bottle was half-empty.

*   *   *

Now she texts Sam: *Everything ok? Can you spare me to run some errands?*

Under control, Sam texts back. *Luv u. Miss u.*

She stares at the text. *Miss u* scrolls across her eyeballs like breaking news on CNN. *How can I tell Sam?* she laments yet again.

*   *   *

In her front hall, she kicks the mail to the side, throws her coat on the floor, drops her pocketbook on the table. Her four-leaf-clover key chain breaks—no surprise—and the keys scatter and roll, one tilting precariously on the heating grate. She doesn't bother to chase after them.

She flops onto the sofa, wrapping herself in the afghan her mother-in-law gave her when Sam's parents moved to a gated community on the Gulf Coast. Its colors are tropical: oranges and yellows and chartreuses and pale orchid. Her mother-in-law, when she knitted it, must have already been dreaming of nicer, warmer places that offered oversized tricycles and pastel cocktails topped by parasols.

Annie doesn't want a nicer, warmer place. She wants what she has now. This job. This husband. This house. This life.

She knows, of course, that people die young. She's donated to bone marrow searches and Kickstarter campaigns for kids with leukemia and a young woman who wanted only to finish her college degree before her heart/lung transplant. She supports a fund for wounded soldiers and one for scholarships to memorialize lives cut short in their prime.

When she checks the mirror, she looks the same as always. She's no Mimi from La Bohème, all skin and bones whittled away from a wasting disease. Okay, she's tired after long hours at the shop. Who wouldn't be? And the dry cough could well come from inhaling onions and Tabasco sauce all day, not to mention the unrelenting cold of February in Maine. Half the town is going around hacking into their lumber-jacketed and down-stuffed sleeves. Is this the bargaining stage of grief Elisabeth Kübler-Ross talks about? Hasn't she always had a sense of doom? *Get a grip*, she tells herself. She's feeling otherwise completely fine. At least she *was* before her doctor's visit.

The doctor.

Her chest x-ray, CAT scan, and PET scan glowered from his monitor. Grasping a letter opener, Dr. Buckley pointed to the white areas on her lungs. He used words like *multiple masses*, *pulmonary nodules, swollen chest glands,* until she covered her ears. She turned away from the tip of his pointer, where the blob overlapped the outline of her lungs like a salami slice annexing a square of cheese. She remembered the pictures of diseased lungs they'd projected onto a screen at Smokers Anonymous. Scare tactics. Okay, she was scared. *Is* scared. Instead she concentrated on the letter opener, on its shiny silver side, its scrolled handle, the engraved words: *To Ambrose Buckley in grateful appreciation . . .* Because his fingers covered the rest of the inscription, she couldn't tell who was grateful or in appreciation of what. A life he saved?

Her life couldn't be saved; that much she had gleaned from what she had assumed was an ordinary appointment. Dr. Buckley had delivered her. He'd brought her into the world, into life. And now . . . Tears spilled down his baggy, grooved cheeks.

She'd protested the biopsy. She needed to think about it. Why go through surgery to confirm what already seemed so clear? she reasoned. After her exam, he'd sent her to radiology, where the techs said nothing and the young radiologist refused to meet her eye.

"There are specialists," he said.

She pointed to the monitor and the report on his desk. "Isn't that irrefutable evidence?"

"I'm not an expert. I would be remiss in not referring you. And at your young age—at *any* age—it is only sensible to seek a second opinion."

"I can't decide anything now. I need some time to process this."

"Of course," he conceded. "Though let me send on your PET scan to the son of a colleague, a thoracic surgeon in Portland, a

rising star. Don't wait too long. There are all kinds of new medical treatments that an old country doctor like me has never even
heard of."

"Okay," she granted. She looked once more at the monitor. At
the digital proof of hard facts that even a rising star could not
refute. "How long?" she asked.

He twisted the letter opener over and over. He studied it so
hard it could have been an exam question on the medical boards.
"What I tell my patients in your . . ." He paused. ". . . in your
situation—in *any* situation—is to get their affairs in order." He
reached over and took her hands. "Dear Annie," he said. "One
thing I know is that your mother and Sam will be a great support
to you."

*   *   *

Now she pulls the afghan up over her head. If only she could shut
out the world as easily as she hides under this blanket. The afghan
smells slightly ripe from the remains of buttered popcorn and
pizza during *Downton Abbey* marathons, in addition to—why not
fess up—that bit of in-honor-of-Maggie-Smith sex. She ought to
take it to the cleaners. Or ask Sam—a rare request, since she'll
have to explain that it can't be put in the industrial machines,
that it can't be commercially dried. It's always easier to do things
herself.

Though how much longer will she be able to keep doing
things?

"Make another appointment for next week," Dr. Buckley
advised. "We should have the thoracic surgeon's report as well as
a referral to a specialist. And I want to check you out. Also . . . we
must talk about what to expect."

What to expect when you're expecting . . . what? She didn't want to know. She fled the waiting room before the receptionist could even grab the scheduling chart.

She'll need to explain everything to Sam. How to work the washing machine, how to care for the silver, what polish to use on the furniture, how to fit the slipcovers over the sofa's arms, how to bolster the desk leg with two and a half matchbooks, how to clean the oven, how to RSVP to a formal invitation, how to repot the philodendron, how to fix the running toilet. He'll have to learn to remember doctor and dentist appointments, to renew subscriptions, to fertilize the lawn, to buy mop refills, to pair socks—an endless list of instructions. Theirs is not an equal division of labor. Sam pays the bills and takes the cars to Gus's Gas for tune-ups. On his way home, he'll fetch clothes already laundered, appliances already repaired. She does everything else. The domestic. The social. The practical. The pain-in-the-neck stuff.

It's what she prefers. She's good at the day-to-day. Sam is nicer, smarter, more loving, but he hammers his nails in crooked, and he never notices if his shoes need new soles. When he was sixteen, his mother still sewed name tags into all his clothes and ironed his jeans while everyone else was courting grunge. During his college years, Sam sent his laundry home and days later it would reappear, pressed, folded, buttons reattached, holes expertly darned, with foil-wrapped Hershey's Kisses tucked between his undershirts. His mother kept both the infirmary and the school dispensary on speed-dial. He'd had a rheumatic fever scare as a child, and though it turned out to be a simple, treatable strep, his mother had declared her strapping son "frail."

To their credit, Sam's parents never complained that he'd married a Unitarian instead of the nice Jewish girl they might have hoped for him. Whoever he picked was just fine. They trusted his choices. They wanted only his happiness. The day Sam's parents moved south, his mother bestowed the afghan on the two of them, then took Annie aside. "Marty and I can leave without worry," she confided, "now that I know my boy is in such good hands."

"That husband of yours is incompetent," Ursula has grumbled on several occasions where Sam has failed to rise to the level of her requests. One involved a complicated dress and a baffling configuration of hooks and eyes. "Though don't get me wrong, I love him to death."

"Just let me," Annie said, clasping a ribbon of black silk at Ursula's shoulder.

"His mother spoiled him rotten. And now you're doing the same."

Sam wasn't spoiled, she knew. He was just the sort of person people wanted to take care of. He was kind and sweet and unselfish, the opposite of Ursula. It was hardly his fault that he had grown used to having so many things done for him, his way magically smoothed by devoted parents who tucked him into bed with prophylactic chicken soup and ginger tea during flu season, who doted on his earnestness, his intelligence, his humor, his good nature.

And a wife who did the same, who felt lucky to do the same, despite a few never-voiced grumbles about a lack of personal space and a husband's occasional neediness. On a balance sheet of debit and credit, Annie had clearly hit the jackpot; she basked in the unconditional love that was Sam's huge return for her small services rendered.

Now she pulls the afghan off her head. She folds it over the arm of the sofa. She thinks back to Dr. Buckley's words: "One thing I know is that your mother and Sam will be a great support to you."

Forget Ursula.

But Sam . . .

Telling him will make it real, put a name on it. And every time he looks at her . . . But how can she not?

She sits still. On the landing, the grandfather clock ticks. The radiators steam. Out in the street, a snowplow scrapes patches of ice. From somewhere—the backyard next door?—a child laughs with delight. She thinks of the joy that day when she and Sam discovered the formula for the Paul Bunyan. Her next step will bring no joy.

Chapter Three

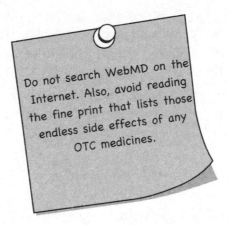

Do not search WebMD on the Internet. Also, avoid reading the fine print that lists those endless side effects of any OTC medicines.

She hears Sam's car in the driveway. Just her luck that he's earlier than usual. She could invent an errand, driving round the block to give herself extra minutes to prepare. Would a few whirls through the intersections of Elm and Main make her revelation easier—or just delay the inevitable? If she were Ursula, she'd be great at picking the right words without any need to rehearse this particular soliloquy. Why couldn't she have inherited both Ursula's talent and her confidence? Has there ever been a daughter so unlike her mother? But then, consolation (or not), Ursula's never had a Sam.

Annie peeks out the window at Sam's Volvo, its bumper sticker flaunting the familiar logo and sketch of the Bunyan. One of its corners is curled and stripped, the *A* in *Annie's* nearly torn off. She's feeling stripped and torn herself. Stripped bare, defenseless, scared.

Which makes what she's about to do even more urgent. At least she's got the starting point. Her sundae gluttony has paid off, not just the predictable sugar high (if only), expanded hips, and oral gratification, but also unexpected dividends: the gift of Mr. Miller's revelations about Mrs. Bouchard's lack of a will has supplied her introductory paragraph, egged on by Dr. Buckley's "get your affairs in order." She'll move from the general to the specific, starting with the will and segueing to her illness. How can she not tell Sam? How can she even contemplate hiding such momentous information from the closest person on earth to her? They've never kept secrets from each other. He would want to know the truth, wouldn't he? Even though she'll be destroying him. Her. Them.

She finds him in the kitchen, reading the paper. And just like that—divine intervention?—he offers her the cue. "I see old Mrs. Bouchard died," he reports, turning the paper inside out to exhibit a dated photo of the deceased, who even in her youth scared local kids enough that hardly any trick-or-treater, Annie included, would venture up those rickety stairs on Halloween.

She takes the chair beside him rather than her usual one across the table. He leans over and kisses her. She smells coffee mixed with onions and pickles.

"Even the obit writer," he continues, "seems to be having a hard time conveying anything good about her, except that she was devoted to her cat." He chuckles. "Well, I hope Agnes inherits a bundle. She deserves every cent, tending to that miserable women all those years."

"I stopped in the drugstore, and Mr. Miller told me. He also told me she died intestate and that heirs are coming out of the woodwork."

"Poor Agnes." Sam sighs.

"Speaking of which . . ." Annie begins.

Sam sneezes. "I think I may be getting a cold," he says. "My throat's a little raw. Maybe I caught your cough."

"At this point, I doubt it's contagious."

"Let's hope. You know how I hate being sick." He puts down the paper. "How was your day?"

"Okay," she says. She pinches her wrist. Why is she such a wimp? Such a coward? Why can't she answer, as intended, *very much not okay* and explain why?

"Did you pick up my stuff from the cleaners?" he asks. "The jacket and pants I spilled hot chocolate all over? Not my fault. Megan bumped into me," he adds.

"They'll be ready tomorrow." How long must they string out these banalities, this preamble, until she can detonate the bomb that will explode their world? She studies Mrs. Bouchard's photo now sneering up at her from the *Passamaquoddy Daily Telegram*. "As I was about to say," she begins.

"Do we have any lozenges left in the medicine cabinet?"

"Sam!" she exclaims. "I'm trying to talk to you."

"Sorry," he says. "Go on."

She goes on. "I think we should make up our wills."

Sam frowns. "Whatever for?" he asks.

She points to the photo of old Mrs. Bouchard. "Because . . ."

He interrupts. "Don't be ridiculous. We're not going to die tomorrow."

"We need to do this."

"Look, even without a will, everything will go to you or me. After we're both dead, who cares? Why bring up such an unsettling topic now?"

"Because . . ." she repeats.

He cuts in again. "We have no children. No one's going to fight over our—ha!—fortune. Besides, we'll outlive my mother and father. And I can't imagine anything felling Ursula."

"We can't be sure."

"It's in the natural order of things for children to survive their parents. We've already disrupted that order once, we've already had a loss . . ."

"Which doesn't mean there couldn't be more losses."

"Statistically"—he considers, his voice pedagogical—"not probable. If you look at insurance tables for life expectancy . . ."

"Statistics are irrelevant when . . . Sam, I could be sick, *very* sick—"

"As could I. This cold might turn into pneumonia. Or even worse. I'd end up bedridden. Tied to an oxygen canister. Sent to a TB sanatorium. Do they still exist? Crack all my ribs from coughing. Have to move to Arizona for the air, give up Bunyans to subsist solely on applesauce and Cream of Wheat, then be forced to take medicines with all those terrible side effects they warn you about on TV ads." He laughs.

"Not funny."

"It is, sort of," he counters.

"I hate to break into your litany of disasters, *imagined* disasters, Sam, especially when you're on such a roll, but I've got something I'm trying to tell you," she persists.

"Okay. I know it's prudent to make a will. I acknowledge you're the practical one in the family, and that, as usual, you're right. We *could* be hit by the proverbial bus or choke on a chunk of cheese. Still, what's the rush? We'll get to that in due course. At the moment, however"—he sneezes, blows his nose on a napkin—"the very thought of making a will, of imagining one of us dying . . ."

"I understand your reluctance. Nevertheless," she ventures, "what if . . . one of us . . . me . . . ?"

He shakes his head. He puts his hands over his ears.

She leans closer. She notes the stubborn set of his jaw, his toddler's hear-no-evil posture. She assumes he can read her as well as she can read him. Does he already sense the train heading toward them, the impossibility of derailing it, the hopelessness of rescuing the damsel in distress now tied to the tracks?

"I refuse to listen any more to these silly suppositions. Annie, I could never live without you. You know that. If something happened to you, well, I'd just . . ." He stabs his thumb against his heart. "There's no way I could go on without you." He rubs his chest. "I plan to grow old with you."

"There's no guarantee, Sam."

"For me, there is. It's what I count on. Otherwise . . ." He lowers his chin to his hands.

She studies him. Tears have started to form in the corners of his eyes. He squeezes her shoulder, pulls his chair back from the table. He points at the newspaper. "Even dead, Mrs. Bouchard still casts her evil spell, provoking this totally unpleasant conversation. Right now, all I want is to swallow two aspirins, get in bed, and take a nap. End of discussion. I love you, Annie. That's all we need to say to each other."

He heads upstairs. As soon as she hears the medicine cabinet squeak open, she walks to the front hall. She picks her pocketbook off the table. She digs underneath the tangle of receipts, Chap Stick, comb, rubber bands, pens, and the matchbook from Gus's Gas for the number to Dr. Buckley's office.

Is there a wobble in the receptionist's voice when Annie identifies herself? "I'll put you right through," says Carolyn Connelly, sparing her the usual *Wassup* and *How's your mom?*

"So glad you called," says Dr. Buckley. "I've got a patient here. Hang on while I step into the other room."

Annie registers the clank of a metal file drawer, the thud of footsteps, the closing of a door. "How can I help you?" Dr. Buckley asks.

"It's about Sam."

"Would you like to make an appointment for me to talk to him?"

"Absolutely not," Annie says, more harshly than she intended. "I don't want him to know."

"Know . . . ?"

"I mean my lungs . . ."

The clock ticks on. The radiator still hisses. Dr. Buckley is silent for so long that Annie wonders if they've been cut off. But then he says, in a measured tone, "He will have to be told."

"I tried. Unsuccessfully. He shut me down."

"Then try again. And tell your mother, too."

"Eventually," says Annie. "But not now."

"This is folly, young lady."

"This is what I want."

More forcefully, he urges, "Something I strongly advise against. For your family's sake. For your own sake." Then his voice turns softer, gentler. "You'll need help in processing all of this. I can refer you to a counselor. And by the end of the day, I should receive the name of a top-notch oncologist."

"No!" Annie nearly shouts. As soon as she hears his intake of breath, she stops. "Okay," she concedes. "Maybe. Though I need to think this through first. I can't make this big a decision so fast. But I can promise you this: the minute I feel sick, the minute I develop symptoms I can't excuse, I'll do everything. Tell Sam, see a specialist, have surgery, sign up for a shrink, undergo chemo, radiation, acupuncture. I'll meditate, write a blog, guzzle carrot juice—whatever. But for right now, for the time being . . ."

"Annie . . ."

"I have to sleep on it."

"Annie . . ." he repeats.

She cuts him off. "If you have a problem with that, let me remind you of HIPAA rules. Of doctor-patient confidentiality."

Chapter Four

Women like flowers. Candy might not be appreciated because of diets and food issues. Jewelry works like a charm.

Annie drops onto the sofa. She scoops up the newspaper crumpled underneath the coffee table. In the lower corner, a headline catches her eye: *Ninety-Year-Old Couple Die Within the Same Hour.* She reads about a husband and wife, inseparable since meeting as teenagers, who "held hands at breakfast every morning even after seventy years of marriage." Tears spill over as Annie pictures the pair's gnarled, nonagenarian fingers clasped over their Shredded Wheat. She studies her own hands, not yet and never to be liver-spotted with age, sporting only a scattering of scars chalked up to workplace injuries.

She considers opening a bottle of wine. Too early. And what good would it do? Dull senses that are already numbed? Depress reactions that are already slowed?

Tell Sam, Dr. Buckley said. There are a million reasons not to tell Sam, ones she should have presented to Dr. Buckley. No wonder she dropped out of debate club. She could never summon an argument on the spot, only after the fact. What the French call *l'esprit d'escalier*. She tried, but he wouldn't listen. Clearly she can't do it. At least not now, when she doesn't have a real diagnosis, when she has no facts. She must protect him, has always protected him. More so since all lioness instincts have been deflected from her nonexistent cubs and onto her spouse. *Sam will support you*, Dr. Buckley promised. What kind of support can Sam offer her in this case? There are no buttresses for dying, only the prospect of knocking the scaffolding out from under both of them.

Sam is incompetent, Ursula complained. That's Ursula's adjective. Annie herself would choose *a tad bungling, a bit clueless*. She sighs, a drawn-out sigh that ends in a cough. What is the word for holding two opposing thoughts in your head? she wonders. Paradox? Cognitive dissonance? Doublethink? Once she knew the precise term, but her formal education is now too far in the past and too blunted by daily life. Yes, Sam gives her support. (How can she live without him?) Yes, Sam is, well, bungling. (How can he live without her?)

Another paradox: as exasperating as Sam's foibles are, they're also endearing. Especially when his apologies make you want to apologize for causing the need for him to apologize in the first place. Annie can always forgive Sam's absent-minded-professor quality because it's impossible to stay mad at him.

Not that she doesn't get annoyed. She scrolls through examples that might forever infuriate a less tolerant, less grudge-bearing spouse. For instance: his hypochondria, his fear that every splinter requires a tetanus shot, his tendency, despite repeated disasters, despite an inability to learn from his mistakes, to leave items on the roof of the car while he's loading the trunk. How many times has he fetched cartons of freshly laundered shirts from the cleaners only to arrive home without them? Retracing his route, he'll either discover the box untouched at the side of the road or flattened by a semi, the shirts inside embossed with the tread of big-rig tires; or worse, he'll find nothing, all missing contents most likely recycled into the wardrobe of a stranger whose neck measures fifteen and a half and whose arms are a perfect thirty-four.

"Maybe whoever swiped them needs those shirts more than me," Sam will note, turning an act of neglect into an act of charity. How can you not love somebody who, except for his own health catastrophizing, sees the glass not just half full but brimming? Yet even the most unrepentant Pollyanna must acknowledge that there are certain things that cannot be changed by a positive attitude.

Annie recalls the coffee mugs plunked on the roof of the car, thus requiring a constant backup of thermal replacements. She remembers the ring of house keys, shop keys, and car keys flying off a bridge and into the river underneath, resulting in a comfortless night at the Comfort Inn because it was too late to get a new key made or contact the neighbors who kept their extras.

And what about the novel Rachel lent her for the trip to a convention of food purveyors in Portland? Stopped at a red light in Monument Square after a three-hour drive on the Turnpike, they were startled by a man pounding on their windshield.

"Ignore him," she warned, "he's probably a squeegee scammer."

Sam rolled down the window.

The man held up the novel. Intact except for a dusting of gravel. "This fell off your roof back there on Exchange Street," he said.

Did Sam feel sheepish? Embarrassed? Ashamed?

No. "Imagine," he marveled, "that book made the whole trip at sixty-five miles an hour along Ninety-Five and only toppled a block away. A feat worthy of the Ripley's Believe It or Not."

She turns her attention to what happened after the baby—the one time when Sam could not weave straw into gold. A nurse had ordered her into a wheelchair, even though she'd been pacing the corridor relentlessly for the three days she was incarcerated in the maternity ward, tortured by the cries of healthy newborns and the chatter of excited mothers debating breastfeeding techniques and diapering skills.

Discharged, she was rolled to the hospital lobby as Sam hurried to get the car. She and the nurse waited and waited. When the nurse checked her watch for the seventh time, Annie suggested she return to her other duties. "Go," Annie ordered. "I'll be fine."

The nurse seemed dubious. "You sure?"

People came and went. Solicitous husbands and attentive family members helped the newly released to their still-running, double-parked cars outside the entrance. Some patients cuddled babies; others clutched overnight bags, pink plastic sick bins, balloons and flowers, and folders of post-surgery instructions. "You still here?" asked a man she'd seen earlier carrying a beribboned fruit basket and now wrapped in his overcoat.

After what seemed like an eternity, Sam appeared, face furious. "You won't believe this," he said.

"Try me."

"They lost our keys."

"Let's call a taxi. I can't bear to stay one more minute in this place."

"Of course not, Annie." He stroked her hand. "How could they . . ."

A man wearing a blue uniform with *Hospital Parking* embroidered on the pocket came up to them. "I'll drive you. We are so sorry. They have never mixed up the keys in the twenty years I've been parking-garage manager. For some strange reason, the key we found left with your Volvo is marked *Toyota*. I can't imagine how . . ."

"Toyota," Annie said.

"Toyota," Sam repeated.

"Check your pocket," Annie demanded.

Sure enough, Sam fished out his key chain, the Volvo key attached. "Oh, hell!" Sam struck his forehead with the palm of his hand. "My fault," he said to the manager. "I gave you the wrong one after I parked the car. And didn't think to check. I've had it in my pocket all this time while my poor wife . . . I feel so stupid. Do let me treat you to a meal, a *week* of meals, at our sandwich shop. Please convey my apologies to the attendants. I'm such a . . ."

"Sam," Annie said. "Shut up and take me home."

All the *how could you especially at this time*s dried up as Sam struggled to hold back sobs. All recriminations vanished as Sam led Annie upstairs to the bedroom, fresh sheets on the bed, flowers on the bureau, a jar of malted milk balls set out on a brand-new wicker breakfast tray with a stack of page-turning mysteries piled next to it. "I was so worried, such a wreck over, well, everything, I must have been out of my mind," he confessed.

And a week later, he ended up in the hospital. "Clinical depression," the doctor diagnosed. "Emotionally fragile," he warned.

Now Annie sticks the newspaper back under the coffee table and thinks about Sam, about how their loss has pulled them closer, not caused the kind of rift other tragedy-plagued marriages suffer. She and Sam resemble puzzle pieces. Apart, their edges are so jagged and jutting, so awkwardly notched, it's hard to get a sense of them—until, fit together, they form a complete and continuous whole.

Like the couple in the newspaper, they've been close from the start. Well, almost, she corrects, depending on how you define *start*. She pictures the redheaded young man whose brass-buttoned blue blazer topped pressed white trousers. Whose side-parted hair gleamed like glass. He was holding a martini in the bar where everybody else was chugging beer and wearing jeans. Charles. Hardly a Chuck or a Charlie, though the other college kids she hung out with that summer addressed him that way. "Are you the last virgin in New York?" he said to her in his tidy bed in his shiny downtown loft.

"I'm from Maine," she said.

"That explains it," he said, pulling her to him with practiced ease.

It was her fish-out-of-water interlude, a time when she and Sam had decided to take a break for the summer. She'd secured an internship in New York between freshman and sophomore year, sharing a hellish Hell's Kitchen one-bedroom, one-bath walk-up with Rachel and the two NYU juniors who answered their need-roommates ad. Untethered to home, family, Sam, she'd discovered an alternate universe that eclipsed her normal world and turned her into a second self she barely recognized.

She'd worked at a now-defunct women's magazine. Hidden from the valuable front-of-the-house real estate just off the elevator, she sorted unsolicited submissions into graveyard file cabinets and sent hope-dashing form rejection slips to the writers of the unread articles. Though it wasn't the glamorous job she had anticipated, its recompense was the glamorous Charles.

"A summer fling," Rachel pronounced. "A rite of passage."

The rite ended in August along with her lease on big-city life. Charles had moved on to a sophomore at Columbia. Besides, she'd had her fill of martinis; she grew to loathe Charles's bay rum aftershave. Right after Labor Day, she was back home and with Sam.

Soon they were inseparable, so much so that they were *AnnieandSam*, one word spoken on a single exhaled breath. They knew they'd be married. Their wedding was already planned for the week after graduation. Though Annie worried about jobs, where they would live, Sam was sure everything would work out. "Minor details," he said dismissively.

She remembers the day the details started to fall into place. She pictures the library at Bowdoin: she and Sam, *AnnieandSam*, chairs pulled up to the table behind the stacks. Sam unloaded a backpack's worth of law school brochures. Annie added articles on entry-level publishing opportunities and the limited market for English majors. They fanned them out.

Sam turned to her. "Do we really want to do this?" he asked.

She examined the brochures: the smiling multiethnic students, the swaths of Frisbee-strewn green campuses, the spires of Manhattan skyscrapers, graduates clutching diplomas underneath hanging scales of justice. She checked out the publishing newsletters with their photographs of newly minted editors, stuffed bookshelves rising to the ceilings of charming offices, cubicles overrun by teetering columns of manuscripts. She shook her head. "No."

"Me neither."

"Your parents . . . ?"

"They want me to be happy." He picked up a sheet, which listed lawyers' starting salaries, a first-year fortune that would sustain, for a decade, an extended family in rural Maine.

"Ursula?" he asked.

"Not an issue. She's already given up on me." Annie studied the chart of salaries. "I don't want to live in New York."

"Me neither."

"Or Boston," she continued.

He groaned. "Or, God forbid, somewhere out west."

She pushed aside the sheaf of papers. "Would it be childish and unambitious of me, not to mention a waste of a good education, to say that I want to go home?"

"Woo-hoo!" he yelped, causing a *shush* from somewhere over by Biographies. He grabbed her. He kissed her forehead, her cheeks, her lips.

"Funny that some people can't wait to get away. But for us . . ." she said.

"We're homebodies," he finished. "Two of a kind. How amazing that we found each other."

"Amazing," she echoed. She turned serious. "But what will we do when we go back to Passamaquoddy?"

He scraped his chair around so he was facing her. Their knees touched. He took her hands in his. He beamed his irresistible-Sam grin. "The most important thing is having decided where we're going to spend the rest of our lives. I have utter faith that everything will turn out okay."

Because for Sam, it always did.

Once upon a time. Before the shadow on her lungs started to cast its shadow on him, on both of them, on *AnnieandSam*.

Back then, she tried to believe him, tried not to counteract his good humor, his trust in the future, tried not to play the pessimist to his Pangloss-like certainty that all would be fine in this best of all possible worlds.

"What's more, we don't have to decide everything this minute," he added.

She refrained from pointing out that they were seniors in college, that they were returning to a town in Maine hit by a depressed economy. That they were liberal arts majors, trained for nothing but careful reading and enlightened thinking and composing a strong intellectual argument headed by topic sentences and anchored by footnotes.

Sam changed the subject. "Talked to my mom last night," he confided.

"And . . . ?"

"She sends her best to you."

"Very nice."

"She filled me in on the gossip, who died, who was arrested for a DUI, who gave the biggest donation toward a stained-glass window for the temple. Betty and George Grismisch, if you want to know." He laughed. "Then there's Evelyn Benoit's new home entertainment system . . ."

Why was he yakking about such things when their prospects felt so precarious—at least to her? "Sam!"

"All right, then, I take it you don't want to know the size of the speakers or where Evelyn eventually placed the unit after two deep scratches on the newly varnished floor."

"No, I don't."

"Well, here's something that might interest you more. Just as we were hanging up, Mom mentioned that the Doughboys might be selling the Three J's."

Shocked, Annie leaned forward. "How could they? It's an institution."

For a few seconds, they seethed in mutual silent indignation at the loss soon to be inflicted on their hometown. Annie picked up a business school brochure. Idly she thumbed through the first few pages of the booklet, a whirl of gray suits and shiny briefcases. She stopped at a photograph of students lined up at a salad bar in a graduate-student dining hall. She took in the vats of gleaming red peppers and bright green lettuce leaves, the crusty loaves that looked as if they'd arrived on the overnight plane from Paris. She knew there was no truth in such advertising, that food was as primped and polished and embellished as photoshopped models in magazines. Nevertheless . . . an idea slowly took shape. Could it work? Would it be possible?

Sam must have been thinking the same thing, because his face assumed a faraway, dreamy look. "The first care package my parents sent to me, freshman year, was a dozen Paul Bunyans. I was the most popular guy on campus for those couple of hours until they were all devoured."

"I remember. I ate one for breakfast."

"Who could forget? We could smell the onions for weeks on my futon."

She smiled. "It didn't bother us, as I recall."

"Because we were otherwise occupied." He smiled back. "Annie, do you really think . . . ?"

"I do," Annie stated with a conviction that wasn't completely an act. "Though"—she wagged a cautionary finger—"taking over the Three J's isn't going to rank high in the class alumni notes. It's basically just submarine sandwiches . . ."

"Which can't be improved on," he said. "Which are artisanal in their own essential submarine-ness."

Annie tilted her chin. "It's a big step. A huge learning curve."

"I know."

"Kind of scary."

"We'll have each other." Sam sat, his head bowed, brow furrowed, fist on chin in classic Rodin position.

Annie waited. She listened to the rustle of papers in carrels, the scrape of books being taken down from shelves and put back. She heard the rumbling wheels of a creaky library cart.

At last, Sam looked up. "The timing of this—right before our wedding, right when we decide to move home. Right when we're casting around for some kind of work, for some kind of future. It's got to be a sign." He put his lips to Annie's ear. "Let's do it," he whispered.

*   *   *

Later that night, she lies awake, rigid, next to Sam, whose oblivious peaceful breaths in this new nonpeaceful world seem an insult. She remembers a movie she once watched on a sleepless night, a real weepie with Julia Roberts, called *Dying Young*; she recalls a *Modern Love* piece in the Sunday *Times* in which a cancer-ridden wife heartbreakingly offers up her cherished husband to, she hopes, a worthy successor. *What should I do?* races through Annie's head. Sam rolls over and tucks his knee into hers.

In the morning she calls Dr. Buckley. "Good girl," he says, and gives her the name of the best oncologist in Portland. "A woman," he adds, as if this is a novelty.

"Dr. O'Brien is generally booked up," she's told when she reaches the office. "She's in high demand." Annie's given a date three weeks from now and is added to the waiting list in case of cancellation. "Is it an emergency?" asks the nurse.

"Not really," Annie replies, relieved to be granted a respite, relieved that the word *emergency* is said in such a routine way. She needs time get her affairs in order, as Dr. Buckley suggested. To prepare Sam. She studies the scribbled telephone number. As soon as she knows what's ahead, as soon as she meets with Dr. O'Brien, she'll tell him.

* * *

Now Annie looks at the newspaper folded under the coffee table. She thinks of the husband and wife who held hands every morning at breakfast for seventy years. She considers all the breakfasts she and Sam have shared: the bowls of cereal, plates of poached eggs, glasses of juice. How many more will be allotted to them? she wonders.

"This has been quite a day," Sam marveled all those years ago as, arms linked, they skipped down the library steps. "Now we'll have a business to leave to our kids. That is, after we die together at ninety-five, wearing matching aprons and slumped over a salami and a jar of peppercorns."

Chapter Five

Don't let your underwear become tattered. Yes, somebody will see it once again.

The doorbell chimes. Annie ignores it. She doesn't feel like a chat with the UPS man or a lecture from the mail carrier about how the postal service is going to hell. She doesn't want to buy Girl Scout cookies or save the whales or sign a petition for more stop signs. She just wants to stop, stop her world from spinning out of control.

The doorbell keeps buzzing. Three long and two short beeps, followed by an interminable blast. She gets up. Does she feel weak? Dizzy?

Rachel is on the porch, stomping her feet, bundled in parka, hood, scarf, mittens, blowing frosty puffs of air. "It's about time," she says. "You can't hide from me. Spied your coat through the window."

Once inside, she peels off her layers, hangs everything up in the hall closet, including Annie's dropped and abandoned coat.

She wiggles out of her boots and one pair of the two pairs of socks she's wearing. These she balls up, then sticks on the tray that holds magazines and catalogs. "I went by the shop to buy Paul Bunyans for dinner. I left them in the car to avoid stinking up your house. Not that the smell isn't Chanel number five to you." She slumps onto the sofa. "You'd think Megan would get sick of them. Anyway," she continues, "Sam said you were doing errands and should be home by now." She studies Annie, who is standing in the entrance to the living room. "You look frazzled. You really should get a humidifier for that cough. It's worked wonders for my sinuses." She unfolds the afghan and tucks it around her legs. "Tea would be nice."

"I'll just put on the kettle," Annie says, not even registering that she's coughed.

Though Sam originally deduced allergies—mold, dust mites—Annie pooh-poohed his diagnosis. Wasn't coughing in winter just the same as sweating in summer? Part of the climate, she argued, but she made the doctor's appointment anyway.

Her mistake.

In the kitchen, Annie pulls out tea bags and sugar. She slices a lemon. She watches for the water to boil. Should she tell Rachel? To unload this burden would be such a relief. Plus, Rachel's a psychologist. Like doctors and priests, she's sworn to secrecy.

She pictures how the plot will unfold: She makes her entrance. As the overture to Act One, she performs a crescendo of coughs. She waits a dramatic beat before she stage-whispers *I'm dying*. Or, rather, *I AM dying*. Rachel goes suddenly quiet, then emits a single strangled sob; she struggles to assume her social worker's voice to express words of empathy, all the while trying to hide her own personal shock and dismay.

Act Two: Rachel holds Annie close and lets her cry; she brings over casseroles with heating instructions on Post-its stuck to the dish; she offers to accompany her to her doctor's appointments and treatments.

Act Three is, of course, the inevitable. Accompanied by a noble, affirmation-of-the-human-spirit consoling and cathartic eulogy.

Now the whistle goes off. Annie pours the water into Annie's Samwich mugs, dunks a tea bag in each, finds a couple of broken biscotti, and puts everything on a tray. Better not to confide in Rachel, she decides. How can she tell anyone without telling Sam first? Such a lapse would be a huge transgression, like breaking her marriage contract or backtracking on a promise or casting herself into a mean-girl role, favoring some, excluding others. Still, protecting a husband must count as an honorable motive. Especially to someone who knows Sam.

She grabs two napkins off the counter top. A hostess gift from dinner guests last summer, they sport rainbows and daffodils and frolicking kittens with the kind of unrelenting good cheer that made her wince when she opened them.

Rachel sips the tea. Annie passes her the plate of biscotti. Rachel shakes her head. "I shouldn't," she says.

Annie looks at her friend, who is as slim and pretty as when they were roommates at Bowdoin together, roommates before she became roommates with Sam.

"Why not?" she asks, scarfing down her own cookie without even tasting it.

"Because, unlike you, I'm searching for a husband. A boy-friend. Someone to date. You have no idea what's it like out there, what the competition is."

"With Ursula as a mother? I know a bit about competition."

Rachel groans. "Remember when she came to visit you at school? She had all your friends, the cool guys, the faculty, the hairnetted ladies in the cafeteria, and Dean Pretty Boy eating out of her hand. *Bejeweled* hand."

"The story of my life."

Rachel sighs. "Including me. Talk about a fair-weather friend; I abandoned you to sit at her feet. And oh, what feet. Those shoes she wore."

"Still wears . . ."

"Can you imagine what she must spend on them?" Rachel scoops out the tea bag and wraps it in the cheerful napkin, which instantly turns brown and sodden. "But Sam never succumbed. He only had eyes for you; he didn't care if you sat around in sweat pants all day and barely combed your hair. While the rest of us wasted hours primping, using up our meal-ticket allowance on moisturizer and eyelash curlers."

Annie did remember. "Ursula was so glad we roomed together. She was sure you'd be a good influence on me."

"Ha! By getting pregnant? I should have taken lessons from *you.* That jerk I married. How could I have missed the signs? Particularly when he kept suggesting I get my teeth whitened because I'd"—she curls her fingers into commas—"quote, look younger, unquote."

"And now he gets to listen to Justin Bieber and Miley Cyrus all day." Annie laughs, amazed to hear sounds of merriment coming from her mouth.

"Megan reports Cindi-with-an-*i* has signed him up for yoga. They have his-and-hers mats. He goes to a stylist instead of the barber. He's got highlights. And he's lasered all the hair off his back and chest."

"Which won't change his essential asshole-ness," Annie says in solidarity. And because Rachel has begun to look a little sad, as though she's missing, if not a hairy husband, then a favorite stuffed animal, Annie shifts the subject. "So, how's work?"

"The usual. Eating disorders. Cutting. Helicopter parents. Divorce. Stepsiblings. SATs. Bad boyfriends. Adolescence sucks."

"Megan turned out great."

"At least one good thing came out of that marriage." Rachel beams. "She did turn out great, didn't she?"

"No goddaughter of mine would dare be otherwise." Annie dumps an extra teaspoonful of sugar into her mug and reaches for Rachel's biscotti. "So, what *is* going on with you and the search for Mr. Right?"

Rachel unrolls the afghan from her legs and pulls it up to her neck. Annie recognizes the impulse. "Please, can I just stay buried here until my hormone levels drop?"

"Rachel . . . ?"

Rachel plucks at a yellow-and-turquoise square. She scrapes something—a pizza crust?—off of it. "I joined Match.com, eHarmony, OkCupid, JDate, and . . ."

"JDate?" Annie interrupts.

"What? A perfectly acceptable gentile girl can't hope for a nice Jewish boy like Sam?"

"Sam? You're always pointing out his shortcomings. You and Ursula."

"Which doesn't mean I don't appreciate him. Your husband has many sterling qualities . . . and those good looks. But . . ."

"But . . . ?"

"You've spoiled him." Shrink-like, she appraises Annie, scanning for defensive twitches or clenched fists. "Maybe because Ursula is so critical, maybe because your father died, maybe because you need someone to mother, maybe—"

Annie holds up her hand. "Spare me the analysis."

"Sorry. My default mode. Nevertheless, Annie, a man like Sam can be trained."

Trained? For what? she wonders. Trained to pick up his laundry? To morph into a social butterfly? She folds her napkin. Trained to live without her?

"And I even drove to Boston once," Rachel continues. "Why? To have lunch with a doofus who wears the remains of every meal he's ever eaten on his tie, who divides the bill in half—on his calculator. A guy in Portland brought along an album of photos of his dead Weimaraner. One jerk handed me his four-hundred-sixty-eight-page manuscript, single-spaced, all capital letters. 'That's how you'll get to know me,' he advised."

Annie shakes her head. "I couldn't do it."

"You'll never need to do it. Sam would never leave you."

Annie brushes crumbs off her knees and onto her plate. "If something happened to him . . . well, I guess I'd just remain an old maid."

"Nonsense. Remember what's-his-name with that amazing loft?"

"Charles?"

"Yeah, that's the one. Leaving Sam out of the equation, you never learned to flirt, even with my fine example and Charles to practice on. Granted, he wasn't around long enough for you to hone any skills. But you're not hopeless. Check out the self-help section of the bookstore. There are instructions for everything. Relationship manuals. Rules for dating, for going after what you want. Rules for playing it cool. I should write one myself."

"That would keep you busy in your two seconds of spare time." Annie steadies her mug. She peers inside. No doubt there are diagrams on how to read tea leaves, too. "Sam and I consulted guides to small businesses and restaurant equipment. I just haven't sampled the kind you're talking about."

"Not even *The Joy of Sex*?"

"Ha! That, of course." Annie points to Rachel's empty cup. "A refill?"

"Thanks, but no. I have to get those sandwiches home. And steam some broccoli for Megan. Since she's been interning at your shop, her nutrition has gone to ruin."

Annie smiles. "Pickles don't count as a vegetable?"

Rachel folds the afghan. "Your mother-in-law certainly chose unusual colors. How she must treasure you to have given you this. I envy you."

"Believe me, there's nothing to envy."

"A decent mother-in-law a thousand miles away? A loyal and loving husband by your side . . . ?"

Annie keeps silent. She pictures Baby Girl Stevens-Strauss, her blue-veined eyelids, her fuzz of hair. She thinks of this fresh new hell she's hiding from her dearest friend. She ducks her head. At least, she realizes, with a perverse relief, she's not going to leave behind a motherless kid.

Rachel reaches for her, pulls her into her arms. "I'm such an idiot. How could I have . . . ?" She pauses, choosing her words.

"You must realize there are specialists in complicated pregnancies. There might be something . . ."

"I got pregnant. I managed to carry one baby to term."

"Why not at least try? Who can discount the miracles of modern medicine? According to that fount of wisdom, *People* magazine, women who've been told they can't have children are having them all over the place. These days, thirty-seven is not too late."

But it is too late, Annie tells herself. After four miscarriages and a dead baby, wasn't the universe telling her something? If you break your leg multiple times skiing, you give up skiing. A no-brainer. And even if it wasn't too late, she knew she could never take a chance on another stillborn. "Enough!" she cautions Rachel. "I'm sure that you in the helping professions think I should have worked through my grief by now, should have moved on to acceptance—"

"I think no such thing."

"—and yet if Sam and I accept what happened, achieve, as you say, closure, then we have *really* lost our baby, have broken our connection with her."

Rachel hugs her tighter. "I know, Annie. I know." Rachel also knows not to mention, as she once did, that studies of childless couples show they are much happier than those with offspring underfoot.

*   *   *

As soon as Rachel leaves, Annie clears the tea things and dumps them in the sink. Without bothering to rinse the dishes or wrap the leftover lemon, she hurries upstairs to the computer. Should she Google metastatic lung disease? She remembers how the obstetrician, after her third miscarriage, warned her away from the Internet. "You don't have the context for all the misleading information you'll pick up," the doctor cautioned. "You'll just get upset."

The last thing she needs is to be more upset than she already is. She takes a deep breath. Is it shallow? Raspy? She can only imagine the other symptoms waiting online, *in* line, for her to discover and, Sam-style, claim as her own. How easy it would be to succumb to medical students' disease. Not that the reality isn't dire enough. Instead, she'll take charge of her life. She'll take charge of Sam's life.

She taps the keyboard. In seconds, hundreds of links appear. She scrolls through them. *A Mourner's Handbook* tops *Healing Steps for Gay Widowers*, followed by *A Short History of Grief*, *The Groom's Instruction Manual*, *Sex Made Easy*, *A Dating Guide for Widows* packaged with *A Dating Guide for Widowers* in a two-for-one deal, *The March Toward Happiness*, a zillion varieties of *How to Lose Weight*. She dismisses *Tools for the End of Life* in favor of *The Right Way to Use a Meat Cleaver*, a possible tax-deductible purchase for a person in the food-service industry.

Her eyes glaze. She turns off the computer.

Downstairs, she assumes her usual position on the sofa. During the one hour that Rachel occupied this same spot, Annie learned a few crucial things from her best friend: Sam can be trained. Rachel envies Annie's marriage. Rachel is a woman in need of a man. There are guidebooks out there, guidebooks to everything.

She decides to take a nap. Is fatigue one of the warning signs? Even under this sword of Damocles, she has to admit that there are still pleasures to be found—a good friend, hot tea, a snowy day, a cozy sofa—and comfort in having come up with a plan. She drifts off as titles clamber across her mind like so many counted sheep: *Instructions for Sam*, *To My Husband*, *How to Do Everything I Did*, *In the Likely Event of* . . .

And then, at last, there it is: *Life Minus Me: A User's Guide.*

Chapter Six

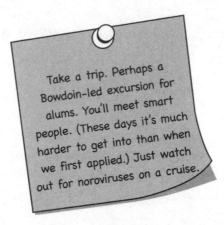

Take a trip. Perhaps a Bowdoin-led excursion for alums. You'll meet smart people. (These days it's much harder to get into than when we first applied.) Just watch out for noroviruses on a cruise.

Annie's in the Samwich kitchen chopping onions when the phone rings. Megan, whose job it is to write down the takeout orders, shouts from the front counter, loud enough to be heard over the gabbing customers and the regulars who monopolize the same three tables every day. "Annie, it's for you. Dr. Buckley's office calling."

Of course Sam's heard this. The whole town has heard this. Why not blare it over the loudspeaker at the high school football field? Annie picks up the extension next to the refrigerator. "I'm at work," she hisses into the receiver, her eyes streaming from the onions.

"Duh," says Carolyn Connelly, Dr. Buckley's receptionist. "I left a ton of messages on your voice mail at home."

Annie is all too aware of those messages. She's been hurrying back early or stopping by her house midafternoon to erase every single one of them before Sam notices the blinking red light and presses play. Not that he usually notices. "I can't talk now," Annie says.

"Doc made me promise to keep you on the line until he can speak to you himself. If I don't, my job will be toast."

"I seriously doubt that." Annie scoops the mound of onion peels into the garbage bin. "I've got work to do. Customers waiting. *Really.*"

"Hold on a sec. He's just finishing with some drug company dude."

"Whoops, smoke's pouring out of the oven. Sorry," Annie says, and hangs up the phone.

Sam walks back into the kitchen. He's wearing one of the white aprons left by the Pillsbury Doughboys tied twice around his un-doughboy waist. Slashes of special Paul Bunyan sauce crisscross his heart.

She points. "That's got to go."

He looks down. "Gee, I hadn't even noticed this mess."

She hands him a clean starched and ironed apron from the freshly laundered pile. "Someone might post a photo on our fan page. For the sake of our public, we have to make a good impression."

He laughs. "Let's face it, our particular public could not care less."

"Then the health inspectors." She helps him into the new apron, double-looping the strings and fashioning them into a natty bow.

He undoes the bow, leaving knotted streamers. "Too metrosexual," he protests. "So?" he asks. "Dr. Buckley's office called? Here at work?"

"Probably figured that's the best place to find me." She pinches her nostrils. "It's about my sinuses."

"That's a relief," he says. "A relief it's not allergies. Remember when I thought I was allergic to tree nuts?" He studies her. "Everything all right?"

"Fine."

"Your nose is red; your eyes are watering."

"I've been chopping onions."

"Maybe that's a chore we should farm out to Megan."

"Great idea." She finds a Kleenex and blows her nose. "Can you spare me for half an hour? I want to get to the dry cleaners before noon."

"Sure," he says. "I left my jacket on the bathroom mat. I'm afraid I dipped the cuff in a puddle of olive oil." He pats her shoulder with the reflexive fondness he must have bestowed on Binky, the still-mourned spaniel who shared his childhood bed and could tap his paws, so Sam claimed, up to the number ten. "That dog was my best friend," Sam would say, then add, sheepishly, "Next to you." Though they discussed adopting a puppy from the ASPCA after they'd given up on babies, they agreed it was too soon and too sad a stopgap.

But now . . . ? What a good prospect for . . . well . . . after. To keep him company when . . . *Get a dog* is a suggestion she must add to the manual.

On the way out, she spots Ralphie Michaud, who is third in line. Thumbs jabbing, he's playing a game on his cell phone and doesn't notice her. "Hi, Ralphie," she says.

He looks up. He grins at her; a dimple punctuates his left cheek. Even nearing forty, he's still cute, with a snaggletooth that only enhances his bad-boy looks. At least he's removed the

piercing he used to flaunt senior year, though she notices a tattooed wing—part of an eagle? an angel?—peeking out from his
collar underneath a crosshatch of black hair. Too bad Annie was
such a prude back in high school, too timid to smoke pot with
him in the hummock of pine trees behind the school.

"How's it going, Annie?" he asks now.

"Okay," she says. "You?"

"Hanging in there. Did you catch the Bruins last night?"

"Afraid not." She stares at his dimple.

"They won four to two."

"Great."

"Dad says you stopped by the store the other day."

"Yeah."

"Hear you started smoking again."

Would a purchase of tampons get reported too? "Not really,"
she protests.

"Trying to keep healthy?"

"You could say that."

He shrugs. From his back jeans pocket, he pulls out his own
pack of Marlboros. "Anyhow, too bad I missed you."

"Oh, well . . ."

"Next time . . ."

"We'll do that." She points to her wristwatch. "Errands . . ."

"See ya," he says.

*   *   *

She drives to Dr. Buckley's office without calling ahead. She'd
just as soon bide her time in the waiting room than schedule an
appointment far enough in advance to allow her the leeway to
cancel it. Also, she doesn't want to give Carolyn the satisfaction.

She gives Carolyn the satisfaction. The minute Annie arrives, she can see the receptionist gloat. "I knew I'd talk you into it."

Lucky for Annie, there are only two people in the waiting room, neither of whom she knows. She opens *Down East* and reads about road repair, vanity license plates, the latest lobster shack, and a Manhattan hedge fund manager's three-million-dollar log cabin renovation at Hancock Point. She turns to the column on tourism. Phew. The Paul Bunyan is still listed as Passamaquoddy's number-one culinary attraction, ahead of Moody's meat loaf, Osborn & Daughters' fried clams, and Geraldine Pritchard's homemade saltwater taffy. She must remember to order the saltwater taffy for the shop; they could branch out, enlarge the menu, add Maine staples like blueberry pie and strawberry shortcake and maple syrup brownies. Thanks to her mother-in-law, she makes a mean blueberry pie, a sellout at school fairs and bake sales.

Maybe they should also consider a real espresso machine despite the old-timers' inevitable complaints and resistance to change. Maybe not. Don't mess with perfection, Sam would say. She sighs. It's amazing the way life goes on, the way one continues to make plans. It's mind-boggling how a person can sit in a doctor's waiting room expecting a death sentence and still clip recipes, ponder menus, and obsess over the choice between the lobster license plate and Robert Indiana's LOVE.

Dr. Buckley opens his office door and steps into the hall, clipboard in hand, stethoscope dangling over his red necktie patterned with blue caducei. He looks up. "Annie?" he says.

"Excuse me." A woman seated across from her struggles to rise out of her chair. She has wispy gray hair and Ben Franklin spectacles and is leaning on a no-frills aluminum cane. "I believe I'm next."

"So sorry, Florence," Dr. Buckley says, "but we have a bit of an emergency here. I promise to be quick."

Annie follows him into the examining room. Dr. Buckley's "emergency" sounds so much more loaded than those same syllables enunciated by the bored voice of Dr. O'Brien's nurse. Annie is embarrassed that she, thirty-seven, with a quick stride and a mass of young-person's hair, is considered an emergency to be triaged ahead of an impaired senior citizen so clearly accustomed to measuring out her days in places like this.

"Well, Annie, we've been trying to contact you."

"So I gather."

Dr. Buckley clears his throat. He picks up his letter opener, a talisman that, Annie concludes, must serve as his Linus blanket in times of stress. She does not envy his job. She does not envy his command of the medical facts he's about to lay out for her. "For the record, I don't approve of your plan not to persevere in telling Sam."

"I didn't expect you to."

His forehead wrinkles in dismay. "You're as stubborn as your mother," he says, "though I could always convince her . . ."

"I am no way like my mother," Annie huffs.

"Hmmm," he replies. He opens a folder on the desk in front of him. "I'm so glad you called the oncologist. The thoracic surgeon's reports suggest you may need a biopsy."

"It all seems so hopeless. Why subject myself to . . . when it's so clear that . . . ?"

He sighs. In agreement? In frustration? He goes on. "Nothing is clear. You're young. There are new treatments all the time. Targeted procedures . . ."

Annie is having a hard time paying attention; what did Dr. Buckley try to convince her mother of? she wonders. She focuses on the caducei. If she gave Sam a tie printed with sandwiches, would he wear it? She lowers her gaze. Now she can read the whole inscription on the letter opener: *in grateful appreciation of saving my life.* Just as she thought. She filled in the blank correctly the last time she was here. Does she earn an A plus? While she's not sure whose life Dr. Buckley saved, she *is* sure he won't be saving hers.

Annie points to a drooping schefflera on the windowsill. "That needs watering."

Ignoring her horticultural advice, he continues. "I'm sure Dr. O'Brien will have a lot of tricks up her sleeve . . ."

"Like a magic wand? Tricks that might mean a cure?" she asks.

"Alas, medicine doesn't work like that. But it is always wise to choose the optimistic path."

"Even if . . ."

"The optimistic path," he repeats. "We'll follow you with scans until your appointment."

"And the side effects of these tricks?" she persists.

"Nothing we can't manage. Though—in all honesty—you will likely lose your hair." He runs his fingers through his own silver locks. His eyes are so sad that she feels terrible for being the cause of his pain.

She touches the top of her head. *Your crowning glory* was one of the few compliments Ursula granted her. Her crowning glory has stayed glossy and thick through thick and thin—the roller coaster of ten pounds up, ten pounds down, adolescent acne and adolescent angst, pregnancy failures, and one unfortunate perm. On a medical spreadsheet of debit and credit, the loss of her hair would result in little gain.

"I feel fine now," she protests.

"Glad to hear it. Though that dry cough of yours is worrisome."

"It's February. In Maine!"

Exasperated, he frowns. "You've got an answer for everything. Did you ever consider law school?"

"And deprive Passamaquoddy of Paul Bunyans?"

"Oh, Annie," he sighs. "Well, at the very least, please stay away from researching symptoms on the Internet. Even my most stalwart patients tend to overidentify. Not to mention all the misinformation out there."

She remembers her obstetrician's moratorium on Googling stillborn babies and multiple miscarriages. "Okay," she agrees. "See how I'm taking your advice," she adds. She thrusts out her forehead as if she expects him to stick a star on it.

Despite himself, he smiles. "And if you won't talk to Sam, then talk to your mother."

"My mother!"

"She *is* your mother, Annie."

A mother missing the maternal gene. Annie can just picture Ursula's reaction. *How can you do this to* me? *How can* I *lose a child?* She'll wail and prostrate herself on her fringed chaise longue and then order a wardrobe of black mourning clothes from Saks.

"If you were my daughter . . ." Dr. Buckley begins.

"With all due respect, Dr. Buckley, I'm not."

She offers him a concession, vowing to schedule a visit a week from now.

In return, he promises to water his schefflera plant. "And don't wait too long to tell Sam" is his parting command.

* * *

Of course she won't tell Sam.

Not yet. She's got three weeks until her appointment, three weeks until an official diagnosis.

First, she has to make sure he's going to be okay. First, she has to write the manual. And when it's finished, as soon as it's finished, then she can begin to train him according to its rules.

Chapter Seven

Change the answering machine to your own voice. Too creepy to hear mine.

Annie sits at her desk. She's taken the day off. Earlier this morning, she stopped by the shop, where Megan was scrubbing out the large industrial coffee urn. Sam was at the bakery picking up rolls, Megan explained.

"Do you need me to help?" Annie asked.

"No, I've got everything under control. It's fun being in charge. By the way, I've been discussing updates with Sam," Megan went on. "Like a cappuccino machine. Make the place more hip."

"Hip won't sell in Passamaquoddy, I'm afraid," Annie said, despite having entertained similar thoughts of improvement herself.

"Why not try? I've got tons of ideas. Scrabble tournaments. Karaoke nights. We could run poetry readings. How cool would that be?"

The only poet in town Annie knows is the self-named Long-fellow Clark, who peddles his "oeuvre" door to door, each stanza written in a cursive so spidery and dense you can't even read it. Though she owns twelve volumes, they could all be the same poem—how would she tell? "Let's not shake the boat," Annie insisted. "The Paul Bunyan is perfect as it is."

"I couldn't agree more. But"—Annie recognized the familiar set of her goddaughter's jaw, just like Rachel's when protesting an injustice—"there's nothing wrong with thinking ahead."

"People around here don't like change," Annie said. Except for a coat of paint, her flea-market finds on the walls, more local baked goods, a new refrigerator, and replacements for the chipped mugs, she and Sam have hardly tinkered with the original Dough-boys template—a policy that food reviewers, local businesses, customers, and tourists applaud.

"We're not talking about adding piped-in Buddhist chants. Or orchids and candles and serving, you know, like, caviar and fifty shades of kale," Megan said.

Annie switched the subject. "Sam reports you're doing a great job."

Megan filled the urn with water and plugged it in. "Annie, I owe you and Sam big-time for hiring me. I was way, way sick of school."

"You may think that now; however . . ."

"Mom only agreed to the gap year because I'm the youngest in my class."

"Because you're so smart. Because you skipped a grade."

"As if smart counts in high school." Megan rolled her eyes. "Right. Okay. I promised Mom I'd go back in the fall. But work-ing here is way more real." She turned to the man who'd just

sidled up to the counter, Ray Beaulieu, one of the indistinguish-
able regulars in anorak and work boots who can extend two cups
of coffee into a six-hour marathon. "I'll have a fresh pot up and
going in a minute, Ray," she said.

"Best decision you made, Annie, was to hire this kid here."

Annie remembered a newspaper piece about a group of senior
citizens who hung out all day at a burger joint in Queens, nursing
cold coffee and free water, monopolizing the tables and causing
lost revenue. The owners wanted to find a way to kick them out
without being labeled ageists. She gazed at Ray Beaulieu chuck-
ling with his cohorts. Not that you could ever kick anybody out
in Maine, except for the drunk and disorderly.

"We're not Queens," Sam had pointed out when she showed
him the article. "Besides, the old-timers give us local color."

Back in the sandwich shop, Megan pushed a mug of hot coffee across the counter.

"No, thanks," Annie said, "I've got stuff to do."

"Take the afternoon off. That cough sounds nasty. I've already
started the sandwiches. We're in awesome shape. I'm working the
whole shift today."

"Won't Sam need . . . ?"

"He'll be fine with it. Any problem, he can blame me." Megan
paused, brightened. "Hey, how about this for a proposal? A date
night here at Annie's?"

*   *   *

Now Annie turns on her computer. *There's nothing wrong with
thinking ahead*, Megan argued. But, let's face it, how far ahead is
Annie going to be able to think? She opens Microsoft Word. She
can't dwell on the bad stuff. She's going to write the manual

today. She's postponed her appointment with Dr. Buckley to start it. As with most dreaded tasks, once she gets to work, she's sure she'll feel better. She's been scribbling notes on Post-its, which she's stuck in the pockets of her jeans, in her purse, in her jewelry box—ideas for the list she's about to compose. But when she gathers them all together, arranges and smooths them out, they're as indecipherable as one of Longfellow Clark's rhymed couplets. Handwriting may be a lost art for those who grew up in the digital age, yet these smears of black ink are Rorschach tests of her mental state, a testament to a tangled mess of tangled thoughts.

No matter. She'll write without a safety net, the way she's been living ever since the diagnosis. Lucky she's not in school anymore. No need to structure a formal outline indexed with Roman numerals and subsidiary letters. Or perhaps she should, to add verisimilitude. The important thing is to set it all down on the page. She can refine it later if she needs to.

And so she starts:

LIFE MINUS ME: A USER'S GUIDE
(In no particular order)

I. DOMESTIC: All the instructions for the machines are in the right-hand drawer in the kitchen under the microwave. Follow the directions for each appliance even though you prefer to wing it. (And we both remember how *that* turned out!) Repairmen's contact info is in the red notebook next to the telephone. Vacuum and dust weekly. Clean out the refrigerator every other week—use baking soda to get rid of smells. That fuzzy white and black stuff is mold = no good! Get sprayed for carpenter ants twice a year. If you feel overwhelmed, call Rachel for help.

A. Dry-cleaning: Only open until noon on Saturdays. Indicate stains with masking tape. Get your clothes tailored—Michelle, Fred's wife, is excellent. Have sweaters cleaned; don't put in washing machine. Get jacket sleeves shortened. And have pants legs hemmed but not cuffed (old fogy). Don't let anyone talk you into leopard-print underwear.

B. Hair: Don't allow the barber to cut it too short around the ears to save money. Makes you look nerdy. Plus it makes your ears stick out (it seemed too cruel to tell you this every time, after the fact). You could also try the new unisex salon on Main Street. Okay, scratch that, you don't have to.

C. Décor: In the back of my closet is that bunch of old maps of Passamaquoddy we found at the Union Antiques Fair. (We got such a great price—you were really quite the bargainer! And remember how that dealer followed us and wanted to buy them as we were lugging them to our car? And remember the fun we had in that seedy motel? How we . . . well, who could forget?) Take them to the framers on Pearl Street, not the cheapo place downtown. Make sure they're matted on archival paper; otherwise they'll turn brown and disintegrate. I think plain oak frames would suit them. Or dark walnut. Ask Mr. Robineau for advice. You could hang them in the study. Just move the bicycle posters to the wall next to the window. Or bring them to the shop. They'll add that bit of artiness Megan is so wild about.

D. Food: My recipe box—wooden, battered, painted with purple grapes and green vines (the latch is a little iffy)—is on the second shelf over the sink. I never got around to alphabetizing the recipes, but your favorites are bunched toward the front. I know you'll be tempted just to bring stuff home from the shop. But don't. You can check out my ancient copy of *The Joy of Cooking*—spotted with remains of a thousand meals, alas—I always meant to get a new one. YOU get a new one! And Mark Bittman's basics will fill in the gaps. Even better, there's an Adult Ed cooking class at the high school—you'll learn tricks of the trade and meet new people. I've heard you get to take home what you make. How great is that!

II.BUSINESS

A. Annie's Samwich: After I'm gone, maybe you DO want to update. Expand. Think about annexing the junk shop next door. Mr. Aherne has got to be close to a hundred. Does anyone ever buy any of his stuff? He should be on that program about hoarders. I bet you could make him an offer he couldn't refuse. I realize we talked about keeping everything the way it is, but the world moves on. (And the fact that it's moving on without me makes me really pissed!) Listen to Megan. A cappuccino machine would be excellent. (But compare prices and check *Consumer Reports*.) You *could* have a poetry night—maybe call the English teacher at the high school for suggestions. Or the librarian? (I suggest Longfellow Clark not be invited, though he'll probably show up anyway.)

Consider live music. A lot of our customers seem to perform in those bands in the bars down by the river. How about a sing-along! And Megan is clued in to the music scene, such as it is.

Date night? Not a bad idea. It may be good for you, too, since you'll get a chance to practice rusty boy/girl skills. You can learn—when I think of all the fun we had, the trips to Bar Harbor, those drive-in double features we barely watched, our walks, the bad food we didn't even notice, that time when we were up to our knees in snow. (Amazing how we could sense what the other wanted.) I'm sure it will all come back.

Most important: DO NOT MESS WITH THE PAUL BUN-YAN. That should remain as ever, no matter how cool the updates of everything else are. I know you agree with me on this, that you would never change as much as a single peppercorn, but I think, for the record, I should mention it anyway just in case a top chef (or new cooking class) wants you to go all gourmet.

B. Ursula: Feel free to ask Ursula for a loan. As you know, I always refused to take any money from my mother, even when we were first buying the place from the Doughboys and she offered it. Don't think I didn't appreciate you agreeing to try the bank when a check really would have helped! (One thing that was so great about you was when it came to me and Ursula, you always took my side.) But now—ha-ha—I won't know, will I? Besides, what does she have to spend it on—Botox and Tiffany? And if she insists you put that picture of her—taken thirty years ago with her boobs falling out of that disco dress—on the wall, well, why not? Most people in town like to claim her as their own. Better Ursula than that other native son who invented the ratchet thingamabob. Rachel will help you find a good place to hang it.

III. SOCIAL: It's important you have a social life. No, a weekend watching the Red Sox on TV with a pizza and beer does not

count. Yes, you and I had a blast, but it was always just the
two of us. I'm afraid we were both too insular for our own
good. Too dependent on each other. Maybe because we couldn't
have a family of our own, we shut everybody else out—our
little unit was enough. You even let old friendships lapse when
we got married—more a guy thing, I think. Women need other
women to confide in. And tell them when they have lipstick on
their teeth. Make yourself get out. You don't have to sign up
for the bowling league, but you could have coffee with some
of the geezers just to shoot the breeze. Excellent practice for
cocktail parties and other social events plus date night at the
sandwich shop. Join some clubs—Toastmasters, local Democrats,
book club (Rachel belongs to a co-ed one. They do *not* read
chick lit!). Join the temple in Bangor and reclaim your roots.
Yes, I get that you hated Hebrew school, but it's only a forty-
five-minute drive, and you'll meet new people. Go to the gym
to keep that perfect body perfect and reduce stress.

A: Find old friends on Facebook. DATE!!! Enroll in Match.com
and JDate. Have Rachel show you how. Better, ask Rachel
herself out. An obvious choice, as you're already buddies
and don't have to deal with the getting-to-know-a-
stranger angst. (This subcategory could also go under
other headers, but you get my point.) Thank God our AP
English teacher is not grading this!

IV. TRAVEL: You and I stayed home and never saw Paree and I did
not regret a single minute of it. Well, maybe a little—I always
thought one of the Greek islands would have been so romantic
for our honeymoon—not that I minded Acadia, cuddled up in
that sleeping bag with you even though it rained 24/7 and our

70

discount L.L.Bean tent leaked—I told you we should have paid full price! We were young, it didn't matter then—later, we were pregnant most of the time, or trying to get pregnant, or becoming unpregnant or far too depressed after, well, I hardly have to tell YOU. Go to the Greek islands and toast me with a retsina (which I never liked, so maybe an ouzo). Megan will be able to handle everything at the shop—she's really competent. Consult Rachel. She loves to travel. She honeymooned in Paris (with the dentist adulterer, so maybe we were right to stay close to home). And she's a whiz with a map.

V. SEX and LOVE: I want you to enjoy lots of both. I want you to find love again. To get married again. Have kids. With my blessing. You will make a fabulous dad. This is my biggest regret (my only one—*almost* my only one—as far as life with you is concerned)—that we couldn't produce little Sams and Annies. And I want you to move on (but never forgetting me, of course— I am not THAT self-sacrificing).

A: Now, the details. Not that I haven't adored every moment of our lovemaking, not that you aren't wonderful, ardent, a virtuoso in the boudoir, as Ursula would say, and not that we've haven't got it down pat and arrived at our well-perfected routine. BUT you might want to investigate some new moves. Who knows what couples are up to these days. Remember before we were married, that time fooling around at Ursula's Park Avenue apartment while she was away getting a new nose and I decided to model some of her naughty French lingerie for you? We snooped inside her underwear drawer and found that Swedish sex book. The one with all the drawings—blue for women, red for men—and proceeded to experiment until you threw out your back. Maybe you could order that book on Amazon.

Let me stress that I have been thrilled and comforted by our sex life, all these seventeen plus years. But new people, new things. And let's face it, everybody's technique could use a tune-up.

VI. MY STUFF: Dispose of it as you will, but please return any jewelry Ursula ever gave me. Give my big gold hoop earrings and silver bangles to Rachel, and to Megan all my hippie-looking beads. Anything else to whoever wants it. Don't sell my car. Have it painted with an image of Paul Bunyan (and maybe the blue ox)—cheerful primary colors would work great—and use it for advertising and delivery. Please save my wedding ring and store it with yours in a safe place. Don't feel you have to wear your ring, but I want you to keep both of them, as a symbol of what we had.

My clothes should go to Goodwill except for a few black items in the closet, dresses from Ursula, which Megan might like and even, oh Gawd, regard as vintage.

VII. Though you know I am not spiritual in any way and do not believe in an afterlife and hated Sunday school as much as you hated Hebrew school and wish to be cremated rather than have you spend all that money on a plot in Mt. Faith cemetery— I still hope (don't think I'm nuts) that maybe in some way I will be reunited with our baby girl.

All of which leads me to the next . . .

VIII. MY MEMORIAL SERVICE: Work on it with Rachel. Either you or she should deliver the eulogy, though if that's too much for you, everyone will understand (especially me!). No way are you to let my mother take over. I don't want Elizabeth Barrett Browning or Ozymandias or some Shakespeare soliloquy. (As Ursula will no doubt point out, she played Ophelia when she was seventeen.) A little music would be nice. You know what I like. But under no circumstances is Ursula allowed to sing. She'll be carrying on in the wings anyway. Assign Dr. Buckley to distract her. I think he's got a crush on her, like half the men in town. Beats me. Display our wedding picture somewhere. I love that photo of us, we look so happy, *were* so happy, even though my hairstyle was totally unflattering. Do serve Paul Bunyans afterwards. And a decent wine. As for flowers, I can't stand lilies or chrysanthemums. Too funereal. (Ha!) You could play "our song," if that's not too painful for you.

Addendum: RACHEL: As I've pointed out, she's very fond of you, and Megan is already part of the family. Rachel is six months older than I am. She could still have a baby. Enough said. No pressure.

And don't forget, my darling, dearest husband, my soul mate, I love you. Have always loved you. Will always love you.

xoxo ME

By the time she writes the final *x*s and *o*s, Annie is choked with sobs. She can only imagine the impact this will have on Sam, Sam who cries at a sunset, at sappy movies, at the awarding of sports trophies, at the national anthem no matter how warbling the rendition. Will he once more end up in the hospital diagnosed with "exhaustion," "a depressive episode"? Is there any way to make this easier for him?

Chapter Eight

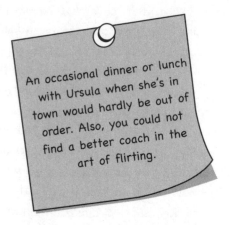

An occasional dinner or lunch with Ursula when she's in town would hardly be out of order. Also, you could not find a better coach in the art of flirting.

Annie drives down Main Street. No wonder she's having a hard time catching her breath—what a horrible morning. She's just spent hours in the community hospital named after a family of founding fathers who summer in the richest part of the state and whose highly privileged portraits sneer down from the walls. It offends her to see those Marie Antoinette smiles. She never voted for any of them, and she blames them for Passamaquoddy's disappearing social programs and high unemployment rate.

She never should have gone. Especially since she's got the big-cheese oncologist marked in her calendar. Talk about overkill. She only did so because Dr. Buckley threatened to send Sam a reminder that Ms. Arabella Ursula Stevens-Strauss's appointment had been ignored.

"HIPAA," Annie warned.

"Not when your behavior is putting your health at risk."

"I could sue you for medical malpractice."

"Be my guest." He sighed. "Or stop this nonsense and come in for the tests."

She'd changed into a robe that could have fit both Paul Bunyan *and* his blue ox. The cat's cradle of tabs and ties was so daunting that a nurse had to help her do them up. She felt small, incompetent, helpless. Maybe this kind of diminution happens to everyone who is forced to enter the uncharted geography of the sick.

She took an elevator down to LOWER 3 and followed a trail of colored arrows that looked like a larger version of the board games she'd played as a child. Stretchers, with and without patients, lined the maze of corridors. Medical staff, badges dangling over white coats, rushed by. She kept her eyes pinned to the floor. No way would she join this club she was too young to be a member of.

In the basement room—freezing, overly bright, and smelling of bleach—she stretched out on a table. While menacing X-ray machines and CAT scans clicked and buzzed above her chest, she struggled to read the impassive faces of the technicians who called her *honey* and *dear*. Was the woman whose lab coat bore an embroidered *Melissa* shaking her head?

"What do you see?" she asked.

"We're not allowed to comment," Melissa reproved. "This is information that can be conveyed solely by your own physician."

Back at Dr. Buckley's office, she sat good-girl-style, hands folded, knees crossed, as he read her films. "No change," he said.

"That's hopeful, isn't it?"

He didn't answer right away. He stared out the window, and then at last replied, "Please keep your next appointment."

* * *

Now she slows her car and pulls into the parking lot next to the new unisex salon. Over the entrance, *Cutting Edge* unscrolls, its curlicued letters painted flamingo pink. A banner, flapping in the February wind, proclaims GRAND OPENING. Silhouettes of scissors adorn the plate-glass windows, which also showcase a bouquet of red roses so big and perfect that Annie assumes they must be fake. She touches her hair, shoulder length, the same style she's worn since seventh grade, except for the tendriled and misguided high-rise edifice Ursula talked her into for her wedding day and one bad perm when she was twelve. Should she get her hair cut?

Despite the instructions she's composed for Sam, she has no rules for the rest of *her* life. Maybe some thrill seekers might choose to climb Machu Picchu or opt for Paris, but she's a home-grown girl. What is *her* bucket list? Eat all the sundaes she wants? Sow the wild oats she hardly sowed? Turn platinum blond?

Such endgame shenanigans might help her detach from Sam, make her less appealing so it won't be so hard for him when she's gone. Or so hard for her to accept that she's leaving him. This will be tough, pushing away, for Sam's sake, the very comfort and love she will need to sustain her . . . she bangs her forehead against the steering wheel . . . when things start to fall apart.

Yesterday afternoon, she folded the manual into thirds, struggling to tamp down the anguish its contents were causing her. She buried it in her underwear drawer. Unlike Ursula's flimsy silk nothings, her underwear is sturdy, 100 percent cotton, bought in multiples at the outlet on Route 15. She'd scooped up a label-designated "hipster brief." It looked neither hipster nor brief, more like what a peasant grandmother would wear beneath voluminous skirts.

What is wrong with her? Besides the obvious, that is. She wants a sexy silk black bikini to turn Sam on; she wants a beige cotton hipster brief to fend him off. She wants her hair to remain the way it is. She wants her hair to change. She can neither stay the same nor simply stay.

She shuts off the ignition, gets out of the car, and slouches through the entrance of Cutting Edge. "I don't have an appointment," she apologizes to a woman chic enough to be the daughter Annie's mother would have preferred.

"No problem." The woman points her fingernails, glitter-glued versions of the French flag, in the direction of a group of zebra-striped chairs.

"Hey, Annie," she hears. She spins around. There, under a matching zebra robe, the top of his head dipped into a basin, a tower of suds dripping onto his forehead, sits—or rather, leans—Ralphie Michaud.

Her mouth opens. He is so out of context that she's knocked speechless. What is Ralphie Michaud doing here? Tattooed, leather-jacketed, a Marlboro still dangling from his lips even in this tsk-tsk-no-smoking interior, he belongs in a Hells Angels gang revving up a badass Harley. It's hard to believe that Ralphie Michaud would choose the *his-and-hers* over the single-sex *his*.

"What a surprise to see you here," he says.

"Not as much of a surprise as seeing *you*."

Streaming rivulets, he lifts his head from the basin and is immediately turbaned in pink terry cloth by a flamingo-smocked teenager. "I mean," he goes on, "your hair . . ."

What *does* he mean? That her hair never changes? That her sole upkeep is a once-every-eight-weeks trim at a place catering to the blue-haired crowd? That she (next to Ralphie himself) is the last person on earth anyone would imagine turning up at a unisex salon called Cutting Edge?

All true. Alas.

". . . your hair always looks great. Ever since high school," he finishes.

Before she can change her mind, she's led to a chair by a woman with red curls, kohl-lined cat's eyes, and the perkiest breasts this side of Barbie. "Dee Dee," she introduces herself, then nods toward the reception desk. "Mimi's my sister." She helps Annie into a robe. She loops a bib around her neck. "The older one," she clarifies.

Two chairs away, Ralphie now sits, riveted by his reflection—arching an eyebrow, testing out a grin. The teenager aims a hair dryer at his sideburns. Dee Dee points. "My daughter, Tallulah."

"I never would have guessed."

She laughs. "I was a child bride."

Annie regards her draped, drab self in the mirror, brown parched earth eclipsed by Dee Dee's radiant sun. "What brought you to Passamaquoddy?" she asks.

"The usual."

"Meaning?"

"A man."

"Did it work out?"

"No. Story of my life. But by the time I discovered what an asshole he was, we'd already moved and rented the shop. Maine's quite the change from New Jersey."

"Do you like it here?"

"The verdict's still out. I miss the malls. But the people are real friendly. They don't have, you know, attitude." She grabs a fistful of Annie's hair and analyzes it. "The raw material is good—thick, shiny, healthy," she says. She pushes it to the side. "So, what shall we do with this?"

Annie likes the *we*, the collaborative effort it implies, the comfort of not having to make a decision all alone. "What do you suggest?"

"How do you feel about taking a walk on the wild side?"

"Just how wild?"

"On a scale of one to ten . . . ? Maybe a nine and a half?"

Annie smells a piña colada. From the corner of her eye, she can just make out Ralphie, dried and coiffed, a dust cloud of aerosol haze circling his head. "Would I have to be sprayed in coconut?"

"We've got lemon. And an incredible fig-ginger combo. You know"—Dee Dee stands back and appraises her—"you have a pretty face, but it's lost under that mop of yours. You are not making the best of your assets. What I have in mind will accent your bone structure and allow your eyes to pop." She adjusts Annie's bib. "We could also add a few highlights for extra pizzazz."

"Perhaps a little risky?"

"Trust me."

"What do I have to lose?"

"You go, girl. It's only hair, right? It's not like it's a matter of life and death."

Dee Dee gets busy. "I had this one client in Jersey, back in my old salon, who said my haircut made all the difference. She met a guy. Got a new job. Lost forty pounds. She was so grateful she sent me six bras. Not your usual box of Godiva."

In the mirror, Annie studies Dee Dee's breasts. "If you don't mind my asking, how did she know your size?"

"She worked in a bra factory. She had the eye. One look and bingo! Those were the best-fitting bras I ever wore." She wheels a cart stuffed with supplies next to Annie's chair. "I gave them to my sister when I had my boobs done."

Now, with surgical precision, Dee Dee lays out her instruments. Scissors—large and small—two combs, one round brush, one flat brush, one paintbrush, a squeeze bottle, a stack of foil squares, a box of clips.

Annie coughs.

"It won't hurt, I swear. I haven't lost a customer yet."

"It's not that. Just nervous, I guess."

"I get it. Some people don't like change. I've been seeing a lot of that since I moved here, people stuck in their ways. Afraid of doing something new. Me, now, I can switch my hair color once a week. Put on a different outfit and become a whole other person. You should see my house. Every day I move something around, change the decor. I've lived in eight cities. Couldn't even begin to count the number of apartments and houses, not to mention"—she picks up a comb—"all the guys I've been with. You know what they say . . ."

"Not really."

"If you don't keep moving forward, you die."

Annie closes her eyes as Dee Dee swirls around her, pulling, cutting, snipping. She tries to zone out. She struggles to imagine sun and sand and an endless horizon stretching into infinity. But all she can conjure is a fast-approaching tsunami, its colossal waves sweeping her away. She shudders.

"Sit still," Dee Dee orders, "or you'll be missing the top of your ear."

Annie squints down at the floor, where there seems to be more hair scattered across the hexagonal white tiles than there is left on her head.

A whiff of coconut signals the arrival of Ralphie Michaud. His just-styled mane is impressively retro, poufed into a semi-pompadour on top and clipped close at the sides. Is the color lighter or just an artifact of the overhead fluorescent bulbs?

"Later," he says. "Dad's due for a root canal and needs me at the store."

"Nice seeing you."

"The same." He flashes his bad-boy grin. "Hey, I've got an idea. Stop by on the way home. I want to check out the big reveal."

"I'm afraid I have to . . ."

"Come on. You gonna make me leave the game before the last inning?"

Surprising herself, Annie agrees.

"That guy has a major crush," Dee Dee remarks as soon as he leaves. "*Major*," she repeats.

"No way," Annie protests, pleased by the observation. "Besides, I'm married."

Dee Dee grins. "So?"

* * *

She is done. Dee Dee holds a hand mirror up to the back and the sides.

Annie barely recognizes herself. Her hair is short, extremely short. Her head is so light she feels as if she's lost ten pounds. And her eyes look bigger, more defined, almost almond-shaped. She smiles. "I think I like it," she says. "It'll just take a while . . ."

". . . to get used to it," Dee Dee supplies. "Cross my heart, pretty soon that *like* will turn to *love.*"

Without complaint, Annie forks over four times more than she's ever paid at her regular hairdresser's, even ignoring the discount earned for loyalty.

Since it is now midafternoon and she's missed lunch, she decides to swing by Miller's Drug before the promised visit to Ralphie Michaud. *Eat dessert first,* people on their deathbeds advise. It's her day for walking on the wild side.

At the counter, she orders a sundae with the works. "And a double scoop," she tells Mr. Miller. "Vanilla *and* strawberry."

"Is that you, Annie?" he asks, his bushy eyebrows knit into question marks. "I barely recognized you. What have you done to your hair?"

"The new unisex salon over on Main."

He *tsks.* "I heard about that. A couple of fancy-schmancy sisters from New York."

"New Jersey."

"Same dif. Unisex! What a world."

"So, you don't approve?" she asks.

He sponges up the spilled chocolate sauce overflowing her bowl and shakes his head. "Has Sam taken a gander at this new look of yours yet?"

* * *

82

In front of Michaud's Quik-Basket, she hesitates. Maybe instead she should go home and tackle the laundry, straighten up the living room. Did she even make the bed this morning? But Ralphie's expecting her. It would be rude if she didn't show up. Not to mention snobby. Besides, why not test Mr. Miller's disdain with a more open-minded, younger-generation assessment?

The instant the ancient rusted-out bell over Michaud's door clangs her presence, Ralphie rushes to greet her. "Annie!" he whoops. "Rock star!" he exclaims. He slaps her five. She smells the sickly-sweet coconut of his saturated hair.

As well as something else. Of course. She identifies it right away. From the stand of pines behind the high school. From campus hideouts, college parties, concerts in the back of bars, everybody's BYOB first-apartment open house.

He takes her hand. "You look so amazing. Really out there." He moves closer.

She inches back.

"I can't get over it. The meta, meta . . ."

". . . morphosis," she supplies.

He turns to the front door and flips the OPEN sign to CLOSED. "Follow me. I've got some A-one weed."

He leads her into the back room. She takes in a sagging sofa, a rabbit-eared TV, a bridge table with a centerpiece of empty beer bottles, piles of *Car and Driver* magazines, a grimy half-refrigerator. A moth-eaten PASSAMAQUODDY HIGH SCHOOL banner hangs on the wall next to a calendar of snowmobiles, stuck on September of two years ago. A torn poster for last summer's La Kermesse Franco-American festival in Biddeford droops beside a photo of a vocalist in full S&M attire whose hair is even wilder, more out there, more cutting edge than her own. What is she doing here?

Ralphie indicates a place on the sofa, brushing it off and raising a cloud of dust. Talk about a men-without-women world! She fast-forwards to her future, post-Annie kitchen, heaped with unwashed dishes, empty bottles, old pizza crusts, back issues of the *Passamaquoddy Daily Telegram*. She watches dust kitties roll around like tumbleweed. She imagines Sam asleep in front of ESPN.

"Earth to Annie . . ." Ralphie says now.

"Sorry. Daydreaming."

She tries to remember the last and only time she smoked pot. She and Rachel and Sam were at a classmate's off-campus apartment. She felt nothing. Where was the buzz? The music of the spheres? Sam complained of a headache and burning throat. "So, we've tried it; now we don't have to do it again," he said. Rachel flirted and giggled and gobbled down all the crackers and cheese. She skipped in circles on the back porch. "You two are so out of it," she accused.

Annie is now certain of one thing: at this minute, she does not want to be out of it. Out of it is what happens when you become a couple as soon as you enter your teens, when you're Old Marrieds even before the wedding bells. Out of it is when you have a yard, designated bedrooms, a separate shower—privileges that most of your community can only dream of. She touches the spiky layers above her ears.

Ralphie pulls a Zippo from his shirt pocket, ignites the joint, inhales. He holds the smoke in, mouth shut, nostrils pinched. At last, he exhales with an orgasmic whoosh. He takes another toke and passes it to her. She is meant to share this—the twisted end he licked, the rolling paper he smacked his lips around. She hopes—shades of Sam—she doesn't catch something. Let's face it, Ralphie's hygiene might not be CDC approved. *Wait.* It hardly matters, considering the top-of-the-line, number-one whammy she's already caught.

She grabs the joint. She inhales. She concentrates on letting no smoke escape, but it scalds her throat; she can't stop coughing. A whole new croaky refrain starts to amplify her recent hoarseness. Does this rasping signal an amateur pothead or the end stages of lung disease?

Ralphie thumps her on the back. "You're out of practice," he consoles. "Try again."

This time she succeeds. When she releases the smoke, she can only admire the long thin plume and its coil of total elegance. She giggles. *Isn't life funny*, she giggles again.

She and Ralphie pass the joint back and forth until all that remains is a torn paper remnant and a drift of dregs.

"Go figure," he muses. "In my wildest dreams, who'd believe that cute, classy little Annie Stevens would one day be sitting on my sofa smoking weed with big, bad Ralphie Michaud?"

"Life is full of surprises."

"I'll say."

"You have no idea."

"Me, I have plenty of ideas." He pats her knee. "Hungry?" he asks.

Though she scarfed down a double sundae minutes ago—or was it hours?—she is starved.

"Wait here," Ralphie orders.

"Not going anywhere," she chuckles, in awe of her own witty riposte.

He returns from the front of the store, arms laden with snack packs of Doritos, Cheetos, Cheez-Its, Twizzlers, and nacho chips. He spreads the treats out on the table.

Like hawks, they swoop. They pounce. They claw the bags open and ravage the contents. "How great to live behind a grocery store," Annie marvels.

"With a dad who spends so much time at the dentist," adds Ralphie, "I get a shitload of personal space."

Annie is sure that if they continue this way, she'll need root canals too. Tooth-wise, though, there's an upside to dying: no more dentists and no reason to floss.

Soon enough, the carcass is picked clean, leaving only scraps. Ralphie bends toward her. The coconut, this close, is revolting. She thinks of Sam, his Sam smell of fresh-cut grass and onions and warm manly flesh. She pictures the bottles of fancy French cologne, *Pour Monsieur*, presents from Ursula, unopened on a shelf and ready for regifting. She remembers Charles's signature bay rum. "How about it?" Ralphie asks.

"How about what?"

"Let's check out what we missed way back when . . ."

"I don't think . . . I mean . . ."

"Then why did you come?"

"You asked to see my haircut."

"What planet are you from, anyway? Give me a break." Ralphie leans closer.

She flinches.

"What a wuss." He smashes his lips against hers. He reeks of the salty, greasy snacks they have just eaten. And the pot.

Her stomach lurches. She pulls away. "No!" she shouts.

He grabs her shoulders. She shakes herself free. "No," she repeats. "Stop it!" She squeezes into the corner of the sofa. She piles empty beer bottles and a bag of Doritos as a barrier between them. How could she have been so stupid, so naïve, to accept Ralphie's invitation? Is she hoping to rewrite the good-girl history of her high school years? Perhaps she's using Ralphie to distance herself from Sam, thus easing the pain of the inevitable distance. Not that she isn't out of her mind, incapacitated by the joint she's smoked and doctor's appointments and grief.

Is this her first #me too moment, however late blooming?

"You *are* a wuss," Ralphie states now.

"A *married* wuss."

He lifts his hands in I-surrender formation. "Big deal. I just knew you'd chicken out." He shakes his head. "You're lucky I'm a gentleman."

"If you say so . . ." she manages.

He goes on. "Maybe your hair is great and all. And you look okay for your age . . ."

"Which is your age too, by the way."

"Like I don't realize this? Though it's a fact: as guys get older, they just get sexier. Take Clint Eastwood."

"I hate Clint Eastwood," she says.

"No surprise there. But the point is, Annie, even though I tried, for old time's sake, and because I didn't want you to think I was rejecting you after you showed up and all, I'm not feeling it."

"*You're* not feeling it?" she exclaims, oddly insulted.

"You figure you're so out of my league."

"That's not the reason."

"Bullshit. I wasn't even tempted to grab your tits," he goes on. He fishes a bottle of beer out of the fridge, takes a gulp, "Here's the thing," he continues. "When we were in high school, all I wanted was, well, you know, to get into your pants. I had this major crush on you. Mostly because you were already taken, which was a kind of test of my lady skills. My *excellent* lady skills. Remember how I used to beg you to follow me into the woods behind the school?"

"I *do* remember."

"It's what Old Hatchet-Face said in English class when we read that book—you finished it; I only skimmed—'we're moving on.' "

"*The Great Gatsby.* 'So we move on, boats against the tide . . .' "

"Whatever." He drums an impatient rat-a-tat on his jeans. "You were always a snooty smarty-pants. The point is, Annie, I'm sure glad I found this out."

"Found what out?'

"That I am so over you. It's just that you and me . . . It's not the same."

"Tell me about it. Nobody's the same."

"I am," Ralphie says.

"And that's a good thing?"

"You better believe it." He studies the poster for La Kermesse.

"Well, I concur, in this futile attempt to rewrite history." She stands up. She pictures her comfortable, tidy house and feels a stab of guilt. "Can I help you clean this mess?"

"Don't bother." He surveys his living quarters. "There's not much to do." As he bends over to brush empty bottles and candy wrappers under the sofa, his shirt rides up, exposing a tattoo of a naked woman—big breasted, slim hipped, tiny waisted. Below the tattooed figure's dainty foot, Annie can just make out a sliver of leopard-print underpants.

He passes her coat to her. "No hard feelings?"

"I have a husband. I have a life. I am very happy. *Very*," she protests.

"Big fucking deal. Whatever. And I'll probably end up getting that cough of yours."

He guides her out of the back room, through the grocery aisles, past shelves now emptied of their unwholesome snacks, and stops at the front door. He flips the CLOSED sign to OPEN. When he turns the knob, the rusty bell clangs a tinny hollow sound, signaling the end of a poorly matched match.

He taps her shoulder. "Can I ask one question before you go?"

"I suppose."

"That kid Megan who works in your shop? Does she have a boyfriend?"

"Over my dead body," Annie says, and slams the door.

Chapter Nine

When at last Annie scrambles into her car and starts the drive home, it's already dark, not the four-thirty Maine-winter seasonal-affective-disorder gloom but the six-thirty dinner-is-ready blackness. In Michaud's back room with its single grimy window, she had no sense of time passing, the lost hours caused by Ralphie's "A-one weed," lost hours she now chooses to dismiss as a bad dream. "Big fucking deal," Ralphie said. Over and over, she rubs her lips with the back of her glove in an out-damn-spot frenzy of un-PC, she-asked-for-it guilt.

She tries to call Sam to tell him she'll be late, but the battery is dead. She forgot to recharge her cell, an uncharacteristic oversight. Maybe her forgetfulness, her brazen dope-fueled visit to Michaud's, her equally brazen new coif have something to do with the disease screwing up brain chemistry. She tosses the useless phone onto the passenger seat. Who knows how many calls have been lost. A ton from Sam, she's sure, who, when she suggests he doesn't have to check in so often, always answers, "But I miss you when we aren't in touch."

Not even her father championed her to the degree Sam does. When she failed her driver's test on account of zigzag parallel parking, Sam criticized the inspector's imprecise instructions. When she broke a glass, he pointed at the sharp-edged counter top. When she (no, *they*) lost the babies, he accused the misaligned stars, not her unreliable uterus.

Before Sam, she couldn't imagine such solicitude—certainly Ursula never noticed her comings and goings, never kept tabs. While her friends resented curfews set by watchful, responsible parents, Annie's freedom felt less like good fortune than neglect.

If sometimes it all seems overwhelming, she has only herself to blame. Lacking a child, did she choose Sam as the repository of her every maternal instinct? After the miscarriages and the still-born baby, Rachel warned that such terrible losses could ruin a marriage. Couples break up over less, she said. She advised them to arrange counseling, join a support group of bereaved parents. They refused. "No one can make us feel better," Sam insisted.

Annie agreed. They didn't need a shrink or a community of fellow sufferers. Annie had a husband. Sam had a wife. That was enough. Better than enough, since, despite Rachel's textbook cautions, they grew even closer. Adrift in their sea of despair, they were each other's life raft. Were they wrong? Should they have reached out rather than turning inward? No, they got through it.

Didn't they?

All beside the point, considering the next thing they will have to get through. An ending. At least for her. And for Sam—a kind of new beginning, however forced upon him, however beyond his control. Here's the Catch-22: she must help him without actually being there to help him.

As she pulls into her driveway, she notices that the first-floor lights are off. It's much darker than their usual nod to economy. Once she's inside, the only illumination seems to be digital— phone, radio, TV, microwave, clock. She's read that sleep specialists suggest these be covered with opaque fabric to inspire a full eight hours and a household's peace of mind. Not that the Stevens-Strauss household is, at the moment, an incubator for peace of mind.

She steps into the hall bathroom and brushes her teeth twice. She grabs a bottle of Listerine and gargles. If she could find any floss in the medicine cabinet, she'd use that too. She scrubs her lips and swivels on Chap Stick.

"Sam?" she calls, dredging her voice in a mixture of warmth, innocence, and cheer. "Honey, where are you?"

No answer.

She switches on the lamps in all the downstairs rooms. She climbs to the second floor. She stops outside their study, its door closed. "My phone died," she reports.

"So I gather," he says from behind the unaccustomed barricade, words stinging like nettles. "Did your watch stop too?"

"Very funny. Open up," she says. Though it's easy enough to twist the knob and simply enter, she knocks.

No response.

"I have something to show you," she pleads.

She's annoyed. She could have been in an automobile accident. Been mugged, been struck with amnesia. She could have been called to the side of a friend in crisis. Could have jumped into the icy river to save a drowning dog. Shouldn't he give her the benefit of the doubt? She's dying, goddammit; doesn't that qualify her big-time for a get-out-of-jail pass? Not that this is an excuse she can use.

"As you very well know, there are no locks," he says now.

She turns the knob. She steps inside.

Sam's at his desk, eyes fixed on a pile of papers.

She clears her throat.

He doesn't move.

"Sam!" she exclaims. She's getting mad now, an unfamiliar feeling that she needs to squelch.

He picks up an envelope. Peering closely, he studies it.

"Sam!" she repeats.

In slow motion, he pivots his chair. He lifts his chin. He stares, opens his mouth, and gasps.

She twirls. "Well?"

"What happened?"

His shirt is buttoned wrong, but she's not about to point that out. "What do you mean?" she asks, keeping her voice reasonable.

"Your hair," he sputters.

"Is there something wrong?" she asks. Is her shame that obvious? she wonders.

"Something? Everything! You . . . you . . . are unrecognizable."

"Don't be silly. After all, you didn't turn me away, did you? You didn't say, whoops, here's a stranger at my door."

"Not funny."

She pushes a stray strand behind her ear. "I guess you don't like this?"

"Like? I'd say just the opposite."

"Isn't your reaction a little strong? I mean, what happened to the person who supports me in everything I do? Must I now ask you what to wear? What shade of lipstick? Do I have to raise my hand for permission to pee?"

"Don't be ridiculous."

"*You're* being ridiculous, Sam. It's only hair."

"No, it isn't. It's the girl I fell in love with."

"That's the problem. You want me to stay the same."

"And what's so wrong with that?"

"Change can be good. It means personal growth."

He tosses the envelope into the wastebasket. "You sound like Rachel. This is personal growth heading in the wrong direction."

"That's your opinion. Other people like it, *love* it."

"What other people? Blind people? Heavy-metal rock musicians?"

"Yeah, Metallica just breezed into Passamaquoddy in their private jet. Come on, Sam."

"Okay, who? Give me a name?"

What's she supposed to answer? Dee Dee, Mimi, Tallulah imported from New Jersey? Ralphie Michaud, from the other side of town? "Everyone in Passamaquoddy," she says. And because she can't bear another lie, she adds, "Except for Mr. Miller at the drugstore . . . and, presumably, you."

"It's your mother, right? Your mother who gave you this ridiculous idea."

"My mother had nothing to do with it," Annie says, surprised to be defending Ursula. "I just wanted a new look."

"Which makes no sense. You have always been fine just the way you are." He rubs his temples. "I was so worried, I developed this banging headache. I imagined all kinds of worst-case scenarios . . ." His eyes narrow. "What is going on with you, Annie? You don't call to tell me where you are. You didn't come to the store. You seem distracted. Lately you've hardly been yourself."

"It's only hair, Sam," she repeats.

"Why didn't you run this by me first?"

"Because," she says, "I'm thirty-seven years old. I can get my hair dyed purple if I want."

"And you will. I'm sure that will be your next step."

"Ah, so that's how you see me."

"All right. All right. Maybe I am overreacting just a bit."

"Ha."

"But to me you could never look less than beautiful, even half-scalped. I'm just saying that I'm surprised. We always make every decision together . . ."

"Maybe it's time we stopped," Annie says, and heads for the stairs.

"If that's what you want," he calls after her.

In the kitchen, Annie grabs a carton of Cheerios. She pours herself a glass of wine. She moves into the living room, eating her dinner straight out of the box in front of the TV.

She clicks on *The Bachelor*. She bets the bachelor would like her new cut. The women on the show sport stylish hairdos and skimpy clothes that expose a lot of shiny bronze skin. However hunky, though, the bachelor can't hold a candle to Sam. One contestant has hair similar to her own. The bachelor runs his hands through it. Lovingly. Though the story's halfway through, she gathers that three women are vying for the same man. Who will go home? Who will win a single long-stemmed red rose? There's a lot of weeping. She wants to weep too. *We hardly ever argue*, she and Sam would congratulate each other. *We agree on everything.*

Once upon a time.

"Aren't you both two little peas in the pod," their condiment supplier remarked at his last delivery, perhaps not intending a compliment.

She hears Sam pound down the stairs and into the kitchen. The refrigerator bangs. She listens to jars opening, spoons and dishes clanging, a bottle cap being popped. She wonders what he's able to scrounge for dinner out of an inventory of cocktail onions, capers, a bruised banana, and a hardened wedge of Parmesan. She meant to stop at the supermarket earlier. At the very least, she could have picked up hot dogs and a can of beans from Michaud's. If she weren't so otherwise distracted. She hears him stomp upstairs.

She pulls her phone out of her pocketbook. She plugs it in to recharge. She returns to the kitchen and brings the whole bottle of wine back into the living room. The woman with the hair like hers now has white orchids tucked behind one ear. Did the bachelor put them there? She drinks two more glasses of Malbec. She turns off the TV before finding out who won the rose.

In the front hall, she grabs her laptop from the bench. Since the document is initialed *MFS*—manual for Sam—it's not something he might consider opening. Even so, she needs to be more careful. She is, after all, married to a man who thinks *his* is *hers* and *hers* is *his* and that the sanctuary of the bathroom is a universal camping ground.

She starts to type:

IX: ADDENDUM TO SOCIAL

    A. Fair Fighting: Do not criticize anyone's looks, weight, hair, clothes, makeup. Especially after they've lopped off their locks or paid a fortune for a new dress, if they are suffering from PMS bloating, if they have issues with self-esteem. Especially if your opinion is not the only one—that is, if other people like the new hairstyle, new dress, or prefer full-figured curves. On the other hand, if you warn the person in advance that, say, purple isn't their color before they buy the purple dress (the way I tell you not to have the barber take too much over the ears, before you go), then that's okay. But after the fact? No way! Remember to separate what is opinion from what somebody else might interpret as just plain mean.

I know you value openness, honesty, transparency. I know you don't believe in secrets. But, Sam, honestly, pure honesty can be just as bad as lying. Lose the I'm-just-telling-the-truth, I'm-only-being-honest, and think before you say something.

I agree we hardly ever fight, and we've been so proud of this fact. Perhaps we should have argued more often so we could have become better at it. For your future relationships (yes, you will have them, and yes, you are a great catch for any lucky woman), remember to watch your words. Also, the so-called experts always say never to go to bed angry—maybe that's overrated. Maybe it's okay sometimes to stew.

B. Independence: Togetherness is great. Nevertheless, a person needs some space. Yes, big decisions should be joint: buying a house, life insurance, car, living room sofa—but a haircut, lunch date, telling someone where you are every minute like you're the other person's GPS—well, that kind of wanting to be close, however admirable, can verge into suffocation, if not turn someone off before they have a chance to know your charms. Despite your aversion to what you see as psychological gobbledygook, you have to be able to accept change. In others. In life. Even in yours truly. The change may be as insignificant (yes!) as a haircut, or as monumental as—here, I've said it—death!

Okay, enuf. There will be more to come. And, by the way, I'm rethinking that never-go-to-bed angry bit. Haven't decided yet, but when I do, I'll stick it in the manual. And it goes without saying that, yes, no matter what, I love you. xoxo Me

She saves the document, then shuts down the computer. She'll print it out later and add it to what's already in her underwear drawer. She grabs her mother-in-law's afghan from the back of the sofa; she wraps herself in it. Under her head, she tucks a needle-point pillow of pine trees a loyal customer stitched for her and Sam. Its balsam stuffing summons up forest trails, morning hikes, campfire breakfasts, snuggling together in one sleeping bag under the stars. Oh, what fun they had. *Had.*

Past tense.

She considers her options. *One:* The usual routine: Climb into bed with Sam. Act as if nothing is wrong. *Pros:* Maybe even have makeup sex. *Cons:* Proximity to her husband's body might tempt her to blurt out recent humiliations, which won't be so easy as a haircut to forgive. Also, she's so angry that she might be tempted to try again to spring on him the harder truth, something that needs careful planning, tact, a thoughtful paving of the way, a whole manual. *Option Two:* Sneak up to the guest room— originally planned as the nursery—and— *Pros:* Let her fury subside while she sleeps in a real queen-sized bed with a goose-down duvet and a stack of P. G. Wodehouse on the night table. *Cons:* While no longer adorned with Curious George–themed curtains and adorable duck decals, it's a room that, no matter how much comfort they stuff into it, still signals a sad and profound emptiness.

She decides on the narrow couch.

She stretches out. The house is now so quiet that she hears only the whirring of kitchen machines and her own raspy breath. *He'll be sorry*, she thinks, and hates herself. She sleeps fitfully, dreaming of a dark forest ending in a lush meadow where a man and a woman hand in hand, hair trailing down the woman's back, dance through fields of daisies under a rainbow-arced sky.

At five in the morning, a ping startles her. She reaches for her cell. *I miss u. Come up to bed*, the text message reads. She pictures the empty space in the bed, the space fit for a new wife, the space fit for a dog. Sam's legs will be looped across her side; one arm will be flopped on her pillow; he'll have rolled himself in her half of the blankets. She imagines the warmth of his arms around her, her body curled into his, his lips in the tangle—less of a tangle now—of her hair. She wants to be up there with him, with her husband, in their marital nest. She unrolls the afghan; she sits up. She searches for her slippers. *But . . .* She drops back onto the sofa. Who more than anybody else on earth needs to start to learn how to be alone?

*   *   *

When she wakes, it's already after nine. She's sure Sam's gone. He leaves by eight, off to the bakery to buy the rolls, to the market for the Bunyan ingredients, to the garden shop to choose flowers for the front counter, an upgrade Megan initiated and one the customers applaud.

She tiptoes up the stairs just in case. He's made the bed—a first. How great, she marvels, then feels immediately disappointed. If she weren't so cowed by the precise military corners (where did he learn that skill?), she'd be tempted to crawl under the covers and snuggle into the hollow left by his body, a space still giving off his particular and comforting smell. Except for his "depressive episode," they've rarely spent a night apart. Even in the maternity ward, when he wasn't sneaking onto her mattress against doctor's orders, he slept—or, rather, passed interminable hours—at the end of her bed in a horrible reclining chair. At one point, the footrest snapped back toward the headrest like an accordion pleat, trapping him. They buzzed the nurse to get him out. A nurse who felt obliged to document this event in Annie's chart (*3a.m. husband stuck in chair*). "I hear there was a little incident in the nighttime," the resident on call chuckled the next morning.

How strange to be pulled in such opposite directions: she wants Sam close; she wants him at a distance. Physicists would document positive and negative magnets. Philosophers would discuss a paradox. Psychologists would diagnose ambivalence. No matter. Some things are too complex—and too unpredictably human—to be explained.

She moves into the study and prints out the addition to the manual. Back in the bedroom, she tucks it in her underwear drawer. The pages are starting to pile up, she notices, and heaps an extra row of socks on top. She showers, careful to protect her hair, which seems to have survived eight hours of tossing and turning crunched against the sofa's nubby linen upholstery. She throws on a turtleneck and jeans. In the mirror, she studies her face. Does she look sick? Ashen? She must admit she appears pretty normal for someone in the throes of normal's opposite.

She heads downstairs to the kitchen. She needs coffee. Toast. Orange juice to erase the fuzz from her tongue. The second she pushes through the door, she sees it—the dozen long-stemmed red roses in the center of the kitchen table. With a note propped up against the vase. *Annie*, enclosed in a heart, scrawls across the front. It strikes her at once: a dozen roses from a husband outclass and outshine a single red blossom from a bachelor.

She opens the note:

Dear Annie,

I am so sorry for acting like such a brat last night. I don't know what came over me. Blame it on my—stupidly—wanting everything to stay the same and my desire to be included in every part of your life. I'm really not one of those stalker husbands who end up on 48 Hours! Of course you don't have to report your every move. Or be available 24/7 by phone and text. And of course your hair looks beautiful. It just took me by surprise. And the lights—so childish of me. (My mother used to do the same thing to my Dad when he was out late with his buddies playing cards—I thought that was so infantile—and here I am copying this awful behavior. Is it in my genes?) I've been so spoiled. So used to having you by my side that I feel totally lonely without you. Unfair to you, I know. And I was worried, imagining God-knows-what had happened. I hardly slept. I am an idiot. All during the night I kept saying to myself, how can I turn away the one person in the whole world I can't live without? Please forgive me.

Love up the wazoo, Sam

(BTW: if you're near the drugstore, can you pick up some Advil?)

Chapter Ten

You always liked the Christmas tree. Keep doing that (as well as the menorah).

The phone rings just as Annie is ready to set out for the shop. Sam making sure she saw the flowers, she supposes. Not that she could ever miss that towering bouquet. But when she picks up, the caller ID displays the name and number of Ambrose Buckley. She's tempted to let it go to voice mail. She checks her watch. Two seconds later and no one would have been home anyway. Her hand on the receiver, she hesitates. No, this is the first day of the rest of her life—her abbreviated life—with its new-dawn resolutions of honesty, transparency, and facing the music. "Hello," she answers.

"Annie?" It's Dr. Buckley himself, unannounced by the customary Carolyn Connelly preamble. "I've received the results of your blood work."

"And?"

"And, fortunately, at present, you continue to be stable. You're in a holding pattern."

"Great," she says. She waits for the other shoe to drop.

It does. "Nevertheless . . ." he begins.

"Nevertheless?"

Dr. Buckley switches to cautionary mode. "Nevertheless," he warns, "things could escalate." He clicks his tongue. "As your family doctor, yours and Sam's, I feel an extra level of personal involvement. Annie, please, you must find a way to tell Sam."

"I already explained . . . I will. Later . . . after I see Dr. O'Brien. It's only a couple of weeks."

"But he should know, and he'll be a comfort to you. In medical school—way back before you were born," he points out—"we used to role-play the various ways to talk to a patient, to convey information, to show compassion, to give instructions. You might try it. Practice will make it easier."

"It never worked the first time; I tried," she says. She recalls his storming up to bed, her night on the sofa, her resolve to proceed slowly, how angry she was. She shudders. "I hardly think polishing up my act will have a new effect." Nothing will make it easier, she knows. She's more than familiar with the struggle to communicate. After all, she's been composing her own manuscript—postscript—now hidden in her drawer. "I'll consider it," she says. "I promise," she lies, already breaking her recent pledge to choose honesty.

*   *   *

By the time she arrives, there's a line outside Annie's, winding down Main Street past Aherne's place and Pappy Rappy's

Electrical Supplies. What a relief. Neither she nor Sam will have the opportunity to initiate any "about last night" blow-by-blow analysis.

"Hi, Annie, how's it going?" the regulars greet her as she heads toward the entrance. She's happy to note that Ralphie Michaud is not among today's customers. She manages a sigh of gratitude.

Sam's behind the counter, wrapping a Bunyan in its signature waxed paper, the shop's name repeated in a series of black elongated triangles. They nixed the logger's ax and the iconic Maine pine for the elegant simplicity of sans serif letters and sharp-edged geometry. A classy presentation for a classic sandwich.

Annie squeezes in beside him.

"Hey there," he says.

She lowers her voice, hoping to shroud any act of contrition from the next-up Mrs. Godfrey, who is already pulling out bills from her wallet. "Hi," she whispers. "Sorry."

"My fault," he says.

"Mine," she counters.

"I was an asshole."

"I was worse."

His face shifts from hangdog to wistful. "How 'bout we split the guilt fifty-fifty?"

"Fine," she agrees. She reaches in her pocket and hands him a bottle of Advil.

"I'm much better," he says.

"Great." She grabs a stack of napkins and sticks them next to the sandwiches. "And thanks for the roses. They're amazing. Really beautiful."

"The least I could do." He rings up the order on the old-fashioned cash register they inherited from the Doughboys, one that antiques dealers making the New England circuit have offered to write a check for on the spot. He turns to her. "Your hair looks nice today," he says sheepishly.

Is this overkill in the make-amends category, she wonders, a blatant lie to ensure company in bed tonight? Or is it a genuine reassessment? Like the coleslaw they first rejected as too sour that is now their favorite condiment?

Mrs. Godfrey steps up to claim her half dozen Bunyans. She passes Sam her recycled Andrew Wyeth shopping tote from the Portland Museum of Art. Annie is glad that this Wyeth depicts a weather-beaten shack rather than the usual maudlin *Christina's World*—a painting that is starting to seem all too personal. "Great hairdo, Annie," Mrs. Godfrey praises.

Fortunately, they have little time for either gloating or apology, so busy are Sam and Annie in dancing their well-rehearsed *pas de deux*. It's a choreography they have perfected, circling each other, layering onions and peppers and cheese, handing off sandwiches, rolls, napkins, paper. Though the space is small, they manage not to step on each other's toes or open cabinet doors into foreheads or drip sauce down their apron bibs.

At last, there's a lull. Only the regulars linger, arguing over municipal taxes and the number of flies tied before the fishing season begins, plus the few stragglers buying sandwiches for dinner. "Don't feel like cookin' tonight," they confide.

"You and me both," Annie replies. She and Sam stand by their product. They're not like those two-faced vendors who sell made-in-China polyester and deck themselves in four-ply cash-mere from Scotland. While big-city experts, ignoring the Bun-yan's local gourmet designation, might denounce it as fast food, Annie can argue that the sandwich *does* cover all four nutritional groups—grains (bread), protein (meat), dairy (cheese), vegetables (onions and peppers) and fruit, if you classify tomatoes as fruit the way botanists do.

Back in the kitchen, Sam begins to fill a request that came over the phone—a family in Florida yearning for a touch of home for their reunion. He calls the FedEx service to schedule pickup and delivery while Annie loads the dishwasher.

Sam squeezes her shoulder. "Are we okay?"

"Of course."

"Can we put it behind us?"

"Absolutely."

Soon enough, she realizes, everything will be behind them. Behind them as a couple. Behind her as half of one. In time, the holding pattern will no longer hold. What looms ahead? Only the unattainable horizon of *Christina's World*. She studies Sam, his strong chin, his wide eyes, the chiseled nose she always dreamed their children would inherit, the rangy body that contains such sweetness, such loyalty, a body that, folded around her, makes her feel safe—until the vulture of disease attacked the tunneled-vision shelter of her nest. She certainly drew the short straw in the lottery that is life: Ursula as mother, her father—too young—collapsing at his desk, miscarriages, a stillborn daughter, this mass in her lungs.

Yet she hit the jackpot with Sam. True, living and working and sleeping with someone can provide plenty of reasons for that person to get on your nerves. A person who will fall apart at a medical challenge. A person who can become a little clingy. A person who holds too strong an opinion about your hair. A person who might have trouble functioning without a book of instructions provided by his wife. Yet with Sam she's known love, has felt cherished, has been happy. For seventeen years they've done more than okay. *You must tell Sam*, Dr. Buckley ordered. Soon, yes, but why destroy Sam's happiness now along with what is left of her own?

She remembers the day they took official possession of the sandwich shop. They turned the key in the lock. Sam carried her over the threshold. They filled a bucket with ice to hold the bottle of champagne they'd bought on the way. Sam unloaded a radio and plugged it in. "May I have this dance?" He bowed. Around and around he twirled her, skirting the cartons of china and utensils, the tables with chairs upended on top of them, while Stevie Wonder sang "I Just Called to Say I Love You." Later, he spread the movers' blanket across the kitchen floor, *their* floor. " 'And I mean it from the bottom of my heart,' " they chorused as they stripped off their clothes.

Now Annie puts away the rest of the rolls. Sam is sponging the counter tops, a job usually assigned to Megan. "Where's Megan?" Annie asks. So full of guilt and apology and her own angst, she hasn't noticed the missing pair of extra hands. She checks the clock on the wall; it's well past the hour when Megan shows up, always on the dot, if not earlier.

"Rachel called to say she'd be late. Some kind of crisis of the teenage sort. Actually, Rachel wants you to phone her." He unties his apron and taps his forehead. "I should have told you the minute you came in. I forgot."

"You always forg . . ." she begins, then catches herself.

Sam hooks his apron over one of hers. She notices that both of their aprons hang sweetly, almost lasciviously, intertwined. He points to the front room. "Do you mind if I join the gang out there for a coffee break?"

"Of course not. You *should* be schmoozing with the customers. It's good policy. I've read that in the fanciest restaurants, chefs make the rounds of the tables every night."

"Ha." He tilts his chin. "I'm not exactly a chef."

"In the world of Passamaquoddy, you're top chef. Iron chef. Master chef. Chef in chief." She looks at him. "Is this coffee-with-the-regulars something new?"

"They started asking me on those days you weren't around."

"Good for them; they're watching out for you."

"Nah. Probably hankering for free refills. But, believe it or not, those guys are pretty cool."

"I believe it. Now scram."

He hesitates.

"Go. I have to call Rachel anyway." She shakes a finger. "Behave yourselves out there. This is an establishment of fine dining, after all."

He touches her arm. "I love you, you know."

Boy does she know. "And I love you," she says. "Now *go.*"

*   *   *

As soon as Sam leaves the kitchen, Annie calls Rachel.

"She's on her way," Rachel says, "finally. She got a ride. Ralphie Michaud came driving down Elm Street just as we were walking out the front door. He said he was going to the shop anyway."

Annie forces out a nonchalant "Oh."

"Such hysteria this morning," Rachel continues. "She broke up with Ben. Or rather, Ben dumped her."

"Ben? I thought her boyfriend's name was David."

"I don't blame you for being confused. I can hardly keep up with them myself. David followed Tom, who was two boyfriends away from Jake, who was a few degrees of separation from the current or currently not-so-current Ben." Rachel sighs. "I wish some of the courting multitudes would rub off on me."

"No, you don't."

"You're right. Who needs all the drama at this age? Fair warning for all the salty tears that are going to end up in your malted milks."

"What happened?"

"The usual. Someone cuter came along."

"No one's cuter than Megan."

"My thought exactly. But this one has huge breasts and parents spending the winter in the Bahamas. Ergo, empty house, full bar."

"I get it. I just hope Ralphie Michaud isn't going to take advantage of her vulnerability."

"Don't be absurd. He's our age."

"So?"

"I'm not worried about Ralphie. Besides, he always had a crush on you."

What should Annie tell her? That she's aged out of crushworthiness? That he's got his eye on Megan? And then have to divulge the source of that information? The *sordid* source? Instead, she asks, "How can I help?"

"The usual. Tea and sympathy. I just wanted to warn you to expect fits of weeping and assorted meltdowns. I doubt you're going to have a very efficient employee today. Remember when Tykie Frye broke up with me?"

How could Annie forget? Freshman year at college. Rachel cried for what seemed like four days straight. They fashioned a voodoo doll from a towel, pasted his yearbook photo on its head, and stuck needles into his India-inked, traitorous black heart.

"Of course you never suffered any of that boy/girl anguish," Rachel accuses.

"Not true. Remember our Hell's Kitchen summer in New York?"

"Oh, that. But it hardly counted, since you always had Sam."

"Poor Megan," Annie says now.

* * *

But poor Megan doesn't appear quite that miserable when she and Ralphie Michaud finally saunter through the door. Ralphie has his arm slung over her shoulder—a little too close to her breast. As for Megan, she's flipping her hair and leaning a hip into him.

"Hi, Annie," she says. Her eyes are bright, not red from weeping. She does not look as if she's been pushed aside by a rival with parents safely stashed in a tropical paradise.

"Hi, Annie," Ralphie echoes, too cool for school. Innocence maps his face—no downward glances, no embarrassed grins. In the acting department, he rivals Ursula.

He also must be experiencing selective memory loss, Annie decides. Early-onset dementia. Or does what happened yesterday bear so little weight in the annals of Ralphie Michaud as to be as forgettable as this morning's reheated Pop-Tart? Perhaps hoping to thrust your tongue into a married woman's mouth counts the same as selling a lottery ticket or filling your car with gas—all in a day's work.

If so, what does it mean for Megan? For her goddaughter, who is newly rejected and therefore raw and vulnerable and clearly on the rebound? It's up to Annie to rescue this Little Red Riding Hood from the pot-smoking predatory jaws of the Big Bad Wolf.

She tosses Megan an apron. "Can you fill the coffee urn?" she asks.

"Sure," Megan agrees. She pulls the apron over her head and wiggles her butt in Ralphie's direction, a signal for him to tie up the back. A signal that Annie intercepts with a maneuver so deft it deserves a Heisman trophy. She jumps on Ralphie's toe, offering no apology. She grabs the apron ribbons and fastens them around Megan's waist with a double half hitch. *Let him undo that*, exults Annie, whose merit badge for tying knots was proudly pinned to the sash of her Girl Scout uniform. She gives Megan a god-motherly push. "Off to work," she commands.

Megan turns back to Ralphie. "Can I make you a cup of coffee? Or a shake?"

Ralphie smiles his slow, bad-boy, pine-woods-behind-the-high-school grin. "A shake would be cool. Chocolate with—"

"No," Annie says.

"Or coffee—"

"No," Annie repeats.

"It'll just take a minute," Megan pleads.

"No," Annie says again.

"But Annie," Megan entreats. Astonishment suffuses her face. Annie is sure Rachel would never offer such a plain, unadulterated no. Instead she would present a list of footnoted pros and cons, all suggested in a calm, uninflected, helping-profession tone oozing concern for the feelings of her daughter, her self-esteem, and her delicate sensibilities.

Ralphie holds up his hands, traffic-cop-style. He steps back. "Relax, Annie. What's going on? A touch of the old PMS?"

"I'm warning you," Annie snarls.

"Okay. Okay. I can take a hint." He turns to Megan. "See you later, kid."

Kid—the only word out of his mouth that isn't a lie. Annie grabs Ralphie's elbow, drags him across the kitchen and through the back door to the patch of gravel where the suppliers make their deliveries.

"What the hell . . ." he says.

"I need to talk to you."

"It's the goddamn North Pole out here."

She hasn't noticed. "What I have to say will take only a minute."

"Long enough for me to get pneumonia."

Though *she* is the likelier candidate for that disease, she doesn't respond. She thrusts her face a foot away from Ralphie's, so close she can smell the beer and tobacco on his sour breath. In the icy, subzero air, they both puff out cartoon clouds of conden-sation. How could she have shared some weed with him? "Stay away from Megan," she orders.

"Who are you to tell me what to do?"

"I'm her godmother."

"Like it matters?"

"Let me remind you, you are twenty years older."

"Big fucking deal."

"She's underage. I could call the police. And also inform them about your drug stash. Illegal. And your sexual assault."

"Bullshit. No one forced you to drop by to visit me."

"And not only the police, but I could enlighten Megan about what happened in that back room. Also her mother. Not to mention *your* father."

"You wouldn't dare."

"Just try me."

"You do that and I'll tell Sam." He smirks.

She's sure he's bluffing. "Tell him what? That you lured me into your back room? That you gave me drugs and tried to thrust your tongue down my throat?"

"You set yourself up."

"Who will believe you? My word against yours?"

He blows into his hands and rubs them together. "And to think I once liked you . . . to think that in high school I even thought of getting *Annie* tattooed on my arm."

"Do I have your word?"

"Only because I'm freezing my ass off out here. With a crazy woman."

"Your word?"

"Only because, to be honest, Megan isn't all that hot." He shakes his head. "And has"—he sneers—"a *godmother* who is one total bitch."

"No car rides, no chats, no coffee, no drinks, no flirting, no dates . . . *nada, rien, nyet.*"

"Okay." He pulls his collar up. "You win. Now can we go inside?"

"Not on your life. Just slink around the shop to your car."

He looks down at the ground. "There's ice on the path. If I slip, I'll sue you."

"Be my guest. I'll make your excuses to Megan."

He gives her the finger. "To think I wasted some of my best weed on you."

* * *

Inside the kitchen, Megan is scrubbing out the coffee urn. "Where's Ralphie?" she asks.

"He had to leave. He remembered he has"—she picks up a sponge, squeezes it out in the sink—"a date."

"A date?" Megan dumps the grounds in the trash and rinses the strainer. "He said he was going to meet me after work."

"He forgot he promised to take his girlfriend to the casino in Bangor."

"He has a girlfriend?"

"He didn't tell you? I think they're almost engaged."

"Hmmm," she says, sounding like her mother. "Interesting. I mean, go figure. He offered to make me dinner at his father's place. He invited me to hear Nat Rathbone and His Blue Oxen play down by the river." She bangs a spoon against the counter. "What a creep."

"You've hit *that* nail on the head, that creep on his noggin."

"I suppose he *is* a little bit too old for me," she allows.

"Not a little. He's your mother's age. My age."

Tears start to fall down Megan's cheeks. She wipes them away with the corner of the apron.

Annie takes her in her arms. "You're not crying over Ralphie Michaud, I hope?" she asks.

"No way. Not that jerk. My boyfriend dumped me today."

"The nerve. David should be ashamed of himself."

"Not David. Ben."

Annie sits her down. She makes Megan a mug of tea, stirring in two spoonfuls of honey. She promises there will be many boys to follow the Davids and the Bens. She holds Megan's hand and lets her cry until the gush of tears trickles to a drip. "Did your mother ever tell you about the time she was dumped by Tykie Frye?" she asks.

At this, Megan perks up. "No," she says.

"Well," Annie begins. "This will make you laugh . . ."

Chapter Eleven

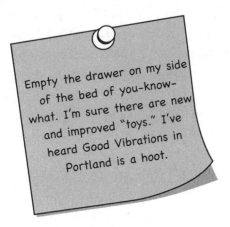

Empty the drawer on my side of the bed of you-know-what. I'm sure there are new and improved "toys." I've heard Good Vibrations in Portland is a hoot.

Annie sits at her desk, a hot fudge sundae melting next to her. She has the house to herself. Sam's checking out Home Depot with Rachel, helping her to decide on a new refrigerator. "You're the appliance guru; go with her," Annie ordered.

"You come too. We'll all get a burger afterward."

Annie had pled chores and going-to-waste leftovers in her own refrigerator. "I couldn't care less about refrigerators," Annie explained. "And Rachel could use the company. Megan's been moping about, lovelorn. While Rachel's love life is zilch."

Her own love life, on the other hand, is the opposite of zilch. Ever since her night on the sofa, she and Sam have turned into honeymooners all over again. These days, sex with her husband seems, like a near-extinct bird, all the more precious for its future vanishing. Why is such a big deal always made about the first tooth, first step, first kiss, first love? From her perspective, it's the *last* of everything that holds more meaning, more power, more poignancy.

How can she be dying when she felt so alive last night, when her supposedly deteriorating body parts resumed their old, instinctive, reliable motions? She clung to Sam while her mind kept telling her to push him away. *Helping Sam to let go is your mission for the time you have left,* her inner voice chimed. *This is your plan, the purpose of all your work on this manual.* But her body disconnected, seeking the one sensation that eclipsed all others.

Now she slurps a blob of ice cream with a flurry of impolite lip smacking. Considering her recurrent sundae-centric visits to his drugstore, Mr. Miller was surprised to see her order "the works" to go. "It'll turn into soup by the time you get home," he warned. "Besides, I'm so used to you perching on your usual seat that I'm thinking of getting a plaque to attach to it." He laughed. "The Annie Stevens-Strauss Memorial Stool."

Memorial, Annie reflected. She managed a thin smile. He didn't realize how unworthy of laughter such a plaque was. Or how quickly he should commission it.

She dangles the cherry by its stem, then plops it into her mouth. She isn't sure that's the way she wants to be remembered, as a four-times-a-week soda fountain customer, as the person who made her mark on a vinyl-covered stool. The list of sundaes she's consumed will be registered in the buy-five-get-the-sixth-free frequent-flier program, adding a few more coils to her spiral of shame. Better not to know the exact number.

There's a lot she doesn't want to know.

And one thing Sam *needs* to know.

*   *   *

She finishes the ice cream. She dumps the Styrofoam cup and plastic spoon into the wastebasket instead of bringing it downstairs to the blue recycling bin in the backyard. Ordinarily she and Sam are careful ecologists, worried about waste and the planet and dwindling resources. They even won, two weeks in a row, a best-recyclers commendation posted on church bulletin boards and the city hall honors list.

On the basis of past good behavior and present dying, she deserves some leeway in the upright-citizen department.

She pictures Rachel and Sam tucked into a booth at the burger joint. She hopes they're managing to find topics of conversation other than refrigerators. They'd be perfect together. What's more, Rachel comes with a built-in child—well, teenager—who despite lousy taste in men nevertheless shows interest in a future in the food industry.

Here's the equation: Rachel has always been the prettier and wiser member of their twosome, while Sam is a hunk in the best possible way, totally unaware of his charms. The opposite of those jerks Rachel has been meeting online. While Sam can be a little clueless socially, Rachel oozes emotional intelligence. Talk about the perfect solution. For Rachel, Sam is the treasure right in her backyard, all wrapped up and tied with a bow and presented with the blessing of the dearly departed. No need to travel to Portland or Boston to meet a date whose photo was taken twenty years ago and who "forgets" his credit card. For Sam, Rachel is the obvious next step. Besides, wasn't it an ancient tradition for widowers to marry their late wife's sister? If so, a best friend can certainly stand in for a siblingless wife. What could offer a stronger validation than near-Biblical backup?

Annie will have to find more reasons to throw them together and absent herself. In the subtlest manner possible. Without

Rachel catching on. Under normal circumstances, Rachel would never consider setting her sights on Sam. And when she's devastated by the loss of her closest friend in these not-so-normal circumstances, she'll balk at taking her place. Annie will have to wage the here-is-your-next-wife ad campaign in the manual. She opens her laptop and starts to type.

After a few halting paragraphs, she stops. She blows her nose on the drugstore napkins, fishes the empty sundae container out of the wastebasket and carries it downstairs to the recycling bin. Though she's not sure she's a believer, it couldn't hurt to strike a contract with God: if she recycles, if she's a responsible member of society and a worthy person, can she buy some extra time? She brushes a dusting of snow off the back porch. In the kitchen, she refolds dish towels and nests the teaspoons in the silverware drawer. *Spooning*, she thinks, picturing her and Sam curled into each other smack in the middle of the mattress, yards of blankets on either side of them.

Back upstairs, she swaps her turquoise earrings for pearl studs. When she checks the mirror, she can almost see Rachel's face morph into her own, like those actresses in the Ingmar Bergman film. Was that the one about death? Perhaps most Swedish films are about death, considering the climate and the dark Scandinavian soul. She shudders. What does Dr. Buckley know about the best way to give bad news? Well, probably a lot; the role of grim messenger is part of his job. Though clearly not part of hers. She is not trained for this. She can't do it. Doesn't want to. Ursula's disappointing daughter is suffering stage fright, acute and incurable.

Chapter Twelve

Don't feel, however sweet a gesture, that you must continue to use our anniversary year for all passwords.

In her bedroom, Annie sticks her underwear back on top of the manual. She should replenish her supply of stretched-out underpants and camisoles. Then again, new bras are as impractical as green bananas to someone who won't get full value for such an expenditure.

Okay, she's had enough, done enough tonight. Sam should be back soon from his excursion with Rachel. She checks her watch. It's after nine. What time does Home Depot close?

She sits on the bed. She picks up Sam's pillow. She smells the lemony scent of his shampoo, the mint of his shaving cream. If only she could hold on to all of this, the smells and touches and sounds; the small things she has always taken for granted now loom so large.

She hears the key turn in the lock. "Annie," Sam calls from the front hall. "I'm home."

She hurries downstairs. He hands her a bunch of daffodils, wrapped in silver tissue paper, price tag ($8.99) still attached. "We went to Lowe's after Best Buy and Home Depot. They carry flowers along with refrigerators and gas grills. Who would have thought?"

The flowers—the first of the season perhaps—aren't the slightest bit funereal. He pulls her into a hug. She smells onions and beer. "Did you have a good time?" she asks.

"Fine," he says, "though Rachel couldn't decide about the refrigerator. We may check out a few more brands." He shrugs out of his coat. "We missed you," he adds. "We both agreed it would have been more fun with you along."

An observation that pleases her, however much it defeats her plan. "A drink?" she asks.

"Why not?"

In the cabinet where they keep the liquor, she half expects to see the expensive bottle of cognac she just finished writing about. Art imitating life? Or the other way around? Alas, no Hennessy VSOP straddles the shelf, only the usual low-end brands of gin and Scotch and a dusty, unopened wild-blackberry liqueur named after a Brontë sister, a bargain-bin, spur-of-the-moment, literary-impulse buy.

She pours them each a finger of Scotch. She fills a bowl with salted almonds. At the kitchen table, they take their customary seats.

"How was your day?" he asks.

"The usual. Errands, paperwork."

"Ah," he says. He grabs a handful of nuts and tosses them into his mouth.

"And you," she asks. "Besides the refrigerator?"

"That was the highlight. I could write a dissertation on the differences between Amana and Thermador." He grins. "Just kidding." He sips the Scotch. "Though I did find out something interesting at work this morning."

She leans forward.

"Old Mr. Aherne reports he's ready to sell. At least according to the guys homesteading our best table. Who, I must say, are an awesome fount of local information."

"Pretty soon you'll join a bowling league." She smiles, remembering their candlepin dates as teenagers, those clodhopper shoes, the greasy snacks, the giant sheets of scoring paper, how cute Sam's butt looked as he started to swing the ball. "We've heard this before, Sam. He'll never leave. And he'll outlive us all." *Especially me*, she does not add.

"This time I believe him. He's hired a service to clear out the property. I saw the truck—"

"There can't be one big enough."

He nods. "Wait till you catch the parade of tractors and backhoes following it. He's got to have a hundred years of accumulated crap in there. But I managed to corner him in the front yard and asked him outright if he'd sell to me."

"You what?" She stares at Sam in astonishment. "You asked him without checking with me first?"

"Just testing the waters. But he said maybe, with that nearly toothless grin of his."

"That doesn't mean . . ."

"I already started running the numbers. And I made a few rough drawings of how we'd expand, connect the two structures, renovate . . ." Sam's eyes scan an imaginary horizon. If he's not counting gold in them thar hills, he's tallying up increased Paul Bunyan sales.

She drops her voice to its throwing-cold-water depth. "Nevertheless," she warns.

He doesn't seem to notice. "And there'd be room for a real cappuccino machine and a space for poetry readings and music nights. Maybe clear a few tables for dancing. We could enlarge the kitchen, improve the menu . . ."

Wait, Annie wants to shout, *this is supposed to happen after I'm gone. On my instructions.* Post-deathbed *instructions.* Instead, ever Eeyore, she grumbles, "What about the money? Sounds really expensive. We can't afford it, Sam." She hesitates. "At least at this time," she clarifies.

"We can't afford not to, Annie, now that he's ready to sell. Remember when *I* was the one *you* had to convince when we first thought of buying out the Doughboys? Now the tables are turned. What if Robineau's or Pappy Rappy's gets hold of the property? Or even"—he shudders—"Wang's?"

Annie winces in solidarity. Wang's Chinese restaurant, run by a family of Greeks, is a place where even the famine-stricken would reject Wang's watery chop suey or gummy chow mein. "No way Wang's," she says.

"My point exactly. We have to act fast."

Will her health insurance cover all aspects of her illness? she wonders. She's sure there will be unforeseen expenses . . . She forces herself to act calm. "And how do you propose paying for this?" she asks.

"Your mother," he says, as casually as if he's offering the weather report.

Annie jumps up from her chair, almost knocking it to the floor. "Ursula?" she exclaims. "We are not asking my mother for anything!"

Sam's expression is mild and reasonable. "Why not? It worked fine before."

"*What?*" She grips the edge of the table. Her cheeks blaze.

Sam's own cheeks suddenly redden. His face turns hang-dog. "Whoops," he says. He flashes his silly-ol'-me smile, eyebrows tilted into pleading commas, chin tucked in adorably.

A smile, which, though usually irresistible, she manages to resist. She sits back down, bursting blood vessels and rising temperature instantly chilled. "What?" she repeats.

"I can't believe I . . ." Sam points to his Scotch. "Loose lips sink ships," he says. "I better cut out the booze." He studies his glass. "This was, was *intended*, as a secret between your mother and me."

Although more than aware of her own hypocrisy, Annie's in full indignation mode. "We have no secrets, Sam," she says.

"This is the only secret I've ever kept from you. Ever. Ever. I promise."

"The nature of which . . . ?"

Sam smacks his head. "I'm an idiot." He takes another gulp of whiskey. She can hear his throat slap it down.

"Just tell me."

"Here's the thing. When we first bought the shop, Ursula gave us—me—a loan." He reaches for her hand.

Annie pulls it away.

"I paid it back," he says. "Ahead of time. With interest. Frankly, Annie, I think you've given your mother a bum rap."

Her fury rises again. Her pulse beats a rat-a-tat in her temple. Such anger cannot be good for her health. For her nonhealth. She takes a few deep breaths, the kind taught in the yoga class she hardly bothered to attend. She's determined not to fight with Sam. Not to spend another night on the couch. Nevertheless, what could be crazier or more upside-down than battling over a mere haircut yet declaring peace when faced with a gigantic betrayal involving her mother, her own personal wishes, her own personal history?

She remembers a story Rachel once told her of a textbook narcissist she met during the supervision phase of her social work studies. The woman had had a stroke. Suffering from aphasia, she lost all language except for one word: Me. *Me! Me! Me!* she screamed day and night, until her daughter could no longer bear to visit her.

She refills her glass, ignoring Sam's signal for yet another shot. She reviews her history with Ursula. She charts the lows:

Ursula: a mother lacking a single maternal gene. Why did she even have a child? Because her then husband, Annie's sweet, quiet, lonely father, insisted on it? Because by the time she discovered she was pregnant, it was too late? Because a baby was a chic accessory, like a bracelet or a pair of opera-length gloves?

Ursula: a mother who once said the following:

> *Don't you tell anyone your age, darling; my public wouldn't believe I have a daughter that old.*
> *Frankly, a touch of anorexia never hurt anyone.*
> *I am so sad to miss your _____ (school play, concert, exhibit, mother-daughter lunch, graduation).*
> *Too bad you take after your father, Arabella darling.*
> *I don't believe that was really pneumonia, just a bad cold.*
> *I'm afraid my lovely new beau doesn't care for children underfoot.*

The nanny spanked you, darling? Well, I'm sure you did something very wrong.

As for when you had your appendix out—you must understand that I am hopeless around hospitals: all those nasty smells, all that noise, that bad food, those dowdy uniforms.

Your Sam is adorable. If only he paid attention to his clothes.

And the worst: *Well, darling, I never wanted to be a grandmother anyway.*

Annie must have gone into some kind of fugue state, because she realizes Sam is still talking; she hears *loan, Ursula, generous, Mr. Aherne,* but the words float around in the atmosphere like atoms unattached to sentences.

"Beep. Beep," Sam says now.

She snaps to attention. "I'm really mad," she says. "Furious."

"I can tell."

"About a lot of stuff. The fact that you asked my mother, who, as you know, I long ago determined not to ask for anything."

"You've made that clear."

"And the fact that you lied."

"Not technically lied. Just kept the secret. For which I am truly sorry. For which I feel terrible. But really," he implores, "Ursula is not that bad. In my dealings with her . . ."

"She likes you, that's why. She thinks you're cute."

"Nonsense. She thinks I'm incompetent. I've overheard her. But she's your mother. She loves you. Of course she does." He shakes his head. "Granted, in her own Ursula-centric way."

Annie looks at her watch. It's ten o'clock. She is exhausted. How odd that sitting at a desk for a couple of hours can wipe you out more than standing on your feet all day making sandwiches. Didn't a famous author once lament that to write was to open a vein and bleed? On top of this, her whole conversation with Sam has sent her reeling. Anger itself opens a vein. It's all too much—that Sam kept such a big secret from her, that her mother is involved . . .

Sam gets out of his chair and comes to stand behind her. He kneads her shoulders, kisses the top of her head. "I'm so sorry, Annie," he says.

"I don't know what to say."

"Ursula . . ." he begins.

"Let's declare a moratorium on all things Ursula," she orders.

The minute he consents, the minute they decide to march up to bed and seek, Annie guesses, the solace in each other that salves all wounds, the phone rings.

Annie grabs it.

"My darling Arabella," gushes the unmistakable voice, words slapping down any moratorium on Ursula.

Annie sinks straight to the floor.

Sam raises his eyebrows, mimes a question mark.

"Ursula," she says in response to both of them.

"You'll have to speak up, darling. I got one of these new little phones. It came with the most delectable silver case. Smartphones, they're called. I'm not smart enough, I told the adorable young man who sold it to me. Of course you are, he said, and promised he'd come to my apartment to teach me the ins and outs. My first lesson is tomorrow. Have you heard of apps? There seems to be an endless choice of utterly enchanting ones."

"Yes, Ursula, I've heard of apps."

"I'm not surprised. You were always good at math."

Annie was horrible at math, not that her mother would know this essential fact about her own child. "Apps aren't exactly math," she informs her.

"Silly me, I'm still counting on my fingers. Fortunately, I have a business manager." She lowers her voice to a stage whisper. "I decided *you* would be the first I'd ring up on my new little thingumajig."

"What an honor."

"I'm delighted you feel that way," replies Ursula, impervious to irony. "Though this is not the only reason I called." She taps a fingernail against the phone. "And oh, how are you? And that Sam of yours?"

"Fine."

"Me too. I'm fine. In blooming good health, I am happy to report. Well, the real reason I called, in addition to finding out how you both are—it's been so long since we've had an actual *tête-à-tête*—is to announce some really spectacular news . . ." She executes a Pinteresque pause.

Annie can recognize a cue when she's handed one. "So, what's your news?" she supplies.

"Ambrose just called. You remember Ambrose, darling, Dr. Buckley . . ."

A cold sweat of dread starts to slick her brow. *He couldn't have, he wouldn't have . . .* "Yes, I know him."

". . . well, darling, Ambrose phoned to announce I have been selected for the Passamaquoddy most-accomplished-citizen award."

Annie starts to breathe again.

Ursula doesn't wait for her daughter's congratulations but jumps right in. "I knew you'd be thrilled for me. It turns out the award is being conferred next week. Though they made the choice ages ago, Ambrose, that dear man, had a devilish time getting hold of me. I've been on set. Then on the West Coast. Then traveling all over with Oliver—"

"Who's Oliver?"

"Never you mind, darling. He turned out to be entirely disagreeable. Best to put him in the past. You know your mother, always looking forward, always looking to the future, never letting little bumps in the road stop her. I am just thrilled, thrilled about the award. After all, *entre nous*, I deserve something for those endless years I languished in that backwater. Not to insult your hometown—I know you and Sam are very happy there—but for me . . . Well, even you must agree that I'm not exactly the typical Passamaquoddy citizen, though I did make the best of it."

"Yes, you do rise to the occasion, Ursula."

"Thank you, darling. Ambrose tells me I'm by far the most notable candidate to receive the award. Some ratchet designer—whatever is a ratchet, anyway?—was the first recipient. Then, before that, a composer who wrote an anthem about the state tree, of all things. Highly unoriginal, if you ask me. Those disgusting needles falling all over the place. I much prefer the charming espaliered chestnuts you find in France. Well, never mind. According to Ambrose, I'm the first woman to be nominated. Oh, I'll have to let my publicist know; maybe he can do something with the first-woman theme. A fish-out-of-water feminist angle. Hang on a sec, darling; I want to make a note to remind myself."

Annie hears the rustle of paper, the scratch of a pen.

"Don't you just love Post-its?" her mother marvels. "Aren't they the most clever, the most wonderfully useful invention?"

"They come in handy," Annie allows.

"And, in case you were wondering, they only give the award every decade, so it is the very definition of exclusive."

Talk about exhaustion. As her mother continues her Ursularian monologue, Annie feels her veins opening one by one. She pictures the blood spilling out on the floor, running in rivulets all over her house. Her mother does it every time. Pricks the wound. Opens the wound. *Causes* the wound. Helplessly, Annie clutches the phone, held prisoner by her mother's elocutionary parries and thrusts.

"What does she want?" Sam whispers.

"We're about to find out," she whispers back.

"What did you say, darling?" Ursula now asks.

"Nothing," Annie replies. "The TV's on."

"Speaking of which . . . I have a small part—small but choice—in the new *Law and Order*." Her mother laughs. "Unless I'm left on the cutting room floor."

"They wouldn't dare."

"Just joking. But the reason I called . . ."

"Yes?"

"Besides to announce the award . . ."

She braces herself. "Yes?"

". . . is to tell you I'm actually traveling to Maine to receive it. In person. I gather from Ambrose there will be a big ceremony at city hall. They'll present me with the keys to the city. As if I'd want them, ha-ha-ha. And a plaque. Ambrose will give a speech. And then some of the city fathers. Is Passamaquoddy actually called a city these days?" She sighs. "Will wonders never cease? At any rate, following all the hoopla, I will offer up a few words . . . you know, the usual . . ."

Annie imagines the blood now all over the floor and creeping, against gravity, upstairs. Her chin is on her chest; her heart is in her toes. She is leveled with despair. Why now? Does Dr. Buckley have a hand in the timing of this?

"So, I want to give you advance notice to get your guest room ready," she hears Ursula say. She feels a roaring in her ears. Her body goes still.

"Arabella," her mother prods.

"It's not really a guest room," she forces herself to answer. "We call it that, but I mean, no guest has ever stayed there." She pictures her mother's customary hotel suites, gilt tables cluttered with orchids, marble bathtubs the size of a small pool, closets bigger than Annie's Samwich Shop. "It's hardly up to your standard. Don't forget, it was meant to be the nursery . . ."

"And high time you got over that," her mother says. "No, on such an occasion, I much prefer to stay with my family. Ambrose offered, but I think it's a little early . . ."

"A little early?"

"In our relationship. Besides, there is only a Days Inn, hardly up to, as you say, my standards, and that B and B with all the Hummel figures in the window." She clucks her tongue; a tidal wave of distaste spills over the phone. "No, darling, your guest room will be perfect. I'll arrive next Wednesday. I always travel with my own pillow and Penhaligon's Blenheim Bouquet candles. It'll save you the trouble of a shopping expedition. Ambrose will collect me from the airport. Oh, my sweet Arabella, we will have such a lovely visit tightening our mother-daughter bonds. Oh, my! Look at the time. I need to get my beauty sleep, darling. *À bientôt.*"

Annie leans against the wall, stabbed, mauled, flattened, a casualty of war, a casualty of Ursula.

Sam scoots down beside her. "What is it, Annie?" he asks.

She can barely speak the words. "My. Mother. Is. Coming. Next. Week. To. Stay. With. Us."

She drops her head to her knees.

Chapter Thirteen

Please do not name any child Arabella.

For the first time in seventeen years, Annie hires a cleaning service. She doesn't even flinch at the price, quoted by the advance man who comes to evaluate the nature of the job. *Major*, he pronounces, requiring a crew of four and the full supply of heavy-duty, industrial-strength equipment. Though he can't be sure—unfortunate surprises often turn up—he estimates a total day's work, including a forty-five-minute break for lunch. As he writes up the agreement, he can barely hide his disdain for the result of her recent lack of interest in keeping up household appearances combined with Sam's casual long-standing attitude toward neatness.

If you think this is bad, go visit Mr. Aherne, she wants to protest. Instead, she meekly signs her name and hands over the deposit for services to be rendered. It's Monday. Countdown: two days—forty-seven and a half hours—until Ursula.

As soon as the cleaners' truck pulls up in front of her house, she heads for the Samwich Shop. Megan's already behind the counter filling sugar shakers and pouring coffee for the early lunch customers who mark their usual spot, reading newspapers and waiting for the rest of their cohort.

"You okay?" she asks Megan.

"Better," she reports. "Much. I figure there are plenty more fish in the sea."

As long as they're not bottom feeders like Ralphie Michaud, Annie does not reply. Oh, to be young, to bounce back from heartbreak, to be resilient in the face of life's blows.

In the kitchen, she's on automatic pilot, chopping, slicing, layering while fixating on the life's blow that is her mother. In the middle of the night, she slipped loose from the tangle of Sam's arms and legs and tiptoed into the guest room. She tried to view the space through her mother's eyes, eyes that would never see the loss inside these walls. She surveyed the sunny, baby-neutral paint, the Van Gogh sunflowers in place of Dr. Seuss drawings. The toys had been packed up and delivered to Goodwill along with the tiny onesies and cheerful bibs. She tested the mattress; it was comfortable enough, of decent quality, though not one of those princess-and-the-pea towering extravaganzas fit to pamper the limbs of a diva like Ursula.

No matter how carefully they'd stripped the room of anything child related, Annie could still imagine rocking Baby Girl Stevens-Strauss, still picture her daughter's face turned toward the window, to where the light danced among the trees. She was real; she existed. Annie had swaddled the motionless body in her arms, had sung to her. If only Home Depot sold smudge sticks to drive out all remaining nursery spirits, or a fêng shui guide to repositioning the furniture and inviting good Chi.

When she could no longer bear the prospect of Ursula on such sacred ground, she'd escaped to the study, opened the computer, and ordered a set of six-hundred-thread-count hemstitched sheets, paying extra for next-day delivery. Still restless, she'd clicked on the manual.

Addendum to Ursula, she wrote. Sam, please feel free to ask Ursula for the money for the annex. You shouldn't ever need to pay her back. Just make a little shrine to her in the shop, maybe hanging over the counter where everyone can see it. Her photo, the Passamaquoddy most-notable-citizen award, a few theater programs from her greatest hits. Hell—why not name a sandwich after her: Ham? Baloney? GORGONzola?

For obvious reasons, I never wanted to ask her for anything while I was still alive. But now, well, there's no incentive to put limits on you out of my own prejudices, my own neurotic principles—ones she probably never noticed anyway. So ask. Speak up. You have my blessing. She owes me big-time. For what, you may wonder? Well, for my not calling in child services! (Okay, a slight exaggeration—she never beat me or forced my hand against a flame or withheld food or a warm winter coat—though she did forbid desserts, *for my own good*, she said.) No, she owes me, and by proximity you (who have suffered from the fallout), for being the most narcissistic mother on the face of this earth. Good enough reason?

Now Annie looks out the window to Mr. Aherne's property. Old tires dot the front yard; a rusted-out Dodge sits up on cinder blocks. Though the dwelling is haunted-house derelict, it could work. It could work, she decides.

Megan walks through the kitchen door balancing a tray of dirty coffee mugs; she rinses them, then loads them into the dishwasher. "Hey, Annie," Megan says, "I hear your mother is coming to town to get the Passamaquoddy award."

"I'm afraid so," Annie replies.

"That is totally amazing."

"Amazing is the perfect word," Annie says, "if you define it as incredible."

"You must be so proud." Megan fills the napkin dispenser. She brushes an anthill of bread crumbs into the sink. "Mom and I wouldn't miss the ceremony for the world. I might be late, though, since we'll all be up to our ears."

"Up to your ears in what?"

"Didn't Sam tell you? They—city hall—have asked us to supply refreshments for the event."

No, Sam didn't tell his wife. A smart choice on the part of the city fathers, she grants, though she's not surprised Sam didn't confide in her. Lately he's been tiptoeing around the subject of her mother, not, she supposes, to keep a secret, but to spare her additional stress. He's seen her rocking in the guest room chair, staring out the window and looking sad before she can hide any melancholy with a fake grin. He's seen her making lists and filling the refrigerator with the low-cal snacks she'd normally scorn. He's felt her tossing and turning next to him, then sneaking out of bed to pace the hall. He's watched her trying on five different skirts and shirts, polishing her shoes, stepping on the scale. "You're perfect just as you are," he reinforces again and again. "Don't let your mother get to you."

"It's such an honor to do the food for the award celebration," Megan now says.

"What are we supposed to serve?" she asks.

"Oh, the Bunyans. They want everything to be iconic to Passamaquoddy: pinecone wreaths, locally brewed beer, Mrs. Gerard's whoopie pies, Geraldine Pritchard's saltwater taffy, Michaud's poutine. They're even printing a couple of Longfellow Clark's poems in the program. Sam's trying to figure out how to cut the Bunyans into hors d'oeuvre size."

"Good luck to him on that one," she says. "Why don't I help?"

Horrified, Megan shakes her head. "Not you, Annie. You're kind of like the daughter of the bride. Or the maid of honor. You'll be all tied up with your mom."

* * *

It's Wednesday. D-Day. U-Day. Ursula's plane gets in at 1:14. It will probably take Dr. Buckley another thirty minutes to gather her luggage, load the suitcases into his trunk, then drive the hour from the Bangor airport until he can deliver the honoree to the scrubbed, fit-for-receiving-royalty manor of Arabella Stevens and Samuel Strauss.

This morning she snared the first appointment of the day at Cutting Edge. "Just a trim," she told Dee Dee, "and a wash and blow dry."

Dee Dee raked a comb through her bangs and clipped the edges. "I know why you're getting your hair done," she said.

"You do?"

"Of course. Your mother's all over the paper." She evened out one side. "But Ralphie told me first."

"Ralphie?" Annie asked, sounding out the word as if it had been Sanskrit or Japanese.

Dee Dee stopped. She held the brush suspended over Annie's head. "In all honesty . . ."

"Yes?"

". . . Ralphie's taking me to the ceremony."

"Oh?"

"I hope you don't mind."

"Why would I mind?"

"Because the first time you came to the salon, well, you know . . . Later, he said it didn't work out." She resumed her brushing. "And now we've had a few dates."

Annie lifted her chin so suddenly that Dee Dee jumped back. "Careful; I don't want to leave a scar for your big day."

"My mother's big day," Annie corrected.

"Ralphie told me what happened that afternoon at Michaud's."

"Nothing happened. I'm married. Happily. You know I would never . . ."

"Don't worry, Annie. I can keep a secret. Discretion is a huge part of the job description for all hairdressers."

What Ralphie told Dee Dee, Annie could only imagine. No doubt a pack of lies, though the truth was bad enough. She cringed at the memory of the pot, the attempted kiss, the sight of the leopard-print briefs. *Forget it*, she instructed herself. At the moment she had other, bigger things to worry about. Let Ralphie date Dee Dee. Her red curls and perky breasts would be just up his pot-smoking, beer-guzzling, unwanted-advances alley. Besides, she was one person who could take care of herself. Not to mention age appropriate. Better Dee Dee than Megan. Better Dee Dee than her.

"So, you don't mind?" Dee Dee asked.

"Not in the least. In fact, you both have my blessing."

"Phew." Dee Dee adjusted an errant lock. "And, by the way, just in case your mother needs someone to do her hair . . ."

*   *   *

Now Annie checks the clock on the kitchen wall: 2:07. Her mother will be here within the hour. Unless—*if only*—her plane is delayed. No such luck; the sky is clear and bright even for February. The few clouds are fluffy and almost pink. She stands in front of the mirror. Well, she's as prepared as she'll ever be. Her hair looks good. She's wearing a dress rather than her usual jeans, earrings, and a strand of silver beads. She's invested in panty hose and shoes with heels.

One good—*goodish*—thing: she's been so busy, so anxious getting ready for Ursula, she has barely thought about her illness.

Until this morning.

Clasping her necklace, she felt a lump in her neck, a swollen node. Here we go, she groaned. She'll deal with it as soon as her mother leaves. At least her appointment in Portland is just a few days away. Lucky for her, Ursula is staying only one night. She can get through this.

Can't she?

*   *   *

She's sitting by the living room window when the car pulls into the driveway. Her heart does a loop-de-loop. Her legs liquefy. *Chin up; get a grip*, she tells herself; besides, compared to what she's already facing, how much fear can a mere mortal like Ursula provoke?

A lot.

Annie smooths her hair, tugs at her dress. She watches Dr. Buckley climb out of the driver's seat and open the trunk. She watches as he extracts three suitcases patterned with *LVs*. Classic Louis Vuitton antiques, her mother once explained, sought out by decorators to be stacked as coffee tables in penthouse living rooms. The way Dr. Buckley struggles with them, it's clear they're meant for redcaps in uniforms or liveried chauffeurs, not small-town doctors used to lifting nothing heavier than a stethoscope.

Now the passenger side door opens; out peeks a sparkly high-heeled boot, followed by a few inches of fur, a pocketbook, a glove, the fringe of a scarf—until the whole Ursula comes into view, clad in her *What becomes a legend most?* mink coat and matching mink-trimmed chapeau. Cars in the street slow and lower their windows. A man on the sidewalk toting grocery bags stops to stare.

And why not? No one can make an entrance like Ursula. All that's missing is the roar of the audience. Or the splattered eggs of PETA picketers.

There's no turning back. Annie moves to the door. She opens it.

"Darling," Ursula calls. Projected to the farthest balcony, it's a voice made to shatter glass. Or a daughter's heart. In seconds, Annie is engulfed in fur and Shalimar. "My baby girl," Ursula clucks.

"Hello, Ursula," Annie says. Even up close, her mother's face is flawless; not a wrinkle mars her perfect skin. Are her cheeks fuller than usual, her mouth more plump? Has she undergone additional nips and tucks since the last time Annie saw her?

Ursula holds her daughter at arm's length. "Let me look at you, darling." Her heavily lashed eyes sweep from Annie's toes to her head and back again. "As for you, Arabella . . . you have not changed one bit."

A compliment? Or a complaint?

"On the other hand," her mother continues, "that is an entirely flattering coiffure. Surely not a product of"—she makes a moue of distaste—"Passamaquoddy?"

"Actually, yes. A new hairdresser just moved here from . . ." She's about to say New Jersey but changes her mind. "New York," she finishes.

"Which explains everything."

Inside the front door, Annie instructs Dr. Buckley to stack the suitcases under the hall stairs, assuring him that Sam will bring them to the guest room when he gets home. Though he protests, Dr. Buckley is clearly relieved to be free of what to Ursula is one day's worth of luggage and to anybody else is enough for a year abroad. "Why don't I leave you girls to get reacquainted?" Dr. Buckley suggests. He pulls out a handkerchief and daubs at his glistening brow.

Ursula puts a hand on Dr. Buckley's arm. "Ambrose, darling, I just adore that you refer to my daughter and me as 'girls.' " Giggling girlishly, she places three kisses on each of Dr. Buckley's cheeks. "À bientôt," she says, and then translates: "See you soon."

Does Dr. Buckley's face redden, or is he just reflecting a transferred layer of Ursula's Crème de Chanel blush?

Annie walks Dr. Buckley to the door. "Thank you for taking such good care of Ursula," she says.

"My pleasure," Dr. Buckley replies. His expression turns medical. He studies her. "How are you, Annie?" he asks.

"Great." Reaching for the knob, she hesitates. Now is not the time to bring up new symptoms. She opens the door for him.

He takes her hands in his. He presses his fingers against hers. "Tell her."

She pulls her hands away. "Impossible," she says. "And don't you dare."

"Only with your permission," he promises. "Still, remember she's your mother. She loves you. She cares about your welfare. She'll want to do her best for you."

*   *   *

After he leaves and after Annie has managed to poke her node a few more times, Ursula returns with a fresh coat of lipstick and a new layer of eyelash fringe. "What a lovely man," she pronounces. "And rather handsome. So dreadfully unfair that age will always flatter men the way it never does women. Of course, it helps that he never went bald. A fine head of hair clearly enhances a man's appeal. What a waste that I didn't fully appreciate him when I lived here. Not that he didn't catch my eye . . . but . . ."

"But you were married?"

"Yes, that . . ."

"And he was married too."

"Not that true love can't surmount a multitude of obstacles. However, to his credit and as a demonstration of his character, Ambrose was always exceedingly loyal to his wife." She sighs. "You and that dear Sam of yours seem to have all the luck."

"I beg your pardon?"

"Your path to true love always appeared smooth as velvet."

"You think so?"

Ursula must register the stunned look on Annie's face, because she hurries to add, "Darling, so many women go through this loss."

"I don't want to discuss it."

"I myself have had . . ."

"You had what, Ursula? You had miscarriages? A stillbirth?"

"No. Not precisely. But I did suffer . . ."

"An abortion, you mean? Abortions? Plural."

"It wasn't easy, Arabella. Not that I intend to criticize, but you can be highly judgmental." She fingers her ropes of pearls. "No, what I mean, what I meant to say—which you rushed to misinterpret—was that your loss obviously has brought you and Sam closer."

"How would you, of all people, know?"

"Because, if nothing else, your mother is extremely observant. It's part of my training in the theater, darling. My studies at the Actors Studio. Why, Lee Strasberg himself praised my powers of perception."

Annie considers presenting her mother with a list of what she did not observe: the signs of appendicitis, of her husband's unhappiness, of a shy and lonely child who couldn't get her mother's attention no matter how hard she tried. But what is the point? She's tired of playing the prosecutor before a jury who will never find her mother guilty of anything but an excess of beauty, an excess of charm.

Ursula bends over one of her suitcases and jabs it with the sharp toe of her boot. "Let's move on to subjects entirely more pleasant. My plan for this visit is only peace and joy. Darling, I absolutely cannot wait one more second to show what I've brought for you."

She unfastens the suitcase. She lifts the top. From under layers of pale-pink tissue paper, she pulls out a silver box. The box is huge, tied with white satin ribbons, a sprig of lavender tucked into the bow. "Shall we take it into the living room and open it there?" Ursula asks.

Side by side on the sofa, mother and daughter nestle against the Maine-themed pillows. Ursula passes the box to Annie. Annie unties the ribbons. She removes the cover and peels away more pale-pink tissue paper. Underneath lies a honeymoon's treasure trove of exquisite lingerie: bras of thin translucent silk flaunt lace inserts placed strategically; garter belts display ruffles with satin streamers threaded through them; slips sport delicate embroidery and wispy straps; panties of lace and gossamer feel weightless; a brocade bustier is a wonder of engineering; a nightgown edged in garlands of organdy flowers could rival any runway bridal dress.

Would a person actually sleep in this confection? Annie marvels. Aside from her long-ago wedding night, what occasion could live up to such delicate underpinnings? A trip to the store to assemble sandwiches? To the market? To the multiplex next to a mall? In bed, wouldn't such delicacy induce fear of rips and tears and thus inhibit spontaneity? "Really beautiful," Annie gushes.

"Indeed! I just knew you'd appreciate my choices for you."

Yes, Annie thinks, *the way you appreciate the* Mona Lisa— *from behind a braided rope.* Would she wear them? She looks closer. *Could* she wear them? She picks up a bra. Could she squeeze her breasts into these fragile vessels? Could she slip these sweet nothings up over her thighs, let alone her big toe?

"I had to guess the size," Ursula confesses. "I hope . . ."

"Perfect," Annie fibs.

"Made in Italy. And France. From a little shop on upper Fifth. I buy all my basics there."

"They look like they belong in a museum," Annie says. "The costume collection of the Met."

"Thank you, darling. I trust you and Sam will enjoy delightful adventures while wearing them."

* * *

Fortunately, Ursula declines Annie's offer of tea and toast or a nip of something stronger. Fortunately, Ursula wants a beauty nap and a long soak in the tub before her big night. From another suitcase, Ursula extracts her pillow and scented candle. Annie ushers her up to the guest room.

On the threshold, Ursula oohs and aahs. "How cozy. How sweet. Such a cheerful yellow color. And those Van Gogh sunflowers always remind me of my trips to Provence. I can practically smell the lavender, darling. I have a friend, one of those financial geniuses, who has an original Van Gogh in his guest bathroom, and every time I sink into that tub . . . Well, no matter . . ." She fingers the hemstitched border of a sheet, turns on a bedside lamp. "You'd almost never know that this once . . ."

"Anytime you change your mind and want tea—or a drink—" Annie cuts in.

"You are quite spoiling me. Such bliss, once again, to be under the same roof."

Annie refrains from mentioning that they were hardly under the same roof when, according to the census, they actually lived under the same roof. "Sweet dreams," she wishes her mother, and closes the door.

She tiptoes to her own bedroom, where she dumps the underwear on her bed. She arranges the silky pieces in proper anatomical formation. She steps back to admire her creation. Which, from a certain point of view, resembles a police outline of a murder victim, a *rich* murder victim. How funny to see something so

French, so Italian, so erotic lying on top of their solid American log-cabin quilt. She starts to laugh.

Until she remembers how little she has to laugh about.

She sneaks into the study. She turns on the computer and Googles the Fifth Avenue lingerie store. Right away, the inventory, with prices attached, fills the screen. She gasps. One of the bras costs $288.97. The nightgown sells for over $600. Even the teeny tiny underpants are in the $200 range. If only she were the math student her mother boasted she is, she'd be able to figure the cost per skimpy square inch. Can she return them? Not if Ursula is the regular patron she claims to be. She bookmarks the site, then clicks on the icon for the manual.

Note to Sam: Put the underwear Ursula brought me on eBay. Make sure you advertise it's brand new and never worn. Made in France and in Italy. If you check out the prices online—Google the label—you'll be shocked. But what a good chunk of dough to put toward buying Mr. Aherne's annex. Though, I must admit, I'm sorry I won't have the chance to model these for you in the privacy of our boudoir! Even if I *could* fit into them.

She collapses on her bed next to the lingerie-outlined crime scene. She buries her head in a silk nightgown. Only twenty-four hours, she tells herself.

Chapter Fourteen

All your love letters to me are in a folder marked Sam in my red file cabinet. Feel free to dispose of them.

When Annie and Sam arrive at city hall, thirty minutes before the ceremony, the parking lot is nearly full. Unusual, since everything starts late in sleepy Passamaquoddy, especially functions open to the public. Though Sam warned her, Ursula insisted on getting there an hour early. "I must memorize the stage blocking and test the microphone," she insisted. "And, of course, the lighting always requires vigorous fine-tuning."

As prearranged, Dr. Buckley came by to pick up Ursula. When Annie opened the door, he stood on the stoop gripping an orchid corsage, bashful as a prom date.

"Have fun, kids," Sam joked. "No hanky-panky. And remember your curfews."

Ursula looked stunning in a long silvery dress, cut low to reveal an acreage of snowy breasts and creamy shoulders. She wore diamonds in her ears, pearls roped around her neck, rubies sparkling from fingers and wrists. Her shoes, silver and buckled with rhinestone clips, added four inches to her height; her makeup confirmed the skill of a professional used to fussing over powders and emollients in backstage dressing rooms.

"Wow," Annie exclaimed. "Far too gorgeous for Maine."

"Nonsense." Ursula twirled around to show the full effect. "Mrs. Astor herself would always wear her best Givenchy, her most lavish jewels, even when she greeted a museum's janitorial staff or held a reception for the disadvantaged or visited a tenement. In fact, I remember her exact quote: 'If I go up to Harlem or down to Sixth Street and I'm not dressed up or I'm not wearing my jewelry, then the people feel like I'm talking down to them. People expect to see Mrs. Astor, not some dowdy old lady, and I don't intend to disappoint them.' " Ursula shook her head in admiration. "She's my inspiration."

Unlike her mother, Annie is no Mrs. Astor. Even in her purchased-for-the-occasion dress, she more closely resembles Ursula's maid or a drab governess. "Don't you have anything else to wear?" Ursula asked when Annie first appeared downstairs.

"I bought this specially. Though the choices *are* kind of limited around here," she replied, deflated.

"My wife is beautiful," protested Sam.

"Which is the only opinion that matters. How lucky to have a husband who views one through rose-colored glasses." Ursula clasped a ruby-and-emerald brooch onto Annie's collar, instantly brightening the whole ensemble. She plucked a piece of loose thread from Annie's shoulder. "Keep the pin."

"I couldn't possibly."

"Don't be ridiculous, darling. This may surprise you, but it's actually my second tier. Costume jewelry."

* * *

Now Sam manages to squeeze their car between two pickup trucks with dice dangling from the windshields and rust patterns like mirror images of each other. He has already spent the afternoon here with Megan and a half dozen hairnetted ladies from the basement cafeteria arranging the mini Paul Bunyans on trays. He's been able to track down some extra-strength toothpicks, which he hopes will hold the layers together long enough for them to make their way intact into the mouths of the citizenry. He's nervous about how easily they may fall apart, considering he's never chopped them into bite-size pieces before. "Though not as worried about my sandwiches as you are about your mother," he concedes. He puts a hand on her arm. "Are you okay?"

"I'm internalizing the little engine that could. *I think I can. I think I can.*"

He squeezes her elbow. "I *know* you can."

She turns to him. "What would I do without you?"

"What would *I* do without *you*?"

Well, he's certainly nailed her biggest worry, which she can't worry about right now. She checks her watch. "By tomorrow afternoon, we'll be free. Less than twenty hours."

"Piece of cake," Sam says.

"For a *normal* family," Annie qualifies.

They follow the Passamaquoddy hordes in their Sunday best up the stairs to the council chamber. Flanking the entrance are a school committee member and a city councilor, neither of whom they voted for. "Hi, Annie; hi, Sam," they chorus.

Annie scans the crowd. The seats are already filled except for a few singles toward the rear. The school committee member, Patti Patterson, a crusader against sex education and the mother of six kids all under the age of eight, steps forward. "You're in the reserved section, first row. VIPs rate the benches with upholstery, not those folding chairs that kill your back."

"I know what you mean," Sam says. "Those chairs can give you sciatica."

The city councilor hands them programs. A photograph of Ursula taken twenty-five years ago shimmers from the cover. "She's quite the looker," he says.

Annie and Sam slide onto the bench alongside Dr. Buckley, the mayor, the mayor's wife, the city solicitor, the city clerk, the head of parks and recreation, the public works chairman, the treasurer, the police chief, the fire chief, the health inspector, and the man who introduces himself as the director of risk management.

If only she had someone to manage *her* risk.

She opens the program to a list of the former recipients, all five of them. She scans the schedule of events: a welcome by the mayor; an introduction by Ambrose Buckley, MD; the presentation of the award; a reception to follow in the multipurpose room. A short biography of Ursula reads like an application for Person of the Year. Annie stops at the last sentence. *She is the proud mother of Arabella (Annie) Stevens-Strauss. Annie and her husband, Sam, are the purveyors of Passamaquoddy's famous Paul Bunyan and are graciously catering the reception following the festivities.*

Annie fixates on the word *proud*. Is that Ursula's doing? Dr. Buckley's? The award committee's? No matter who is responsible, she's touched. And delighted by the shout-out, which counts not only as free advertising but also as a boost for any future expansion plans.

Annie turns the page to Longfellow Clark's poem, "Pine Trees." She reads the first line. *Oh stalagmites of pine, oh conifers of Maine, your fallen needles, your humble cones, your battered bark* . . . She starts to laugh.

Sam pokes her. "What's so funny?"

She points.

"Old Henry Wadsworth must be turning in his grave."

"Shhhh," someone hisses from the row behind them.

The mayor gets up and fiddles with the microphone, which alternates between ear-deafening blasts of static and dead silence. After several people jump to his aid, he makes his speech, which is—surprising for a politician—blessedly short. He lists the former winners, talks about the fine citizens of Passamaquoddy who have put him in office all these years, then turns the stage over to "our beloved Dr. Buckley, who is a special friend of our honoree today."

Dr. Buckley climbs onto the stage. From one pocket he pulls out a few notes, from the other pocket he removes his reading glasses, and then he starts to recount the many wonders that are Ursula. Dr. Buckley lists her beauty, charm, the highlights of her long career. He pays equal attention to Ursula's role as Queen Victoria and her stint at the ironing board in *Look Back in Anger*. The audience seems spellbound: no restless rustling, no unwrapping of cellophaned mints, no texting, no coughing fits. When he gets to her upcoming *Law & Order* appearance, people pull out their iPhones and punch the date into their calendars.

Dr. Buckley talks about his time as Ursula's family doctor, how he looked forward to her visits, how they would chat about art and theater and life until the other patients in the waiting room would start to mutiny.

Annie touches her second-tier pin; she fingers her swollen node. She's sure he doesn't look forward to her appointments the way he once anticipated Ursula's. She can hardly compete with Ursula's *joie de vivre*—which Dr. Buckley now extolls—though in her own defense, Annie argues, without the *vivre*, there can be no *joie*.

At last he seems to be winding down; he's on the final page of notes, the others stuffed back into his pocket one by one. "Let me close with these words," he says, "about Ursula's love of Maine in general and Passamaquoddy in particular."

Suddenly *the hellhole, the backwater, the provinces, boonies, the sticks, the place that time forgot*, which were Ursula's constant declarations of repugnance, are now decoded by Dr. Buckley into terms of endearment: *community, idyll, pine-scented paradise, seventh heaven, cloud nine, civic excellence, neighborhood fellowship*.

"I don't believe this," Annie whispers to Sam.

"She's an *actress*."

"Just like the rest of us," Dr. Buckley wraps up, "our esteemed award winner holds Maine in her heart and in her soul. Though she has roamed far and wide, done more than many of us would have dreamed of in our lifetimes, hobnobbed with people we've only read about, graced stages throughout the world's major cities, she always returns to Passamaquoddy, to the landscape and the people she loves." Dr. Buckley tucks away the last page of his notes, removes his glasses, and blots his eyes. "Please let me close with Dorothy's words in *The Wizard of Oz*." He leans forward, hands tented in prayer formation. " 'There's no place like home.' "

On cue, from behind a velvet curtain strung between one pole bearing the stars and stripes and another the state flag (*Dirigo*, "I lead") appears Ursula, a vision of shimmering silver and sparkling gems, Dr. Buckley's orchid corsage pinned to her wrist.

The mayor rushes onto the stage, carrying the plaque. The audience leaps to its feet, clapping and whistling. Ursula ducks her chin, bats her eyelashes, and raises a beringed and braceleted hand signaling for them to stop.

They roar louder. "Ursula! Ursula!" they cheer.

Would any top-of-the-charts rock star earn a more fervent response? Annie wonders. Not that such a big shot ever performed in Passamaquoddy's city hall. Though her father once told her he saw Roy Rogers on this very stage when he was a kid.

As soon as the audience quiets down, the mayor holds up the award. From her VIP perch, Annie has a clear view. The plaque is oak, with a pine tree embossed on the front; *Passamaquoddy Good Citizen Award* is carved on the top with Ursula's name etched on the bottom. There are smaller Latin words Annie can just make out—the city's motto, she assumes: VERITAS CURAT. Even with her rudimentary high school Latin, she manages to translate: *Truth cures!*

The mayor hands the plaque to Ursula.

Ursula clutches it to her décolleté.

"A few words?" the mayor asks.

"If you insist." Ursula adjusts the microphone so it doesn't block an inch of her perfect face. She speaks without notes. "First, let me thank our wonderful mayor and our beloved Dr. Buckley, one of my first and dearest Maine friends and also a close friend of my late and sorely missed spouse. Special thanks also to my daughter and her husband for their embracing hospitality and for teaching me the true meaning of family." She points to Annie and Sam scrunching down in their front-row VIP seats.

"But my most profound thanks belong to my fellow Passamaquoddians." She waves the plaque. "This is the greatest honor of my career. Why? you might ask. Because it comes from my beloved home, my beloved friends and neighbors, my cherished community. I'm afraid these utterly inadequate words of gratitude will be brief, because, in all honesty, I, who am never at a loss for words—just ask my fellow thespians—am, at this glorious moment, choked with emotion. I feel highly unworthy of this award but so very blessed, indeed, to join the august company of, among others, the inventor of the Quoddy ratchet, who has such a long page on Wikipedia (isn't the Internet marvelous?) and the brilliant composer of our city's anthem. I have, in fact, been humming that tune all day."

"Sing it!" someone calls out.

Ursula laughs. "Better to leave any musical performances to my more melodious colleagues. Alas, I can barely carry a tune. To which you may testify if you ever stand outside my shower door."

She peers down at the audience. "Frankly, no matter the often-elaborate trappings of my profession, deep down I crave simplicity, not fancy bouquets or fancy people or ornate surroundings, but you, the salt of the earth, who know true values, and the town that nurtures those values. These roots, your roots, are my roots. As Longfellow Clark—is there a more perfect name for our local bard?—wrote . . ." Ursula places her hand over her heart. " 'Oh stalagmites of pine, oh conifers of Maine, your fallen needles, your humble cones, your battered bark . . .' "

She waits a dramatic beat, then concludes, "Even before I knew the motto of our hometown, the motto that is written on this very plaque, I seem to have internalized it as my own guiding light, my own North Star. *Veritas curat.* Truth cures. I will cherish these words and try to live by them no matter where life's journey leads me. This I can promise you. Thank you very much."

Ursula bows low, exposing a great deal of breast, then bows to the left, the right, and toward the balcony. She blows kisses in every direction. Russian-style, she applauds the audience. To thunderous cheers, she slips behind the flagpoled drapery.

* * *

By the time Annie and Sam make their way to the reception, the salt of the earth are surrounding Ursula and waving their programs for autographs. Annie and Sam stand in front of the table laden with the mini Paul Bunyans. They are happy to see that more people throng these than Mrs. Gerard's whoopie pies or Michaud's poutine, despite the inadequate toothpicks, as demonstrated by pickle and salami bits littering the floor. She spots Ralphie and Dee Dee over by the bar talking to a couple of the hairdressers from Cutting Edge. They wave to her. It's a sign they've moved on, especially Ralphie. Megan will find more appropriate fish in her sea. Dee Dee is taking her own plunge. All is forgotten or at least forgiven.

"What a wonderful mother you have, Annie. You must be so proud," says the police chief, balancing two plates of mini Bunyans. "For the wife," he says in defense.

Soon enough it seems as if every citizen is coming up to congratulate her on her mother. Annie feels her smile start to freeze into a rictus, her hand sore from being continually pumped, her neck stiff from nodding. So many lipsticked kisses have been planted on her cheeks that she must look riddled with measles. Sam fans out his fingers against her back. "I can tell that you've had it," he whispers.

"Am I that transparent?"

"Only to me, who knows you so well."

"You think I can make my exit?"

"You go ahead. Since I've got to stay and clean up, Dr. Buckley kindly volunteered to drive you and Ursula home."

"It'll be hard to pull my mother away."

"Maybe not. She's no spring chicken, after all, and it's been a long day."

He's right. Even Ursula has had her fill of kudos and the salt of the earth—not to mention a menu that does not include caviar. She's ready to go. "I always try to leave my audience wanting more," she explains. They walk away amid *bravas* and *best speech ever* and *most deserving winner* and *one-person chamber of commerce* and *not changed a whit since you lived here*—compliments Ursula deflects with *veritas curat* modesty.

* * *

"Do come in, dear Ambrose, for a hot toddy or a little nightcap," invites Ursula as soon as Dr. Buckley pulls up in front of Annie and Sam's house.

"If I weren't taking you to the airport tomorrow, I would certainly want to prolong the evening. But now I think I'll leave you two girls the pleasure of a few mother-daughter moments alone." He looks pointedly at Annie. "I am sure you have much to discuss."

"How thoughtful of you, Ambrose. Though Arabella would love you to join us."

"Alas, I have early rounds." Dr. Buckley turns to Annie. "Remind me, what was our city motto?"

"I have no idea," Annie hedges.

"But I do," Ursula says. She unwraps the plaque from its protective tissue paper. "Here it is. *Veritas curat.* Truth cures!" She leans over and awards Dr. Buckley a lingering kiss on the lips. "*À demain*, dearest Ambrose."

Inside, Annie takes out the Scotch they both need despite the reception's continuous flow of jug wine and beer. She pours two fingers into matching glasses and carries them into the living room. Her step is light. Ursula's visit is nearing its end. Soon Sam will be back from cleaning up after the reception. Soon they will all be tucked into their beds. And soon, after breakfast, Dr. Buckley will take Ursula away. Surprisingly, the whole visit has gone without a hitch. Annie has survived.

Or rather—and no small matter either—Annie has at least survived Ursula.

Now Ursula excuses herself to slip into something more comfortable upstairs. "I'll only be a second," she promises.

Annie eyes the Scotch and decides she'll wait for Ursula. She rearranges the books on the coffee table. She plumps up the pillows. She straightens the landscapes on the wall. She peels wax off a candlestick. Soon a half hour has passed. So much for Ursula's only-a-second, but then her mother was always ready to keep an audience—and a daughter—waiting.

Annie changes her mind and sips the Scotch. She yawns. She shuts her eyes. She opens them. She finishes her drink. "Ursula?" she calls.

No answer.

She starts to worry. Ursula, as Sam pointed out, is no spring chicken, despite the spring in her step and her claims of robust health. Maybe the travel and all the excitement were too much for her mother. Maybe Ursula fell asleep. Or worse . . . A *Merck Manual*'s index of Sam-style possibilities parades through her head.

Annie bounds up the stairs. The door to her bedroom is open. Strange, all the gorgeous, expensive underwear Ursula bought her, the underwear laid out and left on her bed like a crime scene outline, is no longer there. Did she put everything away and forget? Has her swollen node metastasized to her brain? Or perhaps Ursula changed her mind about Annie's potential for seduction and took the present back.

"Ursula?" she calls.

Still no answer.

"Ursula," she shouts again. Louder.

She stops in the hallway. From the guest room, she hears muffled sobs. She opens the door.

Ursula is sitting in the dark. She clutches something on her lap.

"Ursula!"

Ursula weeps. "I found this," she accuses, "while I was putting away the lingerie you left strewn so carelessly all over your bed."

Her mother looks up. Mascara rivulets her cheeks. Her face is crumpled, aged. "I know, Arabella. I know," Ursula sobs.

Chapter Fifteen

If people ask about donations in my memory—suggest anything that saves children.

It's amazing how much tension a lone woman in a rocking chair can project. Of course, as Sam pointed out, her mother *is* an actress. And Ursula is in full histrionic mode. Clearly she is mining her past performances of Gertrude, Medea, Mother Courage, and Amanda Wingfield to create this larger-than-life paean to maternal angst and power.

Annie doesn't have a chance. The only role left to her is the disappointing daughter, Laura in the *Glass Menagerie*, crippled, fragile, shy, crushed, as shattered as her glass unicorn.

"How could you have neglected to impart to me such a monumental piece of information?" With the fury of Martha in *Who's Afraid of Virginia Woolf?*, Ursula hurls the manual across the room, where it lands in the spot once occupied by the baby's empty crib.

Annie scurries to rescue it. One by one, she picks up the pages, which have come loose from their clip. She clutches them tight against her chest, feeling like a Madonna cradling, if not a baby, still something she alone gave birth to. "It's private. You did not have my permission to look at this."

"I'm your mother."

"Don't you think I know that?"

"And you are my child. My one, sole, single child."

Any potential others having been peremptorily and conveniently eliminated, Annie does not point out.

Though maybe Ursula reads her mind, because her mother's face flushes. "It was a different time, different circumstances." She shakes her head. "You understand nothing."

Annie holds the manual so close it seems to meld into her skin, her bones, her compromised organs. "You gave up your rights long ago. When you left my father and me."

"You are so quick to judge," Ursula accuses. "You have no idea . . ." She halts her furious rocking, its speed a mounting orchestration of her anger. She lowers her voice. "Now is not the time for recriminations. Let us focus on what I've just read . . ."

"Which you had no right to read."

"In *your* opinion. Yet I did read it. And I am devastated. Utterly devastated." Ursula rubs her hands together; her tear-streaked face and shocked expression appear to spring from genuine emotion not melodramatic artifice. "To think you've carried this terrible, *terrible* burden alone for all this time." Ursula starts to cry again, big hacking sobs deep from her diaphragm.

Annie considers going to her, stroking her hand, putting her arms around her shoulders. Something she would do without hesitation for a perfect stranger in that kind of distress. How odd that reaching out to Ursula seems both harder and unnatural. Annie might as well be a foundling, imprinted to attach to a piece of cloth or a few feathers instead of her own maternal flesh and blood. She takes a tentative step forward.

Ursula weeps. Annie remains silent and watches her. When Ursula's crescendo of cries quiets to intermittent snuffling, Annie goes to the bathroom and brings back a glass of water. She hands it to her. "Thank you, darling. I do apologize for carrying on so. I am quite aware that I can become just the tiniest, teeniest bit overemotional." She sips the water. "May I ask you one question?" she ventures, calmer now.

"Do I have a choice?"

"Were you planning to address a few words to your mother to be read after . . ." She grips the arms of the rocker so tightly her knuckles rise into ridges. "I mean, were you going to include me in that document?"

A message from the grave directed to Ursula has never crossed Annie's mind. She tries to remember a few Ursula references in the manual: suggestions for a loan, selling her gifts on eBay, the usual complaints about her mother's domineering personality. Nothing Ursula—or anybody—would wish to read about herself. She studies her mother's brave, hopeful, drenched ruin of a face. Her heart softens. "Of course," she amends.

Ursula turns ruminative. "Isn't it a shame," she states, "that on a day of such joy, I am tragically forced to receive such shattering news."

Here we go. *Plus ça change* . . . No matter what, it's always about Ursula. Should Annie point out that the "shattering news" came from prying into private property? Should she mention whose fault it is that the day ended in tears? She decides on the high road. "I can't imagine getting sick ever comes at a good time," she says.

"Of course not, darling," Ursula exclaims. "Whatever was I thinking? Too much food and wine. I was never able to drink a great amount." Ursula rises from the chair and walks over to Annie. She holds out her arms. She is about to embrace her daughter when she seems to notice Annie's nearly imperceptible cringe. Maybe her finely tuned and much-touted observation skills kick in, because she reaches for Annie's hand instead. "Please, Arabella, let me be a mother. Let me take care of you."

* * *

It all happens so fast.

After the Niagara of tears and "my poor baby" lamentations, Ursula switches into full action mode. Within the hour, the *late* hour, Ursula has bought Annie a plane ticket and arranged for an appointment with a world-class cancer specialist, one of her admirers, whose unlisted home phone number is shared only among a select circle of intimates.

"But I already have an appointment on Thursday in Portland," Annie protests, "the biggest honcho in oncology."

"I'm sure your Maine physician is more than adequate, darling. Big frog in a small pond, as they say. However, compared to Manhattan"—she makes a *moue* of distaste for the Pine Tree State she has just so lavishly praised—"James is a genius," she marvels. "Cancel," she orders.

Annie calls Dr. O'Brien's office. When she explains, with apologies, that she's consulting someone in New York, that her mother insisted, that she's really sorry but . . . the receptionist interrupts. "No problem," she assures Annie. "Dr. O'Brien's fourth child is due earlier than expected. She pops them out like a Pez dispenser, that one," she chuckles. "Your visit would have to be postponed anyway." Annie hears the click of computer keys, no doubt deleting her. "Good luck," the receptionist adds, before she hangs up the phone.

* * *

Now Annie is packing a bag for New York. "Just the basics. We can get you whatever you need later," her mother instructs.

Annie assumes the basics don't include her extravagant new underwear, which is now folded, strewn with her mother's lavender sachets, and tucked into the drawer shrouding the reassembled manual.

"Like you, I always conceal anything unsuitable for snooping eyes at the bottom of my own collection of *dessous féminins*," Ursula confesses. "That's territory men won't venture into."

For a second, Annie wonders what secrets lie beneath Ursula's satins and silks. Better not to know. She sticks a pair of blue jeans into her suitcase, removes them and substitutes black trousers, then adds the jeans again. She turns to her mother, who sits on the edge of the bed, uncharacteristically ignoring Annie's wardrobe selections. "What do I tell Sam?" Annie asks. "He's just texted that he'll be home in half an hour."

"That your mother has discovered a rare opening in her calendar and is taking you on a-spur-of-the-moment, whirlwind mother-daughter bonding trip to New York. Sam will understand."

"I don't think so. He'll need me in the shop."

"He can hire temporary help. According to the mayor—charming man—the unemployment rate in Passamaquoddy is frightfully high. Sam will be doing a good deed."

"Still, he will have to pay wages he hadn't counted on."

Ursula emits an exasperated sigh. "I will gladly cover any and all costs."

"We would never . . ." Annie starts to protest. But they already have. Or Sam already has. She tries another tack. "He'll be lost without me at home. As you yourself have said, he's not the most competent . . ."

"Only because you've barely given that poor husband of yours a chance. No wonder his skills at independence are rusty."

"Not true. He always welcomes my advice."

"So I gather. You've certainly left him plenty in that book of yours." She pulls a lace-edged handkerchief from the sleeve of her robe and blows her nose. "He may surprise you, how well he will thrive when you're gone." She catches herself. "When you're away in New York, that is."

"I doubt it. We've barely been apart before."

"Then it's high time. Absence makes the heart grow fonder. As exemplified by Ambrose and me." Ursula pats Annie's knee. "Look at it like this. How would Sam feel, once you decide to tell him, if you just stayed in this backwater and, out of inertia, or fear, or ignorance, settled for its provincial medical care and never made an effort to investigate other treatments?"

"I would have. Dr. Buckley did suggest . . ."

"Suggest but not insist? Ambrose is a wonderful doctor and a splendid man; however, he *is* of a certain age . . ."

"Your age."

"Not exactly."

"Younger?"

Ursula scowls. "Not younger. Which is to say, he is probably not up-to-date on the latest medical innovations. And, while extraordinarily gifted, he is hardly a specialist."

"He sent my report to a specialist in Portland," Annie protests, "who suggested the doctor I just canceled."

"No insult to this glorious state and the site of my just-received award. But *really*! No, only in New York can one find medical geniuses. Maybe Boston, but my contacts there are minimal. Besides, how would Sam react if you didn't do everything possible to deal with this—this unfortunate situation?"

"Hopeless situation, you mean?"

"Nonsense! I can't believe a daughter of mine would just throw in the towel before exploring every possibility."

"Except when it's clear that . . . Except when the X-rays . . ."

"X-rays! What could be more old-fashioned? You cannot even begin to imagine the up-to-the-minute technology a major teaching hospital can provide."

"I've had scans and MRIs . . ."

"Not in New York, you haven't."

"Which might turn out to be yet another exercise in futility."

"Arabella! *Mon Dieu!* This is a matter of life and death. Or so I understand from that sepulchral guidebook of yours." With a *tsk* of distaste, Ursula pushes a high-necked flannel nightgown onto the floor. "Though, I hasten to concede, the one thing you did right was not to inform Sam about all of this misfortune."

Startled, Annie stares at her mother. "Dr. Buckley, the *gifted* Dr. Buckley, doesn't think so. At every single appointment, he begs me to spill the beans to Sam."

"Only because honesty is part of his job. A doctor must always promote the truth. I'm sure it's documented in the Hippo . . . Hippo . . ."

". . . cratic," Annie supplies.

". . . Hippocratic oath. But women know otherwise. It's appropriate that this is a confidence shared only between mother and daughter. Men can't handle these things."

* * *

Annie shuts the suitcase. "All packed."

"I am starting to feel much more optimistic than I did earlier," Ursula admits.

"I wish I could say the same." Annie sets the suitcase on the bench at the foot of the bed. She checks the clock. It's almost midnight. She wants only to crawl under the covers and forget everyone and everything. Has this been the longest day of her life?

From downstairs, she hears a key turn in the lock, then the front door creak open. "Hello! Hello! Where is everybody?" Sam calls.

Ursula looks at Annie. She grabs her wrist. "He's home."

"We're in the bedroom," Annie shouts back.

Sam's feet make slow thuds on the stairs, a sign he's as tired as Annie. She knows he will not be happy to see Ursula sprawled on the bed he'll want to jump right into. He will not be happy, either, to spot the battered suitcase, which is distinctly not Ursula's.

He stands in the doorway. He points at the bench. "What's that?" he asks.

"I'm taking my daughter away on a little trip," Ursula explains.

Sam frowns. Mustard splatters his shirt; a residue of flour dusts the knees of his pants. Dark circles rim his eyes, and his shoulders slump with exhaustion. The timing isn't great, Annie realizes, but when is it ever? "What's going on?" he asks.

"Arabella is coming back with me to New York. Tomorrow."

"Tomorrow!" Sam turns to Annie. "Is this true?"

Annie nods.

"But why?"

"Your wife needs a vacation," Ursula clarifies.

"I would love nothing better than for you to join me, Sam," Annie says. "But one of us has to mind the shop."

"And this all has been decided? Tonight?" He looks at his watch. "All between ten and twelve?"

Annie nods again.

"I assume this is Ursula's doing. And that you're just going along with her wishes?"

"Not exactly, Sam. I think it might be nice . . ."

"Nice!" Sam exclaims.

"Well, fun . . . I mean . . ."

"On your own?"

Ursula takes over. "She won't be on her own. I haven't spent much time with my daughter, as you yourself are completely aware, Sam. The opportunity arose, and I was able to make the arrangements."

"How long?" Sam asks Annie.

"Not long," Annie consoles. "If you don't mind . . ."

Sam sighs. He shrugs in resignation. "Sorry I reacted so abruptly. My stomach's a bit upset. Besides, it's late. I'm bushed, and you sprang this on me."

"It was spur-of-the-moment. I was as unprepared as you."

"If this is what you want. If this is your own decision."

"I have not twisted your wife's arm, if that is what's bothering you," Ursula interrupts.

Annie adds, "It *is* what I want. It *is* my own decision. Though I'm sorry I'll be leaving you in the lurch."

Sam relents. "Don't worry. Maybe Megan will agree to more hours. If I need to, I'll get extra help." He brightens. "Hey, you can check out sandwich shops in New York, take photos with your cell, get some ideas we can use when we expand."

"Are you intending to expand?" Ursula asks. "Everyone at tonight's ceremony was just raving about your hors d'oeuvres. I myself, alas, couldn't eat a morsel—terrible stage fright, even a touch of posttraumatic stress. You would think that after all these—"

Sam cuts her off before the floodgates open on dressing room nerves and preperformance rituals. "Any changes we make to the shop will happen in the future. Annie and I have our plans . . . Future plans."

"Of course you do," Ursula says.

Sam turns to his wife. "Frankly, you've seemed down in the dumps lately. Tired. Maybe it will be good for you to get away." He kicks off his shoes. "Just make sure you come back. Promise?"

"I promise, Sam."

*   *   *

In bed, Sam pulls her close. He unbuttons her flannel nightgown. He lifts it over her head. Gently he moves on top of her. There is something so comforting and so comfortable about long-married sex, Annie marvels, with its choreography perfected by practice, with its familiar moves, familiar sighs, familiar smells. How wonderful to know somebody's body as well as your own. *Better* than your own, she corrects, since her once-recognizable body seems lately to belong to a stranger.

Now she nestles her head under Sam's chin. He tucks her hair behind her ears. "I'll miss you," he says. "Have we ever been apart since we got married?" He pauses. "Except for—"

"—that weekend you were at the food convention," she cuts in.

"Motel 6. It was horrible." He rolls onto his back. "Well, we'll find out whether absence makes the heart grow fonder." He laughs. "But after twenty-four hours with your mother, you could be on the next plane home."

*   *   *

In the morning, before he leaves for work, Sam agrees to let Dr. Buckley drive Annie and Ursula to the airport. "For the sake of Ursula's budding romance," Annie argues. Since Ursula arrives at the breakfast table early enough to fetch the newspaper from the front stoop, their good-byes are not the kind of passionate farewells wives give soldiers departing for a war. Annie hopes he doesn't notice she's holding him a little tighter, clinging to him a little longer, depositing a few more kisses on his cheek.

"Off to make the doughnuts," he says. "You two have a blast."

"How could it be otherwise?" states Ursula. She is studying the newspaper, filled with photographs and paragraphs extolling last night's stellar event—the reason for her untimely appearance at the breakfast table, Annie guesses. "I must admit I don't look too hideous," Ursula confides.

Annie leans over to admire a full page's worth of images of her mother holding the plaque and turning her best side to the camera. "Beautiful," she says.

*   *   *

The minute Ursula excuses herself to run a bath, Annie phones Rachel.

"You're kidding!" Rachel exclaims when Annie delivers part of her news. "With Ursula? The Ursula you could barely endure for the twenty-four hours she was in town?"

"The very same."

"But why?"

"She invited me."

"And that's your reason?"

"Well, it is New York."

"True enough. There'll be theater and shopping . . . how bad could it be?"

"My point exactly."

"Still, I'm surprised. For how long?"

"I'll be back in a week."

Rachel clears her throat. "Forgive me for asking, Annie, but . . ."

"Yes?"

". . . is everything all right between you and Sam?"

"Don't be ridiculous. Everything is fine, the same as always. Why would you ever think otherwise?"

"Because this is not characteristic behavior on your part."

"I'm just going to New York. No big deal."

"You're right. Sorry. Though I can't imagine how Sam will survive without you."

"The very reason I called. Will it be too much trouble for you to check up on him?"

"Not hardship duty in the slightest. I'd be delighted."

"And if you're going to the movies or out to dinner or . . ."

"Yes, we'll include him. Megan and I will invite him over. Megan can whip up quite the lasagna. Also, Sam and I have more due diligence to do on the refrigerator front."

"Great," Annie says. "Maybe you can find other stuff to do together. I'd really like the two of you to get to know each other better."

"Come on; you're not making sense. We've known each other forever."

"But always with me."

"Of course with you. What are you getting at?"

"Oh, nothing. Just rambling." She switches the topic. "Though maybe you could encourage him to hang out with the guys from the shop?"

"Those codgers?"

"It's good for him to make friends. He needs more of a social life. I'll remind him to give Bob Bernstein a call."

"The lawyer who screwed up on your contract for the Bunyans?"

"Not really his fault. They could have a drink or something."

"Don't you think Sam's capable of making plans for himself?"

"I don't want him to feel lonely."

"We're not talking about a year abroad, are we?"

"Of course not."

"He'll be fine. I'm always happy to have a handsome man at my elbow. Even one on temporary loan from my best friend."

"Speaking of men . . ."

"Don't ask."

"That bad?"

"That bad. You are so lucky, Annie. I hope you know this."

"Oh, I do," Annie says. "I do."

* * *

When she goes upstairs, she hears Ursula in the bathroom, humming, off-key, "I've Got You Under My Skin." She's pleased she stocked up on imported bath salts and exotic oils and special soaps, no matter their outlandish cost. She can smell one of Ursula's candles wafting the scent of jasmine from under the door—all guarantors of Ursula's long tenure in the tub.

" 'Use your mentality, step up to reality,' " Ursula sings, as Annie tiptoes into the study and turns on the computer. She clicks on the manual. The Reason I Went to New York, she types, a title she's picked after trying in vain for a more felicitous headline.

If you're reading this now, Sam, then the trip wasn't successful. Not that I ever thought it would be. But for once, I think Ursula was right, that I had to try, to exhaust all resources, to see the experts, to have the tests. I understand you are surprised that I sprung this on you so late at night and at the last minute. And maybe a little angry, too, though you were such a good sport, considering I was abandoning you to an empty house and fewer hands in the store. But as much as I longed to stay with you, I also wanted to make sure that I had done everything in my power to grow old with you. I needed to have no regrets. It's important you know that I tried my best.

I don't want you to suffer a shred of guilt—you have been perfect in every way, have always *always* taken care of me—I am so grateful for every moment we shared.

I must admit that the prospect of going to New York, of not having to lie to you every single day, of not feeling like a coward each time I look at you, is an enormous relief.

Yes, Ursula knew, but believe me, I did not tell her. She snooped in my drawer while putting away that ridiculous lingerie she bought me and found the manual. Of course she read it. In a way, it was a blessing, because, lickety-split, she got the plane ticket, booked the appointment with the cancer guru (a friend of hers; no surprise there), arranged everything. So, I owe her this—and the fact that neither of us has to be sorry about not covering all the bases.

Now the hard part: why I lied to you. Or, rather, why I didn't tell you the truth about my illness right away. I tried once. You probably don't remember. In the kitchen, right after I'd seen Dr. Buckley. But you kept deflecting me. And I was so conflicted anyway, I gave up. Maybe you sensed I had bad news you didn't want to hear. I thought about trying again later. But I realized I didn't want to spoil whatever time we had left together; I know how easily you fall apart when someone you love is sick. I can't forget the week you spent in the hospital after we lost our baby—the chance that it might happen again with even worse consequences seems too much of a risk. I couldn't bear causing you such sadness. I knew you'd demand we travel all over the country at great expense, seeking a futile cure. I knew you would insist on any treatment, no matter the short painful weeks we might gain. I didn't want us to live under a cloud of sorrow. I worried you might develop symptoms of your own in response to my diagnosis. I wanted to spare you that. I hoped for our usual routine to continue, for *us* to continue as we were, as long as possible, for *us* to live our lives in the most ordinary but most precious way. And of course, as soon as I received a real diagnosis—I had an appointment in Portland that I canceled to see Ursula's expert—I planned to tell you everything.

It meant the world that we made love last night. Sometimes the body can say what words cannot. This part of our life together has always been a comfort and a joy.

I asked Rachel to check up on you while I was gone, in the hopes—I admit it!—that you might grow fond of her not just as a dear friend. Do stuff with her—movies, dinner, skating. She's great to talk to, not just in a shrinky way. I would be so happy if she and Megan, after the grieving has passed (and it will), became your family. It gives me solace to think that there will be another person in your future, someone you will love and who can love you as much as I have. Well, almost as much as I have.

Please forgive me—and Ursula and Dr. Buckley, whom I made swear not to tell you and is bound by the Hippocratic oath and HIPAA privacy rules—and know that whatever I did, whatever I kept from you, however misguided my actions might seem in retrospect, I did out of my profound love. I have no regrets. And want only that you have no regrets, too.

I hope you will follow the instructions, even if you find some of them annoying and even though they may reflect my bossy, less endearing side. My intention, however presumptuous, was to offer you help after I am no longer there to carry my share of our partnership. I wish you a full and happy life (as I have had with you—just not long enough, alas) and hope you keep me in your heart forever. In one way or another, you will always be with me. xoxo Me

Chapter Sixteen

Get a Dog. A rescue one. A dog won't hog the blankets. Remember how you missed Binky?

Once on the airplane, Annie finds her row and settles into the aisle seat. The middle seat is empty, and the man at the window falls asleep before takeoff, the brim of his Red Sox cap pulled low over his eyes. Ursula sits up front in first class, of course. She already had her ticket, and the difference in price was so huge and the trip so short; would Annie really mind flying steerage? Annie doesn't mind at all. She's happy to have a respite from Ursula, to sit suspended between her past and yet-undetermined future. How comforting to be in the air when you feel so up in the air about everything, to have somebody else pilot you when you have no map, no radar, no signals to point you in the right direction. Now her only task is to nibble the seven packaged peanuts (she counted them) and drink the dwarf-sized can of Diet Coke.

From somewhere behind her, Annie detects the distinct aroma of Paul Bunyans. When she turns around, she spots the telltale bags tucked under two adjacent seats three rows back. She was tempted to join the expat exportation of Passamaquoddy's best-loved resource, carting her own sandwiches to New York, all the better to stuff Ursula's refrigerator—inhabited solely by Perrier and shriveled limes. But she's sure her mother has had her fill of Paul Bunyans. And maybe, Annie decides traitorously, so has she.

* * *

At the luggage carousel, a woman buttonholes Ursula. "You are the spitting image of the actress Ursula Marichal," she declares. "Has anybody else ever told you that?"

Ursula smiles, motioning a skycap to her side and pointing out her bags. "Many people make the exact comparison," she concedes, "which I take as a compliment, as I too am quite the fan."

"Though she's a bit taller," the woman elaborates. "I wonder—is she still alive?"

Ursula's smile drops like a popped balloon. "I very much doubt it," she grumbles. Then she brightens when she spies the black-suited chauffeur brandishing a card with her very-much-alive name on it.

In minutes, the luggage is loaded and they're whisked away in leather-upholstered, piped-in-Brahms comfort to the Upper East Side. In front of the topiaried, awninged entrance to Ursula's apartment building, the doorman greets them, gathers the baggage, and presses the elevator button for the thirty-fourth floor.

Annie is amazed at the way privilege melts obstacles. Ursula's minions include not only skycaps but also chauffeurs and doormen, housecleaners and plant waterers, hairdressers and manicurists, eyebrow waxers, personal shoppers and personal trainers, plastic surgeons and therapists and cosmetic dentists and masseuses. She's heard there are Jamaican women who specialize in removing lice from hair and Polish women who can vanquish excess hair and Japanese women who will thicken thinning hair. Even better, celebrity and wealth can free up the calendar of a medical superstar booked a year in advance and schedule you for the next day right before lunch.

Though—alas—all the advantages in the world can't necessarily save your life.

Now the elevator opens directly into Ursula's foyer, where a gilded table holds a Chinese bowl filled with peonies and, next to it, a silver tray piled high with Ursula's mail, newspapers, and magazines. Annie gazes around Ursula's perfect apartment, once photographed for *Architectural Digest* and the *Home* section of the *New York Times*. Her mother acquired these high-ceilinged rooms in the divorce from the husband who followed Henry Stevens and preceded the one she'd "rather not talk about." It's not much of a consolation, Annie concludes, when marriage to the right wrong man can secure you a Park Avenue classic six but can't guarantee a loving mate like Sam.

Already she's received two texts from him. *Miss U*, one reads. The other, *Do you remember where I put my navy wool turtleneck?*

Miss you too, she texts back. *Second drawer from the bottom, on the right.*

Ursula excuses herself to telephone her agent and her business manager, to check restaurant reservations, to buy theater tickets, and to confirm tomorrow's doctor's appointment. "I really should hire a social secretary," she confides, "but certain things I prefer to do myself." She places her hand on her heart. "I guess it's the Maine in me."

Annie refrains from arguing that the only Maine in her mother is Annie herself and Ursula's Passamaquoddy award, now positioned front and center on the mantel. Where its reflection in the mirror doubles its size and quadruples its significance.

*　　*　　*

In the guest room—Frette sheets, fresh flowers in Lalique vases, a chaise longue covered in pillows with slogans embroidered on them—*A Star Is Born, Broadway Baby, Love in Bloom, Happily Ever After*—Annie unpacks her meager wardrobe; she hangs a dress and two blouses on pink satin-padded hangers. She tucks her utilitarian underwear into toile-lined, cedar-scented drawers. She plops onto the chaise longue and picks up the latest issue of *Vogue*. She decides she doesn't want to read about a socialite's divorce or a model's weight gain or a couturier's labor woes or an artist's architect-designed studio on Long Island Sound. How is she going to get through the next hours until her consultation tomorrow morning?

Not that hard, as it turns out. Leave it to Ursula.

"Are you ready, darling?" Ursula calls. "I've ordered a car." Ursula is already slipping on her floor-length mink.

"Now?" Annie asks.

"It's only two. We have the whole afternoon and evening."

"But I thought . . ."

"Thought what? That we'd sit around and anticipate your doctor's appointment and act gloomy and miserable? Never worry about something you can't do anything about. Always expect the best. Take one day at a time. Enjoy the present. Live in the moment. Let's have fun."

Mottos to stitch on a pillow, Annie thinks. "You sound like a self-help book," she tells her mother.

"And what is wrong with that? Ha, maybe I *will* write a book. My philosophy of life and how it made me who I am."

"A definite best seller."

"Have you got a grudge against being happy?"

"Of course not. It's just . . ."

Ursula eyes her daughter. "Arabella, we're not in Kansas anymore." She sighs. "Perhaps, darling, you'd consider changing into a dress and some halfway decent shoes more suitable for Manhattan."

Annie puts on the dress she wore to the award ceremony. She steps into plain black pumps with medium heels. She grabs her down coat.

Ursula shudders. "Not that." She flings open the hall closet and pulls out a second mink, shorter, lighter brown, only slightly more discreet than the fur now swathing her from ankle to chin. "This."

"I couldn't," Annie says.

"Nonsense. Nothing feels more luxurious against the skin." She scowls at Annie's puffy parka, shapeless and an unflattering shade of green. "You're not one of those PETA people, are you?" Ursula asks. "One night, on my way to the theater, they squirted mustard on me. Can you imagine such rudeness?"

Annie nods in sympathy, though she can't even look at a Davy Crockett hat without picturing the creature that sacrificed its tail. "Not my style," she apologizes.

"You have no style, Arabella," Ursula says, "but we're going to change that." Once again, she reaches inside the closet, this time producing a black wool coat. "Try this."

Annie tries it. The coat is softer and warmer than anything she's ever worn.

"Cashmere," Ursula pronounces. "It's yours."

"I can't possibly accept . . ."

"Indeed you can. It's my everyday coat. Second tier. One I wear to—well, to take out the garbage . . ."

As if Ursula ever took out the garbage.

". . . which otherwise I will give to the maid, who has already inherited several of my castoffs."

Annie sinks her hands into the deep pockets lined with silk; she nestles her neck against the wide collar. The coat is cut to accentuate the waist and flares out at the knees in a series of ingenious pleats. She inspects her Michelin Man polyester, now discarded on the floor like some hulking green animal. "Okay," she agrees.

At the entrance to Ursula's building, the car is waiting, double parked, blinkers flashing.

"I'm going to spoil you," Ursula says.

And so she does.

*   *   *

It's the kind of whirlwind tour that deserves its own description in the *Sunday Travel* section of the *New York Times*. Instead of the usual *Thirty-Six Hours in* _____ *(London, Paris, Beijing, pick one)*, the headline would read: *Eight hours in Manhattan (With Ursula)*. Annie opens her laptop and Googles the *New York Times* font; she switches to Georgia and starts to type.

Eight Hours in Manhattan (With Ursula)

By Annie Stevens-Strauss

Ursula's Manhattan is a rarified place, catering to the glitterati who expect red carpets, first-rate service, and head-of-the-line placement. During these eight Manhattan hours, no urban woes dare to be visible. If there are signs of blight, trash blowing along the sidewalks, graffiti on the walls, Ursula refuses to see them—"Let's not spoil this trip with such unpleasantness," she says, and rolls up the window. The one thing Ursula cannot control, however, is the stop-and-go traffic, but from the padded back seat of a town car with newspapers, a split of champagne, and a single rose in a bud vase, it's easy enough to ignore honking and fumes. For any country bumpkin taken into her silken bosom, the volcanic force of her personality wills troubles away.

2:30 P.M.

1) GET YOUR MAKEOVER AT BERGDORF'S

The country mouse is dragged to the makeup counter, plopped onto a high stool, wrapped in a paper bib, and attended to by a patchouli-scented woman whose forehead is so bronze, whose lips are so red, whose lashes are so thick, whose eyelids sparkle with so much gold that in Passamaquoddy, Maine, she would be scorned as a lady of the street or—equally bad—a foreigner. Fortunately, her hand is lighter on somebody else's face. Even better, Ursula perches on the next stool offering up a constant stream of directions: "a little less there"; "a little more here"; "wow, she has cheekbones!" All is not disastrous, as the woman pronounces the mouse's hairdo "very flattering." (Kudos to Dee Dee at Cutting Edge.) She assembles tubes and pencils and wands and multicolored unguents with a how-to chart. Despite increasingly vociferous protests, Ursula hands over her platinum credit card. The daughter, now sprouting cheekbones, has been transformed from provincial dustbin to urban icon who can't pass a mirror without checking her reflection. Narcissus, anyone? The cost? Priceless. Astronomical.

4:00 P.M.

2) FASHIONISTA

Onto the elevator and up to Designer Clothes. A hushed and sacred space with plush carpets, subdued lighting, and vast sofas. Skinny salespeople (do they ever eat?) in black are primed to indulge every whim. Ursula's personal shopper—Aurelie, five stars—brings them each a flute of Prosecco. She orders Annie to stand up, all the while inspecting her like a prize hog at a 4-H club. But Aurelie is discreet. "Not hopeless. *Pas du tout*," she whispers to Ursula.

By the time they have finished the Prosecco, Aurelie is back with a handful of frocks. She leads Annie to a dressing room mirrored on all walls. Since Ursula insists on coming with her, Annie regrets the safety pin holding up the bra strap that she meant to sew. One look and Aurelie knows what fits, what flatters, what dazzles. Annie pirouettes. "A metamorphosis," Ursula marvels. "We'll buy them all."

Aurelie arranges to have the dresses delivered so that such special customers (clients, she calls them) won't strain their delicate arms carrying the packages to the waiting town car.

5:00 P.M.

3) TEA FOR TWO

Ursula ushers Annie across the street to the Peninsula Hotel. Suggestion: ask for a banquette by the window overlooking Fifth Avenue and view the stylish natives along with the sneaker-wearing, tracksuited tourists. Perhaps, however, you have to be Ursula to warrant such prime real estate, with its banquette for six offered to just the two of you. Thus cossetted, you might deem all of Manhattan this lush and decide that the grim reaper, like the ragged, the dowdy, the rustic, could never reach you here. From a three-tiered silver-fluted tray, mother and daughter nibble on cucumber-and-watercress sandwiches minus the crusts and Scottish smoked salmon dotted with caviar. They sip Darjeeling from translucent cups. It's impossible to contemplate darkness when in front of you towers a platter of scones, Devon cream, tartlets, and lemon curd. "This is the life," sighs Annie. "This is life," corrects Ursula.

7:30 P.M.

4) BROADWAY: *THE BOOK OF MORMON*

The perfect choice for someone whose usual theatrical experience consists of high school productions of *Our Town* and an annual *Pirates of Penzance* put on by the out-of-tune Passamaquoddy Savoyards. Have a glass of wine in the lobby first, surrounded by patrons who saw your mother as Blanche DuBois back in—well, no need to state the exact year. Third row center—house seats, of course. Annie swears that the actor who plays Elder Cunningham looks down from stage right and winks at Ursula. The musical is hilarious, irreverent, joyful. How can you contemplate illness amid such entertaining affirmation of the human spirit? At intermission, Ursula buys Annie the CD and an outrageously expensive box of mints. A piece of advice: bring your own mints.

10:00 P.M.

5) APRÈS-THEATER DINNER: DANIEL'S

You could be in Paris at this top-rated, best-of-Manhattan restaurant. Sheer beauty, sheer luxury, sheer gourmet ecstasy. Ursula and her daughter are greeted by the chef himself, who plants kisses on each of their cheeks, then personally leads them to the premier table. Spoiler alert: one can easily get spoiled in the company of Ursula.

Where to begin? To start, Annie has the wild-mushroom fricassee topped by quail eggs and white asparagus tempura. Ursula chooses frog legs—a bit too anthropomorphic for Annie, though Ursula gobbles them up. This is followed, for Annie, by the Dover sole and, for Ursula, by the veal with braised cheeks and crispy sweetbreads. For dessert, they share the floating island, surrounded by passion fruit confit and garnished by a black sesame praline.

Has a meal ever been more celestial? Though Annie protests—where could she find the ingredients? how would she have the time, or the skill, or the stamina?—Ursula buys her Daniel Boulud's cookbook. Chef Boulud presents Ursula with his memoir, *Letters to a Young Chef,* which he inscribes to her with many references to *amour* and *bisous.* "If only Sam were here to experience this meal," Annie says. "Next time," Ursula replies, and Annie doesn't have the heart to argue.

Midnight

6) AND SO TO BED
Into the waiting car and uptown to Ursula's apartment. People still crowd the streets. Unlike Passamaquoddy, this is a city that does not sleep. Annie puts on her flannel nightgown. Ursula drapes herself in a negligee ruffled with marabou feathers. She kisses her daughter goodnight. "Sweet dreams," she says. "Thank you," Annie replies, and because the words sound so inadequate, she adds, "*Merci beaucoup.*" "*Mon plus grand plaisir,*" answers Ursula.

* * *

Annie crawls into bed and checks her cell phone. There are several texts from Sam: *Where are you? What's going on? Hell, it's awfully late. Whatever has Ursula done with you? Are you getting my messages?*

She listens to her voice mail: three calls. More of the same. *So, where are you?* he asks, his voice registering successively louder. *I assume you've turned off the phone,* he declares. Then, unconvincingly, *I hope you're having fun.*

She opens her email. Sure enough, there's a message from him:

Hi, Annie. I already miss you like the dickens. Our bed is going to be one lonely place tonight, though I can spread out and snore to my heart's content. While you've been living it up in the big A, Rachel and I have been checking out refrigerators. You'll be glad to know that she finally made a decision. She's picking the Amana. It's got some neat features, like an icemaker on the outside and a water filter, and it will be delivered next week. We grabbed a pizza afterwards at Pat's. Not great, but even I couldn't look at another Bunyan. Rachel's a lot of fun. No wonder she's your best friend. There's that concert at the auditorium which you and I ordered tickets for. I assume you won't mind if I go with Rachel. It's nice to have her company. We may take in a movie later on. We invited Megan, but it seems she's got a new beau, a student at Bowdoin. Rachel's pleased he's not some townee with tattoos and piercings. There's a new Clint Eastwood playing at the Bijou. Not your favorite, but Rachel's game. She's a good sport. BTW, I think Mr. Aherne will actually sell his place. I've been drawing up more plans for the annex. I really like doing this; the drafting, the designing. Perhaps I'll take a course in architecture and blueprint-making or whatever it's called. One of the codgers, Jimmy—the short redhead in the overalls and lumber jacket—has a niece who's a single mother and needs a job. I may interview her to help out. I doubt Megan will be making a career out of ringing up our cash register. Right after you left, I twisted my back, but I've been alternating ice packs and a heating pad and am almost as good as new. How long are you planning to stay with Ursula? Give me a call. I should be home from the movies by nine at the latest. Unless Rachel and I go for a nightcap—Fat chance. Where would we get a nightcap here? Lotsa love, xxxoooxxxooo, Sam

Annie is so exhausted that she can only manage to text back *More later. Ursula's worn me out. Try a couple of pillows under your back. Miss you, too,* then add a cut-and-pasted exact configuration of Sam's own *x*s and *o*s. She sets her phone in the charger, pulls up the satin comforter, and then turns off the light. Tomorrow is the doctor's appointment. Tomorrow she'll wake up to reality. But she's grateful to her mother for this magical interlude. And relieved it's too late to call home. She feels guilty because, well, she's had so much fun. And ashamed, too, that in the last eight hours—*Eight Hours in Manhattan (With Ursula)*—she's barely thought of Sam.

Chapter Seventeen

Do not leave keys, books, shirts—fill in the blank—on the roof of your car.

In a curtained-off cubicle, Annie lies on a hospital bed waiting for an open lung biopsy. She's wearing a johnny and matching drawstring pants, all huge. Ursula has double-wrapped the johnny and tied it, obi-sash-style, then rolled the pants into cuffs. Annie fears the whole effect is less Japanese minimalist and more J. Alfred Prufrock AARP. "One size fits all," Ursula scoffs. Which does not include Ursula and her progeny.

In truth, her mother's nose is out of joint, her toilette restricted by the fragrance-free environment—no perfume, no hair products, no vanilla-smelling lipstick, no lilac hand lotions, no face creams, no powders, not even deodorant.

An unscented Ursula is now sitting on a patched vinyl chair at the foot of Annie's bed. A handful of fashion magazines and a screenplay peek out from her Hermès tote. She plans to get a lot of work done during Annie's surgery. She may even run across the street to investigate a just-opened boutique. "Retail therapy," she claims. Annie's not to worry—of course there is nothing to worry about—since Ursula can be summoned in an instant if she's needed.

Ursula *is* needed. Without her, Annie would never have managed to get through any of the preop tests—the X-rays, ultrasound, blood work, lung function, EKGs. Even her teeth have been subject to scrutiny. "Those molars, those incisors, could shatter during intubation," the tech explained.

If Ursula hadn't been at her side, Annie doubts she would have survived the consultation with the surgeon either. Ursula grabbed her hand while Dr. Albright recited the legally mandated, cover-your-ass litany of everything that could go wrong—*the lung could collapse, the heart could be punctured, there could be unknown metastases calling for us to remove parts of the organ, the risks of anesthesia itself, the risks of intubation, pulmonary aspiration, air leakage into the lungs, perforation of the esophagus . . .*

"Nonsense," Ursula cut in.

Dr. Albright, reading robotically from a script, made no eye contact. Ignoring both of them, he continued. . . . *the chance of an infection, a severe hemorrhage into the lung causing respiratory compromise, a blood clot to the brain . . .*

"Just shoot me now," Annie said.

Ursula reached over and patted Annie's knee. "Health care is so utterly ridiculous these days. If you need the teeniest splinter removed, they threaten to amputate the whole limb."

*   *   *

Now researchers with clipboards and consent forms surround her bed. Will she help her fellow sufferers and donate her freshly excised tissue? Permit her blood to be syringed weekly? Allow the monitoring of her lungs? All for a new study.

What kind of person would not rush to volunteer her body to advance medical science? Annie asks herself. *What kind of person would prefer only to be left alone?* The answer's clear: somebody like her. Somebody who lacks a social conscience and a sense of responsibility to her fellow man.

Ursula takes charge. "Just say no, Arabella," she decrees.

Another nurse approaches, lugging an additional stack of forms. "Do you have a living will?" she inquires.

"Leave my daughter alone," demands Ursula.

As soon as these intruders disappear, Annie notices—by looking underneath the curtain that does not reach all the way to the floor—several pairs of feet crowded in the adjacent cubicle. The voices attached to them first murmur, then rise. "Don't worry," says one, "because you are in God's hands."

"Give yourself up to God," advises another.

"Everything happens for a reason," confirms a third.

"Good lord!" Ursula stage-whispers, not loud enough to impinge on any First Amendment rights.

Kaleidoscope-like, the brown oxfords, white sneakers, black clogs, red boots, and tan moccasins reshuffle into a circle. A prayer circle, obviously, because Annie hears "Our Father who art in heaven, hallowed be thy name." When at last the beseechers reach "Amen," she figures—hopes—they're done.

No such luck. They segue into "O my God, relying on your infinite mercy and love, grant the forsaken life and good health and overturn the diagnosis and steady the hands of the healers."

Annie's heart races. The incantations coming from the next bed underscore the prospect of life's end more strongly than any surgeon's recitation of dire consequences. Why is she putting herself through this torture? She remembers the Jewish prayer for the dead at the funeral of Sam's aunt Edie, a lament her mother-in-law described as an act of loving-kindness, helping the soul ascend to heaven. Annie doesn't want to ascend to heaven but prefers to stay here on earth for as long as possible. "Into your hands, I commend my body and my soul, while all the trees of the field applaud and I shall go forth in joy. Amen," the worshipers behind the curtain chant.

"Jesus Christ!" Ursula mutters.

As if "Jesus Christ" is his cue, a man in a somber suit and tie pulls aside one drapery panel and steps halfway into their cubicle. "I'm the chaplain," he announces.

"Go away," Ursula orders.

"Are you sure?"

"Never surer."

"You may regret . . ."

"Go!"

The chaplain turns to leave. "Just remember"—he smiles beatifically over his clerical shoulder—"God comes, bidden or unbidden."

By the time the intake nurse arrives, Annie's blood pressure registers as "off the charts." "I'll give you a little something to calm you down," the nurse offers as she sets up an intravenous line.

Within seconds, Annie understands why people become drug addicts. A warmth and peace descend. The hospital hustle-and-bustle fades. Ursula turns into a blur. The voices next door mute into a celestial choir. The curtains waft slightly, like tropical trees in a breeze. In the distance she hears wheels rolling, machines pinging, rubber-soled shoes squeaking. Somebody laughs. Is her departed soul ascending to heaven? If so, it's not all that bad. Annie giggles.

Into this nirvana steps Dr. Albright, the reality check. He's wearing full surgical scrubs in the noxious green color of Annie's just-discarded coat. He smells of bleach and ammonia. The operating room is ready for her.

A vision of Sam springs up in front of her eyes. Sam! Right now he seems so far away. He *is* so far away. For the first time in decades, he has no idea what she's going through.

How sad it's come to this: she's in a New York hospital bed facing death while Sam is assessing refrigerators in Maine. At least there's the manual. Her no-longer-living living will. If she had her laptop with her now, she'd type her own prayers for Sam. Ask him to forgive her her trespasses and instruct him to go forth in joy. *Amen.*

"How soon will you know, James?" Ursula asks Dr. Albright.

"The frozen biopsy will yield preliminary results right away. Final pathology will take up to a week."

"But you'll inform us of the preliminary diagnosis?"

He nods. "Though we have to wait for the complete report to be absolutely sure."

Then he does something that, in her drug-induced haze, Annie assumes she might be imagining: he squeezes her hand. Is this a gesture of empathy? Sympathy? A once-more-unto-the-breach salute? A final farewell?

*   *   *

She awakes in yet another hospital bed, in yet another curtained cubicle. Her first thought: she must be alive. Her throat is sore; her chest hurts—dull aches blunted through layers of cement. She assumes the anesthesia has not yet worn off. She runs her tongue over her teeth; she seems to have all of them still. At the foot of her bed stand two figures: Ursula and the surgeon. They're either the masks of comedy and tragedy, Annie supposes, or a mismatched couple accidentally assembled from separate wedding cakes.

"The best news on the face of this earth," Ursula cheers. She claps her hands.

"Not so fast," Dr. Albright cautions.

Annie looks from one to the other.

Ursula takes over. "Tell her."

Dr. Albright picks up a clipboard. He is still wearing his green surgical scrubs but has removed his cap. She doesn't like Dr. Albright, she decides in kill-the-messenger despair. She forces her wandering mind to focus on the words spilling out from between his lips.

"According to preliminary reports—let me stress *preliminary*—it appears as if there are no signs of malignancy," he says.

She tries to lift her head. "Could you repeat that, please?"

"No sign of malignancy. So far. To be absolutely sure, we will have to wait about a week for the final report."

"Which means . . . ?"

"I assume the final report will corroborate no evidence of malignancy," he concedes. He turns to Ursula. He smiles. "Just don't quote me on that."

Annie must be shamelessly fickle, because now she likes Dr. Albright just fine. He has a cute chin, she realizes, with a hint of a dimple in it. "Did I just hear . . . ?"

"You did."

She takes a breath. It hurts to inhale. But even though her rib cage is getting sorer by the minute, a warm bath of relief floods her from the top of her head to her now-wiggling toes. Her whole body unclenches and floats. *I have to tell Sam*, is her first thought, followed by *I can't tell Sam what I haven't told him in the first place.*

"Though," the surgeon continues, "you do have two granulomas on your lungs. Suggestive of sarcoidosis."

So here it comes.

"Which seems confined to the lungs, and is the cause of your nonproductive cough and your lymphadenopathy as well as myalgia . . ."

"Excuse me?"

"Enlarged nodes and muscles aches. The reason for your Maine physician's"—his cute chin tightens with scorn—"alarm. According to our tests, it presents as a small inflammation. We can treat you with prednisone. Often the symptoms improve even without treatment."

"You mean, I'll live?"

"Very likely."

"Unimpaired?"

"Probably."

"How did I get this?"

"We don't know the cause. It can be chronic or can simply disappear. It looks entirely manageable in your case. We'll recommend a pulmonary specialist. You'll need to be checked annually to head off any flare-ups."

Annie falls back against the pillows. "I thought I had lung cancer," she says.

"It can be hard to tell on X-rays and scans. Especially without further tests, especially in the hands of one unfamiliar with this disease . . . such as a general practitioner."

"A very experienced, caring one," huffs Ursula.

"Who sent my films to a thoracic specialist; who referred me to an oncologist," Annie says in defense.

"In Maine?" Without waiting for an answer, he continues, "Evidently, you didn't follow up with more state-of-the-art technology. Fortunately, you came to me, to this hospital," Dr. Albright says.

"And you are a veritable miracle worker, James," Ursula declares. "As soon as Arabella is settled, I will phone Ambrose with the good news."

The drug must be wearing off, since Annie is starting to feel crummy, however elated and relieved. Considering the alternative, her new diagnosis doesn't sound that bad. She wonders if God came through for the person in the next cubicle, if the prayers worked. Maybe God, however unbidden, came also to Annie Stevens-Strauss. "What about the patient in . . . ?" she begins to query Dr. Albright. She stops, remembering the strictures of confidentiality, strictures she used to her own advantage. "When can I go home?" she asks instead.

"You'll stay a few days in the hospital. Then we'll discharge you to your mother's care." He nods at Ursula.

Dr. Albright walks to the side of the bed and pats Annie's blanket-swathed leg. "No traveling for at least a couple of weeks."

She's too tired to protest. "Thank you," she manages. "So much," she appends. She must remember to send him a half dozen Bunyans and a package of whoopie pies as a token of her gratitude. Right now, all she wants to do is sleep.

"I've arranged a private room for you, darling," Ursula says.

"That's not at all necessary."

"With a view of the Hudson River," Ursula adds. "And a restaurant delivery service."

Chapter Eighteen

Laundry—you know not to mix darks with whites, not to leave change in your pockets, not to overdry your pants or they'll be ending at your knees, and to clean the lint trap with each washing. I don't have to tell you this, right?

Annie is back in Ursula's guest quarters, back in the lap of luxury, though the hospital's private accommodations were by no means a hardship post. She's been sprung, thanks to Ursula's promises of devoted care and Annie's time off for good behavior: that is, peeing, walking, crackle-free breathing, acceding with grace to needles and pills and saline infusions, a healthy appetite unmarred by Jell-O or tapioca pudding but still leaning toward the throat-friendly and easy-to-digest. Further aiding her escape, an entourage from Dubai, having booked a whole floor, needed her room for their food taster.

Ursula has perfected a Florence Nightingale worthy of a standing ovation. Bouillon in lacquered bowls appears at her bedside on the hour. Pillows are plumped into clouds of down the second she leaves the bed for the bathroom, where a bath is drawn with scented oils, lit candles around the rim, towels as thick and as soft as Ursula's mink. Though Ursula has had two tote bags full of best sellers and recent DVDs delivered, Annie wants only to sleep and to eat one of the delicious and medically soft concoctions Ursula orders from restaurants bearing a Zagat rating of twenty-two and above.

One night, Ursula reads to her from a collection of Alice Munro's short stories. The rise and fall of her mother's syllables stirs a distant memory. Did Annie as a child once listen to this same voice narrate Eloise's antics at the Plaza, Wilbur the Pig's testament to Charlotte, or Marmee's advice to Jo, Amy, Beth, and Meg? No, the drugs and the perfection of her sickroom must have confused her; it was her *father* who always read to her, who nursed strep throat, pneumonia, her recovery after her appendix was removed, who acted out the stanzas of Dr. Seuss and the adventures of Winnie the Pooh.

Now Ursula appears with a glass of freshly squeezed orange juice on a silver tray.

"You are taking such good care of me," Annie says.

"I *am* your mother."

"And a Mother Teresa as well."

"*Au contraire.* Those shapeless robes and not a lick of makeup and all that praying and hugging and blessing . . ." Ursula straightens the edge of a sheet and tucks a blanket under Annie's knees. "Not that I don't appreciate the compliment." She studies her daughter. "Would you like to check your email? That husband of yours must be jamming up your inbox, not to mention all those phone messages. Thank goodness for call waiting and my voice service. Otherwise I'd miss theatrical opportunities and reporters waiting to interview me."

The prospect of opening her laptop and typing on a keyboard when her wobbly body and woozy brain are so out of sync looms like Mount Everest. "Not now," she says. "Maybe tomorrow when I have a little more energy and my head isn't so fuzzy." She drops her fuzzy head into the down cloud and shuts her eyes. During the days before surgery, she emailed Sam frequent tourist reports along with selfies of her and Ursula against a backdrop of skyscrapers and traffic, labeled *We're not in Passamaquoddy anymore* and illustrated with winking, smiling emoticons. Now that she's returned from the hospital, however, the pinging computer and ringing phone stab like yet another surgical slash, oozing guilt and signaling a to-do list beyond her current capacity to do. What to say, how to explain, pose even more difficult challenges than the torturous exercises—reaching, stretching, bending, deep breathing—the nurse printed out for her on discharge. Still, even Ursula, the queen of little—and not so little—lies, has had a hard time inventing excuses: *She's out. She just stepped into the shower. She's at the theater. She popped over to the Met. I sent her on an errand to Saks. Oh dear, you just missed her. She's getting her hair done.*

As a result of Annie's failure to return his calls, Sam's messages on her cell, Ursula's cell, and Ursula's answering service have become increasingly anxious and annoyed. She can hardly blame him. Still, she can't call him back; her sore, constricted throat and labored breaths are too much of a giveaway. Hearing her, he'll be on the next plane. And then what? He'll see her in all her postsurgical collapse, the bedridden proof of her—and now Ursula's—subterfuge. His predictable sense of betrayal and his hypochondriacal catastrophizing will set back both of them.

Ursula promises to coach her, has suggested diaphragm-expanding exercises followed by the arpeggios that opera singers use to warm up. She has offered to hire the vocal therapist who helped Julie Andrews speak again. Because of her not-yet-healed lung, Annie is sure the calisthenics won't work. They've tried cough syrup and prescription-strength lozenges to mask her hoarseness, but she still doesn't sound remotely like herself. "You need to answer Sam," Ursula says.

"Not like this," Annie croaks.

"Tell him the truth."

"That I lied? He'll never forgive me."

"Once he realizes you've returned from the valley of the shadow of death . . ."

"I will, when we're face-to-face, when I figure out the right way . . ."

"Here's the plan: as a temporary stopgap, why not explain you caught a bad cold. And now have laryngitis. From which you are, in fact, truly suffering. Airplanes are notorious, even in first class, for the bad quality of the air, for spreading germs. Many actors actually choose to wear a mask during flight to protect their voices for upcoming performances. Frankly, I am running out of pretexts to offer up to him."

"Will you do it?" Annie asks with John Smith/Miles Standish cowardice, dismayed at how quick she is to toss the hot potato to Ursula. "Email him that my cold's so bad I can't talk? That I'll call as soon as my voice permits?"

"Is there anything I wouldn't for you, darling? And I assume"—she places a pledge-of-allegiance hand over her heart—"you want me also to send your love and add that you miss him?"

"Please." Of course Annie misses Sam. But in an abstract way, as through a haze. From here on her sickbed, from here with the lights of Manhattan twinkling outside her window, from here with Ursula exuding maternal concern—real or staged—Sam belongs to another world. "Out of sight, out of mind," she sighs.

"Nonsense," Ursula remonstrates. "It's more likely *you* are out of *your* mind." She frowns. "Perhaps James missed your lungs and sliced into your brain."

"Ha," Annie says. "Very funny."

Right now she's focused only on her immediate concerns: sleep, pain, how rubbery her limbs seem, the steady stream of soothing cups of tea with honey that Ursula tips to her mouth when her hands are too weak to hold them, her struggle to speak without a rasp, her total exhaustion. Even following the birth of Baby Girl Stevens-Strauss, when she fell into a black hole, when the world swallowed her up, she never felt such fatigue, fatigue that, at the moment, leaves little room for Sam.

Yet, she reminds herself, how lucky that through her present fog shines a future bright and hopeful enough to offer—knock on wood; she bangs the bedpost—a normal life-span's worth of years with him.

* * *

The phone rings. Not Sam this time, but Ambrose. After the initial medical explanations, Ambrose's apologies, and Ursula's insistence—with Annie's full consent—that nothing was Dr. Buckley's fault, Ursula and Ambrose's conversations have become less health related and more personal. This afternoon, Annie falls asleep listening to her mother whisper "*J'adore*" and "*Bisous*" in a throaty Marlene Dietrich voice.

*   *   *

When she wakes again, it's dark; she's been asleep for six straight hours. Ursula is curled into a wing chair across from her daughter's bed, reading a script illuminated by one of those miniature book lights advertised in the back pages of the *New Yorker*. In the big chair, Ursula looks tiny, like a Tennant illustration of a shrunken Alice.

"Can you actually see?" Annie asks.

"Oh, you're up." Ursula clicks off the light, shuts her script, turns on the lamp next to her. "These little devices are devilishly clever. You can read in bed while your inamorato is snoring away . . . How are you feeling, Arabella?"

"Better."

"Your color appears much improved. I must confess you looked paler than my whitest linens. I was quite alarmed." Ursula moves closer to Annie; she adjusts the pillows behind Annie's head. She sits on the bed. Annie smells all her lovely, expensive Ursula creams and perfumes and is grateful for their proximity. "Would you care for more tea? Perrier? I have some divine—soft—biscuits from Fauchon. Dinner will be delivered in an hour."

"I'm fine," Annie says. She studies her mother, who has been at her side since before the surgery and all these days after, now a week and a half. "It must be so boring for you, stuck home with me like this."

"Not at all," says Ursula. "*Pas du tout.*" She squeezes Annie's knee underneath its layers of sky-high-thread-count Egyptian cotton bedding made in Italy. "For the first time in ages and ages, I've got my little girl all to myself."

Considering what she owes her mother—her life, her happiness, a Manhattan idyll, her five-star recuperation, a Bergdorf wardrobe, newly revealed cheekbones, food of the gods—it seems crass to point out that she is no longer a little girl, let alone that, in fact, it is the first time *ever* that Ursula has had her to herself.

"Are you up to a little chat, darling?" Ursula asks now.

Actually, no, Annie wants to reply. Her mother's "little chat" will not be so little, she realizes. She'd rather watch *Top Chef* followed by *Kitchen Nightmares*, followed by another nap. Still, because she knows Ursula will do most of the talking, she answers with a grateful "Sure."

Her mother folds her hands in her lap and crosses her legs at the ankle, her prim *The Country Girl* stance belied by her glittering cocktail ring, a gift from a departed/deported Brazilian lover who had something to do with mines. "While you were asleep, I've used the time for reflection . . ."

"About?"

"About Sam."

"Not again."

"There are other issues. Besides the increasingly arduous burden of keeping the facts from him." She pauses. "Even more serious ones."

"Such as . . . ?"

"I worry you take him—his loyalty—for granted."

Annie groans. "You don't need to worry. As I've already pointed out, I know my own husband."

"I'm sure you *think* you do."

"What do you mean by that?"

"One can claim one knows somebody, Arabella, but one can never really know another person, deep down."

"Except for Sam."

Ursula reaches for her hand. Though the Brazilian lover's ring digs into her palm, Annie's instincts warn her not to pull away. "As your mother, I have my concerns. Let me remind you, darling, I read your manual."

"Which was *not* meant for your eyes. Let me remind *you*."

"Water over the bridge." Ursula cocks her chin. "Or is it water *under* the bridge? I am never sure." She folds her fingers over Annie's. "But I'm very glad I did. Otherwise . . ."

"And I am indebted to you for the result," Annie concedes, "though not the method you used to achieve it."

Ursula lets that go; she has more important things to discuss. "Sam . . ." she says.

"Yes?"

"It seems to me that, when you thought you were going to die—oh, the tears I shed at those passages, darling; I was a veritable Trevi of despair—you determined to throw Rachel in your husband's path."

"That's true . . ."

"For the noblest and most unselfish and purest of reasons. And out of profound love. But now?"

"Ah, you're afraid Rachel and Sam are having a tryst behind the Amanas and Sub-Zeros?"

"That's not quite . . ."

"Or at Rachel's house. Or in the back row of the movie theater? Or"—she curls her finger into quote marks—"in my own marital bed?"

"You certainly are direct, Arabella. I myself would not have been so blunt. Nevertheless, even without showing Sam the manual, you've set particular things into motion."

"What are you getting at, Ursula?"

"Your suggestion of concert dates, of dinner, and yes, buying that refrigerator . . ."

"So, you've been listening to my phone calls too?'

"One's voice carries, darling. You get that from me."

Annie doesn't bother to argue that at the moment her voice can barely project across a breakfast tray. Instead she says, "There is nothing wrong with friends of the opposite sex sharing a movie or a dinner. *Platonically.* Whatever I planned was supposed to happen while I was dying and after I was dead. When Sam was widowed and free. Now he's not. Now I'm not dying . . ."

"Which is certainly a marvelous outcome," Ursula interjects.

". . . thus, I can't conceive in this short time of anything . . ."

"One person's short time is another person's eternity, believe me. You've been in New York for what Sam must view as frivolous reasons. And for far too long. Not to mention incommunicado. No doubt he feels abandoned and angry. He's handsome and charming and somewhat naïve. The perfect combination. When the cat's away . . ."

"Not Sam! And not Rachel—she's my best friend."

Ursula raises her chin. "Ha."

"Trust me, if a woman flirted with Sam, he would never act on it. His only response, if someone came too close, would be a fear of germs."

"Don't be so sure. Rachel is divorced. Sam is alone and, may I point out, somewhat helpless. You had to leave instructions about dry cleaners and the washing machine and a million domestic details any other grown man would be completely capable of handling."

"*You* don't know how to handle such things."

"I pay people to do them for me. Sam doesn't. And Rachel is attractive and competent"—she nods at her daughter—"though not as attractive and competent as you, of course."

"More attractive and more competent," corrects Annie, "but Sam wouldn't notice that either."

"Don't be so sure," Ursula repeats. "You are not setting up a playdate for a child."

"You're just jaded by the life you lead, Ursula. Which is not my life. I have complete faith that Sam would never do anything behind my back, even if he's a little pissed at me."

"You cannot possibly comprehend what is going through his mind."

"I do. He's dreaming of sandwiches, and espresso machines, and how to expand the shop."

"The temptations . . ."

"I hate to disagree with you, but there are no temptations. No X-rated scenarios. Except for a touch of hypochondria and a tendency toward cluelessness, Sam's a rock. Like Daddy."

"Like your father?" Ursula's eyes widen. Her brows arch. "You have no idea."

"What do you mean?"

Ursula adjusts an earring, fluffs her hair—stage business to draw out a dramatic pause. She clears her throat. "Maybe now is the time to express to you some hard truths, Arabella."

"About your lovers? Your husbands? Your own infidelities? Your inconvenient pregnancies? The way you treated my father? The way you were never there?" The words spew out. Shocked at her own nerve, ashamed of her ingratitude, Annie gasps. Her incision starts to pull.

Underneath her expertly applied makeup, Ursula's face grows ashen; her mouth forms a sad downturned crescent. "Mea culpa. Mea culpa," she confesses. "But that's not the whole story." She stands up, teetering on her I-could-have-danced-all-night stilettos. "I fear I'm upsetting you. It can't be good for your recovery."

"I'm fine. Finish what you started."

Ursula clip-clops across the room and stops at the door. "First, let me get us a little something."

Annie hears glasses rattle, the slamming of a cabinet, the squeak of a drawer. Ursula returns carrying two snifters and a bottle of Courvoisier. She pours a small shot of brandy for Annie and a larger one for herself. She drains her glass in one gulp, refills it, and resumes her seat on the bed. "Where was I?" she asks.

Annie realizes it's a rhetorical question; she's sure Ursula can pinpoint the precise syllable where she left off. She's stalling. Annie sips her own brandy and holds the warm liquid on her tongue. "My father," she prompts.

Her mother twists the cocktail ring round and round her finger. "As I stated before, darling, you can never really know someone . . ."

"Shall we agree to disagree?"

Ursula taps the end of Annie's bed as if she's punctuating a sentence. "Let me start by saying that your father was the love of my life. So much the love of my life that I agreed to move to Passamaquoddy to be with him. Though it was a struggle. I still had to work."

"You mean you wanted to. You mean the theater was your life. You mean you couldn't wait to get out of Dodge."

"No, I had to. I was the breadwinner."

"That's not true. Daddy held an important job."

"He ran that business into the ground."

"I don't believe you. His office was huge and gorgeous . . ."

"I flew in my decorator. Your father chose items from the Sotheby's catalog. He had good taste. Expensive good taste." She pauses. "Didn't you ever wonder why he employed no assistants, no secretary?"

"Because he was a perfectionist. Because he liked to do everything himself."

"*No!* Because he couldn't afford it, because there was hardly enough work for a secretary, because we had to draw the line somewhere. His job"—she sketches quote marks in the air—"was all smoke and mirrors, darling."

Annie remembers as a child visiting her father's office downtown; he'd set her up at an ornate desk, give her scissors and paper, point out the sharpened pencils in their silver cup. "You can be my secretary," he'd say. She'd stare at somber oil portraits of other people's ancestors, old county deeds framed behind wavy glass, her father's diplomas and civic awards lined up in a neat row, her own baby photos scattered on tables, the Al Hirschfeld cartoon of Ursula—nine Ninas hidden in her hair and chinchilla collar— the first thing you saw when you opened the door. She'd wait for the phone to ring, practicing in a somber voice, "Henry Stevens Insurance. May I help you?"

But the phone rarely rung, and when it did, it would be her father calling from the inner office to ask if she was ready to go out for a father-daughter lunch.

Her mother's eyes mist. "In fact, I was so much in love that he was the only person with whom I actually considered having a child."

Annie stays silent. She knows Ursula didn't want her, that when she discovered she was pregnant it was too late to do anything about it, that she despaired over her burgeoning stomach, the potential loss of any ingenue part, that she worried about the ugliness of maternity clothes and how to lose the post-delivery fat and remained convinced that her job was the most important thing to her. Not that her father ever came right out and said all of this. Yet, if her mother was an expert at reading lines, Annie, the only child of a mismatched couple, learned at an early age how to read between those lines.

"I was worried about being a mother, worried whether I was good enough, worried that I'd have to be away from my baby. After all, my only experience as a mother of children was playing one—in aging makeup, of course. And the mothers I played—Gertrude, Medea, Amanda Wingfield, Mary Tyrone—were hardly role models. All of this colored my, well, my earlier decisions. A gypsy life was not for a child, especially with my other—how should I put it?—more iffy relationships. Until I met your father, who represented the rock I spent my whole life searching for."

Yes, Annie agrees, her father was a rock, a stable, reliable parent, the only constant in an ever-changing, unpredictable, foundationless household.

"When at last you were born," Ursula goes on, "the most beautiful baby on earth, a miracle, you wrapped your little fingers around mine and held on for dear life. I was over the moon." Ursula pulls a handkerchief from her pocket and wipes away a tear. "Henry wanted to call you Abigail, which means a father's joy. But I insisted on Arabella—a Dutch name signifying beautiful—since, in all fairness, you were your mother's joy too. Then the nurse put you in your father's arms; you had your father's eyes. You looked at him; he looked at you. That was it. I was the third wheel, the uninvited guest."

"Because you were away, always traveling, always working."

"Out of necessity. To feed you, to clothe you, to send you to school, to give you piano lessons and toys. And later, of course, I wanted to. I did love my work, and I needed to escape . . ."

"To escape from the constant demands of a helpless baby."

"Oh, darling, not from you, never from you. I always avoided any temptation to topple your father from the pedestal you put him on. But perhaps it's time to face facts."

Annie has had enough. Why can't she just burrow under the covers, stick the pillow over her ears? "I don't want to hear anything more," she says.

"Hardly surprising. Nevertheless, right now you need to. I've been beating around the bush long enough. I'm going to come right out with it before I lose nerve."

As if Ursula would ever lose nerve. "If you must," Annie concedes, "though it doesn't mean I'm going to believe you."

"The same old story." Ursula sighs. "Hortense was my best friend—now I utterly shiver at such a cliché—my sole friend in Passamaquoddy. In retrospect, I realize her appeal for me was partly due to her name. Hortense and Ursula in a world of Peggys and Bettys and Sues. "Stupidly, I asked her to look after Henry while I was away."

"Which is only natural."

Ursula shrugs. "You'd think that, wouldn't you? Those checks I wrote to the Passamaquoddy Community Players, all those boring, mortifyingly bad performances I attended. Hortense was a terrible, wooden Auntie Mame, though I never told her so; in fact, I acted as her coach, for which she never expressed the slightest morsel of gratitude. Instead, she ignored all my instructions about timing and inflection. So amateurish." Ursula pours more brandy into her glass and nods at Annie's.

Annie closes her fingers over the top of the snifter. "I've had enough."

"Haven't we all," her mother groans, her body a study in world-weariness. She leans forward. "And yet with Henry, for a while, I enjoyed being a part of a community, a respectable mother and wife, so enchantingly ordinary. A woman like others, with a best friend, with neighbors and rosebushes in her front yard and tomato vines in the back. Naturally I would have done the gardening myself if I didn't need to preserve my hands for my career."

Ursula holds up her beringed, pampered hands, hands that at bedtime are swabbed with lotions and placed into white cotton gloves, hands that hide from daylight like vampires, the skin silky soft and pale, the nails perfect ovals varnished scarlet three times a week—hands that have never pruned a rose or planted a tomato seed.

"I was in love," Ursula continues. "Blinded by love."

"What are you getting at, Ursula?" Annie asks, hurrying along the narrative. Despite her own efforts at denial and her mother's tendency to dramatize, she has a pretty good idea of where this is going. She remembers Hortense—squat and dull, a horrible Auntie Mame, an ingratiating, phony adult—*call me Auntie Hortense*, she used to order Annie, who nevertheless could not bring herself to add the *Auntie* in front of the *Hortense*.

"What's embarrassingly ordinary is how it ended. The same old scene I've played on stage for years and years. Yet I, like the most preposterous ingénue, never saw it coming. Hortense having dinner and drinks with Henry. Hortense even taking you to rehearsals, letting you play with that spoiled, yappy terrier of hers. Bringing you lollipops."

"Rachel is not Hortense," Annie insists. "There is no comparison."

"How can you be so sure?"

Annie cuts her off. "I never liked Hortense. I could tell she was a fake, even as a kid."

"And rightly so. You were precocious that way. Like me, though I suspected nothing. But then, who can ever know what is in another's heart? I thought I did."

Had Hortense and her father been looking at refrigerators too? Annie wonders now. Did it always start with kitchen appliances and then move on to mattresses—the testing of them, the sharing of them?

Ursula pats her daughter's knee, tented under its downy duvet. "It gets worse," she warns. "Little did I anticipate what a failed businessman Henry turned out to be. Why? Because, frankly, he was almost as good of an actor as I was an actress. Did I, in my wildest dreams or worst nightmares, imagine I was going to have to support this man who appeared so established in his career? Never! Alas, he had no head for commerce—though he had a head for many other things, which I prefer not to enumerate."

"Ursula!" Annie squirms like a teenager.

"I realize how hard this is for you, darling," Ursula grants. "Nevertheless, it's best you know everything. *Alors*, I helped out quietly, from behind the scenes—no one caught on; his facade was so grand; a big shot in the chamber of commerce and those other silly men's clubs with their secret handshakes and adolescent rituals. On his walls hung as many awards as those arrayed along my own mantel."

"Because he was respected," Annie feels obliged to add. "Because he earned them. I used to dust them as a child. When I visited his office. When he let me play secretary and took me out to lunch."

Ursula's voice softens to a whisper. "How could I point out that the emperor had no clothes?" She squeezes Annie's knee again. "I blame myself. I loved to travel; I got tired of Maine; I longed for my apartment in New York. And I had the theater. Henry liked being married to an actress, liked my comfortable bank account, my celebrity, and obviously grew to like that I was so much out of town. I gather there were more dalliances beside Hortense. All, of course, while you were at school. Your father always protected you."

Annie covers her ears. "I've heard enough."

But her mother's on a roll. "I never even confronted Hortense. Who, I learned later, ran off with a tree surgeon to Edmonton, Alberta. Imagine!" She shakes her head. "My only choice was to leave. Even though"—she strokes her daughter's hair—"even though you, my daughter . . ." Her throat makes a choking sound, strangling her words.

"It didn't matter. As Daddy said, we were complete, the two of us."

"Of course it mattered. If you only . . ." She straightens up. "It's my own fault for throwing Hortense in my husband's path—also for doing too much for him when he should have been standing on his own two feet. Enabling, they call it." She stops. She waits a beat. She looks at Annie. "Enabling," she repeats. "The way you enable Sam."

"That's not true," Annie says.

"I threw Hortense into your father's path," she states, "just as you're doing with Rachel."

Annie jams her fist against her mouth and turns her head to the row of windows framing a fairy-tale world of twinkling lights.

For a long time, neither of them speaks. The hall clock chimes. The radiator pipes clang. An elevator glides. Her mother's controlled, drama-school-steady breaths rise and fall from deep within her diaphragm.

Ursula breaks the silence. "It's all right, darling. You don't have to say anything. Your face speaks for itself. Volumes."

As if on cue, the doorman's buzzer sounds. A deus ex machina just in time to save them both from awkwardness. Ursula walks to the front hall. Annie hears muted voices, the clank of silverware, the click of a closing door. In the lighted apartment across the avenue, she can make out the shapes of a family sitting down to dinner under a sparkling chandelier. A family of four or five. Not two. A *normal* family. Parents. Children. Are they laughing? Finishing each other's sentences? Are they discussing schoolwork? The mundane events of each person's day? Though she can't see it, she imagines a fire crackling in the fireplace, a dog curled on its hearth, a homemade apple pie in the oven, wafting the scent of nutmeg and cinnamon.

Ursula reappears. "Voilà!" she says.

Annie turns toward her. The tray she is carrying bears the most architecturally gorgeous hamburgers and most sinfully divine, salt-encrusted *pommes frites* that Annie has ever seen.

Ursula puts down the tray. She twirls. She snaps her fingers. "Forget the pâté and quenelles," Ursula says. "Sometimes a girl just needs a lift."

* * *

Later, after the last French fry lies abandoned in its soggy puddle of ketchup, after Ursula has eaten two of the toothpicked quarters she's chiseled from her own burger—proving that she can transform anything into elegance—and after Annie has devoured hers whole, Ursula piles the leftovers onto the tray. This she places on the floor outside the bedroom door as if she's expecting room service to whisk it away. Once more, she settles into the curve excavated by Annie's knees and reaches for Annie's hand. "Are you okay?" she asks.

"I guess," Annie allows. "Nothing that a hamburger and fries can't cure," she says, her tone a mixture of good-sport effort and an appreciation for her mother beyond mere food choices. Is she okay? She's not so sure. What about Sam? And Rachel? Though she remains convinced that neither of them would ever . . . Would they?

Then there's the puzzle of her mother and father. Up till now, she's always been so sure about who was the good parent and who was the bad.

"Oh, Arabella," Ursula says now, reading her mind. "You must feel utterly overwhelmed. Especially after what you've just been through. I dreaded telling you. I hated to cast a shadow on your image of Henry. But it became imperative. It seems so clear to me that your marriage is at risk, that you need—yes—a *mother's* advice." Ursula snuggles closer, wraps her arms around Annie. "My darling baby," she croons. "The lawyers I consulted assured me I would win custody. Which I longed for. You have no idea."

Annie looks up at her mother, whose face now bears the same ravages of loss she so famously demonstrated in *A Doll's House* when she played Nora, forced to abandon her children for what she thought was their own good.

"But how could I take my daughter away from the father she loved?" Ursula pleads.

Chapter Nineteen

Do not subsist on Paul Bunyans. Eat your vegetables. Pickles are not a vegetable. Your mother's blueberry pie recipe is in my wooden index box—you can do it!

For the first time since the surgery two week ago, Annie wakes up neither sore nor woozy—a good sign, since today's her postop appointment with Dr. Albright. If she receives a clean bill of health, she'll be able to go home. When she turns her head, she's astonished to see a breakfast tray magically transported to the night table. She smells freshly roasted coffee; she admires the buttered toast slotted into the silver rack the staff at the Connaught gave Ursula when she checked out of the Grosvenor Suite; she marvels at the hothouse tulips in their crystal vase.

The chink of ice reserved in Annie's heart for her mother is starting to thaw. Not that Ursula is turning into Marmee or Ma Ingalls. Did she ever sew on a button or drive a carpool or chaperone a field trip or carve a pumpkin? Did she stay up all night applying a cold compress to a feverish brow?

Well, nobody's perfect. Even her father, it turns out.

Except for a few minor flaws, the person in her life who *is* perfect, perfect for *her*, is Sam. Any complaints about him—his messiness, his forgetfulness, his inattention to detail, his medical students' disease, his dependence, his occasional thin skin— count as inconsequential given her changed circumstances. Maybe she purged any grievances by committing them to the manual; her illness and subsequent return from the dead seem to have put such concerns into perspective. Lately she's been focusing on all the good things, both the big ones—love and friendship and values and ethics and kindness—and the small, sweet moments too—the time he hired a calligrapher to copy onto parchment one of her poems, which he framed as a Valentine's Day surprise; the time he took her father's watch to be repaired, adding a smaller wristband so she could wear it; the time he secretly packed up the baby's layette and donated it to Newborns in Need.

She clears her throat and attempts the first paragraph of the Gettysburg Address. *To form a more perfect union* is actually audible. Her voice sounds stronger, if not still quite her own. It's the right moment to call Sam. She reaches for the phone. She yanks her hand back. Shouldn't she wait until the official medical okay? Until she has all the facts? She sprints out of bed and performs a series of increasingly vigorous jumping jacks. No chest pain. No breathlessness.

She wants—rather, she *needs*—to hear Sam's delight when she tells him she's coming home. She'll save the real story of her illness for when she can see him in person, confront him head on.

He'll be furious she kept things from him, but if all goes according to what Dr. Albright indicated at the hospital, he won't be able to help but be overjoyed at the outcome. Ursula's right. Anyone who passes through the valley of the shadow of death should be forgiven all crazy behavior. Under such circumstances, whose thinking wouldn't be skewed? Who wouldn't panic and act illogically? Sam will understand. Won't he? She misses her own lumpy bed with its trough down the center encouraging her and Sam's nightly slide into a full-body collision; she misses her work, neighbors, best friend, customers, car, empty streets, the sounds of taxi-free silence, frosted sidewalks, sludgy drifts of snow. She'd exchange any number of Ursula's sachets and candles and eau de cologne for a whiff of Sam.

It's not as if she'll be giving anything up. She's sure that, in the future, she and Sam will visit Ursula, attend Broadway plays and eat choucroute garnie and sushi and tandoori lamb, admire Rothkos and Sargents, watch the ballet, walk in Central Park, explore the High Line. They will laugh about those weeks when they were so foolishly forced apart. And then they'll return home.

Always home.

She decides not to wait. She picks up the phone, a cream-and-gold French model with a rotary dial repurposed from a stage prop. The numbers spring off her fingers as if they've been coiled, ready to pop.

After five rings, the machine clicks in. She checks her watch. He must have left earlier than usual. "Hi, it's me," she addresses the recorder, noting that her voice, though improved, is still exhibit-A hoarse. "I'm sorry about not returning your calls or messages. That's why Ursula emailed you—I've been stuck in bed with this cold"—she coughs—"which I must have picked up on the plane. It's turned into laryngitis, so it's hard to talk. But I do see the light at the end of the tunnel. Love you. I'll try you later at the shop."

When she finishes the coffee and toast, she wraps one of Ursula's ostrich-trimmed, chin-tickling robes over her nightgown and opens her laptop.

My darling Sam, she types, I tried to call. I actually have a voice. Feeling much better and hope to make plans to return soon. Let's discuss, when we can talk on the phone. Meanwhile, though, there's serious mother-daughter bonding going on here—all to the good. I know you'll approve. Will explain in detail when I get home. I miss you desperately. Truly, madly, deeply. Thinking of special souvenirs you might like from New York, but hoping the best souvenir will be me. xxxooo Annie

She presses send, then tiptoes into the living room. Her mother is a night owl, sleeping until noon, cosseted by her black-out draperies, her black silk eye mask, and her white-noise machine.

Surprise! Ursula is sitting upright on the sofa, fully dressed, her makeup and hair impeccable, reading the *New York Times*. "It seems wide-legged trousers are in again," she informs her daughter. "I find them terribly unflattering. Here"—she peers closer at the pages, nose wrinkled in distaste—"they're paired with cropped tops that expose the navel. Really, who can carry off such styles except teenagers?" She looks up. "A restful night?"

"Very. I feel so much better. How about you? You're up early."

"I refuse to fritter away any mother-daughter moments in the arms of Morpheus. Besides, now that you have been staying with me, I find myself turning in somewhat earlier than is my usual modus operandi."

"I'm sorry."

"Nothing to be sorry about. In fact, I owe it all to you that those dreadful bags under my eyes have entirely vanished. Which means I no longer have to recline for an hour every day with cucumber slices on my lids." She folds up the newspaper and sets it on the coffee table. "It's rather mild for the end of February. I thought we might have a brisk walk in the park—or as brisk as you feel up to—before we go to see James."

Even though she's three states south, Annie dresses for a Maine winter: sweater, turtleneck, tights, corduroys, two sets of socks. While Ursula fusses with her own wardrobe—what scarf matches what gloves match what hat—Annie returns to the bedroom and phones Sam at work. It's not Sam's voice but Megan's that announces "Annie's Samwich Shop." Annie's shoulders sink with disappointment. She leans against the bed. In the background, she catches the rattle of cups and dishes, the burble of the coffee machine, the broad-vowel chatter of the regulars.

"Hey, stranger," Megan says. "You sound like you have a cold."

"It *was* pretty bad, but I'm on the mend. Can I speak to Sam?"

"Whoops. You just missed him."

"Where . . ." she begins, then stops. She doesn't want Megan to think she's one of *those* wives who track their husbands like an on-the-case sleuth. Or a female Sam. "I called to tell him I'll be coming home by the end of the week," she explains.

"Phew," Megan says. "That's good news." *Just a second. You're next*, she informs a complaining customer. "He'll be totally relieved," she tells Annie.

"I hope so. How are things in the shop?"

"Hanging in there. But we're all kind of lost without you."

Before she can savor this sentence or ponder the collective *we* versus the singular *he*, a woman's voice shouts, *Coffee with half-and-half. They're in a rush*, accompanied by the screech of sliding plates, clumping footsteps, the tap of a knife against the cutting board.

"Sorry, Annie," Megan says now. "It seems like the whole town has just burst through the door."

"I'll leave you to it. Will you let Sam know I called?"

"Glad to. See you soon."

"And give him my love," she adds, but Megan has already hung up the phone.

*   *   *

The minute she and Ursula step outside, Annie feels like an animal released from captivity. She and Ursula walk hip to hip, her multilayered arm linked through Ursula's mink-swathed one. They cross Fifth Avenue and enter the park near the skating rink. "Shall we watch for a while?" Ursula suggests.

"Oh, yes," Annie agrees. She used to skate with Sam, back in high school when they flooded the old fairgrounds parking lot; they were both good skaters, evenly matched, gliding along, hands around each other's waists, the loudspeakers blasting out tinny golden oldies whose lyrics seemed both utterly profound and intended only for them: "Love Makes The World Go Round," "Love Me Tender," "I Can't Stop Loving You." Later, they shared hot cocoa behind the creaky carousal while Sam warmed her mittened hands between his own. "Isn't this great?" he marveled.

Everything will be great again, she consoles herself now. Once she's back. This surprising new lease on her life will make her marriage even better than before. Maybe they should renew their vows, have a party to celebrate, rent out city hall . . . She pictures champagne and mini Bunyan hors d'oeuvres, their toothpicks more tightly secured. And a gooey multitiered cake.

"Isn't this great?" Ursula exclaims, interrupting Annie's reveries. They are standing at the rink's rim, the whole skyline of New York City stretching before them. Down below, crowds weave in and out, some skaters clinging to the side walls, some swirling around with the grace of the professionals in the Ice Capades, which performs at the Passamaquoddy arena every January. A lithe woman executes an axel jump. A young man grabs her and waltzes her across the frozen floor. "Yesterday" plays from the loudspeakers. Annie lifts up her cell phone to take a picture to send to Sam.

A little girl squeezes in beside them. An adorable, rosy-cheeked moppet, perhaps four or five. She's bundled into a velvet-collared red coat with matching leggings, like a nineteenth-century portrait come to life. "Mummy, I can see," she calls.

"That's terrific, Annie."

Annie spins around. A woman directly behind her is patting the back of a sleeping infant snuggled into a BabyBjörn pouch. Annie has one packed away, still in its unopened cardboard box.

"Just be careful. Don't bother the people next to you," the child's mother instructs.

"She's no bother," Annie insists. She kneels down next to the little girl. "You know what?" she says. "My name is Annie too."

The little girl's eyes widen in amazement. "It is?"

Annie nods. She smiles at the mother, who smiles back at her, unconcerned, it seems, about strangers who could be potential kidnappers or pedophiles. Maybe she recognizes Ursula and assumes such an eminent person would be above suspicion—despite, in the way of sophisticated Manhattanites, never acknowledging Ursula's *People*-magazine celebrity.

"I have a little sister," young Annie informs her.

"So I see. What is *her* name?"

"Esmé. After a story."

"I've read that story."

"I'm named after someone too. My grandmother. She's really Ann."

Annie leans forward. "I'll tell you a secret," she whispers. "I'm really Arabella."

"That's silly."

"Isn't it? I much prefer Annie."

"I'm going to take skating lessons next week. I think I will be very good at it."

"People named Annie are good skaters," Annie says.

"I know." She points to a mound of melting snow. "There's not enough to make snow angels. Do you like to make snow angels?"

"I do. Where I come from, Maine, it's usually so cold and snowy that you can make snow angels for a very long time."

"That's a good place to live."

"It is."

Just then the baby, Esmé, wails.

The mother struggles to take her out of the carrier, but the strap catches on her sleeve.

"Can I help you?" Annie asks.

"That would be wonderful. Would you mind holding her while I adjust this thing?" She passes the baby to Annie. "Fair warning: she's a howler."

Esmé lives up to her reputation. She howls. Blood-curdling cries that elicit glowers of accusation from the surrounding tourists. The baby's face turns red, scrunches up; hot tears squeeze out from the corners of her eyes.

Annie nestles her against her chest. She strokes her back. The baby shudders and quiets down. Annie caresses the velvety cheek, the silky fuzz sticking out from her hood. Esmé sighs, settles her body into Annie's, and falls asleep.

"You're a baby whisperer," the mother says. "You must have children of your own."

Annie nods. What a fraud she is, pretending she's refined her calming skills on wiggling offspring she's actually borne. What a demonstration of impostor syndrome. She hugs the baby closer. Is there a purer bliss than snuggling a sleeping infant?

"Careful," Ursula comments. "You don't want to awaken her." Her eyes on Annie are sharp, assessing, hard to read.

At last the mother has adjusted the strap. She holds out her arms. It's not easy for Annie to forfeit the coveted weight of the child and pass her back.

"Thank you so much," the mother smiles. "Annie, say good-bye to the nice lady."

The little girl turns to Annie. She extends a fluffy angora-gloved hand. "Very nice meeting you," she says with a half curtsy.

"Very nice meeting *you*," Annie replies.

"Maybe you can come back sometime and watch me when I really learn how to skate."

"I'd like that."

"Though I don't think Esmé will be good at it."

Annie laughs. "Because she's not an Annie. Only Annies have all the right moves."

*　*　*

At the surgeon's office, Dr. Albright listens to her heart and lungs. He checks her incisions. "Excellent healing," he grants, adding in a tone of self-congratulation, "the scar is almost invisible."

Ursula, who has followed her into the examining room without asking permission, agrees. "You could sew for the best Paris couturiers, James."

"I'll keep that in mind," he jokes, "if my day job doesn't pan out."

He's sent Annie for an X-ray, which he now clips to the light board. "Just as I predicted. No evidence of sarcoids. You can stop any medication. No heavy lifting for a month."

"A clean bill of health," Ursula gloats.

"Clean as the driven snow. I'll refer you to the pulmonary specialist right down the hall—top man in his field—to make sure all continues to stay well. You should schedule regular check-ups every six months at first and then annually."

"A perfect excuse to visit me," Ursula says.

"I hardly need an excuse."

"We'll be seeing quite a lot of each other—your trips to New York." She straightens her scarf. "As well as my own excursions to Passamaquoddy . . ."

Annie stares. Has she missed something?

Ursula flutters her lashes, then flashes a cat-who-swallowed-the-canary grin.

Annie turns to Dr. Albright. "I assume there are pulmonary specialists in Maine?" she asks.

Ursula answers for him. "None better or more renowned than right here at this hospital. A truth to which you can surely agree, darling, now that brilliant James has saved your life."

"You're right," Annie acknowledges. She means it. She is not taking any more risks with her health. She's sticking with the hospital that saved her. Maybe God can come unbidden, but sometimes you just have to do the bidding yourself.

"Accordingly, you'll travel to New York for the specialist and dear Ambrose can take care of any other little problems at home," Ursula summarizes.

Home. Now that she's won the get-out-of-death card, Annie can pass Go, collect her bill of health, and proceed to home.

"I guess that's settled, then," Dr. Albright concludes.

"I can't find the words to express . . ." Annie begins.

"I'm glad we had such a fine result." He shakes her hand.

Annie heads for the door.

Ursula grabs her elbow in midstep. "Just one more thing . . ."

"Yes?" the doctor asks.

With no preamble, no gentle paving of the way, no waiver from the party concerned, Ursula announces, "My daughter wishes to have a baby."

"Ursula!" Annie exclaims. Astonished and horrified. Embarrassed and appalled. She yanks her arm from her mother's grasp. "Let's go."

Ursula will not be moved. "She's had several miscarriages. How many, darling?"

"It doesn't matter," Annie mumbles. "Dr. Albright is a *lung* surgeon."

"And one stillbirth. Heartbreaking." Ursula daubs at her eyes.

Dr. Albright has already punched numbers on his phone. In Annie's haze of fury, she can only pick out scattered words and phrases: *The Knicks Sunday. A favor. Daughter of Ursula Marichal. Yes, that one. Find time. I owe you.*

"Stanley. Dr. Stanley Feld, fertility specialist, on the twenty-second floor, will see you next week. On the way out, stop at the desk and my nurse will write up an appointment card."

* * *

In the taxi back to Ursula's apartment, Annie's mother puts her arm around her. "The nurse informed me that the fertility specialist is booked years in advance," she crows. "Even Kuwaiti princesses and Olympic medalists have to wait in line."

"The power of Ursula Marichal," Annie says, "to bring people back from the brink of death, to secure them doctor's appointments beyond the reach of mere mortals or royal personages."

"Nonsense," Ursula protests faux-modestly. "Yet, it is truly amazing how quickly we managed to see James and then this renowned . . ." She pulls the card from her pocket, not having trusted it to Annie. "This Dr. Feld."

"But," Annie says, "I promised Sam I'd be home in the next couple of days."

"Arabella, what's a little more time away when . . . ?"

"Not that there's a chance."

"Of course there's a chance."

Annie thinks of Esmé; she can still feel the heft of the child in her arms. Muscle memory. Could this doctor work a miracle?

"At least tell Sam about this new development," Ursula urges.

"Not yet."

"It's your marriage, Arabella. Far be it from me to give you advice."

"Yes, you're pretty stingy with your advice," says Annie. She studies the peppy weather woman on the screen underneath the taxi's sliding-glass window. *A storm coming from the north*, the woman announces. She thinks of Sam's loss-of-baby nervous collapse. "On top of everything else," she continues, "how cruel to raise Sam's hopes. And imagine his downward spiral if those hopes get dashed." She needs to address him face-to-face, analyze that cherished face, then calibrate her words in response to emotions only she can decode. She looks at the map of a snowbound East Coast. "With a little luck, I can plead bad weather."

"In my opinion, weather is entirely less reliable than a relapse into bronchitis or pneumonia," Ursula states.

Annie leaves a message on their home voice mail when she's sure Sam will be at work. "It's me. I won't be able to get back as soon as I thought," she says, lowering her voice to a near whisper. "Not to worry," she adds, "but my cold's taken a turn for the worse. And they're predicting a storm. I'll let you know the second I change my ticket. Miss you. Love you."

*   *   *

A half hour later, he calls her back.

"Where were you?" she asks.

"How are *you*?" he sidesteps, and without waiting for her answer, he continues, "Here's the plan. Just book the next plane out. It's only a couple of hours in the air, and I'll pick you up in Bangor. A little husbandly TLC, and I promise I'll have you as good as new."

Annie's torn. She wants Sam. She wants to go home. She wants to give in. She wants to give up. Is it selfish to ask for more? Why not be grateful for what she has?

Yet again, she pictures Esmé and her big sister. How can she not take the chance, no matter the odds? "If only I could," Annie says, the lies tripping off her tongue with practice-makes-perfect dexterity. "They're worried about bronchitis," she explains, then produces a volley of coughs as evidence. "Ursula's doctor has already made a house call to check me out."

"Are you on antibiotics?"

"Penicillin."

"That should solve the problem. In twenty-four hours, you'll be fit to travel. I'll come bring you home. This is getting ridiculous."

"The doctor doesn't want me on a plane."

"Then we'll go by car."

"To Maine in this weather? Besides, he's afraid the bronchitis might turn into pneumonia. I need more rest."

He shuffles some papers—a calendar? "Okay. In that case, I'll fly to New York and stay with you. I'm sure I'll be a better nurse than Ursula."

"That's sweet but unnecessary," she replies. "You'd be surprised, but I've got Ursula waiting on me hand and foot. I think it's a role she's really embraced. Why rain on her parade"—she turns coy—"even though I'd pick your particular style of nursing anytime. Besides, you're busy in the shop."

"Screw the shop. Give me the name of Ursula's doctor. I'll ask Ambrose to call him and check things out."

"Too many cooks. Besides, I could be contagious. I wouldn't want you to . . ."

"For you, I'll take the risk."

"It's just a few more days, Sam."

He sighs. "I'm not going to argue any longer, Annie."

As they say good-bye, Annie tries not to dwell on how quickly Sam gave in.

Chapter Twenty

You do not like your dress shirts starched. Light starch is a myth. Though flannel can look rugged and virile, you're a dream when you're spiffed up.

Annie's soaking in Ursula's yacht of a bathtub, bubbles up to her chin. She's tried out all of Ursula's loofahs, her sponges, her boar-bristle brushes, her mitts made of Turkish toweling. Surrounded by steam and heat and unguents whose labels promise all manner of life-changing, body-changing, stress-changing benefits, Annie sighs and sinks deeper into the water. She rubs her scar, which she plans to treat with one of Ursula's stretch mark–vanishing creams as soon as she climbs out of the bath.

If only Sam were submerged under these bubbles next to her. In the early days of their marriage, they used to enjoy baths together in a tiny old tub perched crookedly on porcelain claws. Limbs pretzeled, they nonetheless managed feats of acrobatic lovemaking, their contortionist positions guaranteeing giggles, soap-stung eyes, and tailbones bumped against the chipped enamel. Back then, they could occupy a single twin bed, share one desk, watch TV while hammocked into their lone butterfly chair. When did they start to require more acreage: a queen-sized mattress, a vast sofa, his-and-her toiletries?

It's hard to ignore the distance between her and Sam, one she can't blame just on geography. Her texts are answered in monosyllabic *okays*. As a crackerjack interpreter of symptoms, perhaps he doesn't believe her fake coughs and contrived croakiness. Is he having more fun with good-sport Rachel than she imagined? Impossible. Perhaps he's just fed up. *What a tangled web we weave, when first we practice to deceive*, Miss Mullen used to quote in high school English class, citing Sir Walter Scott as the author of lines they assumed Shakespeare had composed. Everything will be okay, Annie concludes. She can untangle that web. She can risk putting her marriage on hold until next week. Afterward, at peace with childlessness, she can return to Passamaquoddy and resume her old life. But now, better to have exhausted all possibilities before her biological clock ticks its last tock.

She gets out of the tub, dripping onto the bath mat appliqued with Monet's lily pads. She spreads the stretch mark oil over her scar, a salve that smells surprisingly of licorice. She wraps herself in Ursula's towels, thick and toasty from their heated rack. It's time to take action. If good deeds can assuage guilt, she knows what she has to do. In the bedroom, she pulls on jeans and sneakers. She Googles family-run mom-and-pop sandwich shops. She is amazed to find the biggest cluster not in Manhattan but in Greenpoint, a neighborhood unfamiliar but—she checks—easily accessible. She pores over Google maps, studies directions and subway station charts.

As soon as she steps out from the hallway, Ursula gazes up from her script. "Darling," she says, "you look dressed for herding cows."

"I'm off on a few errands," Annie explains. She grabs the cashmere coat from the closet, wishing Ursula hadn't given away her parka, so better suited to today's Brooklyn-bound trudging mission in due diligence.

"Shall I accompany you, Arabella? I can be ready in half an hour." Ursula folds down the corner of a page. Her voice turns hopeful. "Do your errands include Bergdorf's?"

"Greenpoint."

"How brave. Never ventured there myself. Isn't it in an"— Ursula grimaces—"outer borough?"

"So it seems. I won't be long."

Ursula returns to her page, where she squiggles a few lines in the margin with her gold-tipped lapis lazuli fountain pen. "For such terra incognita, darling, you'd be wise to engage my car service."

*　*　*

Annie takes the subway. Following her maps and the phone's GPS, she strolls to 86th Street for the express to Grand Central Station. Schoolchildren in blazers and plaid pleated skirts scamper up and down subway stairs and platforms, trailing backpacks and musical instrument cases. If eight-year-olds can figure this out, there is no reason for a thirtysomething country cousin to be daunted.

For a second, her eyes alight on a tall, redheaded man waiting on the platform. Her breath catches. Could it be Charles, he of the summer fling all those years ago? Charles who so expertly rid her of her virginity in his downtown loft? The string of what-ifs now parading through her brain is hardly surprising, given her recent tensions with Sam. She remembers the elegant way Charles held a martini. How he could summon a cab with just a nod. But when the man bends his head to his newspaper, Annie notes the unfamiliar profile. Of course not. Besides, after twenty years, she'd never recognize him. The current Charles could have lost his hair, developed a paunch, grown a beard.

She asks directions from a teenager swaying from a strap of the Queens-bound 7, nose buried in *To Kill a Mockingbird* and oblivious to the rocking of the train and the jostling elbows of fellow passengers. She's told to get off at Vernon/Jackson and walk over the Pulaski Bridge to Greenpoint.

"Is Atticus Finch your favorite character?" she asks.

He rolls his eyes. "Boo Radley." He turns back to his book.

Annie doesn't get lost. She crosses the Pulaski Bridge, a name embodying the essence of the melting pot. Compared to Manhattan, the "borough" looks almost rural. The low buildings with their peeling clapboards, their chain-link fences, the sidewalk's human scale and inviting shabbiness, provoke pangs of homesickness even without a single pine tree breaking through the asphalt or shading a tiny front yard or shedding its needles onto a grate.

After a detour due to faltering map-reading skills, she finds the cluster of sandwich shops off Franklin Street. Mecca!

At the first shop, a scratchy sign displays print so small she almost has to press her nose against the dented tin to read its name: *Little Hanoi*. A dry cleaner? A local Laundromat? She walks inside. She takes in the rickety metal tables and back-challenging stools, the tattered calendar pages of Vietnamese bicyclists and fishermen tacked to the walls.

Behind the tiny counter, two people, squeezed together like
conjoined twins, are taking orders—husband and wife? There's a
pot boiling and a griddle smoking on a two-burner hot plate. A
toaster oven rests on a table next to a dorm room–size refrigerator.
A tower of baguettes fills a tray. The whole place is bathed in
beguiling smells, the components of which Annie can't identify
except for the general piquant deliciousness. She's suddenly raven-
ous. She joins the line behind a woman in jeans and a replica of
her own lamented down coat. "Excuse me," she asks, venturing a
timid tap on the woman's shoulder.

The woman turns around. She's about Annie's age, no-non-
sense, glasses, not a stick of makeup, hair pulled up into a
scrunchie that even Annie knows is unfashionable.

"What's the best sandwich?" Annie asks.

"Your first time?"

Annie nods.

"But you've eaten a banh mi before?"

"I'm afraid not."

She studies Annie with are-you-from-Mars disbelief. "You
don't live nearby?" she asks.

"Maine."

"Order the special," the woman advises. "I visited Bar Harbor
once. You can get better lobster rolls here in New York."

She orders the special. A man just paying the bill offers her
his chair. The other occupants of the table are three women who
are chattering exuberantly in what Annie assumes is Vietnamese, nasal consonants rising, dipping, and sounding argumenta-
tive though the women are smiling. It's a good sign, she notes,
that transplants are seeking their native cuisine on these
premises.

She pulls out her phone and photographs her plate before she samples it. As soon as she takes a bite, she's amazed by the unfamiliar yet mouthwatering combination of flavors. Screened by her backpack, she disassembles the sandwich and examines the ingredients. The bread has been hollowed out to allow space for liver pâté, cucumber, chili peppers, jalapeños, thin slices of pork and beef, daikon, pickles, carrots. There's a method to the layering having to do with natural proximity, eye appeal, and alternating tastes. Just like the Bunyan.

She reconstructs the banh mi, careful to keep the right order. She and Sam can make this at Annie's; they can experiment with downloaded recipes and add their own touches. It will be like the good old days when they were building and rebuilding the Bunyan. When they were so much in love. History can repeat itself. Why not branch out, introducing banh mis gradually to Mainers resistant to change? She assumes Sam in his shop-expanding mood will also want to expand the menu. And at the very least, he'll appreciate her helpful "research," and the fact that Ursula's haute cuisine palaces have not blinded her to the street food of East Asia, or that, however distracted, she never stopped trying to improve their livelihood.

Annie grabs a copy of the takeout menu. With the permission of the owners, she photographs the counter, the minimal cooking facilities, and the owners themselves, each hoisting two fingers in a V-for-Victory sign. "You *New York Time?*" the man asks.

"I'm afraid not," Annie says.

"Is okay. Person at *New York Time* give four star."

* * *

By the time she stops in at Meatball Magic, Annie's perfected her culinary detective moves. She orders the special, photographs it, sifts through the delectable segments. What brilliant chef came up with the idea of serving a meatball sub in a brioche topped with mango chutney and a fried egg? The combo is a revelation. She wraps up the remaining sandwich and, back outside, hands it to a homeless person, who asks, "Got a Pinot Noir to go with that?"

She visits more shops, talks to more proprietors. As soon as she explains her profession, describes the Bunyans, they, in a gesture of collegiality that should be an example to the Doughboys, share sandwich-making tips and foist on her samples of homemade mozzarella, fried eggplant, barbecued pork, house-roasted turkey, tuna melt, chicken parm, and cashew pesto until she needs to unbutton the top two buttons of her jeans.

By the end of the afternoon, she's chock-full of ideas, takeout menus, and a camera roll documenting scrumptious and unusual treats. A bonanza of new and exciting possibilities to surprise Sam.

*　*　*

She's about to cross—or, rather, waddle—back over the Pulaski Bridge when she spies one last shop on the corner. Joe and Mary's Café, according to Yelp, hits all top-five foodie lists.

Nevertheless, no customers wander in or out, no chalkboards on the sidewalk list the day's special, no plasticized clips from reviews are taped to the front door. When she peeks through the window, she sees empty tables and chairs and, in a corner, one lonely broom leaning against a wall. A man wearing a tattered shirt slumps on a stool in front of the counter. Despite a fancy cappuccino machine next to a stack of cartons, he's gripping a takeout Styrofoam cup.

He spots her and gestures for her to come inside.

Annie hesitates, then pushes through the door. "Sorry," she says, "it looks like you're closed."

"You could say that."

"I read all the raves for Joe and Mary's," she explains, "so I wanted to see for myself. I—my husband and I—run a sandwich shop in Maine and are trying to broaden our menu."

"Good luck to you with that," he says. "I'd offer you a cup of coffee"—he points to the cappuccino maker—"but the machine's been sold. Just waiting around for it to be picked up." Looking as lonely as the broom in the corner, he gestures to the seat opposite him. "I'm Joe, by the way. The Joe of Joe and Mary's."

"I don't mean to intrude."

"I'm glad for the company." He rubs his bristly chin. "So, you run a shop with your husband?" he asks.

"Yes."

"And that's going okay?"

"So far."

"And you work night and day together, side by side, a team totally focused on a single goal?"

"That's a way of putting it."

He frowns. "In the beginning, everything always seems so fucking great."

"It still is," she insists, though she wouldn't take an oath in a court of law.

"Mary and I . . ." He holds up two fingers; he crosses them. "We were that close."

"And . . . ?"

He turns his head away. "Life can really suck."

Uncertain how to respond, she waits.

"She died," he says, his voice muffled by the cup he's holding up to his mouth. "Cancer."

Annie's hand flies up to her lung.

"We thought we had it beat."

She notes the collective and now vacant *we*. She sees he's only a little older than she and Sam. She observes the way his fingers are still locked in their sad gesture of togetherness.

"How awful," she says. "I'm sorry."

"We were high school sweethearts. Were never apart, not for one single day."

"I can only imagine . . ." She *can* imagine.

For a few minutes, Annie and Joe sit in silent solidarity. She scans the dusty surfaces and the smeared windows, which must have sparkled when Mary was alive. A pink apron printed with cupcakes hangs from a hook on the back door.

He's the first to speak. "I know she would want me to carry on with the shop. Continue our work. In fact, she made me promise I would." He shakes his head. "But I can't."

"I understand," she says. She herself could never run Annie's without Sam; she'd feel she was missing some essential limb, that with each movement she was stepping into negative space; every spoon and mug and smell would bring a sharp stab of painful, unbearable memory.

"Heart's not in it. It was Joe and Mary. You can't slice a couple down the middle like you can a submarine sandwich."

"Do you have kids?"

"Didn't get around to it. If only . . ." He rubs at his eyes. "I hate having promised Mary something I can't fulfill."

"I'm sure she'd understand."

He shrugs. "All beside the point now. Take it from me. You never know. You may be sailing along and then . . . *wham.*" He looks at Annie. Perhaps he reads something in her face, because he softens. "Apologies for being such a spoilsport."

She gazes around at the ghost town of the restaurant. "What will you do next?"

"Haven't got that far. Have to settle up the shop, clear the inventory. Hey," he says, slightly more animated, "anything you need?"

"Not really."

"Wait until I show you my combi. Cadillac of stoves. It'll do everything—your steaming, your bread making, your crisping, your soufflés, your sous vide . . ."

"Sous vide?"

"Never mind. Your grilling, your browning, your defrosting, your chilling, your éclairs, and pizza, and roasts. Hey, you can cure your own beef, smoke meat and fish, make pâtés, add a crunchy shell, dehydrate fruits, cook all sorts of custards and eggs, create rolls and loaves and doughnuts and croissants—completely fail-safe. The only thing it won't do is wrap your sandwiches and deliver them. What a masterpiece of German engineering."

"Like the ultimate driving machine?"

"Better. Mary and I ordered it just before she died. I'll give you a great deal."

"I'm not sure . . ."

"You won't go wrong. It will take over so much of the work, you can dismiss half of your employees. Mary always wanted to vacation in Maine. She'd be glad if the combi ended up there."

Joe escorts her into the back kitchen. "Feast your eyes on this!"

Annie beholds a magnificent gleaming structure that looks like the brainstorm of a mad scientist. Joe points out the bells and whistles, all computerized. He presses the buttons and turns the dials. He explains the staggering multitude of functions. He hands her an encyclopedic stack of manuals. "It's fully self-cleaning, too. At the touch of a switch."

Struck by what Ursula would label a *coup de foudre,* Annie falls in love. She runs her hand down the machine's stainless-steel body, cool and sleek to the touch. She tweaks its handle, solid and substantial against her fingers; she pulls open the doors, which unfold gracefully on hushed ball bearings. She fondles the shelves, so many, of such infinite variety. It's a fantasy made real. Oh, the things she—they—could do with this. As the come-hither centerpiece of the annex's redesigned kitchen, its seductive qualities would lure more and more customers. She wants it. She has to have it. She must possess it. Also, she'd be doing a favor for a person in need.

"How much?" she asks.

"Remember you get a tax write-off," he says. He shows her the original bill of sale with its shocking parade of zeros. "I was planning to put an ad in the papers tomorrow afternoon."

"How much?" she persists, panting with desire.

She doesn't bargain; she doesn't say *Let me think this over* or offer up the unfeminist *Let me consult Sam.* Instead, she writes a check on the spot, which Joe agrees not to cash until she transfers funds from her bank account. It's less than half the cost, he points out.

She trusts this sad, recently widowed man, this perfect matchmaker between a woman and a kitchen appliance, a man whose last name—the ironic, kick-in-the-pants Fortunato—she only discovers as she signs over the check.

Has she lost her mind?

Joe promises to call a delivery company and make the arrangements for the combi's journey to Maine. They shake hands. "I can't believe what I just did," he confides. "Mary would have killed me for letting it go for such a song."

"I can't believe what I just did either," Annie seconds.

*　*　*

As she comes out of the subway at 86th Street, her cell phone rings. *Rachel*. Another stab of guilt half a level below the first circle of hell that represents her guilt over Sam slices into her gut. She can offer up plenty of good excuses to justify avoiding her best friend. How can she confess the truth when she's assigned Rachel a major on-the-page role in the manual's duplicity?

She plops herself on the nearest bench, spreads out her bags to discourage seatmates, squares her shoulders, and presses answer.

"Will wonders never cease; it's the elusive Annie Stevens-Strauss," taunts Rachel.

"The one and only," Annie replies.

"Megan reported you had a cold. You sound just fine. I hear honking. Is it fair to assume you're off the sickbed and on the town?"

"Yes, I'm out and about. What's new with you?"

"I called to tell you to come home."

"Ha. That's getting to be a bit of a refrain."

"For good reason. Last week, I ran into Ed Duvall and he looked like hell. It seems his wife went to Boston to visit her mother, met up with an old flame, and returned wearing a fur coat with divorce papers peeking out of its pocket. You should have seen Sam's face when he heard this."

"Sam knows he has nothing to worry about. I'll be back on Friday. I've already changed my ticket."

"Make it sooner."

Annie straightens up. "Is there an emergency?"

"Let's just say, trouble in paradise."

"Excuse me?"

"It's the new hire. Twenties, a real looker, a single mother with an adorable little girl she brings to the shop. Megan reports some flirting going on there."

"Not on Sam's part . . ."

"Don't be so sure. Megan is really concerned."

Annie grabs the edge of the bench. "But . . ."

"But, indeed. Megan says she's a terrible employee. Muddles the orders, calculates the change wrong, is late most of the time. She's surprised Sam hasn't let her go."

"Maybe he will."

"Yeah, right. So far, she keeps screwing up and he keeps her on. Fishy? You need to nip this in the bud."

"Sam would never . . ."

"Don't be so sure," Rachel repeats. "I haven't seen that much of him."

"You haven't?"

"Not since I bought the refrigerator. He's bowling and taking some class at the college to help him design the annex. He seems to have renewed ties with that lawyer who did the paperwork for the sale of the shop."

"All of which I wanted for him."

"*Some* of which," Rachel amends. "Granted, in certain ways, your leaving has had its benefits. He's demonstrated impressive personal growth."

"Now you're sounding shrinky."

Rachel ignores this. "People change. Even Sam. Hang on a minute," she yells to someone talking in the distance. She turns back to Annie. "Don't take any chances. Just come home."

Maybe it's time to confess to Rachel about the fertility doctor. To explain that her trip to New York isn't a sybaritic orgy of self-indulgence. Rachel, after all, has been privy to her failed pregnancies and lost babies. "I'll come home," she begins, "as soon as I keep a doctor's appointment scheduled for next week."

"Aha," Rachel says, "so Ursula has convinced you to get rid of that bump on your nose?"

"What?"

"She asked me once if I thought you'd be upset if she suggested a bit of rhinoplasty. I said of course you'd be upset. A lot of my career, as you know, involves working through body issues. I counseled Ursula that it would be folly to suggest there's a problem when you have never noticed one."

"Until now, thank you very much." Annie moves her finger to her nose and tests the bridge. "Sam loves my nose," she protests.

But Rachel isn't listening. The background voices grow louder now. "Forgive the distraction," Rachel cuts in. "Megan's here with her boyfriend. Of whom, by the way, I fully approve. And believe it or not, I have a date later. With someone I met online. Not the usual loser. I'll clue you in. That is, if I ever see you again."

"Rachel!"

"Coming,'" she yells to Megan. Then, "Is any of this getting through to you? Annie. Just cancel your appointment and book the next plane."

Chapter Twenty-One

Ditch the socks. Going sockless is the latest fad for guys, according to the NY Times Styles section. You do have cute ankles—show them off (but not in February).

She needs to go home.

Back in Ursula's apartment and relieved to find it empty—Ursula having posted an *off to Bergdorf's* note near the telephone—Annie looks up train, plane, and bus schedules. She could fly the shuttle to Boston and catch a Greyhound to Passamaquoddy; she could take a train to Brunswick, hop on a bus, then find a taxi. She could rent a car for the eight-hour-plus drive from New York. Could she manage such a trip on her own only two weeks post-surgery? The daily flight to Bangor is filled; the one to Portland doesn't get her far enough north. What a nuisance to live in a place with neither airport nor train station, its residents stranded like those remote tribes anthropologists spend years in the bush studying. Somehow she'll get there.

She sinks onto a damask, pillow-festooned love seat. She shuts her eyes. Not that she wants to kill the messenger, but she'd gladly obliterate the message that has arrived in the guise of her best friend.

Don't worry in advance, her father—the unrevised first-edition Henry Stevens—used to warn. As if it's a prescription she could fill. Funny, Sam's developing a social life, going out, learning a new skill, following her directions in the manual. *The manual he has never read. Will never read.* Maybe the words in her underwear drawer transferred themselves to Sam's brain subliminally while he was asleep on the other side of the room. She pictures winged paragraphs perching along Sam's neurons like birds on a cable strung between telephone poles.

And the new hire? What a ridiculous term, conjuring up images of a cowgirl in a crappy western, pushing through the saloon doors with a *Howdy, pardner* and ordering a sarsaparilla. It's a twist that even the ever-suspicious Ursula didn't anticipate. But she's young, she's pretty, she's flirting with Sam, to the extent that Megan felt compelled to tell her mother—and she has a small child. Would Sam be tempted? Would the new, improved Sam choose another woman because of a dowry that includes a ready-made kid? Perhaps she doesn't know her husband as well as she thinks she does.

In her mother's bedroom, she finds the card Dr. Albright's nurse filled out, the card Ursula insisted on keeping. She dials the number for the fertility specialist. "Dr. Feld's office," a voice answers, "please hold."

She holds. Music blasts her ear. "Tea for Two." Followed by "God Bless the Child."

She doodles on Ursula's notepad, engraved with her name above the masks of comedy and tragedy. She draws sundaes and sandwiches, sperm and eggs, and a rough sketch of the combi until she hears a click, followed by *Your call is important to us and will be answered in the order in which it was received.*

"Time is of the essence," she yells into the receiver. Since it's impossible to leave tonight unless she charters a private jet—absurd even for Ursula, who would have to be the mistress of a Greek shipping magnate—she hopes to be squeezed in during morning hours before train, bus, car, plane, sled, or wings of a dove deposit her where she's meant to be.

Your call . . .

"Fuck," she shouts. She's covered four pages of Ursula's notebook with sandwich designs, added mustaches to comedy and tragedy, and trimmed her cuticles by the time an actual human being finally breaks in on "Sweet Child of Mine."

"May I help you?" the voice asks.

"Yes, this is Arabella Stevens-Strauss. I'd like to switch next week's appointment to tomorrow morning, if at all possible. I've been called out of town on an emergency."

The voice drops several degrees in temperature. "Do you have any idea?"

"Any idea what?"

"How people wait years to see Dr. Feld. They travel from all over the world. From Thailand. From China. From Saudi Arabia. From New Zealand. The doctor is booked solid well into next spring." She clicks her tongue. "And beyond!"

Beyond what, Annie wants to ask, *the great beyond?* Instead, she clamps her mouth shut. To explain she has to hurry home to save her marriage will not cut any ice with Miss Icicle.

The voice rustles some papers. "Ah, I notice you were referred by Dr. Albright and that you're the daughter of . . . never mind."

Apparently, any blood ties to Ursula Marichal are not enough to win an earlier appointment with Dr. Feld when the wife— *wives*—of a Saudi prince must wait a year to put their legs up in stirrups on Dr. Feld's paper-covered examining table.

Now Annie hears the tapping of a keyboard. "Well"—the receptionist's voice warms slightly—"because you *were* sent by a renowned colleague, perhaps Dr. Feld can turn you over to a physician he trained."

"Oh, that would be wonderful," Annie gushes, eating crow. "Would Dr. Feld be able to recommend someone in Maine?"

The voice sniffs. "Maine? How . . . unusual. I'm going to put you on hold."

Annie has nearly finished the *New York Times* crossword by the time the voice comes back. "You're in luck. Dr. Feld supervised a brilliant OB-GYN who's an ace at high-risk pregnancy and fertility. He now practices at the Maine Medical Center in Portland. I've secured you an appointment for tomorrow afternoon."

"I am so grateful," Annie genuflects. She adds the name and address to her scribbled transportation notes.

She's about to book herself on a plane to Portland at a last-minute inflated premium rate and figure out the connections later when she hears Ursula's key turn in the lock.

"*Bonjour*, darling," her mother says, Bergdorf's bags dangling like ornaments off a Christmas tree, "I've had a most satisfying little shopping expedition—" She stops, studies her daughter. "Is something wrong?"

A litany of what's wrong pours out in a mishmash of choked sobs: Joe's Mary who died, the combi, Sam's entreaties devolved into disdain, Rachel's call, the new hire, the canceled appointment, the urgency to get home . . .

She's sure Ursula will advise her to reinstate the appointment, provided the next wait-listed candidate isn't already on a plane from Beijing. What's a few more days, she'll point out, when you're granted an audience with the guru of gynecological excellence? A New York guru. But her mother surprises her. She drops her bags at her feet and rushes to the phone. "Of course you must go home, darling. ASAP. One lesson I learned from your father is absence does *not* make the heart grow fonder. I'll be damned if I'll see my own marital history repeat itself with you and Sam. Ever since that enchanting wizard of a technician put the car service on my speed dial, I find it requires only seconds to make arrangements. Let me engage a driver to take us to Portland and then on to Passamaquoddy."

"Us?" Annie asks.

"Naturally. What kind of a mother would leave you on your own at such a critical time?"

She's about to reply *the Ursula kind of mother*. She's about to add *I can't have a houseguest in the room down the hall when my marriage is under threat*, but Ursula is already a step ahead. "I'll stay with Ambrose, darling. Perfectly proper," she appends, "as it's hardly our first date."

*   *   *

The car pulls up to the medical building on Congress Street with fifteen minutes to spare before her scheduled appointment. The driver parks in the loading zone, where he opens up his copy of the *Wall Street Journal*. No doubt he's a man with ambitions beyond chauffeuring aging actresses and anxious daughters across three state turnpikes.

Just inside the lobby, Annie and Ursula find the directory for Reproductive Medicine and Fertility Care Associates. Given her reprieve from lung cancer, is it greedy to tempt the gods by asking for more? Why can't she just return to the way things used to be: her solid marriage, her endearingly clueless husband, her fraught mother-daughter relationship, the unchanged and perfect Bunyan formula, the sad yet hard-won five-stages-of-grief acceptance of her childlessness?

When the elevator stops at the third floor, Annie freezes.

"Arabella," Ursula coaxes, her voice a mixture of familiar impatience salted with a new, unfamiliar layer of compassion.

"I don't know what's the matter with me."

"Perfectly understandable. You're scared."

"More like catatonic."

"Nonsense," Ursula protests. "Without dismissing your genuine concerns . . . we've come this far; we cannot stop now."

It's the *we* that comforts Annie. The plural that tells her she's not alone. Now Ursula's firm push between her shoulder blades propels her over the threshold and toward whatever waits along the fluorescent-blazed green-and-white checkered corridor.

* * *

Nobody makes eye contact in the waiting room. They're here for similar failures: failures in reproduction, failures at motherhood, failures of biology, when all over the world sperms are fertilizing eggs and babies are populating continents. They want what for most of their sex is easy, intrinsic, ordained by nature. They are the small percentage excluded from the nursery, the playground, the PTA. They are the untouchables.

And she's one of them.

All her medical records have been faxed ahead—Dr. Albright, Ambrose, the hospital accounts of her miscarriages, of the stillborn Baby Girl Stevens-Strauss. It's a chronicle of catastrophe, a bad report card, an F in pregnancy, an F in childbirth. And, who knows, an F in good-wifery as well.

She studies the pictures on the wall: sailboats, rainbows, gardens, beaches—intended to comfort those who can't be comforted. Her eyes stop at a painting of a saint. *St. Gerard Majella* notes a plate attached to the frame. His golden-haloed head lifts toward heaven; lilies festoon his feet, and he clutches, instead of the expected cross, a white handkerchief. An odd image to adorn a doctor's office, but perhaps it's a reminder that there are more things in heaven and earth than are dreamt of in medical philosophy.

Next to her, Ursula pretends to study a script, though she hasn't moved beyond the single page her flamingo-colored fingernail marks. Annie takes out her phone and Googles *Saint Gerard Majella*. No surprise—he's the saint of happy childbirth. A few months before he died, he dropped a handkerchief in the house of family friends. When the daughter tried to return it, he told her to keep it, that she might need it someday. Lo and behold, years later, close to losing her baby and her own life, she called for the handkerchief. Abracadabra! All pain disappeared, and she gave birth to a healthy child.

Annie clicks on the link to the Saint Gerard Store where she can buy an embroidered linen *Hope Faith Prayer* facsimile for seven dollars plus tax. She's just about to enter her Mastercard numbers when her name is called.

Ursula marches into the doctor's office ahead of her. Her mother's wish to be present for such a personal and private appointment is not subject to negotiation but, in Ursula's opinion, a fully ratified constitutional right.

The baby specialist, Dr. Revere, has a baby face—bright, open, red cheeked, blue eyed. His hands are as pink and dimpled as those of the Doughboys, setting Annie off on a mental tangent of awkward analogies between sandwich making and gynecological inspection. She forces herself to stop. What matters is skill and knowledge. She'll have to trust that Dr. Feld trained his infant protégé well.

Dr. Revere stands up and introduces himself. He shakes her hand in a strong, firm clasp. He smiles, displaying a set of grown-up, chunky chipmunk teeth.

"I really appreciate your fitting me in," Annie says.

"No student, past or present, of Stanley Feld's would ever dare refuse his request." He nods at Ursula.

"This is my mother, Ursula Marichal," Annie says.

"You look familiar." He checks the folder on the desk in front of him.

"My mother's an actress," Annie explains. "Maybe you saw her on the stage?"

"I imagine you're far too busy saving people's lives," Ursula offers.

"That's rather a grand way of putting it. Unfortunately, it's true, a doctor's schedule doesn't leave much room for such pleasures." He slicks down a cowlick, which pops right back up. "Of course, big cities offer more distractions than Maine. The reason I chose to live here."

Ursula points to a photo of five towheaded children in a silver frame. "Are these yours?"

He grins. "Guilty as charged."

Annie remembers Dr. O'Brien's fourth baby, the Pez dispenser analogy. Are doctors more fertile than the normal population? Scientists should do a study on this phenomenon. She wonders if it's unseemly to display photos of five children when his patients struggle for just one. Unless his wife had issues of her own and the kids are the happy-ending evidence of a cure.

"Such enchanting little faces," Ursula trills. "And what could be a better advertisement for your practice."

"Talk about a handful." He smiles, then steers them to a cluster of seats by the window. Annie perches on the chair, the supplicant before the altar, the beseecher of St. Gerard, hoping for a miracle-producing handkerchief that not just anybody can purchase with a Mastercard.

Through the mullioned panes, she can see gulls circle. She spots boats in a harbor and a man in a yellow slicker hosing down a dock. There's a world beyond these walls, she reminds herself, even though, right now, their little triumvirate feels vacuum sealed.

The doctor grabs a fat folder from the desk and sets it on his lap. "You've accumulated quite the file."

She sighs. If only she were medically uninteresting.

Now Dr. Revere executes a getting-down-to-business flurry of throat clearing. "I've gone through your reports and tests, but I prefer to hear your history in your own words."

Annie points to the file balanced on his knees. "Isn't it all in there?"

"I find I learn the more crucial data from the patient herself." He tilts his chin in Ursula's direction. "If you'd rather your mother . . ."

Ursula huffs. "My daughter does not keep secrets from me."

Annie is not about to turn on the one person who made it possible for her to come this far. It is comforting to have a familiar ally in unfamiliar territory. In an uninflected, un-Ursula voice, Annie narrates her most recent medical challenges: the lung biopsy, the diagnosis, the disappeared masses; then the pregnancies, miscarriages, the dashed hopes, the stillborn child.

Though she's determined not to cry, it's hard to ignore the boxes of Kleenex on the doctor's desk, on the table between their chairs, on the shelf that bears the portrait of his kids. What better testament to all the tears these walls have witnessed. It must be the power of suggestion, because she starts to sob, triggering a chain reaction as Ursula herself turns into a veritable Niobe, out-weeping her daughter and infuriating her.

Hey, I'm the patient here, Annie wants to shout. She remembers her father's funeral, how Ursula demanded all the comforting even though she was no longer married to Henry, even though Annie was the only daughter and real mourner. *For a time, I truly loved Henry Stevens*, Ursula had written in her journal. Was she playacting the grieving widow, or did her mother, in her own Ursula way, also feel bereaved?

Dr. Revere waits a few tactful moments, then taps the folder. "It is a very good sign you were able to get pregnant," he says. "A very good sign. It tells us that so many things are actually working."

"What a refreshing point of view," grants Ursula, daubing at her streaked mascara and blotched rouge.

"I need to do a pelvic exam. Would you mind waiting for your daughter here, Ms.—Miss—Mrs.—"

"Marichal!" Ursula harrumphs.

"Yes, Mrs. Merryshaw. She'll be in the next room." He points to a half-open door.

"My daughter requires my support."

The doctor raises a questioning brow.

Annie shakes her head.

"Once my nurse comes in to assist, it might get a little crowded," Dr. Revere explains. "I can send for some coffee, if you'd like."

"My mother would love a cup of coffee."

"Espresso?" Ursula asks.

"It can be arranged."

Not that Miss Ursula Marichal (slash Merryshaw!), member in good standing of the Actors' Equity, would ever tolerate plain old American java bubbling in an ordinary percolator. Still, espresso must seem like a small request compared to what Dr. Revere's mentor might feel obliged to supply—a whole lamb on a spit or bowls of Beluga caviar.

Ursula turns to her daughter. "Even when you were a child, Arabella, you never wished me to give you a bath; you were that modest."

Annie doesn't point out that it was her father or the babysitter or the nanny who gave all baths. Could she imagine her mother toweling dry a dripping, howling two-year-old?

Ursula continues. "Of course, we theater nomads are used to sharing dressing rooms, walking around half-naked while the dresser straps us into a corset or a slinky slip. We view the body as just one of our many instruments."

"Yes, well, I wouldn't know about such things"—the doctor smiles—"though maybe I should. At any rate, I'll perform the exam and send your daughter for blood and urine tests. The labs are just down the hall. She'll be out shortly."

Dr. Revere is quick and efficient. Annie watches him through the crevasse of the mountain made by her knees while he wields his nearly painless speculum with a maestro's grace. "Okay. All done. Why don't you change back into your clothes and we'll have a chat. Your mother will be just fine in the waiting room."

Dressed, she sits in the chair in front of his desk like a penitent schoolgirl while he writes notes in that kind of scrawling penmanship peculiar to doctors—sentences she couldn't decipher even if she *could* read upside down.

He poises his pen above his notepad. "A couple more questions. Have you ever observed a lacy rash on your wrists or knees?"

"Actually"—Annie touches her father's watch, its restoration a tenth-anniversary present from Sam—"wristbands and bracelets tend to irritate my skin. I do get rashes, though I've never paid that much attention to the shape."

"Any swelling in your legs or arms?"

"Not really. Well, maybe a bit from being on my feet all day." She looks at his bright eyes, his dimpled hands, his neat desk, her fat folder into which he is now tucking his notes, the two rows of diplomas on the wall behind him. "Do you have any idea what's wrong with me?"

"Whatever ideas I might have will need to be confirmed by the tests. There are some syndromes—one in particular—that fit your situation and are treatable. There may be hope."

Her breath stops. "You mean . . . ?" It is all she can do not to leap up from her chair and grab the doctor's arm, snatch his notes, plead with him to reveal his thoughts. *Hope.* Wouldn't it be the height of medical malpractice to grant hope to a patient when there is none? Especially without the saintly intervention of a handkerchief?

Dr. Revere hands her a sheaf of orders for the lab. "It will take about a week for the test results. I will call you as soon as we have the answers."

She rattles off her cell phone number, her home number, the number of the shop. She asks him to read them back to make sure they're correct.

"Your inability to carry a baby to term could be caused by a number of things—many, as I pointed out, *very* treatable." He flashes his chipmunk teeth at her. "Do not give up hope," he repeats.

Annie grabs a tissue from the box on his desk. She pumps his hand. Loudly and profusely she thanks him. Silently she thanks St. Gerard.

Chapter Twenty-Two

Don't you dare switch your lemon shampoo, even if Ursula (or someone else) brings you some rare elixir made from the underbelly of a nightingale.

They arrive in Passamaquoddy at six. The car drops Annie at home before driving Ursula to Ambrose's house. He's cooking her a special welcome-back-to-Maine dinner, she informs her daughter. "What are your plans?"

Annie shrugs. "I'm sure Sam has made some."

She doesn't tell her mother that she texted him an hour before with their ETA. *Busy at the shop*, he texted back. *Be home late. Sandwiches, milk, and eggs in the fridge.* There were no *x*s and *o*s, no *can't wait*, not even a signature.

In a way, she's glad for some time alone to decompress, to unpack her bag, hang her new frocks in the closet, line up her new cosmetics on her half of the bathroom sink. Who's she kidding? She wants the chance to snoop. She's anxious to take the measure of the enemy.

He's left the lights on. A good sign, she hopes, that there'll be no replay of his fury the night she got her hair lopped off. A cursory glance around the first floor reveals her mother-in-law's afghan folded at the end of the sofa, not on the rug where she and Sam used to practice Kama Sutra maneuvers; there's one mug in the kitchen sink without—she checks—a lipstick blot along the rim. She looks more closely. Nothing seems out of order.

A light is blinking on the answering machine. She presses play. It's Gus of Gus's Gas announcing that the cable Sam ordered has arrived. She listens to two weeks' worth of old messages: appointments about the annex, a rescheduled city-planning meeting, a bowling date with the geezers, political solicitations, a notice about class assignments posted online, Megan hoping to switch her hours, quotes from suppliers, and then this—a young, lilting voice: *Hey, Sam, just wanted to say that Isabel is real thrilled with the awesome teddy bear. It's wicked cute. She's working on a thank-you drawing. You are the best.*

The kernel of hope Dr. Revere lodged in her heart now shrivels and dies.

She trudges upstairs. She sniffs the sheets for a trace of something else buried in the toothpaste-and-sweat-and onions-and-lemon scent of Sam. The familiar smell of his body pitches her into a reverie of longing for times past. She collapses onto the mattress. She clutches the pillow, all the while searching for makeup smears and inexplicable strands of hair. She doesn't recognize this cliché of a crazy, jealous wife. In fact, she hates herself.

In the bathroom, she checks the shower for foreign shampoo and soaps. Sam's not that stupid. If he were up to any hanky-panky, he would never carry out such deeds under their marital roof. Not that Sam would ever initiate any infidelity. She blames the new hire—who would have taken advantage of both the absence of Sam's wife and Sam's anger at his abandonment.

She goes back to the bedroom and inspects her underwear drawer. The manual is still there, untouched beneath the intact shield of camisoles and bras. Her most recent supplements, paper-clipped or stapled, creased and tattered, lie just as she left them, a messy tumult of messy emotions.

She opens the door to their closet. She notices three snappy oxford shirts and a navy blazer with the price tags still on. She crouches down next to the shoe racks. Stuffed behind one is a shopping bag from Passamaquoddy Toys and Games. Inside the bag are several packages gaily wrapped and tied with pink satin ribbons. Though not quite lipstick-on-the-pillow evidence, these gifts signal—what? That Sam's winning the favors of the new hire though her child? That Sam's winning the favors of the child through her mother? Either way, little Isabel will have to create a lot of drawings as thank-you notes for so much bounty.

The timing couldn't be worse, not that the timing could ever be good for such a betrayal. *Don't give up hope*, Dr. Revere said. What does Dr. Revere know about maternal emptiness or marital mishap?

She thinks of Ursula. Who must now be sitting down to Ambrose's lovingly prepared meal. Lobster and champagne, Annie predicts. Not a waxed-paper-wrapped Bunyan and a half gallon of milk. There will be fresh flowers on the table and fresh sheets on the bed. Not last week's linens, however cherished their unlaundered pheromones. No doubt Ambrose will have tucked away photographs of his late wife, better hidden than the toy-store loot now in plain sight behind the Birkenstocks and moccasins.

Has she sunk so low that she envies her own mother's AARP romance?

In the kitchen, she takes out the sandwich. She doesn't bother to put it on a plate. After days and nights of gourmet menus, she couldn't wait to devour her go-to comfort food. Now she can barely look at this culinary reminder of all that she and Sam have achieved; the careful tiers of salami and pickles curdle her stomach. She shoves it back into the refrigerator and finds a half-drained bottle of wine. She fills a glass. Like a soldier anticipating the encroaching battle, she waits for Sam.

* * *

By the time he arrives, she's finished the bottle and has uncorked the next. Even so, her senses stay on highest alert, tuned in to the sounds of a switched-off motor, the scuff of boots against the welcome mat, the jangle of keys, the creak of the hall closet. She's slathering on a new layer of lipstick when he comes into the kitchen. She jumps up and opens her arms.

He stays in the doorway. "You're home," he says, stating a fact.

Uh-oh. So much for the joyous return of the native. She drops back down onto the kitchen chair. She tucks her elbows against her ribs. "That might be a reasonable assumption," she replies.

"There's quite the fancy black number hanging in the closet—a coat I've never seen before."

She remembers Ed Duvall's wife's incriminating fur, divorce papers stuck in its pocket. "A gift from Ursula," she explains.

"What happened to your green parka? The one you've worn forever?"

She shrugs, loath to admit the garment was so scorned that Ursula wouldn't pass it on to her maid. "Time for a change."

He shakes his head. "Too many changes." He points to the table. "I left you a Bunyan."

"So I saw. Thanks."

"And the drive back?" he asks, making polite conversation.

"Uneventful. Ursula hired a car." She sips the wine. "How are things at the shop?"

"Fine," he says.

"Megan?"

"Fine."

"And the new person?"

He doesn't answer, his attention focused on a stack of mail.

"Let me guess," she says. "Fine?"

"Good enough." He starts up the stairs.

She follows him. "Sam," she entreats, "we need to clear the air."

He stops. "Not now, Annie."

"I have to explain . . ."

"There's nothing to say."

"But there is. A lot. Just give me a chance." She holds on to the banister. She forces herself to sound both cheerful and casual. *Fake it till you make it*, Rachel would advise. "Aren't you glad to have me home?"

"Sure."

"Is that all?"

"Let me put it this way: I was sad when you left. Yes, okay, actually miserable. And surprised—well, shocked—that you didn't want me to come get you." He climbs another step. "Especially when you were sick. When you *said* you were sick," he amends.

"But I was. From even before New York . . ."

"Come on, Annie. I live with you, remember. I would have known. And now I do."

"What do you mean?"

"It felt more than strange—suspicious, even—that you rejected the comfort of your own husband." He studies the gas-and-electric bill. "Do I really have to spell it out for you?"

"I guess you do."

"If that's what you want. All right. I assume you came home because it didn't work out."

"*It?*" she parrots.

"Do you think I'm stupid?"

"Sam, I have no idea what you're talking about."

"You're getting to be as good an actress as Ursula," he says. "It must have rubbed off during all that time you spent with her."

"Sam!"

"Come on, Annie. I'm not that thick. There is only one reason for you to leave me and the shop and your home for all that time, ostensibly to be with your mother—"

"Ostensibly?"

"—your mother, whose company, may I point out, after half an hour, drives you up a wall."

"You don't understand."

"Oh yes I do."

"You have no idea. I was sick," she pleads again.

"So you've already said. What was it? Bronchitis? Tuberculosis? Ha! I know when someone's faking it." He turns to her. Fury knits his brows and twists his mouth. "You look pretty healthy to me. I'm sure Ursula is an expert coach. As you also said, you needed a change. Who is he?"

"Sam, there never . . ." She stops. She's such a fool. How can the truth be worse than what he's now accusing her of? "Just listen," she shouts.

"No, don't tell me. I don't want to know." He takes the stairs two at a time. "Frankly, I feel sick myself. I'm getting into bed. I refuse to hear another word." He slams the door.

Annie's heart pounds against the wall of her chest. Stunned, she staggers back down the stairs to the living room sofa. She unfolds the afghan and wraps herself in it. No matter how many tight, mummy-like layers bind her body, she can't get warm. So much for her noble wishes to spare Sam a dying wife; so much for her desire to handle things on her own. It's her fault. All she wants is to run up to him. Fling her arms around him. Go back to how they used to be. Instead, released from a death sentence and offered the flickering possibility of a child, she feels no joy but only the continuing and agonizing need to protect Sam. From her own lies. From hope.

It's hopeless. She remembers their last fight over her haircut and her Ralphie-induced lateness. This one, she's pretty sure, will not end in a bouquet of roses and a loving note of apology. How does she argue her case against such a wrongful conviction? And what's the point? After all these struggles, and with the best of intentions, this is what it boils down to: a soap opera starring Arabella Stevens-Strauss as a loyal wife, failed mother, stalwart citizen, and phoenix risen from the ashes of a misdiagnosis, who has fled to New York for a wild love affair. Aided and abetted by her mother. At the end, she returns, a woman spurned. Hester Prynne without the consolation of Pearl.

Could anything be more ridiculous? And yet . . . She finishes the wine. She sticks the glass in the sink. He will never forgive her.

On second thought, can *she* forgive *him*? Maybe he's accusing her of what he himself is guilty of. *Displacement*, Rachel would label it. Perhaps he's decided that if their marriage is bad enough for him to wander, then, symbiotic pair that they are, she must be looking elsewhere too.

She gets her laptop from the front hall. She brings it back to the kitchen table. She strains to hear any sound of Sam in the study, in the shower, in the bedroom. Each activity has its particular noise: the faucet when he brushes his teeth, the desk chair sliding in front of his computer, his shoes dropping one by one at his side of the bed, the sprung-spring sigh of the old mattress, the window creaked open for a gust of freezing fresh air, the good-night snap of the turned-off light. But everything is silent. Hushed. The stillness, an admonitory finger wagging *bad girl*. Oh, Sam.

She clicks on the document. Oh, Sam, she writes, what have I done? Why don't I just force you to hear me out? I gave up too easily. Meg Ryan would keep at it. She'd run into the street in a bathrobe and chase after an angry Tom Hanks.

Here's what I'd say to you, in my bathrobe on the sidewalk playing Meg Ryan: I thought I had cancer and was afraid you couldn't live without me. I worried you'd be so deeply affected you'd get sick yourself. Stupidly, vainly, I was sure you couldn't go on alone. I tried to tell you and was relieved when that didn't work. I felt I had to protect you. I went to New York—to see doctors, NOT to have a love affair.

And once the lung cancer diagnosis was dismissed, I saw a fertility specialist. And there is a possibility . . .

probably remote, but I might have some kind of syndrome that could be corrected. So we could try . . .

Or, rather, we could have tried. I didn't tell you that either, as I didn't want to get your hopes up. The doctor will call at the end of the week.

I can't make you stay with me out of guilt. I can't live the kind of lie I've discovered not only my mother but my father also lived. And here I am, deceit, like my bone structure, built into my DNA.

Of course you're angry. It's not a surprise that you feel justified in keeping things from me. It's my fault, Sam, that we've moved so far apart. I abandoned you. I don't—can't—blame you.

Is there a way to find each other again? I wanted you to need me, felt you always needed me. But, irony of ironies, it's me who needs you.

She's crying now, yelping sobs that make her chest heave and her ribs ache. She can wail as loud as she wants. Sam can't hear. Sam *won't* hear. The last time she cried this hard—the last two times—were when her father died and when she and Sam lost their child. They both wept together then. "We still have each other," Sam pledged. "No matter what, we will always have each other."

What to do next? Should she sleep on the couch yet again? Perhaps she needs to claim her rightful place in their marriage bed.

She sticks her just-composed, just-printed entry into her pocket. In the hall, she opens up the unopened suitcases, still standing where the car service driver dropped them. The first thing she sees, tucked between her folded clothes, is "Eight Hours in Manhattan (With Ursula)." On some dark day in her Maine assisted-living quarters, when she's old and feeble, when Ursula has moved on to that great theater in the sky, it might be a hoot to read of her adventures with her mother. Why not add these pages to the manual; they could serve as comic relief, as a travel diary, as a restaurant-and-shopping guide and, most important, as testimony for the defense. *Her* defense. After all, what better evidence than her minute-by-minute account to prove the impossibility of squeezing a lover into such a jam-packed schedule?

Of course, there's no longer a purpose to the manual. Any after-I'm-gone incentives are now irrelevant. But still, it has helped to write everything down. Words on paper are an attempt to make sense of things, to explain herself to herself.

Soon enough she'll stop. She may find it a relief to discontinue this chronicle of hard times, however unresolved and uncompleted the final chapter. Her attempt to impose logic on something as illogical as life has become an exercise in futility.

Now she searches the luggage for the gossamer nightgown Ursula bought her in Bergdorf's. She strips off her clothes and pulls it over her head. She checks her reflection in the mirror. Who is she kidding? Sam? Herself? She looks like a child playing dress-up. Like an actress in costume for a bedroom farce. Or— she gulps—a woman having an affair. What's more, the scar over her lung is clearly visible above its skimpy neckline. Not that Sam won't eventually discover this incriminating evidence himself. She traces its faded red ridge. Or maybe he won't. She slides out of the nightgown and tucks it back into its tissue-paper nest. She'll give it to Rachel, who can carry off seductive froufrou— and may actually have need of it.

Underneath a pile of socks, she finds a stretched-out T-shirt printed on the front with *Passamaquoddy Little League*, on the back *Annie's Samwich Shop, Proud Sponsor of The Clamshells*. As official benefactors, she and Sam attended all the games, lugging folding chairs and thermoses. "In the future, we'll watch our own kids play," Sam said, "while turning into those obnoxious, rah-rah parents columnists write cautionary editorials about."

Now Annie sticks her finger through a hole in the T-shirt's seam. With good reason, Ursula must have dismissed this item as worthy of neither a maid nor a Salvation Army donation box. She slips into it, soft and familiar and perfect for sleeping. Correction: for someone who once had no trouble sleeping.

She remembers to remove the printout from her jeans pocket and tiptoes up the stairs. Gingerly, she turns the knob to the bedroom door. The room is dark except for the slice of streetlamp shining through the crack between the drawn shade and the window frame. She can make out the shadowy hump of Sam on his side of the bed, face turned toward the wall. She moves to the bureau, where she slides open her underwear drawer. She adds the new pages to the others, spreads her camisoles on top, and pushes it shut.

Sam is hogging the covers; her exposed fraction of the bottom sheet feels like a glaze of ice. She tugs at a corner of the blanket, releasing just enough to cover one breast, one elbow, one hip. The hulk that is Sam rises and falls with each breath. "Sam," she whispers.

No response.

She inches closer. She stretches a toe under the covers until she finds his ankle. He flinches. She pulls away. She moves her head next to his pillow. She can smell his hair. Though she longs to nuzzle his neck, she can't risk such a gesture. She turns onto her back, arms tight against her side—a familiar position, like slipping under a scanner or sliding into the MRI tunnel, immobilized, hammers pounding above her, trying not to press the panic button clutched in her right hand.

Trapped.

"You're doing great," the technician coached from her distant, glassed-in booth, spinning her buttons like a DJ spinning platters. "Try not to move. Only ten more minutes. Think pleasant thoughts. Summer. A beach . . ."

What did Annie picture during the eternity of ten minutes? No beach. No palm trees. No piña coladas. Instead, she imagined snow piling on her roof and lacing the windows, icicles fringing the eaves, snow angels etching the drifts, the radiators clanging with steam. And her in bed with Sam. Sam's arms around her.

Snug. Protected. Safe.

Now, lying rigid in her own tunnel of misery and regret, she struggles to ignore the impending call from Dr. Revere. No matter what the news, it'll come too late. Her husband can't even bear the touch of her toe against his ankle. She needs to face the truth: that she's been replaced by a woman with an instant family who is young enough to ensure many more years of fertility uncompromised by unpronounceable syndromes.

For a long time she stares at the ceiling, its vast blackness a perfect metaphor for her mood. Once, full of hope and the future, she and Sam pasted stars in the baby's room, fluorescent stars that Sam meticulously applied, consulting an atlas of the constellations, insisting on an exact replica. "When our baby opens his or her eyes, he—or she—will behold the delights of the universe," Sam said.

They scraped the stars off after their little girl died. There would be no delights of the universe for either of them.

*   *   *

In the middle of the night, Sam flops over and drapes an arm around Annie. Annie, still awake and fused into MRI paralysis, holds her breath. His hand skirts her biopsy scar and finds her breast. For an instant, a flame of joy leaps up inside her. Only to be doused when he recoils, looking stung by his own instinctive gesture. She hears a muffled, sleep-slurred "Sorry."

Sorry? For touching his wife?

"Didn't mean to," he adds, and inches so far away from her that she's afraid he might tumble to the floor.

She touches her breast where his hand rested. The one spot of warmth along her chilled flesh. Funny that, in a long marriage, you never forget the old moves, the same way you never forget how to ride a bike—even if you haven't climbed onto your ancient Schwinn in seventeen years. Perhaps the body remembers when the mind has moved on.

Moved on to other breasts, other bodies in bed.

Chapter Twenty-Three

Set up speakers in the shop with some cool contemporary music that does not involve either the Maine Stein Song or the golden oldies they play at the ice rink.

It's after nine when Annie wakes up. Sam's side is now empty. He's slipped off to work without a peep. She wonders if he remembers how he reached for her in the middle of the night. How an unconscious repetitive motion must have kicked in despite his conscious resentment. She rubs her jaw; it aches, no doubt from grinding her teeth, a sign of repressed anger, according to Rachel.

Rachel is right. She's angry, a teeth-grinding, insomnia-inducing fury too strong to be repressed. She is mad that her husband won't touch her, mad that while she was away seeking a stay of execution, he was at home performing his own execution on their marriage.

She drags herself out of bed and starts to reach for her robe. Before she can grab it, she spots Sam's robe puddled on the floor. She picks it up. She slides her arms through the sleeves, which hang several inches beyond her hands, the hem dragging behind her like a bridal train. She winds the belt around twice and knots the frayed ends.

She hitches up the bathrobe, then pads down the stairs. On the kitchen table sits a waxed-paper Bunyan wrapper scattered with onion and pepper scraps. She hardly requires the little gray cells of Hercule Poirot to conclude that Sam ate last night's discarded sandwich this morning—*the funeral-baked meats did coldly furnish forth the breakfast table. His* stomach was clearly not affected by any kind of estrangement. She turns away from the table. Right now, even an invalid's dry toast and soft-boiled egg seem unpalatable.

What will she do today? Perhaps she should call her mother. The sensible thing would be to act as if this is just another ordinary morning.

She should push aside all worries about a failing marriage, her own mistakes, the fertility report. Rather, she'll clean the kitchen, shower, dress, go in to work, keep to a regular schedule. She'll pretend that everything is all right on the yet-again fake-it-till-you-make-it principle.

Plan in place, she is loading the dishwasher when the phone rings. "You're back," accuses Rachel. "It's about time."

"And good morning to you too."

"Was I ever going to hear from you?"

"We got in late—latish. And then I overslept. In fact, just woke up." Annie adds the beans to the grinder and presses STRONG. "How did you find out I was back?"

"Megan bumped into Ambrose at the market. He had the longest grocery list she's ever seen. For your mother."

"Yes, well, he's excited to wine and dine her. Unlike some people."

"Meaning . . . ?"

"Never mind."

"I'm glad you listened to my advice and hurried home. I was worried."

"And with good reason, I gather."

"Difficult to tell. But now that you're here, everything will sort itself out."

"I'm not so sure. Sam's barely speaking to me."

"Not surprising. You *have* been away for more than two weeks. With a mother who drives you nuts."

"Sam pointed out the same thing. He resents my going. He's been so aloof since I came back." She tightens the belt on Sam's robe. "Frankly, I'm angry at him too."

"Turning the tables—a common coping strategy."

"Rachel!"

"You expected him to fling his arms around you and jump for joy?"

"Sort of hoped."

"Me too. That would have been the quick fix."

"No such luck. Considering the alarms you raised, I hardly anticipated the red carpet treatment. But I didn't count on the total cold shoulder either. Isn't the way he's acting a little suspicious?"

"Not necessarily."

"There are children's presents wrapped up in the closet."

"Which signifies nothing."

"Come on. You're the one who warned me to hurry home, who told me Megan . . ."

"When I thought about it later, after I talked to you, I wondered if Megan and I were overreacting. There's no real evidence.

Just Megan's report of a little flirtation. Not that I've ever known Sam to flirt."

"You told me Megan doesn't dramatize."

"What matters, Annie, is that you're here now."

"Last night he moved so far away from me he might as well have been sleeping on the floor."

"Understandable," Rachel says. "It's human nature. I remember when Ted and I went off once on vacation, trying to repair our marriage. We left Megan with her favorite babysitter and tons of treats. Still, we had to wrench our way out the door while she clung to our legs. Three days later, the babysitter reported Megan inconsolable and we cut our trip short. From the minute we returned, she ignored us. Wouldn't even open the gifts we brought her. Our very presence, instead of instilling happiness and relief, reinforced the fact that we'd been away. It took almost a week for things to get back to normal. Both my child development books and the pediatrician confirmed this was a common way for children to behave after a separation."

"But Sam's not a child."

"Don't be so sure. He's certainly having a toddler's little tantrum. My advice to you is to keep to your ordinary schedule, act as if nothing has changed."

"What other choice do I have?" Annie pours the coffee into a mug that reads *World's Best Wife* and adds a teaspoon of sugar.

"That's the spirit," Rachel cheers. "I am sure everything will be fine. *Really*," she adds. "Whoops. Look at the time! I've got a meeting at school. I'll call you tonight to confer. Wait, no can do. Have a date."

"Talk about burying the lede."

"Ha! Yes, lots to discuss. We'll speak soon."

Annie finishes her coffee, strips off Sam's robe, and heads for the shower. She takes extra care with what Ursula would call her *toilette*. She lathers the lavender soap from her forehead to her toes until she smells like a field in Provence. After she shampoos, she glops on conditioner, waiting more than the suggested three minutes before rinsing. She shaves her legs and armpits—areas that ordinarily remain untouched until bathing suit season. Instead of slicking her wet hair back, she blow-dries it into waves. She applies makeup, hewing to the chart the cosmetic expert diagrammed. She outlines her eyes in a smoky charcoal and pats blush on the apples of her cheeks. She pulls on old jeans and a new cashmere gray sweater that accents her shape rather than flour-sacks it. She's ready to face her public, as Ursula would say.

* * *

There's a commotion in the parking lot behind Annie's Samwich shop. A huge van—*Maine Moose Movers*—looms over the asphalt eyesore, blocking a line of cars from exiting. Horns blast. Motors idle. Drivers shout out of rolled-down windows at the self-appointed amateur attempting to direct traffic. Stopped on a ramp halfway between the ground and the open back of the truck rests a crate the size of a hippopotamus. This tilts on a dolly, which, Annie hopes, has a fully engaged and heavy-duty brake. Sam seems to be arguing with the movers, identifiable by their antlered hats and Moose-decaled fleece jackets. A crowd of onlookers has assembled. Among the regulars, Annie picks out a young, oh so young, woman whose logo-dappled apron designates her as staff. Sam is waving his arms and shaking his head.

Annie turns off the ignition, climbs out of the car, and heads toward the van.

"I didn't order this," Sam is saying.

"Here's the bill of lading." The mover, whose bulk is a credit to his profession, sweeps a clipboard under Sam's nose. "It's got your name and this address and"—he points a stubby finger—"it says right here, *paid in full*."

"Well, you'll just have to take it right back where it came from. There's obviously been a huge mistake." Sam nods toward the shop. "What the hell's in that crate anyway? A herd of moose?"

"Ha-ha-ha," a second man, skinnier but hardly skinny, replies. "A real jokester, that one."

"Beats me," the first man says, shaking his head so hard the antlers bob and sway. "Some kind of kitchen supply thingama-bob." He leafs through the clipped pages. "Called"—he peers closer—"a combi."

Sam's eyes snap open; his jaw drops. His face, bathed in a beatific glow, softens with longing. Smitten, he stares at the crate the way he used to gaze at Annie; *the eighth wonder of the world*, his expression would convey. "A combi," Sam swoons, lingering on each letter like a poet declaiming his favorite line of iambic pentameter. He heaves a sigh of loss and regret. "It must be meant for another restaurant."

Annie steps forward. She is starting to feel more hopeful. Forget moral integrity. Forget marital pride. Forget honorable intentions and ethical actions. Maybe she can *buy* Sam's affections. Maybe the way to this particular man's heart is through the shameless bribe of a multipurpose, cutting-edge miracle of technology. "Excuse me," she interrupts.

Sam nods in her direction. "Do you have any idea what's going on?"

"Actually, I do."

"Would you mind explaining?"

"Well," she begins, "since you—*we*—hope to expand, part of my reason for going to New York was to do some research . . ."

"You could have fooled me."

She forges on. "So, I took the subway to Greenpoint. It's in Brooklyn."

"I know that."

"Which is the center of a lot of new and fascinating family-owned restaurants and cafés."

"I know that too. Wednesday's dining section of the *Times* actually gets distributed here in the boonies."

"Isn't the subway dangerous?" Ray Beaulieu, a local, cuts in. "All those pickpockets and juvenile delinquents and terrorists and crazy people ready to push you onto the tracks?" He jiggles his folded copy of the *Passamaquoddy Daily Telegram* as if its pages bear witness. "I hear they've got rats."

"The subway is perfectly safe," Annie says. "Though there *are* rats," she points out, the *look what I go through for the sake of the shop, for the sake of you* subtext directed toward Sam.

"I've seen them myself," chimes in the Maine Moose mover. "They're as big as raccoons. And the teeth on them . . ."

"I visited some amazing places," Annie continues.

Does Sam even hear her? His eyes are glued to the combi crate. He touches a board of rough wood the way she herself stroked the combi's stainless-steel surfaces. She glances at the young woman. Who looks bored. What other two people in this world would be so enraptured by an oven as she and Sam? Who else would bond over an appliance?

"So . . ." She waves a hand at the combi. "I wandered into a little shop called Joe and Mary's. Joe was selling the business.

Mary, his beloved wife, had died after"—she picks a number—
"*seventeen* years of marriage. Just like us, Sam," she embroiders.
"He was heartbroken. *Heartbroken.*"

"Sounds like my wife's brother's cousin," Ray Beaulieu puts
in. "Missed the whole fishing season when his wife passed. And
he couldn't stand her."

Annie ignores this. "He offered me the combi, hardly used,
for a great price. I wrote out a check on the spot."

"You didn't think to consult me?" Sam asks.

"You weren't exactly available to consult. Anyhow, I knew
you'd be thrilled."

"There's no way of your knowing that," Sam objects, even
though his whole face, his whole posture, states otherwise.

Despite last night, his resentment, her despair, Annie experi-
ences a sense of triumph.

He's not going to give her any credit. On the other hand, his
quick signature of the bill of lading, his directions for unloading
(*easy, careful, watch the top, don't chip the surface, secure the shelves*),
his negotiations with Maine Moose Movers to cart away the old
ovens and a storage cabinet to make room for the behemoth, his
excited comments to the audience at large (*I'll have to go back to
the blueprints and reconfigure stuff*), and his acceptance of the
accompanying colossal user's guide, which he clutches against his
heart like a politician's spouse hugging an oath-of-office Bible—
these are all signs that Annie has done something right.

* * *

After a series of Herculean feats, the combi at last rests in its place
of honor. Sam beams with paternal pride. He swabs a rag all over
the Moose Movers' fingerprints, rubbing until the surface is back

to its pristine radiance. Perhaps the oven is taking the place of a pet. Or a baby . . .

Or a wife.

"Hey, any more coffee?" shouts a customer from the front room.

His combi-worship put on hold, Sam instructs the new hire to fill the coffee cups and clear the tables. He makes a perfunctory introduction—"Annie, Juliette. Juliette, Annie"—as they crowd together in the kitchen with combustible three-on-a-match proximity.

Annie shakes Juliette's hand. She is pretty, her good looks only slightly mitigated by the wad of gum she's working at the side of her jaw. Annie tries to read Sam's body language, to calculate the degree to which her husband is playing the role of Juliette's future, past, or present Romeo. But right now, all feeling, wonder, romance, passion, and attention are directed at the combi. Sam is opening drawers, pulling out shelves, punching buttons.

Annie glances down at Juliette's open-toed, shiny red platform shoes. "Joe, the guy I bought it from, says the oven does so much of a kitchen's work that you'll be able to let some of the help go," she informs Sam.

Sam's not listening. He slaps the side of the combi. "Boy, you're a beauty," he croons.

*　*　*

By the time Megan arrives for her four o'clock shift, Annie's on automatic pilot. There is something to say for the comfort of slicing, dicing, chopping, peeling. She's so far into the zone that when Megan hugs her, she jumps, startled, brought down to an earth she'd rather not visit yet.

"Sorry," Megan says. She gives Annie another hug. "I've missed you so much." Then adds, *"All* of us have."

What should I do next, Sam? Where should I put this? Is it half-and-half or whole cream Mrs. Murphy likes? Juliette now asks, questions aimed exclusively toward Sam, though she and Megan could easily answer them.

Does Sam sound a little impatient with her? Only because he hates to be disturbed when he's concentrating on something. Now he's in a corner studying the instructions with the intensity of Ursula memorizing a script.

A second later, the plate Juliette is drying clatters to the floor. Sam stops reading, inserts a spatula to mark the page, and fetches the dustpan for her. "Oh, I am such a spaz!" she cries.

"Don't worry about it," he says.

"You are a saint. I'm not sure why you put up with me when I screw up so much."

Neither is Annie, but then there's the child and that dewy, glowing skin . . .

As the dinner rush nears, Sam, clearly reluctant, puts down the combi guide to get to work. There is no touching, no banging of hips, no affectionate pinch of the butt or pat on the shoulder, no napkin handed over when the onions spark tears, no sloppy kiss when everyone else's back is turned. He doesn't even use her name—*Pass the salt*; *Can you hand me another dish towel*; *Where's the olive oil?*—his phrases designed to avoid any direct form of address. She remembers a *New Yorker* cartoon: a woman chops onions. More and more tears flow until the woman plunges the knife into her own heart. Annie can identify.

She escapes to the bathroom at the rear of the shop; she refreshes her lip gloss, combs her hair. The light's dim in this unisex, purely utilitarian space, which insists that all employees wash their hands yet offers only a stingy sliver of soap. Perhaps they'll build a designated ladies' room in the newly expanded area, with a box of soft tissues, dispensers of hand cream and liquid sanitizers, and a vase of real flowers. Perhaps Sam can add this amenity to his blueprint. In the middle of smoothing her eyebrows, she stops. Will she still be on-site to enjoy soft tissues and fresh flowers? Will there be a spot in the blueprint for Sam's wife? She sits on the toilet for a long time, contemplating her place or lack of it.

At last, she returns to the kitchen. "If you hand me that pot, I'll put it away," she offers.

He doesn't answer, only bisects his loaf of bread with a violent karate chop of his knife.

"Not that way," Megan cautions Juliette, who is assembling a Bunyan. "Onions first."

Juliette strikes her forehead. "You'd figure by now I could have got the hang of it."

Does Sam roll his eyes? Or is it her imagination? But when Juliette drops the sandwich spreader on the linoleum tiles and doesn't rinse it off before sticking it into the jar of mayonnaise, Sam does roll his eyes—and then some. "Jesus!" he exclaims. He grabs it from her, shoves the spreader into a pot of water already boiling on the burner, and throws the whole jar of mayonnaise into the trash.

"My bad," Juliette apologizes.

"Please go out front and clear the tables," Sam demands. "Can you at least manage that?"

As soon as she leaves, Megan shakes her head. "Not that it is any of my business . . ."

"I know," Sam replies.

"You're too nice," Megan remonstrates.

Sam shrugs.

Now Sam turns toward Annie. "Can I talk to you for a minute?"

Her chest balloons with hope, then deflates with dread. "If you want."

"I'll go help Juliette," Megan offers. "I'm sure she can use an extra couple of hands."

The instant the door swings shut, Sam, with no preamble, declares, "I want you to fire Juliette."

"Whoa," Annie says. "Maybe you could explain what this is all about."

"Nothing to explain. Even without your being here a full day, not to mention the last weeks, you must have noticed what a terrible employee she is."

"You've had more than two weeks of her incompetence. Why now?"

"As you pointed out, the combi can take over a lot of kitchen chores. Besides, you're back." He straightens the napkin holder. "Or so it seems."

Annie notes the lack of gratitude for her return or any expressed hope that she'll stay. His tacked-on *or so it seems* sounds both snarky and unfair. Well, she too can play the snarky game. "You want me to do your dirty work for you?"

"She's a single mother with a little kid. A sweet child . . ."

"What's that got to do with it?"

"It's hard to kick someone when they're down."

"Tell me about it."

He steps back and bumps into the combi. He rubs his elbow. "I've already got a job lined up for her in a nursing home. Ray's sister-in-law's brother-in-law. She won't like it as much . . ."

"I bet."

"Though the chores will be more basic."

"Than pouring coffee and spreading mayonnaise?"

"And she can bring Isabel. Will you do it or not?"

* * *

In the front room, Annie spots Juliette lounging at the table with the lumber-jacketed habitués. "A refill?" asks Remi Arsenault, dangling the coffeepot over Juliette's cup. Ray Beaulieu passes her a plate of pastries.

Annie taps Juliette on the shoulder. "Excuse me," she says, "Could I have a word with you?"

"I guess . . ." Juliette dunks a doughnut into her mug, then licks it. She looks up. "It's Annie, right?"

Annie nods.

She points to the plate. "Do you want a maple glazed? They're real good. Still warm . . ."

"Not now." She takes Juliette's elbow. "Let's step outside."

"It's wicked freezing out there."

Annie considers, then dismisses the bathroom as undignified for conducting serious business. "We can sit in my car," she offers.

* * *

In the parking lot, the two of them pile into the front. Annie turns on the heat to full blast. She can see deep ridges in the asphalt where Maine Moose Movers unloaded their truck and then drove off, considerably lighter than when they arrived. "So, Juliette . . ." she begins, aiming for a casual tone.

"Hey, now I get it," Juliette cuts in. "You're Sam's wife, the one who left him."

"Hardly. I went to New York. To visit my mother."

"Yeah, right, he was that pissed you were gone." She leans closer to Annie, within whisper's length. "Hey, are you two still . . . ?"

"Very much so."

"Can't hurt to ask, right? For a middle-aged dude, he's pretty hot." She switches on the radio dial and spins through the stations. "Too bad you don't have satellite."

Annie reaches over. She twists the knob to off.

"It's only news anyhow." Juliette digs in her purse. She brings out a lipstick. "So, you think he was just being nice to me?"

"He *is* nice."

"Since I mostly know scumbags who only want you-know-what, it's kind of hard to decide when a non-scumbag is just a good person treating you with respect"—she angles the rearview mirror toward her chin, smudging the glass—"or whether there's something more."

"What made you imagine there might be something more?"

"Besides being nice? He's real amazing with Isabel. He's even coming to her birthday party next week. He's bringing cupcakes."

"He likes kids," Annie confides with a pang.

Juliette's eyes move to Annie's stomach. "How come you and Sam don't have any?"

"That's a rather personal question."

"Just wondering. Me, any dude just looks at me and I get pregnant."

The pang grows stronger. Annie adopts her sternest schoolmarm voice. "Juliette, let's get to the point of this conversation. There's a reason I needed to talk to you."

Juliette draws a Cupid's bow on her lips. "I know. You're going to fire me."

Annie's mouth opens in astonishment. "How did you . . . ? Why would you . . . ?"

"Because I suck at this job. A no-brainer. If you ask me, Sam's got way too big of a good heart to tell me, so he wants you to do his dirty work for him. Men," she spits out.

"Men," Annie echoes.

"I expected him to sack me that last time I screwed up all those orders. I was pretty much cool with it, because once I left the job, Sam wouldn't be my boss; he'd be fair game. I mean, how would I know that you, the *wife*, could be coming back?"

Annie is starting to feel sorry for Juliette. *Been there, done that*, she's tempted to confess to her fellow sufferer. Instead she says, "Sam talked to one of the customers about a position for you in a nursing home."

"Yuck. Bedpans and stuff? Old people? No way. I've already found myself a job, cocktail waitress down at Gabe's. Better salary, and I hear the tips are totally awesome."

Annie bends forward. She clutches the steering wheel to keep from laughing. Wait till she tells Sam. She stops. Not that she tells Sam anything these days.

"Anyhow," Juliette adds, her hand on the door handle. "Nice meeting you. What the hell . . . who'll miss me if I take the rest of the day off." Halfway out, she turns to Annie. "And if by any chance . . ."

"Don't even think about it," Annie says.

* * *

"All done," Annie reports when she returns to the kitchen.

"So fast?" Sam asks.

"She's already landed another job: cocktail waitress at Gabe's."

"That dive? I guess no good deed goes unpunished."

She tries to read his face—is he relieved? Sad? "Is that all you have to say?"

"Thanks."

"Actually, firing her wasn't that hard."

Pressing her advantage, Annie turns herself into the anti-Juliette, a whirling dervish of efficiency, arranging silverware, sorting the spices, refilling the salt and pepper holders. "It's been quite a day," she says.

"I suppose." He doesn't look up.

She taps a drum roll against the oven door.

He looks up.

"I take it you approve of the combi?" she asks.

"It's fine."

"I supposed as much," she persists. "The second I saw it, I knew."

Is she mistaken, or does he almost smile?

Could it be that Sam is only mad at her, not infatuated with someone else? Does she sense a thawing? She leans against the counter, alternately exultant and confused. If she dares to assume that the combi-sized obstacle of Juliette has been knocked down, there still remains a slalom's worth of other hurdles rising up to block her path.

Sam steps away. His mouth takes a sudden downward twist. His eyes don't meet hers but stay pasted to the shelf of condiments. "And just who went along with you to help you pick the combi out?" he asks.

Chapter Twenty-Four

Renew your friendship with Bob Bernstein; it really wasn't his fault about the missing recipe. Someone you were Bar Mitzvahed with deserves a second chance.

It's Thursday. Annie has already spent three sleepless nights in solitary confinement on her side of the bed. Now she waits for Ursula to arrive for tea. While Ambrose is holding office hours, Ursula wants to visit her daughter, whom she hasn't seen once since they returned to Passamaquoddy. "You know what it's like when you first fall in love," she explained, coy as a teenager.

The last thing Annie needs right now is to discuss love with her mother.

Or the lack of it.

Does Thursday count as the end of the week? she wonders. Dr. Revere could call her today with the results of the test. Or tomorrow. Perhaps he's the kind of compassionate man of medicine who might even contact an increasingly impatient patient over the weekend. So far, she's managed to keep the lingering prospect of fertility reports at bay. Given the impasse between her and Sam, what's even the point?

For a nanosecond on the vast spectrum of time and on the not-so-vast-and-now-shrinking spectrum of her marriage, she thought everything was going to be all right. Once Juliette was eliminated as number-one perpetrator of crimes against a lawful wife, hope surged. But if Annie's suspicions about Sam were eased, Sam's resentment and doubts about her obviously remain unchanged.

On the surface, her defense appears to be, in Juliette's words, a no-brainer; she has only to stand up and shout, *But there is nobody else; there never has been. I am innocent of your accusations.* She can't because, if she is innocent of one thing, she is guilty of so many others. Not that he will even let her plead her case.

She thinks back seventeen years to their wedding day. The details are still fresh, etched into high relief. The morning before they were married, they struggled for hours over the precise wording of their vows.

"We will always tell each other the truth," Annie promised. "No matter how painful, or hurtful, or embarrassing, or how big or how small."

Sam laughed. "Do we have to sign with our blood?"

"I don't want to be like my mother. I'm serious."

Now Annie checks her watch. Ursula is already twenty minutes late. Surprise, surprise.

She has time.

Upstairs, she pulls open the closet door. The first thing that draws her eye is the shopping bag of packages meant for Isabel. Notwithstanding the innocent birthday-party explanation, they're still a kind of affront, which does not say much for her character. Well, Annie is quick to admit that hers is a character studded with flaws.

She forces her gaze from the presents. She fetches the step stool. On the top shelf, she finds the box tied with the streamers from her bridal bouquet; the ribbons are yellowed and brittle, the lid dusty. She should have wrapped the contents in archival tissue and sealed them in plastic. An endless list of *shoulds*.

She remembers the photos she and Sam arranged in the white album embossed with wedding bells. Together, they lingered over each one. Snapshot after snapshot of the two of them, barefoot on the beach, her wearing an ivory Mexican wedding dress she'd ordered from a catalog, Sam in a matching guayabera. That morning she'd picked wildflowers and woven them through her hair. She'd fashioned a daisy chain for Sam, which he'd slung around his neck. Ursula had been appalled at such makeshift informality; Sam's parents, puzzled.

Now she brings the box to the bed. She unties the ribbons, lifts the lid. It's all there, the invitations they hand-addressed in their best Palmer method script, using fountain pens with a mixture of blue and green ink the color of the sea; the dried Queen Anne's lace and baby's breath; the flat rocks they picked; the shells that decorated the picnic tables; the bird whistles they gave their guests; the pipe-cleaner bride and groom that crowned the lopsided cake, assembled—crooked layer by crooked layer—by a first-year culinary student. She studies the photos. Have two people ever looked happier, more certain of the future?

Toward the back of the album, tucked into a satin pocket, she finds the vows. Her handwriting, even with the ink faded, appears more vigorous than it does now. Two decades ago, she pressed her pen hard against the paper to form emphatic sentences; the letters at the ends of her words curled upward in optimistic swirls. She unfolds the page:

> I promise always to tell the truth, to open my heart and soul to you. I believe there is nothing we cannot confide in each other. I promise to let you in on my innermost fears and feelings, secrets and dreams. I promise to grow along with you, to be willing to face change together as we both change, keeping our relationship alive and exciting and honest. And finally, I promise to love you in good times and in bad, with all I have to give and all that I am, in the only way I know how—completely and truly and forever.

She reads the words again. She remembers how the Dough-boys fled to Florida without leaving the recipe for the Bunyan, astonishing Sam. "It was a *contract*," he protested. "A binding document."

"*I'll* never let you down. Scout's honor," she swore with a three-fingered salute.

Now the doorbell rings. Ursula. Suddenly Annie realizes she looks like hell. Ever since her first day back, her whole carefully calibrated New York appearance has taken a downhill dive, along with any prospects for reconciliation. She pushes her tangled hair behind her ears. It's too late for a comb. She sticks the box back in the closet and hurries to the bottom of the stairs.

"So sorry, darling," Ursula apologizes, swanning in, a whirl of fur and cashmere and pearls and a tartan shawl—her interpreta-tion of country attire. "I had to make Ambrose lunch."

"Really?" Annie asks. She hangs up her mother's coat and fetches a mug of tea from the kitchen.

Ursula flinches at the choice of the mug over a proper cup and saucer. "Well, yes, I ordered scads of yummies from Zabar's—how did we ever survive before FedEx? Nevertheless, I needed to assemble everything. Then add a *billet doux* to the little brown bag. Ambrose, in case you want to know—"

"Would it matter if I didn't?"

"—is turning out to be quite the ardent swain. We are happy as clams. I have finally, at long last, got something right."

Annie looks at her mother and feels a stab of affection for the woman whose larger-than-life quality, always an embarrassment, has allowed her daughter to live. She's grateful for Ursula's problem-solving abilities and her thick everybody-who's-anybody Rolodex, enhanced by big fat checks. Without her mother's car and driver, she would never have seen Dr. Revere. Or made it back to Passamaquoddy in time. She stops. In time for what?

Now Ursula extols Ambrose's virtues, their life together, her plans to renovate the house, Ambrose's thoughtful attempts to erase any trace of his dead wife and Ursula's insistence that he keep one small portrait (though not in a prominent place), she is feeling that secure. "I'm not at all jealous of his past," she adds.

"Very evolved of you, Ursula," says Annie.

Ursula gives her daughter an appraising look. "And what about you?" She takes in Annie's default dowdiness, her unkempt hair. Ursula's no fool. "The reason we rushed home in the first place?"

"False alarm. The new employee, pretty and young, did seem to have her sights on Sam, but he took no notice of her."

"Because he is so in love with you," her mother pronounces from her own Cupid-saturated pedestal.

"Not exactly."

Ursula leans forward. She puts down her mug. "What is the matter, darling?"

"Nothing."

"Very much something, if you ask me. Just tell your mother, Arabella. Out with it."

Annie comes out with it. She catalogs Sam's distance, the bifurcated marital bed, his anger at her abandonment, how she thought the combi might be the way back to his heart only to have her hopes dashed by his suspicions of a lover in New York. "Imagine, *me* with a lover!" she exclaims.

"Imagine," Ursula concurs. "I've never heard of anything so ridiculous."

Should she mention her single New York fling as a single nineteen-year-old? No matter. She plows ahead, talking about the agony of waiting for the fertility report, and how either way it's something she can't share with Sam. She describes her loneliness, the loneliness of carrying secrets.

Ursula shifts to the sofa. She takes Annie in her arms. Annie smells French perfume and Italian soap embellished with a tang of smoked salmon left over from Ambrose's lunch. Ursula strokes her hair, "Darling, darling," she soothes. She hands Annie a lace-hemmed linen handkerchief, so inadequate for even a single snuffle that Ursula hurries into the bathroom for more generous supplies. She passes Annie a wad of Kleenex, then extracts one tissue for herself; she daubs at her own eyes, which brim with a few select diamonds of tears, not the waterfall cascading down Annie's face and splattering her mother's Clan MacDougall–clad chest.

For a long while, Annie lies against her mother's breast. It's amazing how perfectly she fits here. How comforted and protected she feels. Has her mother ever held her like this before?

"There, there," Ursula croons.

Annie nuzzles closer. "Oh, Mother, how did I ever get myself into such a mess?"

Ursula's head springs up, dislodging her daughter.

"What?" Annie asks.

"Arabella!" her mother exclaims. "Annie," her mother corrects. "Do you understand what just happened?"

Uh-oh, Annie thinks. Did she ruin her mother's thousand-dollar dress? "Not really," she says.

"You called me *Mother*!"

"I did?"

"For the first time ever!" Ursula shakes her head in wonder. And then, as if this miracle is too fresh, too fragile to make a big fuss over, she tucks her chin back against her daughter's hair and says, "It's not too late." She releases Annie, stands up, and starts to pace. "Pretend you have a script. All you have to say is something like this: 'I thought I had cancer. I thought I was going to die and wanted to spare you. Ursula—my mother—took me to New York for a second opinion,' et cetera, et cetera . . . until you arrive at the all's well that ends well." She flings the corner of her shawl over her shoulder like a matador. "We can rehearse until you learn the lines and feel entirely comfortable voicing them."

"It's not that simple . . ."

"I beg to disagree. You'll be so sympathetic and convincing he will fall to his knees in relief, overjoyed that instead of an Act-Three-Camille death scene, his wife survives." Ursula mimes what Annie assumes is a tubercular courtesan rising from her sickbed. "Off the bat, I can name several plays in which a husband forgives his spouse all trespasses—Chekhov, alas, not one of them. But then you have done nothing wrong."

"In Sam's view I have. Besides, it's not a play. It's real life. It's my marriage."

"A play always springs from real life, darling." Ursula squeezes Annie's hand. "Promise me you'll consider this."

"It's hopeless."

"Won't you try?"

"I already did. He wouldn't listen."

"Your approach was wrong. You hadn't mastered your pacing and technique."

Annie shakes her head no.

"You were always stubborn, Annie. Even as a child, once you made up your mind . . . I remember the day . . ."

"This is not helpful," Annie breaks in.

"Then your only choice is to give him the manual and let him read it for himself."

"Never! It's proof of all my mistakes."

"It's proof of your love for Sam."

"Sam won't see it that way."

"Don't be so sure. Just tell him everything," her mother repeats.

"I can't. Do you remember my wedding?"

Ursula shudders. "How could I not?" She looks down at her leopard-skin boots. "All that sand everywhere."

"It was a *beach*," Annie counters.

"Which, alas, continues to be a popular venue." Ursula groans. "At least yours wasn't vegan like the Viola in my former company, who—can you imagine?—carried a wilted arrangement of red and white radishes. Accompanied by barefoot bridesmaids clutching the most unappealing bunches of kale."

Despite herself, Annie laughs. "My bouquet was a gorgeous assortment of wildflowers Sam had picked that morning." She shifts into serious mode. "What I was about to point out, talking of weddings, is how Sam and I worked and worked on our vows, and their central theme was honesty and the need to be open with each other."

"But you wrote those vows ages ago, darling; you can't expect to be held to the same standard today for promises you made when you were mere children and incredibly naïve. There must be a statute of limitations."

"Not on vows."

"Believe me, I have made plenty in my time. And now I can't remember a single one. And neither will Sam."

"Oh yes, he will."

"Aren't you a tad too scrupulous? He can hardly hold on to any resentment when you tell him about the cancer and the doctors and all those tests and terrible tribulations you've suffered through."

"Suffered through without including him. That makes it even worse."

"Not the way I see it. In my own wide-ranging experience, men are more than happy to be spared any unpleasantness."

"That was my intention. Though I did try, maybe too half-heartedly, until I gave up. After that, I planned to tell him when I developed symptoms. Until then, I hoped to spare him. To protect him from making himself sick over all of this. But Sam isn't like any of the men you know."

"Don't be so sure." Ursula changes the subject. "Suppose you receive good news from the fertility tests?"

"And use a possible pregnancy to trick him? That is, when we're, if we're . . . you know." She refills her mug. "Didn't you once play a scheming character who trapped her man that way?"

Ursula turns wistful. "There were so many . . ." She finishes her tea. "Very well. Don't say that Ursula Marichal doesn't realize when to throw in the towel." She reaches into her tote and pulls out an enameled art deco compact. "Oh dear," she frets, a woe-is-me wrist pressed to her forehead. She rattles the bag; she digs around some more. "Where is that . . . ?" She pats her pockets, turns them inside out. "Could I have left my favorite lipstick in the guest room the last time I visited? It seems a lifetime ago. I'm going to have a look."

While Ursula's upstairs, Annie carries her mother's mug into the kitchen and sticks it in the sink, scouring off a scarlet lipstick print. She should have offered her mother a shot of brandy, not an Earl Grey tea bag dunked in a Gus's Gas giveaway mug. Hell, she could have used a shot of brandy herself.

Soon enough, Ursula reappears. She makes her entrance, all smiles. She holds up a gold tube of lipstick sparkling with a border of rhinestones. "*Voila!*" she exclaims, waving it with the kind of triumph with which she'd hoist an Oscar, if she ever won one. "I found it on the windowsill, of all places, rolled behind a drapery. What a relief. It's a special color created solely for me by Antoine on the Champs-Élysées. Brilliant. Half red with peachy undertones and a tinge of purple." Ursula unzips her tote and drops it in. "Actually, the color will suit your complexion, darling."

Annie is pretty sure that no amount of red and peach and purple, however brilliant, could even begin to mitigate the toll her return home to Passamaquoddy has taken on her skin. Let alone her heart.

Ursula checks her watch. "Alas, I have to tootle back; I'm expecting the delivery of a new mattress I ordered for Ambrose's bed. I guess you might say, *our* bed." She giggles. "No wonder his mattress was such an excruciating torture; it was constructed entirely of horsehair. Imagine!" She brushes her lips against Annie's check. "I love you, Annie," she says.

"And I love you too, Mother," Annie replies, astonished that she means it.

Chapter Twenty-Five

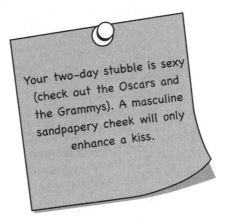

Your two-day stubble is sexy
(check out the Oscars and
the Grammys). A masculine
sandpapery cheek will only
enhance a kiss.

The day after Ursula's visit, Annie's in the kitchen poaching eggs. Sam's at the breakfast table, head buried in the newspaper. Despite her earlier adamant refusal to follow Ursula's advice, she's decided to try again to tell Sam. Agitated, she lay awake all last night, pondering the pros and cons. She was awestruck by the mathematical formula he must have calculated to position himself at the greatest possible distance away from her while still sharing the same bed. Alongside the silent rebuke of Sam's body, she mapped out stage directions, considered pacing and technique, invented her lines, practiced her delivery. She was sorry she had so blithely declined her mother's expert coaching.

At three in the morning, Sam stomped out of bed. "I'm going to the guest room," he announced, "I can't sleep with all your thrashing about." He picked up his pillow.

His departure gave her a greater incentive to fess up. A wall was one thing, but absolute secession terrified her with its prospect of permanence. What next? The living room sofa? Someone else's sofa? Someone else's Sealy Posturepedic, horsehair or not? How easy it might be for him to get used to a separate room free of what he viewed as a hulking betrayal on the far side of their joint mattress. Maybe her mother was right—*oh, please, let her mother be right.*

She looks at him. His eyes are glued on the paper. She pulls apart an English muffin, toasts it to golden perfection, butters it, settles an egg on each half, grinds pepper, adds a sprig of parsley, and slides the platter next to the Corn Flakes.

"Don't have time for these," he grumbles.

"Oh, come on," she coaxes. She sits across from him with her own plate, a little less perfect, a little less culinarily accessorized. She ticks her teaspoon against her coffee mug. "Can this meeting please come to order."

He doesn't raise his eyes from the paper.

She clears her throat. "Sam," she says.

More silence.

"I have something to tell you," she persists.

He turns to the sports section.

"Sam," she repeats.

"I don't want to know."

"How can you be so sure until you hear what I have to say?" she asks, her voice tuned to a reasonable and conciliatory frequency. From the pages covering his face, she can see that Marden's is having a sale on single sheets. *Buy one get one free*, she reads.

"It doesn't matter. Whatever happened belongs to the past," he says.

On closer inspection, the sheets have clowns on them. "Nothing happened. It's not what you think."

"Fine."

"I need you to hear me out."

"Some things are best left unsaid."

She points to his plate. "The eggs . . ."

"Not hungry." He slides back his chair.

"Are you thinking . . ." Her throat constricts. She forces out the words. ". . . our marriage . . . ?" Okay, if she hasn't quite expressed the inexpressible, the question is still a trial balloon floated up in the air between them, hovering.

"I'm thinking of nothing but getting to the shop before the morning rush." He stomps out of the room.

She studies her own plate; the yellow yolks look like accusing eyes or, worse, mocking embryos. Her stomach sours. So much for Ursula's advice. So much for her own intentions. She scrapes both their plates into the sink. She listens to Sam gather his papers, zip on his boots. She did try, she can assure her mother. She even rehearsed, offering up as stage props his favorite eggs. What could be a more direct, more impossible-to-misinterpret line of dialogue than *I have something to tell you?* It's not her fault that her full court press didn't result in a score.

How can they continue the way they are, tiptoeing on the very eggshells now discarded in her sink? You don't have to be Rachel to know that buried resentments can cross sandbag-sheltered, barbed-wired boundaries, ready to flare into battle at any trigger—a plate of eggs, a haircut, a few gifts on the closet floor, a frown. Despite Sam's insistence that what happens in the past stays in the past, she's sure he doesn't mean it. The one thing she *is* sure of is that she cannot live like this.

She rinses the dishes and stacks them in the dishwasher. Then again, maybe deep down she's relieved she didn't get to deliver the self-incriminating soliloquy. What did she expect? In Sam's view, her dishonesty about something so crucial to his own life might loom as a more profound breach of trust than the cliché of a fling.

Still, he's never proposed a status change; he's never told her not to come into the shop or suggested she check apartment listings in the *Passamaquoddy Daily Telegram*. Maybe, in the end, she won't be exiled to single sheets with clowns printed on them.

But will that be enough?

In a little while, she'll take a shower and head for Annie's. When her whole world is falling apart, she can still make a sandwich, still rinse a cup. Working alongside Sam, she can hope the repetition of old habits and familiar rhythms will at least deaden pain, if not restore a marriage to the glow of its former prime-of-life past.

From the driveway, she hears the car turn over, once, twice. After a few more gasps, the engine goes silent, a barometer of freezing weather. And a sign, also, that the Volvo is long overdue for a tune-up. In light of all the recent drama, she's let so many chores slide—the ice dams on the roof, the worn upholstery on the sofa, the toilet upstairs that runs no matter how hard she jiggles the handle.

Yet again, the car emits a puny spurt, then stops. If the ignition won't catch, she and Sam may be forced to drive in together. At last, trapped shoulder to shoulder in the self-contained capsule of her car, just the two of them, radio off, heater warming up, windows fogged with their frozen breath, she can try once more to tell him.

The car sputters three more times before it catches. She hopes he remembered the scarf. She hears tires skid along the gravel.

A split second later comes—oh, no!—the sound of squealing rubber, followed by a screech, a bang, crunching metal, the blare of a stuck horn.

Chapter Twenty-Six

All you need is love.

In the hospital waiting room, Ursula grabs Annie's hand. Annie clings to her. Without Ursula's steady grasp, she'd be floating up in the air like one of Chagall's women with nothing to anchor her to reality.

The reality is this: Sam is in surgery. Has been for the last two hours. Ambrose has reassured her that his injuries, though multiple, are not life threatening. She doesn't believe him. It's all her fault. If she hadn't tried to tell him the truth, he would never have left in a huff, anger propelling him to a reckless back out from their driveway onto the street and right into an oncoming garbage truck. Fortunately, no one in the garbage truck was hurt. Unfortunately, Sam was hurt, very hurt. An ankle broken in three places, a shattered collarbone, cracked ribs, a concussion, bruises, contusions. When she saw him loaded onto the stretcher, she barely recognized him.

Oh, what has she done?

"But none of them life threatening," repeats Ambrose, his eyes shooting superhero spine-bracing bolts into her crumpled slump of misery.

She is beyond comfort. This is worse than exhaustion, his depressive episode. *It's all my fault* cycles through her head. *All my fault.*

In the ambulance, she struggled to find an inch of bruise-free flesh to kiss. "I'm so sorry, so sorry; I love you, Sam," she wailed over and over, until the EMT explained that the patient was not only in shock and thus unresponsive but in fact couldn't hear her at all.

What if he *could* hear? He needed to know how she felt. That she loved him. That she was sorrier than she had ever been in her life.

She grips her mother's hand tighter. Although it must hurt, Ursula doesn't flinch. Ambrose excuses himself to make some calls, leaving the waiting room empty except for the two of them.

Only a half hour ago, three sisters sat here, marking time until their brother's hernia operation finished.

"You look familiar," one said to Ursula.

"The spitting image of Aunt Ethel," the other supplied. "And as interfering," she added when Ursula climbed a chair to change the channel on the overhead TV, tuned to a talk show about knitting wardrobes for pets. Unable to switch the station or lower the volume, she finally yanked out the plug. Causing the sisters, three abreast, to march out in protest.

On a normal day Annie might have apologized for her mother's peremptory behavior and disregard for a democratic consensus. Remorseful, she would have switched the TV back on.

However, this is not a normal day, and she is glad to be spared the details of Marmalade's tricolor sweater or Duke's angora-and-mohair booties.

Now Annie turns to her mother. "I tried. He wouldn't listen."

"It's okay."

"It will never be okay. Whatever he expected me to say upset him so much he crashed the car. It's all my fault."

"It was an accident."

"He could have been killed."

"But he wasn't, darling."

"Will he ever forgive me?"

"Nothing to forgive. You love each other. That's all that counts."

"I'm afraid he doesn't love me anymore."

"He does. You'll have to take it on faith, Annie. A mother just knows."

They sit in silence. From the corridor outside, gurneys rumble by. Announcements squeak from the loudspeaker. *Will Doctor Otten please report to operating room three.* An elevator pings. Nurses laugh. An orderly whistles.

Ursula cuts in. "I could fetch coffee, which I suppose will be completely undrinkable."

"Sure."

"Would you like a muffin or a banana? It seems as though we haven't eaten for hours."

Annie pictures the eggs scraped into the garbage bin and Sam's accusatory bowl of Corn Flakes. A breakfast—or nonbreakfast—that seems a century ago. "Just coffee, thanks," she says.

Alone, she flips through a stack of magazines. She avoids the medical ones: warning signs of prostate cancer, spinal stenosis treatment, physical therapy for Parkinson's disease. She ignores the rainbow-illustrated brochures on gratitude and thankfulness. She picks up a woman's magazine three months out of date. She turns to the page titled *Ten Steps to a Good Marriage*. She looks at number ten—*Forgive and Forget*—and slams the magazine shut.

She's just about to return it to the rack and exchange it for a *People* when Ursula reappears, carrying two Styrofoam cups. "Oh, the lines," Ursula complains. "It would have taken me far less time to walk outside and find the nearest espresso bar." She hands Annie the coffee. "Any word?"

Annie shakes her head.

"I called Ambrose's cell, but his phone was engaged." She looks at her watch. "It's been three hours. By now, they must be finishing."

They sip the coffee, bitter and too weak, but it gives them something to occupy their hands and mouths. Too bad she didn't learn to knit an outfit for a pet, a little snowflaked ski sweater for the dog she advised Sam to get after her demise. Ursula grabs a leaflet on what a woman should do if she feels abused. She glances at it, frowns, and deposits it in a bin marked RECYCLABLES.

When the door opens, they both jump up, but it's only a nurse searching for the three sisters whose brother was just wheeled into the recovery room. "Try the cafeteria," Ursula says.

"The hernia is all repaired," the nurse informs them.

"What *excellent* news," replies Ursula with phony glee. "Do you want to take a stroll?" she asks Annie.

"Not really."

"We might discover some amusing trinkets in the hospital shop. Or up-to-date magazines."

Annie stares through the window at smokestacks and heating units, cement mixers and soaring cranes. You'd think whoever designed the waiting room would offer a more soothing, more uplifting view, she imagines, but maybe that's part of the plan for the new annex now under construction. Would it make her feel better to look out on parkland or streams or distant mountains? No, an unlovely gray industrial scene suits her unlovely mood.

Will anything make her feel better?

Actually, yes. Because the minute she turns from the non-view, a green-scrub-suited surgeon appears, flanked by a grinning Ambrose. "All done," Ambrose says. He wraps a protective arm around Ursula. He nods at Annie. "That Sam of yours is a trouper."

The surgeon introduces himself and shakes hands all around. Clearly exhausted, he plops onto an adjacent chair. "We've repaired the ankle," he tells them. "Two plates, several screws. Your husband has got a lot of hardware in there, Mrs. Strauss."

"Stevens-Strauss," Annie auto-corrects.

"Yes, well, he will be out of commission for quite a period and will need extensive physical therapy."

"And the rest of his injuries?" Annie asks.

"Set the collarbone, stitched up the cuts, taped the ribs. The concussion is minor, although we are watching him. He'll be fine. Still, the recovery won't be easy. That crash did quite the number on him."

"But he'll be all right?"

"In my opinion, yes."

Annie hopes his opinion is buoyed by a host of successful surgeries under his belt and a first-class medical degree. "How can I thank you?" Annie says. For starters, she'll send a donation to

the new annex fund. And deliver a box of sandwiches to the nursing staff. Ha, if she keeps pushing Bunyans on medical personnel,
maybe they'll install a branch of Annie's in the completed addition. She'll have to take this idea up with Sam. Now that she *can*
take it up with Sam.

She shifts her attention back to the surgeon. "I am so grateful," she says.

"All in a day's . . ." He waves a dismissive hand, a hand—she
shudders—all too recently soaked in her husband's blood.

"Can I see him?"

"He's in his room now. Under heavy sedation. He's not going
to remember much for a while."

Trailed by a chorus of praise, the surgeon departs, no doubt
to collapse onto one of those stacked bunk beds prevalent in TV
doctor dramas and often shared with a glamorous nurse. How
lovely to be that appreciated. How satisfying to repair a human
body.

If only a marriage could be repaired that fast.

"Shall I accompany you to see Sam?" Ursula offers.

Annie studies her mother, who, for once, no matter the brilliant red-with-peach-undertones French lipstick or the Swiss
moisturizer composed of the stamens of edelweiss, has not been
able to mask the strain of the last few hours. "No, you go home
with Ambrose. I need to do this on my own." She hugs Ursula.
"Though I could not have managed without you, Mother."

*   *   *

On the third floor of the patients' wing, Annie pauses, her hand
on the knob to 37A. She is happy that his is the only name
scrawled across the chalkboard that hangs from the door. She

supposes she has Ambrose to thank for the privilege of a single room. Yet one more way that Ursula has indirectly smoothed her path.

Sam looks like a horror-film mummy, all wrapped in white. His plaster-cast leg hangs suspended from a trapeze hooked to the ceiling. Bandages circle one shoulder and crisscross his forehead. His arm, which is propped on two pillows, rests in a sling. All other exposed body parts, in various degrees of swelling, range in color from yellow to black-and-blue to red. At the base of his throat, peeking through the V of his johnny, she can make out a triangle of unspoiled bare chest. Has she ever seen anything so poignant? So perfect? If only she could put her lips to that tender, beckoning hollow. "Sam," she whispers.

He's asleep, his eyes shut. She pulls up a chair next to him. There's a box of tissues on his bedside table. She wipes her eyes and nose. "Oh, Sam," she says. She scoots her chair closer. She squeezes his unbroken, though scraped and battered, fingers. It's been so long since she's held his hand.

After a while—minutes? hours?—he opens one eye. His face, however distorted and puffy, seems infused with wonder, with delight. It's the face of the boy who asked her on a date, the face of the bridegroom who handed her a perfect shell he found on the beach, the face of the lover who joined his body to hers. "Ann-eee," he marvels, his voice slurred with painkillers. "Don' go."

Hope soars and mingles with relief. Is she off the hook? Has she been tried and found innocent? Has he traveled back to a time before all this stuff happened? Perhaps he has developed selective amnesia; perhaps the trauma of the accident has obliterated bad memories.

If only.

"I'll never go," she promises. "I'll never leave your side."

The nurse comes in to check his vitals, give him more meds. She's got a large grandmotherly shelf of a chest and wears sneakers with sparkles on them.

"Are you sure he's okay?" Annie asks her.

"A bit battered, but he'll be right as rain," she says. She points to a recliner in the corner. "That chair folds out into a bed, if you want to stay the night, though I wouldn't promote it as comfortable."

"Yes, thank you. I'm not leaving my husband."

"From the look of you two lovebirds, I'm hardly surprised."

As soon as Sam nods off again, Annie rides the elevator down to the hospital shop and buys a toothbrush and toothpaste. When she returns, the nurse is placing a huge vase filled with purple gardenias on the table in front of the window.

Annie doesn't have to check the card to know that the flowers came from Ursula. The nurse hands Annie a pillow and extra blanket. "Your husband is lucky to have such a devoted wife."

Has she ever been more content to be a devoted wife, to sit by someone's side and hold that person's hand? Has she ever been happier to help someone sip water through a straw? What a joy, what a privilege, to adjust Sam's covers and stroke his cheek.

"I love you, Sam," she says.

"Luff you do," he manages.

*　*　*

Three days pass like this, in the overheated hospital room with the terrible food, gloomy view, and health aides interrupting every hour to take Sam's temperature, squeeze on a blood pressure cuff, or give him his meds or a bedpan or a sponge bath. Aside from her honeymoon, Annie can't remember three days of such sheer bliss. Yes, the recliner is a torture rack, the same kind of contraption Sam got stuck in when he was sleeping at the foot of *her* bed all those years ago. Yes, she could use a shower and shampoo. Yes, she's monopolizing him, banishing all visitors. He's not up to company, she cautions everyone. He sleeps, he eats, and in between, his voice muffled, thick, he speaks her name. "Luff you," he whispers. "Ann-eee," he repeats.

In the middle of the third night, he calls for her.

"Are you okay?" she asks, alarmed. It's four in the morning. He pats the mattress. "C'mere."

She squeezes next to him on his good-leg/good-arm side, careful not to disturb any wounds. He rests his hand on her thigh, moves his cheek against hers. "Good. Dow can thleep," he says.

She has barely a foot of space, but even if she were allotted a mere centimeter, she'd still grab the chance to snuggle up to him. Turned on her hip, she Velcros her body to his. Curled into the warm, sweet arc of her husband, she feels her own wounds heal.

*   *   *

On day four, all is right with the world. Their marriage is no longer a house divided against itself. She goes home to retrieve some clothes, take a shower, pay the bills.

Casseroles and bottles of wine crowd her front stoop; get-well cards stuff the mail slot. On the hall table, the answering machine blinks at double speed. She presses play: Rachel announces she's available night or day, Juliette promises brownies and a drawing by Isabel for Sam's hospital wall, neighbors volunteer to run errands. She presses stop. She doesn't have the time—or inclination—to spool through any more of these.

She takes a long, hot shower and shampoos her hair; she rubs her skin with lavender lotion; she slips on a silk shirt Ursula gave her; she finds a pair of clean, nonfrayed jeans; she applies lipstick and blush and mascara. She throws in a load of wash.

The minute she enters Sam's room, she senses the change in the temperature. Though the radiator is hissing, the climate is frigid with anger and accusation. "Oh, it's you," Sam says, his voice wintry, his syllables enunciated shards.

She pastes on a small smile. "Is something wrong?"

"You need to ask?"

"How are you?" she asks anyway.

"Actually," he says, his eyes turned toward the window as if he can't bear to look at her. "I'm much better. My memory is coming back."

"That's good, isn't it?"

"Depends on your point of view." He scowls. She notices he's been reading the newspaper and is holding his cell phone. Back to business. Slightly hampered, yet still back to business. And back to holding a grudge.

"If you don't mind shutting the door behind you when you leave," he continues, "I think I'll take a nap. Thank you for all your help till now." It's a voice you'd use to address a stranger who picked up an umbrella you dropped in the street. "I'm fine on my own," he adds.

"Sam . . ."

"Please, just go."

She staggers out to the corridor, where she bumps into Ursula, carrying another lavish bouquet. "Annie!" Ursula exclaims, staring at her.

Annie covers her face with her hands. "It's all come back. He wants me to leave him alone."

Ursula gives the bouquet to a passing nurse, requesting delivery to the children's ward. "The surgeon did explain that any memory loss was temporary," Ursula reminds her daughter.

"I know. But for a while Sam seemed so great, so loving, I just hoped . . ."

"And why not hope? It's human nature, darling." Ursula shakes her head at human nature. "Do what Sam says. Go home," she orders. "Everything will seem better later."

"As in the sun will come out tomorrow? Not for me, I'm afraid."

"Do I detect a note of self-pity? Why not call Rachel and have a heart-to-heart. Don't worry, darling."

"Don't worry?" Annie repeats, incredulous.

*   *   *

Once home, Annie worries. She doesn't want a heart-to-heart with Rachel. She has no guts left to spill. She is capable only of doing practical, mindless work. She sorts the mail. She checks the blinking answering machine and scrolls through more inquiries about Sam's health, political solicitations, offers from snow removal companies, notices regarding financial services, and a Chinese robocall, erasing each in turn. She sets up appointments for physical therapy. She contacts the visiting nurse association and arranges for a caretaker to assess the ways the household can accommodate Sam's convalescence.

She switches on the television to CNN. The world is at war, people are trapped in mines, there are riots in the cities, thousands are dying in Africa, an earthquake is hitting Japan, forest fires flare in the West, the elms in Central Park are developing a blight, Boston is topping the record for worst winter ever, Maine fishermen can no longer count on a supply of cod, bridges are crumbling, racial violence is erupting in the heartland, ISIS is setting off bombs—on and on, each mounting disaster matching her own mounting misery.

*   *   *

The phone wakes her. She must have dozed off on the sofa, because it's dark outside. Insomnia and oversleeping are both symptoms of the same distress, she once read in some magazine, maybe in a magazine in the waiting room of the hospital she's just been banished from. CNN is now describing the latest national security breach, reminding her how her own sense of security has been so recently breached. She reaches for the phone; she checks the ID. It's Sam's cell.

She can hardly understand him. He's sobbing and nearly out of breath.

Panicked, she sits up. "Oh, no! Sam!" she exclaims. "What happened?"

He sobs harder. "I read it," he weeps.

"Read what?"

"The manual. Ursula gave it to me."

"She gave you . . . ?" she begins, then stops.

She drops back onto the sofa, speechless. Overwhelmed. A series of journalism-school questions loop through her head: *how, why, when, what, where*—all focused on Ursula, the already identified *who*. She needs to pose these queries—and more—to Sam now. She opens her mouth, ready to release a veritable third degree's worth of them lined up behind her throat. But the words won't emerge.

"Annie. Are you there?"

In a flash, it all comes back to her. She pictures Ursula traipsing down the stairs, waving a lipstick she supposedly left on the guest room windowsill, chattering away, all the while lugging her big heavy tote. A star performance. A lesson in diversionary tactics. The old bait and switch.

"Annie?"

"I'm here," she manages.

"Why didn't you tell me?"

"I tried . . . ages ago when I suggested making a will after old Mrs. Bouchard died. This ploy was supposed to open up our conversation. But you shut me down. Though, frankly, I was relieved, as I'd been so worried about how such news would affect you. I tried again, the first night I came back from New York. But you refused to listen."

"I was such a jerk . . ."

"And the other morning at breakfast, I started once more to explain . . ."

"While I was too busy rejecting the eggs I really wanted."

"You were so angry."

"I had no right."

"And then you ran out and crashed the car and . . ."

"Oh, God, Annie, I've been a pigheaded ass."

"Me too."

"Never you," he declares.

"The accident was all my fault. I provoked you."

"No. It's mine. I am an idiot." She hears a door squeak open. *Not now*, Sam says to whoever has entered his room. He waits until the door slams shut before he continues. "I figured you'd met somebody else. Otherwise, why would you spend so much time away from me and with a mother you can't stand?" he confesses.

"Whom, believe it or not, I've learned to love. I, on the other hand, suspected that Juliette . . ."

"You're kidding!"

"I'm afraid not."

"That child? Come on, Annie."

"I see that now."

"How could I ever have doubted you?"

"I was hardly forthcoming. It's not your fault."

"I'm an idiot," he says again. "Acting like a total prick while you've been going through hell. And all alone." He coughs. His words, when he speaks them, sound strangled. "To think you thought you were going to die. To think you wanted to spare me."

For a while, they both linger in silence, their breaths synchronizing in and out, in and out, straining to control the chaos of emotions.

"Oh, Annie," Sam says at last, "Is there any chance . . . ?"

She grabs her car keys. "I'm on my way." She laughs, giddy with relief. "And Sam, save me some room in that bed of yours, please."

She finds her coat hanging from the banister. She slips it on. Once again, she pictures Ursula skipping down these stairs. The interfering Ursula who yanked the TV cord in the waiting room. The interfering Ursula who got her daughter to the specialists. The interfering Ursula who stole the manual and hid it in her tote. The most annoying woman on earth.

Who deserves to be canonized. Would Annie in a million years have predicted that it would be Ursula who would save her marriage, save her life?

"Now for some good news," she hears the CNN commentator report, "the Dow rose and the trade deficit has shrunk."

She turns off the TV. As she starts to pull on her gloves, she spots the voice mail button still flashing. She must have skipped one. Or another call came while she was on the phone with Sam. She hesitates. Why bother when she's in such a rush, when it's no doubt more spam? She presses play: *My message is for Ms. Arabella Stevens-Strauss from the office of Dr. Felix Revere in Portland. We've been trying to get in touch with you all week. Could you please call us back?*

Epilogue

Plus me . . .

So here is the last entry in the manual. Even though I'm going to live (hooray!), every so often I scribble instructions for Sam on Post-it notes. I guess I got into the habit. But now Sam can do the same, advise me to stand up straight, to go easy on the jalepeños when I make chili, and to stop micromanaging. Maybe on New Year's Eve we can exchange our notes as suggested resolutions for our future selves. Still, I'm afraid my once vast library of better-you guides has been taken over by parenting how-tos.

Talk about burying the lede! Hope Albright Stevens-Strauss and Abigail Revere Stevens-Strauss, the twins, are now six months old. To say they are the joy of our life is an understatement.

It turned out that my previous miscarriages and stillbirth were caused by a disorder that could be treated with low-dose aspirin and heparin. Antiphospholipid syndrome. What a mouthful. The pregnancy was uneventful, though Sam quite cheerfully tolerated his own swollen ankles and first-trimester morning sickness. As matron of honor at Ursula and Ambrose's wedding, despite Ursula's frenzied consultations with the personal shopper at Bergdorf's, I still looked like I was draped in a gigantic, expensive tent. I must admit that I relished every varicose vein and every successive urge to pee that ornamented my pregnancy. My badge of honor, my utter, blessed normality.

Ursula insists the children call her *Mémé,* the French nickname for grandmother, which to her ears doesn't sound so golden-agey. She says that now that she's playing grandmothers on TV, she might as well be one. She delights in the twins, spoiling them with fancy European clothes and toys, reading to them from children's books well over their admittedly genius comprehension, but they love the sound of her voice. Hope laughs and Abigail grins, showing off her brand-new tooth. They are beauties, Ursula gloats. And they are—the best of Sam, mostly Sam, but also the best of me. Ursula draws the line at changing diapers, however, but otherwise she's been exemplary.

As has Sam. Whose enthusiasm more than compensates for a lack of skill. Frankly, his diapering turns out lopsided and tends to leak. And because he's so afraid of soap in his daughters' eyes, their hair is never sufficiently rinsed. As soon as he leaves the room, I refasten the diapers and get the shampoo out on the sly. He never even notices the difference. I'm trying to teach him that scrapes and bumps are part of normal growing up. He's making progress. Yesterday he put a Snoopy Band-Aid on Abigail's "boo-boo" and only slightly flinched at a tiny bubble of blood.

Has there ever been a more doting father in the history of fatherhood? He leaves the shop early, dawdles in the morning to gobble Cheerios with his girls. Fortunately the combi has taken over a lot of the previously time-consuming chores. "Best purchase ever made," Sam congratulates me.

I mailed Joe a photo of the combi with Sam and me and Hope and Abigail posed in front of it. He sent a postcard back that he was doing okay and that the photo made him happy, would have made Mary happy too. And that he's so glad the combi found a great family to appreciate it.

Our expansion has been successful. *Down East* magazine raved about us, and tourists are making a detour to Passamaquoddy just to sample a Bunyan, our famous banh mi, and the meatball sub with the egg on top and to soak in our friendly Maine atmosphere. We hired more staff, more competent staff, and the place is buzzing. We plan to hold the girls' first birthday party there. We're surprising them with a puppy we've already picked out from the ASPCA, a puppy who is the spitting image of Binky, Sam's childhood pet.

After Sam and I reunited, I wanted to burn the manual on the principle that we no longer needed it, that it had served its purpose and was a thing of the past. I wanted to erase any reminder of that scary time, of how stupid I'd been, how stupid we both had been, how close we had come to losing everything that mattered to us in this world. But Sam said no, he wanted the manual, wanted to be able to refer to it on how to lead his life, how not to fall back into his old unsociable and slovenly ways. What is most important about the manual, he feels, is that it's a tribute to real love and a guide to how to make a good marriage great.

It was a long recuperation, but Sam is okay now. When the weather is damp, he feels it in his ankle, and he still doesn't have full range of motion in his shoulder. But when we think of what could have resulted from that horrible morning, we are both so grateful, grateful to be alive and to have each other.

Other news: Rachel and the guy she met online are still dating. "I'm cautiously optimistic," Rachel says. Megan got into Bowdoin early admission. Sam and I will come along with Rachel to parents' weekend in the fall for a little trip down memory lane. As a side note, Rachel swears she was never worried one bit about Sam and me. I have refrained from quoting her back when she was handing out warnings and advice. It's amazing how easy it is to rewrite history. And to forget.

My lungs are as clear as a bell, Dr. Albright claims; a spontaneous recovery from sarcoidosis is not unusual, and I am one of the lucky ones. Still, I plan to go to New York once a year for checkups. Ursula kept her apartment and is always thrilled to accompany me. Since Ambrose is semiretired, they are dividing their time more equally between Maine and Manhattan. In the spring, the whole family will head for the city—Sam and I and the girls and Ursula and Ambrose. Sam is already researching child-friendly restaurants. He hopes to show the twins the Egyptian rooms at the Met, even though Ursula and I tell him they're still a little young.

The whole family—who would have thought it? And that there would be so many of us?

The other day, Sam heard from Ray Beaulieu's brother-in-law that Juliette left her cocktail waitress job because of the hours. It turns out that she's quite the hit at the nursing home; they are willing to overlook her barely dissolved tapioca and deficient dusting technique for the pleasure of gazing at her young face. And Isabel acts as official mascot; because of her, they have less need for the therapy dogs, which used to visit regularly from the animal shelter and were not always that well house-trained.

Sam's coming home early this afternoon while I drop in on Dee Dee and get my hair cut. Since the kids, and to Ursula's chagrin, my hair has been a mess. I'll find out about Ralphie Michaud. Thanks to the passage of time and Sam's tendency to see the whole interlude as hilarious, I can now say his name without cringing.

Sam has an architecture class tonight. He's got a real gift for design. His new plan for Annie's is brilliant. I'm encouraging him to go out more. We both need a little independence, I say. We both can benefit from our own space. "Yes," he agrees, "I read about this once in a manual." And we laugh.

I can't even form the words to describe what it feels like to hold my own babies, our babies, to my breast. Or the looks on their faces when I go into the nursery and they see me, their mother. Dare I confess (something I'd never reveal to Rachel) that some nights—okay, most nights—we take them into our bed and we all sleep together, one tight little family knot.

Well, I hear Hope rustling in her crib. In seconds, Abigail will be up too, forming a little duet of wails, which means it's time to shut down. I wish I could conclude with some profound observation on everything I've learned so far. But, let's face it: the real lesson is love, isn't it? Love and life.

xxxooooo Me (Annie Stevens-Strauss)

Acknowledgments

Thanks to:

My smart, charming and patient agent, Mitchell Waters.

My editor, the savvy Faith Black Ross, and the always good-natured Alcove team, Melissa Rechter and Madeline Rathle.

Ellen Feld, MD and Lisa Weissmann, MD, for invaluable medical know-how.

The incomparable Elinor Lipman, first reader, hard marker, best of friends, whose generosity to fellow writers (and me) is legendary;

The brilliant Stacy Schiff, for manuscript insight and endless empathy.

The late, great (adored and deeply missed) Anita Shreve, a cheerleader for this novel and all my others.

Acknowledgments

Friends, neighbors and my circle of fellow writers who provided food and drink and strong shoulders during these last sad and difficult months.

My lovely sons, their lovely spouses and children: Daniel Medwed and Sharissa Jones, Mili and Clementine; Jono Medwed and Marnie Davidoff, Mirabelle and Gabriel.

My equally alliterative sister, Robie Rogge, a fount of support and good humor

And finally, my beloved husband, who died unexpectedly last year before we knew the manuscript was actually going to be a book and who would have beamed with pride. Let me repeat the dedication, so long ago, from my first novel, Mail:

For Howard, whom I met in nursery school, who thought writing was noble work, and who never once, in all our years together, said go get a job. This is for you, kid.